D0652319

"You're sensational," he rasped. "You're the last woman on earth I'd ever want. But I think sometimes, if I can't have you, I shall go out of my bloody mind."

His hands moved over her with unquestioned skill, wrenching her mind from her plot as his mouth nibbled her cheek, her ear, her neck. He dipped his dark head and kissed her with unchecked passion, until she was kissing him back with a rashness of her own.

Then, her body on fire, she opened her eyes and saw his face. The hated Blackwood face with the piercing midnight eyes above a mouth so blatantly sexual, it should have been against the law. But she was never one to revere lawful commandments. The obscure, the forbidden, those were the realms of her soul. She was as undeniably drawn to that illicit mouth as she would be to a priceless necklace locked in the most impenetrable vault. Not for any wish to possess it. Just for the fun of knowing she could . . .

PRINCESS OF THIEVES

Books by Katherine O'Neal

THE LAST HIGHWAYMAN
PRINCESS OF THIEVES

PRINCESS
OF THIEVES

KATHERINE O'NEAL

BANTAM BOOKS
NEW YORK · TORONTO · LONDON · SYDNEY · AUCKLAND

PRINCESS OF THIEVES
A Bantam Book / December 1993

All rights reserved.

ISBN 0-553-56066-2

Published simultaneously in the United States and Canada

Bantam Books are published by Bantam Books, a division of Bantam Dou-
bleday Dell Publishing Group, Inc. Its trademark, consisting of the words
"Bantam Books" and the portrayal of a rooster, is Registered in U.S. Patent
and Trademark Office and in other countries. Marca Registrada. Bantam
Books, 1540 Broadway, New York, New York 10036.

For Bill,
for Janie,
and
for Barbara:
without whose help,
patience, and
inspiration,
this book would never
have been written

PROLOGUE

She was running again . . .

Running with burning feet as her shoes beat a frantic rhythm on the hot pavement. Running with a beating heart and heaving lungs as the footsteps gained on her. Closer . . . closer . . . almost upon her. She summoned her last ounce of strength and surged ahead through the dark night, wearing her panic like a beacon. Amidst the narrow maze of Chicago's back alleys, there was nowhere to hide.

She knew little about her pursuer. Was he armed? Angry enough to kill? She only knew he was stronger, faster, larger than she. She felt like a bird with a broken wing being stalked by a determined cat—to be pounced on and devoured around the next corner. She couldn't fight him on his own terms—not with swiftness of foot or brute strength. She'd have to use her wits. But to do so, she needed time. Time to recover herself, to catch her breath.

Abruptly, too exhausted to continue, she ducked

into a doorway and flattened herself against the door. As she held her breath, keeping her face in the shadows, the man plunged past her. She caught a glimpse of the thick club he carried as a weapon. Where he'd found it, she couldn't guess. Not that it mattered. Her only concern was to see that he didn't have a chance to use it on *her*.

When he'd passed, she gulped air into her lungs, fighting back the fear. She couldn't stop trembling. She couldn't catch her breath. But then, she hadn't known what it was like to catch her breath since she was thirteen. She wasn't even sure she remembered how.

The receding footsteps grew suddenly louder. He was coming back this way. From this direction, he'd spy her, huddled in the doorway like a trapped animal. She had to flee. She must find some way to seize the offensive. Picking up her skirts once again, she dashed into an alley with the intention of running out the back way.

But as she dove through the laundry strung across the alley on lines, she came up against a brick wall. She'd been running so furiously, she could barely stop herself from plowing into the enclosure. Darting about, fitfully seeking an exit, she eventually gave up and collapsed back against the wall. The small space closed in on her in the steamy night. The alley stank with the smells of refuse and cheap perfume. Above, the laughter of women shrilled through an open window. She could hear the footsteps coming closer, heading for the alley. Ominously, they stopped, leaving only a chilling silence. As she peeked out from between the clothing, her heart ceased as abruptly as the footsteps. Her pursuer stood at the face of the alley, his gaze darting about him as he beat the club against his palm with mighty whacks.

There wasn't time to reflect. She was a clever woman who lived by her wits. Never had she needed an idea more than she did now.

If she was going to get out of this alley, she'd have to risk everything. This particular escape called for a bluff so daring, it could mean the end of her freedom and her quest. She peered through the laundry once again to see the man making his way cautiously down the long, dim alley toward her. In the face of impending danger, she knew what she had to do.

Wrenching off the red wig, she fluffed her blond hair and hurriedly ripped her dress so she could step out of it. Then she pulled a frock from the line. Belatedly, she realized it was a whore's gown—bright green satin strewn with feathers and beads. She slipped it on, assuming her role as effortlessly as she donned the disguise. There wasn't time to fasten it. All the better, she decided. She put her hands on her hips, stepped through the curtain of gaudy laundry, and sashayed toward him with a come-hither smile. Miraculously, with her stance, with her attitude, with the alteration of her features, she had transformed herself from a dowdy street thief to a woman of surprising beauty whose very skin radiated sensuality in the stifling heat.

As she waltzed toward him, her lips pouty and gleaming in the absence of light, the strap of her dress fell from her shoulder, baring her skin. Using the accident to her advantage, she shrugged it toward him, moving closer to rub it against him as she let out a soft purr. He stared at her, transfixed by the vision that had so unexpectedly crossed his path.

"You weren't perchance looking for me, were you, darling?" she asked in her natural English-accented voice.

"I—I was looking for a redhead," he stammered.

"I could be a redhead—*for the right price*." She let the shimmer of her hair graze his shoulder in a suggestive slither. "I could be anything you want."

He seemed rattled by this sudden change of events. She knew her effect on men, knew the distraction her

sensuality could cause when she so desired. She was counting on it. "No—I mean—Did you see a redhead running
this way?"

"Have you lost one?" she asked, coolly teasing him
with a smile.

He swallowed hard, sweating, struggling to stay focused as she allowed her backside to brush his hips. "She
robbed me."

She halted the swaying motion. "You don't mean to
tell me you've no cash?"

His voice came out in a soft growl. "She cleaned me
out, the—"

"Then, little man, whatever are you doing wasting
my time?" She put her hands to his back and gave him a
shove. "Out with you. And don't come back till you've the
price of my company!"

He seemed as startled by her rejection as he'd been
by her invitation. Shaking his head as if to clear it, he
headed out of the alley in the other direction, seeking to
regain his advantage—and his prey.

When he'd gone, she rounded the corner and sank
onto a nearby step. For all that she'd outwitted her pursuer,
the encounter had shaken her. Never before had she come
so close to capture. If not for the dress hanging on the line,
her head might have been bashed in. Her escape had been
sheer luck, not good planning. Next time, she might not be
as fortunate.

Fishing in her discarded clothing, she withdrew the
wallet she'd pilfered from the man and counted the contents. She had enough money for a train ticket, a hotel
room, and a few meals. The impermanence of it all hit her
once again. Once it had been fun, besting arrogant brutes
with her brains. But more and more, she felt lucky to be
alive.

Feeling lonely and discouraged, she tossed aside the

billfold and stuffed the money into her bosom before rising and heading for the train station. Like every other city, Chicago had become too hot for her.

SHE'D ASKED THE ticket agent for the next available destination. A train for St. Louis was leaving in three minutes, and one for San Francisco in ten. She'd chosen the latter. It didn't much matter where she went. She'd been in a hundred train stations, heading for a hundred different destinations. She'd been on the road for so long now, pursuing a man who was as clever as she in the ability to vanish. She'd followed him over from Europe and lost him along the way. The trail had been frustratingly cold now for more than a year. She'd searched New York, Philadelphia, Boston, even the cowtowns of Kansas—anywhere she thought such a man might hide. But she hadn't found a trace.

Now she was tempted to give up. She was tired of it all—of chasing a phantom who might not even exist. For all she knew, he could have left the country long ago. He could even be dead. Sometimes, she thought the whole thing was a delusion, something she'd made up during the long, lonely nights on the road to keep herself sane. To keep focused. To give herself a reason to go on.

She'd never been to San Francisco. Perhaps she *should* give up the chase. It was likely she'd never find him. Not after so long. Maybe she should go to San Francisco and start a new life.

Doing what? a voice inside her asked. *Doing what?*

She was making her way toward the platform when she spied a newsstand. She didn't like the path her thoughts were taking. Perhaps if she had something to read . . .

Suddenly she stopped. At first she couldn't be sure what had captured her attention. It was just a blurred photograph of a group of men on the front page of a newspaper. Looking closer, though, she understood. One of the men was in the act of raising his hand to shield his face, as if seeking to hide. Because she, too, never allowed herself to be photographed, the odd motion had caught her eye. Acting on instinct, she took up the paper and brought it closer. Could it possibly be him? She couldn't be sure. But what she could see of his face looked as much like the man she'd been seeking as anyone could.

The shock of seeing him hit her like a blow. The pain she'd thought had eased with time seized her heart so that she doubled over. As if someone had kicked her in the stomach when she wasn't expecting it. The heartache, the horror, the memories, flooded her vision so she momentarily lost sight of him in the white blaze before her eyes. She must be strong—she had to be. Yet in that moment, she felt shattered anew. Would this living nightmare ever cease? Not, she determined, bracing herself against her newly raw emotions, until she'd extracted her revenge.

As her vision cleared, she could taste again the sweet lust for vengeance on her tongue. Her fingers trembled, hungering for the feel of his throat beneath them. She clutched the newspaper so hard, it crumpled beneath her hands.

She looked up to find the newsboy staring at her. "Who are these people?" she asked, smoothing out the page.

"The Van Slykes are the publishers of the *New York Globe-Journal*. They're making a tour of some New York slum."

Skimming the caption, she read of the Van Slykes' desire to help the poor of New York, then found at last what she'd been looking for. The man with them was identified simply as Archer, editor-in-chief.

It *could* be him. From what she knew of his past, it made perfect sense. Still, she couldn't be sure. Was it worth a trip to New York to find out?

Studying the picture in a daze, she began to walk away. "Hey," the boy called. "That'll be a dime."

"A dime!" she cried. It was a scandalous price for a newspaper.

"It costs more, 'cause it comes all the way from New York. But believe me, lady, it's worth the price."

Worth the price. If Archer was the man she'd been seeking for eight wretched years, it was worth any price.

She paid the boy and headed back the way she'd come. Somewhere up the line, she heard the last call for her train. Ignoring it, she returned to the ticket agent. She stood in line in her feathered green dress with a wildly beating heart. It didn't matter that her attire was inciting stares. All that mattered was she'd rediscovered her purpose. She knew what she had to do.

When it was her turn, she slid her ticket across the counter and asked, "When is the next train for New York?"

CHAPTER 1

Suddenly, the crowd parted, and there he was—Bat Masterson, pride of the Kansas frontier, standing in the plush drawing room of the New York mansion.

It made an incongruous sight. The moneyed elite of New York, in their sleek dinner jackets and jeweled gowns, crowded around him like pups pawing over a bone. Saranda knew it was a perilous situation, calling for stealth, subtlety, and quick thinking to avert any trouble that might arise. But then, those were qualities that came naturally to her. In truth, the danger thrilled her as much as the challenge.

It wasn't that she thought this most welcome of guests would purposely give her away. But in that moment of recognition, who could tell what else might slip from him? He was, after all, the only person in the city who knew her real identity.

He was as attractive as she remembered, in a reckless, irrepressible sort of way. More appealing, perhaps, since he'd aged a little and didn't look like such a boy. Two years younger than her twenty-five years, he still radiated the same Huck Finn quality of deviltry that had made him a favorite on the frontier. He had the same short mop of black hair parted on the side, the thick but neatly trimmed mustache, the wide forehead and lean cheeks. He was of medium height, slender, but with a body toughened by the rigors of the frontier. Always fastidious about his appearance, he dressed like his own peculiar version of a dandy. But he'd toned down his image considerably, adopting undertaker black instead of the bright colors and red Mexican sash that had been staples in his wardrobe when she'd known him two years before. He looked somewhat awkward amid the glitter of New York society—not like a man who could single-handedly back down a saloonful of drunken cowboys on a Saturday night.

He still carried his gold-headed cane, she noted. Originally, he'd used it to aid him in walking after he'd been shot in a saloon fight over a girl; by now it was a symbol as much as anything. No one could brandish a cane like Bat. But she'd forgotten that cool, sighting-down-the-barrel look in his light grey eyes. It was a look that could make a woman tremble or, clashing like steel, stop the hearts of the roughest men.

He glanced at her with the impartial appreciation he'd bestow on any beautiful woman. It was clear, for a moment, that he didn't recognize her. Then his face changed. A look of wonder softened his features, and he took an impulsive step toward her.

"Sarand—"

"Sarah," she corrected him in the perfect mid-Atlantic American accent that wasn't her own. "Sarah Voors, Mr. Masterson," she repeated, willing him to take the hint.

He studied her for a moment, not entirely sure. She'd always been a chameleon, rarely looking the same twice, unless she made an effort to do so. He'd never known such a changeable woman. She had the remarkable ability to become anything she wanted. She could stand out as the most stunning woman at a gathering, or she could just as easily disappear into a crowd. The shade of her skin seemed to change with her clothing. Her eyes appeared sometimes blue, sometimes grey, sometimes even green, depending on the effect she was after. Her only impediment to her gift for invisibility was her silvery-blond hair—so shimmeringly unique in shade that she was forced to cover it with wigs to disguise her identity. She had one of those faces he wanted to watch all the time, changing like a mountain whose beauty shifted with the light and whose colors varied as often as Saranda's eyes.

Now, she was dressed in gold, looking like something the conquistadors would fight and die for. Her features looked altered, her face wider than he remembered—no doubt the result of her mastery with a pot of rouge. But her hair was her own, the color of moonlight, swept up in sophisticated curls, with soft ringlets gracing the creamy satin of her bare shoulders. Her eyes appeared a deep, mystical blue, alight with hidden amusement, like a secret password for him alone, watching him carefully to see what he might do. Her lips, always so enticing, were parted in a "let's-see-if-you-get-it" smile, so that her white teeth gleamed at him in playful challenge. She looked every inch the aristocrat she was no doubt pretending to be. Yet she couldn't—or hadn't bothered to—hide the bewitching sensual femininity that belied and softened the inner fire and determination. She gave the impression of lush, willingly offered flesh while at the same time holding herself aloof. Like a present a man might open when he'd proved himself worthy of the deed.

It was all he could do to keep from sweeping her into his arms and giving a good old western yelp for joy. But her

manner—and the gauntlet she was clearly throwing him—
held him at bay.

"Haven't we met before?" he prodded, testing her to
see if she'd waver in front of an audience.

She didn't skip a beat. "I think not, Mr. Masterson. I
would have remembered a man of your—reputation."

Her lips, forming the word, made it sound as if his
reputation were born of adventures she'd never dream of
sharing. But he knew her well, and he caught the subtle
message. Saranda understood Bat's renown as an invincible
lawman was as much a con as her pretending to be the
estimable Sarah Voors. But he did have another, more
rightly deserved, reputation—one of remaining loyal to,
and protecting, his friends no matter which side of the law
they were embracing at the time. With the soft, dewy glim-
mer of her eyes, she told him she was counting on him to
come through for her now.

"But tell me, Mr. Masterson," she continued in a
playful voice, "how do you like New York?"

"I like it fine, Miss—Moors, was it?" He raised a
brow, throwing back a challenge in return.

"Voors, Mr. Masterson," she corrected with a knowing smile. "It's a Dutch name."

"Well . . . how delightful—and unexpected."

"Is it? I should think a man of your vast experience
would have learned to *expect* the unexpected."

"Being invited to New York out of the blue was
rightly unexpected. I always wanted to come to the big
city—" A thought struck him, and he peered at her more
closely. "Say, you wouldn't have anything to do with me
being here, would you?"

All around them, people were watching. She was the
most beautiful woman at the party, he the celebrated guest.
Conscious of this, she flashed him a femininely timorous
smile that was quite unlike her, and blushed in the charm-

ing, self-deprecating way ladies in fashionable New York society did when pretending not to flirt with handsome gentlemen. "Me, Mr. Masterson? Don't be silly. What influence would I have over the *Globe-Journal?*"

Which meant she'd arranged the whole thing. It was an astonishing revelation. *The New York Globe-Journal* was one of the most influential newspapers in the country. When they'd wired him in Dodge City, offering him a week's visit to New York—all expenses paid, with a great deal of money thrown in as incentive—in exchange for an exclusive interview about his adventures on the frontier, he'd been understandably flattered. And just the slightest bit confused. His reputation didn't extend much beyond Kansas and parts of Texas and Colorado. He couldn't figure out how they'd known to ask for him. But, adventurer that he was, he wasn't about to turn down such an enticing offer.

Now it all made sense. At least he knew why they'd sent for him. But if his pride was ruffled by the truth, seeing Saranda again was more than enough compensation.

But how had she arranged for him to come? And to what purpose?

"Where I come from," he drawled, wondering if it was possible to pierce her veneer, "you can't always tell who has influence and who doesn't. Folks change names like they change their clothes. Fact is, in Dodge, folks change their identities so often, it's assumed they're giving false names. It's got so we don't even ask anyone what their name is. We just say, 'What do you want to be called?' "

"Indeed? Dodge must be a dangerous place, with so many desperadoes on the prowl."

"Dangerous, ma'am?" He grinned as he recalled some of her more celebrated escapades in Dodge. "I reckon a woman like you could hold her own."

"A woman like me, Mr. Masterson? At the mercy of all those ruffians . . . ?"

"As a rule, men respect women on the frontier. I've even known a con woman or two who used that fact to her advantage."

How far could he take this, he wondered, before she began to squirm? "I knew one once—what a beauty she was—best in the business. So notorious in the underworld that her very name struck awe in their hearts. She took the rough men of Dodge for every plug nickel they were worth."

"How absolutely scandalous! You must tell us more. Was she really the best you ever knew?"

His eyes softened appreciatively on hers. "She was more than that," he said softly.

"And what became of her?" she challenged with a fearless abandon that sucked the breath from his lungs.

He shifted, realizing once again the eager faces all around them were listening, riveted, to every word. Glancing about at the sumptuous surroundings, wondering again what she was doing here, he replied sincerely, "That, little lady, is something I'm waiting to find out."

CHAPTER 2

A large man in his fifties, with the assured air of a man who knew his place in the world, stepped over to them. "Mr. Masterson, I see you've met my future daughter-in-law, Miss Sarah Voors."

Bat looked at Saranda, then back at the man standing beside him as if he couldn't fathom what he was hearing. Jackson Van Slyke was one of the wealthiest men in New York, and certainly one of the most influential. It was his newspaper, *The New York Globe-Journal*, that had sponsored Bat's trip East in return for an exclusive interview. Bat was a stranger to the big city, but it hadn't taken him long to discover that his host personally owned quite a chunk of it. On the frontier, they'd say he was rich enough to be called Mister.

Bat looked about him at the imposing surroundings. The Van Slykes' Fifth Avenue mansion boasted high, vaulted ceilings and arched doorways leading from one spectacular room to the other. It was decorated in the cool blues and whites of the Delftware pottery that graced the surfaces of tables, curios, and mantels throughout the house. Beside them rested an enviable assemblage of Netherland knickknacks in silver, pewter, and crystal. Ancient Dutch rugs covered cold tile floors, and tapestries lined the walls. Paintings by Rembrandt, Vermeer, Jan Steen, and Frans Hals were displayed as casually as family portraits. Overflowing with flowers and palms, it was quiet, peaceful, well ordered, and serene.

There was no doubt that the inhabitants were fixed in a way few people ever dared to imagine. Upon his arrival in New York, Bat had done his homework. Jackson Van Slyke inherited a great deal of money from his father, but had amassed more by competing with John Astor to buy up every available lot of real estate on the island of Manhattan. Unlike the deceased Astor, however, Jackson was a man who believed in giving back to the city that had made his family a power in their new country. He was, everyone assured Bat, a humanitarian first and foremost.

A most interesting place for Saranda Sherwin, royal successor to a family of con men and thieves, to turn up.

"Who's the lucky fella?" Bat asked.

"I have that honor," said a young man stiffly, moving to Saranda's side.

"My son, Winston," Jackson Van Slyke introduced him with pride.

Bat turned to look, wanting to see the man who'd won Saranda's hand when *he'd* been so unsuccessful at it. Winston was twenty-six, but already his hair had turned salt-and-pepper grey, giving him the serious appearance of an older man. The family resemblance was unmistakable. His face was delicate, open, like his father's, but gullible in a way one wouldn't expect from the son of such a powerful man. His eyes were a gentle shade of aquamarine, and his wire-rimmed spectacles bridged his nose. He wore about him the vulnerable aura of the ultimate sucker, Bat decided. As Winston gazed at Saranda, he blushed, as if he still couldn't quite believe his luck.

"Mr. Van Slyke," Bat greeted him carefully. "You're getting hitched?"

Winston was bemused. "Hitched? Well, yes, I suppose I am. Next week, in fact. Perhaps you could lengthen your stay and attend the ceremony. We'd be delighted to have you as our guest."

"Well, now, it's not that it ain't a sight I'd even pay to see. . . . It's just that my duties as sheriff . . ." His voice trailed off as his gaze drifted back to Saranda. He wanted her as much as he ever had. He'd loved her once, been rejected by her, and had accepted it long ago. Still, she was the most infuriatingly tempting creature he'd ever known. What kind of scam was she pulling this time?

Saranda glanced back over her shoulder in an imperceptible gesture he knew was meant only for him. He saw that she was standing beneath a portrait of a woman who looked so much the way she did now that Bat glanced at it, shifted his gaze to stare at Saranda, then looked back at the painting again in disbelief. "That's not you, is it?" he asked her hoarsely.

"That's my mother," Winston explained. "Lalita Van Slyke."

"I'm sorry for staring. It's just that your—Miss Voors could be her."

Winston's eyes softened with deep affection as he looked from the portrait back to his fiancée.

His father elaborated. "My wife died when Winston was just a baby. Sarah came into our lives and filled a void of loneliness no other woman could have filled."

It was obvious that the Van Slykes cared deeply for Saranda. He wasn't sure which of them looked at her with more love in his eyes. More baffling still was the fact that she returned their smiles with what seemed to Bat to be genuine affection.

Jackson broke the tender silence. "As you know, my dear, we've asked Mr. Masterson to come and illuminate for our readers his life on the frontier."

"Then the man you'll want to talk to is Archer, Mr. Masterson," she said.

Bat watched her intently. There had to be more to this than she was letting on. If Saranda wanted him to meet this man Archer, he wanted to know why.

"Yes, he should be here any—" Jackson turned at the commotion at the other end of the room. "Oh, here he is now."

An excited murmur rushed through the small crowd as they turned to behold the man who'd just made his entrance. He was tall and devilishly handsome, with black, tousled, thickly curling hair that made all the women present want to reach up and brush it into place. He gave the overall impression of a man of unstoppable action, a man you couldn't help noticing when he swept into a room.

As Bat watched, Archer's gaze roamed over the heads of his admirers and came to rest at last on Saranda. His eyes hooded, he swept her with a look of such intimacy that it bordered on impertinence—a daring, possessive glimpse that quirked his handsome mouth into a slow, impudent grin.

Bat glanced back at Saranda, astonished to see the expression on her face as she gazed at the newcomer. Her eyes were glittering, her lush breasts rising and falling with sudden explosive breath. Her skin took on a rosy hue, and she looked even lovelier, if that were possible, than the moment before. She looked as if, with Archer's arrival, she'd suddenly come alive. She looked, Bat reflected resentfully, and with more amazement than he cared to admit, like a woman in love. Gazing at the melting look of sensuality in her eyes, he felt himself go hard.

"In his own way," Saranda was musing, "Archer's as much of a legend as you are."

"I don't doubt it," Bat grumbled, feeling that his thunder had been stolen out from under him. "But who is he?"

"Archer?" asked Jackson, as if he assumed everyone would know him. "Why, he's the man who made the *Globe-Journal* what it is today. He's my managing editor, my right-hand man, and—if I had anything to say about it —would be my adopted son as well. He's the one who'll be interviewing you over the course of the week."

"He's like something out of fiction," said Saranda, casting Bat a pointed look. "Arrived from out of nowhere three years ago and took New York by storm."

"It was, in fact, Archer who suggested we bring you to New York," Jackson explained.

"Then I'm obliged to him. Does he have a front name?"

Saranda smiled. "No one knows. He writes for the paper under the name 'M. *Archer.*' "

A pretty young socialite with dark curls and bright pink cheeks said in a dreamy voice, "I once heard someone ask him what the M stood for. Do you know what he said? It was delicious, really. He just flashed one of those grins of his and said, 'Mister.' "

They chuckled approvingly, as if not knowing added a happy measure of spice to their lives. Bat turned back to Saranda with a questioning look.

"He's quite the man of mystery," she said. "Speaks with the faintest trace of a proper English accent, but no one really knows who he is."

That, Bat suspected, was a clue. Normally, Saranda spoke with an English accent herself, but she was disguising it with incredible skill. So Archer was English, just as Saranda was. What did it mean?

"I think," said another young woman, "he's an impoverished nobleman. He talks like a prince."

Saranda broke into a gleeful grin.

"Well," said Bat with an impressed whistle. "Sounds like a man who don't use up all his kindlin' to get a fire started." They gave him a blank look, as if he were speaking a foreign language. "Can't hardly wait to meet the man," he explained.

Saranda's mouth twitched. "I promise you, it will be worth it."

"Well," said Jackson jovially, "let's go see him. It looks as if Archer could use some rescuing."

They moved across the room to where a man had cornered Archer, speaking to him in a low, urgent tone. He was a man of corpulent girth and an air of authority that spoke, along with the impeccable tailoring of his evening clothes, of his wealth and position. Like many moguls of his day, he wore his bulkiness like a badge, as if to show the outside world he was a man who could well afford the finer things in life, and as much rich food as he damn well pleased. His head was nearly bald, with just a few solitary strands of red hair, but he made up for it by wearing fringed Dundreary whiskers that nearly met at his chin.

"Perhaps we could talk about this later, Sander," Jackson said in a soothing tone. "In private."

Unhappily, the man dropped the subject, but it was clear that he was waiting to get Jackson alone.

Jackson made the introductions. "Mr. Masterson, may I present Sander McLeod, one of our more prominent businessmen. And this is Archer."

Archer stepped forward with a bold, unmistakably self-assured smile, shaking off the confrontation with McLeod as if it were unimportant. "Sheriff Masterson, it's a great pleasure to finally meet you. I apologize for not greeting your train. The paper keeps me busier than I'd like sometimes."

He extended a large hand. Bat shook it, taking the opportunity to study the man at greater length. In his mid-thirties, he was as sleekly dressed as the rest of the men, the black of his evening suit and the white of his shirt setting off his dark coloring to perfection. But there was something different about him. Beneath the polished veneer, he radiated an innate sense of strength and virility, a manly, rugged vigor reflected in the hawklike nose, the prominent brow, the eyes, dark and flashing as the midnight sky, piercing like spears. His jaw was sculpted, solid as granite. Clean-shaven as he was, his beard was so heavy, Bat could detect the threat of a dark stubble. His mouth, large, obvious, firm, and sensual, had teeth so white and strong, they reminded Bat of a wolf's. There was a dimple on either side of his mouth. No demure little thumbprint, either, but long, vertical creases that, when he smiled, gave him a mischievous, wicked look. It was an arrogant smile, a ruthlessly confident grin that, when combined with the penetration of his gaze, caused the ladies present to fan themselves unconsciously. Yet, despite the intoxication that accompanied his presence, despite the fact that the air around him seemed to crackle with an enviable vitality, he looked at Bat as if he were the only person in the room.

He spoke charmingly, as if nothing gave him greater pleasure than to shake hands with the Kansas lawman he'd been waiting all this time to meet. He'd moved through the roomful of socialites with a polished ease that he wore like his natural birthright. But there was that puzzling something . . . It seemed to Bat that he looked more like a Gypsy than an English gentleman. That would explain the swarthy features, the air of the pirate about him.

"Your visit should be quite interesting, Mr. Masterson," Saranda said in her American accent. "I believe Mr. Archer has a number of amusements planned."

"We thought we'd take you on a tour of the city, naturally," Archer said with an ingratiating smile. "And the newspaper, if it interests you. Tomorrow night there's a masked ball to raise funds for the Museum of Natural History. Madame Zorina will be there, giving readings."

"Who," Bat asked, "is Madame Zorina?"

The fat man who'd confronted Archer earlier snapped out of his black mood and joined the conversation. "Madame Zorina," he said, "is only the most famous fortune-teller in the world. She's coming all the way from Hungary to be with us tomorrow night. It's a great honor."

"I'm obliged for all these *honors*," said Bat, who couldn't care less *how* famous this Madame Zorina was. "But just out of curiosity . . ." He glanced at Archer. "Why me?"

"Why you?" Archer's voice was so deep, it rumbled in his chest. Smacking faintly of an aristocratic English accent, it was the antithesis of the gentle, effeminate sneer of the majority of British men. It was aggressive, decisive, vigorously forward-moving, like the rest of him. As he spoke, he seemed to hypnotize with his voice. "You might as well ask why Wild Bill? Or Buffalo Bill Cody? Ned Buntline may have originated the concept, but it's become an image that ignites the fires of our imagination. The lone man poised on the sun-drenched street, sixgun in hand, fighting the loneliest battle—to bring law and order to Dodge City, the toughest town of them all. Sheriff Masterson, it's what legends are made of."

Bat had the grace to blush. "Well, it ain't all that glamorous," he admitted. "I mostly chase after horse thieves."

"Let's not be *too* modest. We need our heroes, Sheriff, like we need music to soothe our souls and great pictures to rest our weary eyes. Life is a dull existence without something to believe in. Our heroes inspire us. They make us dream that we, too, might rise to the same heights of glory. That we can transcend the pettiness of our inclinations and do something noble for the common good. You, Sheriff Masterson, are as important to our huddled masses as Shakespeare and Sarah Bernhardt."

Stunned by this tribute, Bat glanced around him at the glowing faces, readily accepting the fiction this man so convincingly stated as fact. It was an era of culture and sophistication in New York City, but in February of 1878, gunmen still prowled the streets of western Kansas, and shooting a man before breakfast was a common occurrence. Everyone here believed it, had been primed for it.

"I never figured it that way," he said with a grin. "By God, Archer, I've an inclination to shake your hand."

There was a burst of applause as Archer obliged him by stretching out his hand. Caught up in the spell he was weaving, Bat clasped it as Saranda looked on and pursed her lips.

A quartet began to play in the adjoining ballroom, giving Bat the opportunity he'd been waiting for. Turning to Winston, he said, "I'd like to have the honor of a two-step with your fiancée, Mr. Van Slyke—if it wouldn't inconvenience you."

"Not at all."

Taking Saranda in his arms, he whirled her safely away from the crowd. "What goes on here?" he asked.

She gave him an impersonal, artificial smile for the benefit of onlookers. "A fetching greeting, I must say, for a long-lost friend." Her voice sounded completely different in her natural English accent—lilting, breezy, richly sensual.

"Don't put me off, honey. You're pulling some doozy

of a scam, and I'd like to know what it is before I trip over my own tongue."

"I can't talk now, Bat. Besides, it's too complicated to go into. It won't be a minute before Winston cuts in. He always does," she said quickly.

"They're all in love with you, I reckon, these city men."

"Every one." She laughed at his disgruntled look. "Don't pout, darling. I shall find a way of disclosing everything tomorrow."

"Tomorrow's too long to wait, for a fella with his spurs tangled up."

"What confuses you, pray tell?" Her smile was teasing now. She was enjoying stringing him along.

"I didn't notice much excitement when you looked at your intended. But, by God, did your eyes light up when this fella Archer appeared. What goes on here?"

Other couples joined them on the floor, swirling about them in their finery. She put her mouth to his ear and confessed in a voice crackling with excitement, "Archer is an imposter." Then she drew back and stared into his eyes, waiting for his reaction.

"Imposter? Who is he?"

She glanced about to make sure no one was looking. Winston was already heading their way, weaving through the dancers with the intention of cutting in. Before he could reach them, she whispered heatedly, "He's the blackest bloody con man England ever produced. And I'm out to destroy him!"

CHAPTER 3

Bat awoke with a start, lunging for the gun he always kept hanging from the post of his bed. The holster was there, but the gun was missing. Alarmed, he shoved himself up and stared at the apparition before him.

Saranda sat at the foot of his bed in a white lace nightgown and filmy wrapper that hung open in soft folds. Somehow, she'd managed to light a small gas lamp just enough so the slight illumination spilled over her like starlight. She held his sixgun in one hand, the bullets in another. Dangling the gun from her fingers, she whispered with a provocative smile, "Is this what you're looking for?" Playfully, she rattled the bullets in her palm like dice.

Without cosmetics, she looked young, fresh, disarmingly natural. Her sensuality was innate, not studied. Her skin glowed with an inner radiance and an odd, unsettling aura of innocence—considering her line of work, and the all-too-obvious fact that she was sitting on his bed in the middle of the night in a nightgown that did little to hide her womanly curves. The shadowed V of her cleavage drew his gaze. He barely had time to wonder if he really could see her nipples through the lace before he noticed something equally significant. She had tucked within the peekaboo bodice a number of crisp new bills that he recognized as those given him by Jackson Van Slyke. Glancing at the dresser, he saw that his billfold had been rifled, some of the same new bank bills jutting out from the pocketbook as if replaced in a hurry.

She noticed his gaze as it returned to her bosom and chuckled softly. "I thought it only fair that you share your profits, since I was the one who arranged for you to come. Consider it a percentage for services rendered."

Same old Saranda. Yet she seemed completely different from the woman he'd spent the evening with earlier in the presence of strangers. Gone was the sophistication of Sarah Voors. Her silvery hair hung about her face and shoulders in dishabille, appearing like a halo of moonbeams in the shimmer of the lamp. Her eyes appeared lighter, more of a smoky bluish grey. They were huge in her face, compelling in their remote mystery and taunting sensuality. She seemed lusher, more astonishingly beautiful, without the magnificent "costume" she'd worn earlier.

"How'd you get in here?" he asked, still dumbfounded by sleep, still marking the possibility that he was dreaming. He was in one of the many guest rooms in the Van Slyke mansion. As was his custom, he'd locked the door before retiring. He knew she was staying the weekend, to act as hostess to the assemblage of other overnight guests. But to get in, she'd have had to sneak down the hall from her own room without being detected. Next she'd have had to pick the lock, light the lamp, go through his wallet, retrieve his gun, and shake out the bullets, all while he slept. Out of necessity, he'd become a light sleeper, always ready to pull his weapon at the slightest sound. In all his years on the frontier, in the company of hard men, he'd never met anyone capable of getting the jump on him. It unsettled him now to realize the extent of her abilities.

She held up a small steel file. "Tricks of the trade," she whispered with a smile. "But you disappoint me, darling. I had imagined you'd be happy to see me."

He glanced down at his long johns, feeling awkwardly at a disadvantage. "This strikes me as a situation that could get a man killed. What if your intended comes looking for you and finds you in my room?"

"That's what makes it all the more fun. But you needn't worry. If you keep your voice down, no one will know. Besides, Winny's too much the gentleman to visit my room before the wedding. Oh, Bat, it *is* good to see you." She crawled across his bed and wrapped her arms around him, hugging him tight. She smelled clean and refreshingly like a woman but without the distracting fragrance of perfume. He remembered from the old days that she never wore any scent in case she needed to make a quick getaway. She'd told him once of a man who'd been caught because the woman he'd fleeced had recognized the smell of his cologne.

"I thought we were going to talk tomorrow," he said, not daring to touch her. He'd forgotten how soft she was, how tempting her skin.

"It *is* tomorrow. Did you fancy a reunion chat over breakfast with our guests?"

He reached up and took her arms from his neck, pushing her away. "Let me look at you."

She rose to her feet and stretched out her arms for his perusal.

"You're still the prettiest thing this side of the Great Divide."

With the instincts of a woman who knew the power of her sensuality, she played to his aroused state by twirling around so he could get an eyeful. "Then you think I look all right? Fashions have changed since I saw you last. I'm afraid these tight sheaths don't quite suit me. I have a wretchedly rounded bottom that keeps wanting to show itself when I walk. Much more suited to bustles. What do you think, Bat? Is my body *too* unfashionable?"

She dropped the lace wrapper to the floor and walked away from him a few steps, so he could see every curve of her swaying backside enticingly outlined against the clinging lace. He groaned miserably when he realized she was wearing nothing underneath. Smiling, she paused to look back over her shoulder at his disgruntled stare.

"You damned temptress. You have the most fetching —fanny of any woman alive, and you know it."

She stroked it consideringly with a slim hand. "It's my best feature, actually, my bum—fashionable or not. A pity it can't be shown off to advantage these days."

Bat was sweating. He loved her, of course, had since she'd first burst into his life like a shower of shooting stars. But he knew he was no match for her. She appealed to the shamster side of him—the one that allowed him to straddle the fence and change sides of the law, depending on who was wearing the badge. He'd considered himself quite a rascal in those early days, but meeting the legendary Saranda Sherwin had quickly shown him what an amateur he really was. He'd come to think of her—in her own way —as royalty of sorts. Not that he hadn't tried to live up to her. He'd done everything he could to get her to share his bed. When at last she'd appeased him that one and only time, she'd proved to him what she'd been warning him all along. Much as he hated to admit it, she was too much woman for him. And he knew it.

To ease the blow, she'd confessed that she'd never been in love. She was incapable of it, she explained. She could see men only as partners in crime, as Bat had been, or suckers to be fleeced.

Realizing they had no future, he'd been strangely content to play the brother, which was how she'd treated him. At least under normal circumstances he was content. But he hadn't seen her in a long time. Suddenly, seeing her in his bedroom, looking so ripe, so sweet, so damnably tempting, made his hands itch to reach out and touch the luscious backside she was caressing. The proximity of her scantily clad flesh tested the limits of his restraint.

He swallowed with difficulty. Very quietly, he said, "Put your robe on, honey. You think I'm made of stone?"

Her eyes softened, and she retrieved her wrapper. "I suppose it's cruel of me to tease you. I do it only because I know your feeling for me as the infatuation it really is. One of these days you'll find a woman who's worthy of you, and you'll forget all about me."

It wasn't a subject he wanted to pursue.

Footsteps sounded in the outside hall. They both froze, their eyes fixed on the door. Bat was planning what he'd say if they were caught when the interloper moved on. Bat's body sagged as he released a pent-up breath.

Saranda turned to him with a delighted grin, infuriating him with her coolness.

"Why'd you bring me here?" he asked gruffly. "It appears to me it took some doing."

She shrugged, as if it had been the easiest thing in the world. "They were going to bring some gunfighter anyway. I just planted the idea in Winny's head, and he took it to—Archer. I thought if they were going to bring someone, it might as well be you. Knowing what a gambler you are, I assumed you could use the money. And I doubted you'd be adverse to the publicity. But mostly, I missed you. I wanted to see you again."

"I'm flattered." He glanced nervously at the door.

"Now, why don't you tell me what you're up to, before they come looking for you? And hand over that Colt, would you?"

She handed the gun to him, and he proceeded to replace the bullets as she wrapped the lace robe about her and sat cross-legged at the end of his bed.

"Where to start?"

"Start with Archer. Who is he?"

"Mace Blackwood."

She said it as if it should mean something to him.

"Blackwood . . . Why does that sound familiar?"

"The Blackwoods are a family of confidence artists that stretches back as long as mine does—at least three hundred years. Our families have been feuding almost as long. It's become a tradition to outcon the other family, preferably without the other knowing they're being duped. Until Lance Blackwood crossed the line."

"Who's Lance Blackwood?"

"Mace's brother." Her voice showed her contempt. "I can't tell you all of it. Suffice to say, the Blackwoods are evil incarnate."

"Unlike *your* family."

She leaned forward, speaking in a low, defensive tone. "I may come from a long line of clippers, just as Mace Blackwood does, but we Sherwins had a code of honor we never broke. We never conned or stole from people who didn't deserve it. In over three hundred years, we never once killed anyone to get what we wanted. We had style, we had finesse. My mother was fortune-teller to the aristocracy."

"Sugar, you don't have to justify your family to me."

"I'm not justifying them. I'm merely pointing out a crucial difference. Not only are the Blackwoods capable of murder, they resort to it at the drop of a hat. Bat, Lance Blackwood killed my parents."

"I see," he said softly. He knew what Saranda's parents had meant to her—particularly her father—and how losing them at the tender age of thirteen had scarred her.

"He blamed my mother and father for his own parents' death. You see, they were involved in what was for them their biggest con ever. Lance was to impersonate the son of a wealthy American on a cruise down the Nile. One of those special cruises, you know, invited guests from the aristocracy, that sort of thing. His mission was to steal what jewels he could off the other guests. But something went awry. He kidnapped the real American as planned, but killed him instead of releasing him after the job. My parents found out about it and informed the authorities. The Blackwoods had stepped over the line, you see, by committing murder. My father was adamant that a good confidence artist never resorts to violence—we don't need to, if we know our business. So he put a stop to the job before anyone else could get hurt. The upshot of it was that the three of them were captured. Lance escaped—no doubt with the help of his brother, Mace—but the parents were hanged. No loss to the world, certainly. But they were vilified over the length and breadth of England. The London *Times* took it on like a personal vendetta."

"So Lance got even, is that it?"

"Anyone else might have realized it was his own actions that brought this about and take responsibility. But Lance was quite mad. He'd been blinded in one eye somehow. Spent most of his time taking it out on the world at large and us Sherwins in particular. Blamed his incessant failure as a hustler on his deformity. It never once occurred to the bastard that he was incompetent—or out of his mind, which of course he was." She shuddered, remembering.

"Where's Lance now?"

"Dead. He died trying to escape England when his ship went down at sea."

"And Mace—"

"Is the last living Blackwood. The best of the bunch. My father, who was the greatest confidence man of his time, claimed Mace Blackwood was the best he'd ever seen. The veritable crown prince of the Blackwood line. His hoaxes are as notorious as he is. After his parents died, he went to Oxford, of all places."

"Oxford University?"

"Indeed. Faked credentials, assumed the accent, and in time became more like them than they were themselves. They didn't know what hit them. In swift succession, he became captain of the rowing team, the debate club—you name it. Editor of the newspaper. He was, in fact, the first to challenge the administration in print. That's where he acquired his impeccable speech. The rest of his family spoke like East Enders. But that was just the beginning. After leaving England, he cut a wide swath through Europe, bilking untold treasures from wealthy noblewomen who were more than willing to part with their jewels in exchange for his presence in their beds." Her tone had turned acrid. She took a moment to alter it. "To date, no one has successfully nicked him. That's where I come in. I'm going to bring him down once and for all."

"Is that why you've become engaged to Van Slyke?"

"It's one reason, yes. I spent years tracking Blackwood all across Europe before he sailed for America. I kept losing track of him. Though I never told you, that's the reason I was traveling through the West when I met you. I knew that sooner or later, I'd run into him again. Finally, I found him here in New York. He'd assumed the role of Archer, and as you can see, had everyone fooled—particularly the Van Slykes. It's the biggest con he's pulled to date—and the most successful."

"So you saw your chance," Bat murmured.

"I knew if I could get close to the Van Slykes, I could put a stop to Blackwood's scuttle. It wasn't until I saw a picture of Lalita—Winny's mother—that I knew how to go about it."

"So you made yourself over to look like her, knowing if the son didn't fall for you, the father would."

"Something like that. Although it all sounds rather coldhearted, when you say it aloud like that. It *was* at first, I readily admit it. All I cared about was making Blackwood pay for what his family did to mine—for *destroying* mine. But something happened along the way. I discovered what everyone learns after getting to know the Van Slykes— they're two of the kindest and most decent men who ever lived. They genuinely love me and want me to be a part of their family. Bat, do you know what that means to me?" Her voice was soft, emotional.

"I reckon I do."

"So it isn't just about destroying Blackwood anymore. It's about protecting the Van Slykes from him. He's got them so bamboozled, Jackson was going to leave the *Globe-Journal* to him! Until I came along. Not that I'm being noble. By destroying Blackwood's con, I shall not only protect the Van Slykes, but I shall wreak my revenge as well."

"Just how are you planning to do this?" he asked.

"By becoming so indispensable to the Van Slykes that my influence supersedes Blackwood's. I shall become a voice they trust and listen to. Gradually become more and more involved with the newspaper, so I can undermine his authority. Then I shall have him disgraced and fired. So publicly, he'll never be able to pull another con."

"If that doesn't work?"

"Then I'll expose him for what he is."

"If he doesn't expose you first, you mean. Does he know who you are?"

She paused. "I'm not sure. Sometimes I suspect he does. Certainly he will by the time I'm through with him. I want him to know that it was a Sherwin who brought about the end of the Blackwood dynasty. In any case, he realizes I'm a threat to him. He's doing everything he can to keep me from marrying Winston." She burst into a smile so dazzling, he narrowed his eyes just as he would against the glare of the sun on the prairie. "Guess how he's doing it."

Bat shook his head. "Tell me."

"By trying to seduce me so he can go to Winston with the news and destroy my hopes of a wedding ring."

"Is he succeeding?"

Her smile widened appreciably. "I'm having an absolutely marvelous time allowing him to think so."

"What does that mean?"

"It means I'm playing along with his scam. He's trying to hoodwink me into his bed, and I'm convincing him I'm mighty tempted and may just capitulate at any moment. When the truth is, I'd sooner seduce a rattler."

She said it so vehemently, he had to wonder. Some instinct told him there was more to this than she was admitting. "Sounds a mite tricky, if you ask me."

"That, dear friend, is the beauty of it. Where's the challenge if it's predictable? If you want the absolute truth, I've never had more fun in my life."

"I saw the way you looked at him. And I have first-hand knowledge of what that look does to a man. You're lucky Blackwood hasn't forced himself on you."

She got up suddenly and moved to the window. In the white lace, with her blond hair streaming down her back, she looked suddenly vulnerable, like a skittish bride.

"Has he?" he asked in a harsher tone.

"Mace? No. But it was his idea that we be masked at the ball. Just the sort of notion that would appeal to a confidence man, wouldn't you say? The hiding of identities. All in all, it should be a smashing evening. Madame Zorina will be there, which should be fun. My mother studied with her, but I've never met her. And I have a sneaking suspicion Blackwood's going to make his move. With the wedding a week away, he doesn't have much time."

CHAPTER 4

Saranda arrived at the ball dressed in a clinging velvet gown of deep cobalt blue. The neckline was plunging, the skirt tight about her hips, then draped in cascading folds to the hem that brushed her matching slippers. Deep blue flowers, scattered over the skirt, dipped saucily to adorn the flowing train. She wore about her throat the Dutch blue diamonds that had been passed down through the Van Slyke family for generations. Jackson had given the necklace to Lalita as a wedding present, and Winston had insisted Saranda wear it tonight. No one had seen the jewels since Lalita had died nearly three decades before. Now the legendary necklace sparkled at Saranda's throat, dipping to accentuate the pale crests of her bosom, making her intensely aware of her exposed skin as it brushed against her when she walked. Master thief that she was, she felt enraptured by the sensation of the jewels on her flesh. As they warmed to her body's temperature, they became a part of her, inspiring her creativity, lending her a new and heightened consciousness of the possibilities of the evening. In all her travels, to the capitals of Europe and beyond, she'd never so much as had her fingers on such exquisite gems. Wearing them made her feel more alluring, more sensual, more womanly, than she'd ever felt before.

But it was the mask that excited her beyond all else. Of black velvet, decorated simply with jet beads, it shielded her identity more completely than any disguise ever had. It erected a barrier between her and the other guests, providing a wickedly stirring sense of anonymity that appealed to the con woman in her. Hidden behind this tenuous impediment of velvet and ribbons, she felt devilishly alive, throbbing with a sense of adventure, in her true element for the first time since meeting the Van Slykes. Anything was possible tonight. And before the evening was over, she intended to put Mace Blackwood in his place.

She surveyed the crowd, all dressed in evening finery with similar masks concealing their identities. Once they'd successfully traversed the bridge over the mud surrounding the museum, they settled in to the mood of the festivities. Fashioned from pink granite, the American Museum of Natural History had been opened two months earlier with a celebration attended by President Hayes. Built at the far corner of Central Park, it had been considered a bit of a gamble. Quite a way from downtown, surrounded by little except vacant fields, the museum posed the question of whether anyone would brave the inconveniences for the sake of science. But, at Jackson's and the *Globe-Journal*'s instigation, society had come to the rescue, determined to infuse a certain glamour while raising funds for the completion of the museum.

That there was much to complete was evident, even as the guests enjoyed the music and elegant tables laden with food. In sections, scaffolding stood against the walls, awaiting completion of projects once the fashionable party was little more than a memory. Certain walls were completely bare, others half-hung with displays. Some crates lined the corners of one room holding specimens and sculptures that awaited pedestals. A guard stood vigilant, sentinel against undue interest in the artifacts, but not adverse to accepting an occasionally offered glass of champagne from one of the wealthy patrons.

Unaccustomed as New York society guests were to masked balls, they were all aquiver tonight, dancing to the orchestra as they tried to ascertain who was hiding beneath each mask. The gimmick had been Blackwood's idea, and as such it had taken on an enchantment it might not have had if it had come from other quarters. As Archer, he was such a popular and dashing figure in society, his women admirers immediately seized any idea of his to their breasts and promoted it with the enthusiasm their husbands might lend to a campaign of war. The men, because they respected "Archer" and desired to please their women, somewhat less enthusiastically followed suit.

As the Van Slyke party entered the hall, they were immediately noted by the crowd, because of the presence of Bat Masterson. The first of Archer's articles had appeared that morning in the *Globe-Journal*, making much of the cane Bat always carried and the derby he always wore. Though he'd been outfitted at the newspaper's expense in evening clothes, he walked in brandishing his cane like a baton and was immediately swooped down on by a bevy of giggling female admirers. They drew him away, chattering all the while, firing questions about the colorful exploits they'd read of earlier in the day. Blackwood had painted a fiery picture of a legendary gunfighter who fought for justice with a smoking sixgun, single-handedly standing against the rowdy elements of the West to bring law and order to the wildest town in America. In his hand, Bat was drawn as a man who put his life on the line for the good and decent citizens of the vast frontier, a man deserving of awe, respect, and fear.

"Christ," Bat had told Saranda when he'd read it. "I'd best not let Wyatt get ahold of this. He'll laugh himself silly."

He wasn't sure, before the ball, that anyone would believe it. So it came as quite a shock when he found himself a celebrity for the first time in his life. The women crowded around him, demanding dances, so he was at first overwhelmed. But he rose to the occasion with the speedy reflexes that had been touted in the paper. To Saranda's amusement, he was soon cavorting the society butterflies about the dance floor, leading the ladies in more of a western two-step than a Fifth Avenue waltz.

Now that Bat was taken care of, Saranda turned to her fiancé with a warm smile. "Winny, look, isn't that Mathilda standing in the corner? She looks so lonely. You should go dance with her. She's always been sweet on you, you know. I'm afraid it will break her heart when we marry." She took the lapels of his jacket in her slim hands and looked flirtatiously into his face. He wore his grey mask somewhat awkwardly over his spectacles, so it was difficult to see his eyes. "Should I give you up to make her happy, do you think?"

Winston colored to the roots of his salt-and-pepper hair. He'd never been adept with women, always too shy to believe anyone would be attracted to him for himself alone. It was one of the qualities that endeared him to Saranda more than any other. While he'd been warned that women would pursue him simply because his father possessed such wealth and power, he considered himself a man of limited wit, and therefore unappealing to the opposite gender. Unlike his ideal, "Archer," who could charm the birds from the trees, he never knew how to respond to a woman's teasing. It was just this sort of flirtatious bantering from Saranda that made his heart swell with love for her. It made him feel more interesting, and, remarkably, more manly in her presence.

The last thing he wanted was to leave her side. But he was a man of great compassion. He knew what it was to be shy and alone in the shadows at a party. Saranda's reminder that Mathilda might be lonely touched his heart and made it impossible for him to refuse.

He gave her a tender smile. "You're so sweet," he said. "So kind to everyone. Sometimes—"

"What, Winny?"

"Well, sometimes I think you can't possibly be real," he confessed. Then he kissed her hand with restraint, as if unsure of his rights as her fiancé. Saranda took a slow breath as she watched him leave. Naive as Winny was, he didn't know how close he'd come to the truth.

Once he'd gone, she was free to search out her prey of the evening. It shouldn't be too difficult. Blackwood was such an impressive-looking man that it would take more than a mask to disguise him. She studied the dancers, dismissing them with practiced eyes. This one was too short, that one was blond. . . . No, he wasn't dancing. She turned to survey the back of the room and saw a figure who might be him. He was tall with wavy black hair and the body of an acrobat—something that had been passed down through his family by the Gypsies, who, generations ago, had infiltrated the ranks of his English ancestors. He wore a plain black mask that made him look utterly masculine, dangerously sensual.

As if he'd felt the persistent heat of her gaze, the masked man turned to face her. Saranda gasped softly, trembling at the unexpected sense that she'd become the target of his desire, that she was no longer the huntress in search of her prey. Her instinct was to escape, to run from the power he exuded, the threat he represented. . . .

There was a wide stone staircase at the end of the hall, leading up to a second level. She headed for it on shaking legs, hoping she could escape before Winston caught sight of her.

People were wandering up and down the stairway on tours of the museum. Before she made it halfway up, she felt a hand on her arm. She whirled. It was Mace Blackwood. His midnight-blue eyes took in her jittery state with one swift glance from beneath the unadorned black shield of his mask.

She'd run from him, but now that he'd caught her, she was inexplicably happy to see him.

"Had enough of the party?" he asked in his Oxford-inflected voice.

Feeling incapable of speech, she nodded.

"Perhaps you'd care to join me on the terrace. We might step outside and look at the mud."

He smiled charmingly, but her mind was working too feverishly to respond. Now that she had a moment to catch her breath, she recalled her reasons for going after Blackwood in the first place and strengthened her resolve. As he guided her, his hand at her elbow, up the staircase toward the outside door, she took the opportunity to collect her wits and devise a plan of attack. The last thing she could afford at this juncture was to have Blackwood perceive her vulnerable state. She must behave as if nothing out of the ordinary had transpired.

She reached up and fingered the mask at her eyes. It gave her a sense of comfort, a contrivance by which to shield her jumbled emotions from the penetration of his gaze. She could do what she must, what she'd planned for so long. She had only to look at his face . . . and remember the pain. . . .

She overheard McLeod, the fat man who'd been at the Van Slykes the night before, complaining to a woman in a brightly colored mask. "But you don't understand. The only reason I came tonight was to see Madame Zorina. Now you tell me she decided not to come?"

Saranda was distracted enough that the comment barely registered. She was disappointed, naturally, for she'd been eager to see the famous psychic. But she had all she could do to concentrate on the task at hand.

They stepped outside, into a gust of wind that cooled her cheeks and brought a semblance of sanity to her mind. She looked around. They were standing on a stone terrace overlooking the back of the museum. A scaffold had been shoved against the wall, with some buckets of paint atop and some ropes dangling down the sides. She put her hands on the rough railing and drew a deep breath, steeling herself for the battle to come. But in the midst of taking a breath, she leaned over too far and was unnerved by the sensation of the balcony protruding out over nothing but empty space below. She was afraid of only two things in the world—prison and high places. A wave of dizziness flooded through her, and she straightened abruptly, shaken but determined not to let him see her weakness.

He leaned back against the rail so he was facing the pink granite wall of the museum while she looked in the opposite direction, out over the empty fields. As long as she didn't look down, she told herself, she'd be fine.

"I see your interest in the mud is short-lived," she commented to cover her nervousness.

"Why pretend? We both know the mud was an excuse to get you alone." His voice was hushed in the night, oddly thrilling.

"Ah, but you plucked me from the crowd with such careless abandon. Given the masks, have you considered that you've made a mistake? I may not be who you think I am."

He swiveled his head and looked into her glittering eyes. "Perhaps I'm not, either."

"Under the circumstances, perhaps I should demand you remove your mask and prove your identity."

He turned back to her and took the larger blue diamond of her necklace in his hand. His warm knuckles brushed her flesh as he did, sending unexpected shivers up her spine. With a playful grin, he asked, "And what will *you* remove, if I take off my mask?"

"You should be horsewhipped for your impertinence." She jerked away so the necklace fell from his hand. In the process, his hand brushed against the yielding velvet of her breast. She hadn't meant for it to happen, but taking advantage of every opportunity, she raised herself up just a bit, ever so slowly, encouraging his hand to graze her at a more leisurely pace.

"And you should be spanked," he said in a suddenly husky voice. "For encouraging such impertinence from the best friend of your fiancé."

Saranda moved away, sashaying past him with arrogant female grace. "The last man who tried to spank me is now wearing an eyepatch and a new set of teeth."

Her hand was caught from behind, captured with a gentle, halting pressure. She froze, her back still to him.

He turned her around slowly, yet with the inexorably determined gaze of a man who had no intention of being denied. The look that passed between them was electric, raw and crackling with hidden truths. She could feel him touching her before he did, feel her skin tingle as his eyes roved with familiar longing over the lush, seductive curves of her body.

Suddenly, he stepped closer, his body touching hers. She felt blistered by a sudden invading heat. In the flare of his eyes beneath the mask, she detected a rampant spark of maleness, a brightly burning blaze. She could almost smell his need of her. As if she'd pushed him to the limit. As if, by her playing him on her string, all the red-blooded urgency of his desires had suddenly seared his well-built armor, devouring his sense and caution in the hellfire of his arousal. His body as he pressed into her was like a furnace, bent on combustion, ignited by the amorous torment of her gambit. She felt it scorch her, as if her clothes had suddenly burst into flames. Alarmed, she moved back until she came up short against the wall at her back, the scaffold at her side, the dangling ropes brushing her face. She had time only to swipe them aside before he was upon her, crushing her against the stone with his body.

Beneath the elegance and impeccable tailoring of his evening clothes, he had the physique of a cat burglar—that acrobatic Blackwood body, firmly muscled yet with a litheness of movement that easily lent itself to the traversing of rooftops in the dead of a moonless night. The lean yet powerful grace, the massive shoulders, the sinewy arms . . . His hands grasped her arms, pressing them back against the cold wall on either side of her head, sliding them up to entwine his fingers with hers in an act of intimacy that shocked and thrilled her all at the same time.

"Thanks for the warning," he said in a deceptively lazy voice. "If I ever decide to spank you, I'll take precautions beforehand."

With a swiftness that caught her off-guard, he wrenched her hands above her head. Holding them taut in one hand, he grabbed one of the ropes and looped it repeatedly around her wrists so they were anchored high above.

"What are you doing?" she cried, her sudden panic causing her voice to tremble.

She could feel the intensity of his gaze. He softened

it with a lift of the corner of his mouth. In the moonlight, she saw the dimple crease his cheek. His teeth, as his smile widened, shone white and strong. Shuddering, she turned her face away.

With his other hand, he traced a finger along the outline of her mask. "Didn't you wonder why I chose masks for tonight?"

"I don't have to wonder. I know why you did it."

"Do you?"

"Because you wanted to seduce me, and you're too cowardly to do it to my face."

She struggled against the ropes, the frustration of her helplessness acting in an incongruous way as a stimulant to her senses. With her arms anchored so, her breasts rose high, swelling and threatening to spill from the confines of her dress. In the night air, the diamond necklace felt cold against her suddenly heated skin.

He chuckled softly. "Is that what you think?"

"Who but a coward would have to resort to binding a woman's hands just to—"

"To what? Kiss her?"

His hand crept around her, and he crushed her to him, lifting her feet off the floor, as he bent to capture her lips with his own. He kissed her deeply, impaling her against the solid barricade of his chest. He had a deliciously wicked kiss, so passionate, so thoroughly devouring, that she felt she was being consumed, in a flash, by a brushfire, a force of nature without compunction, without mercy. She lost track of her thoughts, of her role, of her plans. He was like Mars, the ancient god of war—bold, confident, impatient, giving all of himself to the burning interest of the moment. His lips moved over hers, invading, claiming her. Under the fierce assault, she felt her body go limp as she fought against the ropes in a futile effort to bring her hands to his face. She was drowning in sensations so volcanic, she forgot to breathe. Clutching at her bonds, feeling the roughness of the hemp dig into the flesh of her wrists and palms, she fought to keep a hold on reality as her head spun and her limbs turned elastic, molding themselves to his frame.

When he raised his head, leaving her mouth parted to the cold night air, she slumped against the ropes, stunned by the discovery his touch had forced on her. His kiss intoxicated her beyond anything she'd ever known. She hadn't expected it, wasn't accustomed to being swept away by men—no matter how enamored they were of her. It frightened her, left her gasping for badly needed air. Perhaps, she rationalized desperately, she'd been rattled by her earlier fear of heights. . . .

"I love masks," he whispered in a voice hoarse with the same maddening passion that was pulsing through her veins. "A mask is passion's best friend. Once masked, you're freed from your inhibitions, from your sense of self. In a way, it's the same freedom and exhilaration when you wear the disguise of a great flam."

It was as close to a confession that he was a con artist as she was likely to get. His words recalled the rumors that had followed Blackwood across Europe and kept the tongues of the underworld wagging. He was, they claimed, the greatest lover in Europe. The thought of it made her limp with need. His mouth, whispering with hypnotic power, nuzzled the sensitive flesh at the side of her neck, sending shock waves of sensation through her hungry body that made her want to turn her mouth to his and part it in another searing kiss.

"A mask gives you a sense of control," he continued, his lips obliging her by moving toward her mouth. He held himself away so that, unbidden, she leaned forward, whimpering for his kiss. "It aids the pretense. Ropes, on the other hand, take away all control, destroy all pretensions.

A woman like you should lose control occasionally. Surrender to the moment . . ."

He leaned over to kiss her once again. But just as his lips touched hers, just as a low moan rushed from her mouth to his, he drew back. Some instinct told him they weren't alone anymore. Saranda was too insensible to realize what was happening as he turned his head, saw the open door, then straightened up, suddenly cautious and distracted.

"You'll have to excuse me," he said abruptly, unwrapping the rope from her wrists so she fell against him in a heap. Setting her on her feet, he added, "This will have to wait for another time."

He moved toward the door, closed now, as if to leave her without another word. Then, thinking better of it, he returned and said, "Meet me in the Park. Tomorrow at five."

She just stared at him, unable to believe what was happening. Was he leaving her—after all that had happened? Could he calmly walk away after rousing her to such a fevered pitch that she could barely make out his features in the blur before her eyes?

He grabbed her neck and pulled her close, kissing her hard. "Promise," he commanded.

She nodded weakly, leaning closer for another kiss. But once she'd promised, he moved toward the door with swift efficiency and left her standing alone in the moonlight, her wrists chafed and her heart pounding in her brain.

She didn't see him again that night. But occasionally her fingers wandered to her lips, where his kisses still burned like a brand.

CHAPTER 5

Saranda was accompanying Winston as he gave Bat a tour of the *Globe-Journal*. Already, they'd viewed the composing room, the pressroom, the city room. It was intended as a perfunctory jaunt, but Bat surprised Winston by showing interest in every aspect of the paper. He'd had little formal education, having left his parents' Illinois farm at an early age to follow a life of adventure, but he'd read widely on a diverse range of subjects. Writing, it turned out, was a particular fascination of his, as was the power of the press. He'd witnessed this power firsthand during his visit. After just one article in the *Globe-Journal*, he'd found himself lionized as a folk hero.

Because of his interest, and the questions he asked, their circuit of the paper was taking longer than expected. Bat stopped to chat with everyone from reporters and editors to the printers and engravers in the back shop. No one escaped his inquiries or his easy grin. Everyone, having read the report of his skill with a smoking sixgun, stared at him with an awe that he found at once flattering and discomfiting.

They'd been touring the executive offices when they came at last to a door with a stenciled sign that read:

M. ARCHER
EDITOR IN CHIEF

Saranda had known they'd pay him a visit sooner or later and had spent the time preparing herself. What had happened the night before now seemed like a dream. She couldn't believe she'd behaved in such a ridiculous manner just because a man had kissed her. Well, not just any man; Mace Blackwood, her sworn enemy. She'd never reacted to anyone in such a breathless manner before. It embarrassed her, making her question her sanity. *What had she been thinking?* The trouble was, she hadn't been thinking at all. In his arms, she'd been reduced to a rush of sensation such as she'd never experienced before. By the sight of his wolf's mouth lowering itself to hers. By the sound of his voice rasping in her ears. By the feel of his arms as he demanded from her a response no man ever had. It unsettled her. She'd always known he was a formidable foe, known he had the ability to fool anyone alive. The humiliating realization hit her that, for that brief moment in the moonlight, he'd duped her as well. His golden tongue had lulled her into a senseless state of surrender that was unlike anything she'd come up against in all her years on the con.

But it wasn't going to happen again.

Winston opened the door without knocking. They caught a quick impression of a massive office dominated by a cluttered desk and lined with wooden file cabinets on three sides. The corner office looked down over Park Row, where the other New York papers made their homes. But it

was the atmosphere that captured their attention. Blackwood was standing behind his desk, glaring at the man
seated opposite him. It was the same man Saranda remembered complaining about the absence of Madame Zorina.
She knew he was Sander McLeod, whose wealth and influence rivaled Jackson's. She knew, too, that Blackwood, in
his guise as Archer, had been systematically exposing the
underhanded tactics of McLeod's powerful business friends.

"I can recall a time," McLeod was saying heatedly,
"when the *Globe-Journal* stood up for the rights of the underdog without libelous attacks on the fine and decent men
that have made this city—hell, this country—great." He
was clearly agitated, gesturing with a fist that looked like a
blacksmith's hammer pounding away at an anvil.

"By decent men, you wouldn't be referring to men
like your friend Grant?" Blackwood demanded.

"The General is one of the greatest men I've ever
had the privilege to know. I served under him in the War.
Why, if it weren't for him—"

"If it weren't for him, we wouldn't have had the most
crooked administration this country's ever seen."

"Grant has done more good for this country than a
man like you will ever know."

Blackwood raised a brow. "A man like me, Mr.
McLeod?"

"It's misguided editors like you who are responsible
for his leaving office."

Blackwood lowered his eyes deceptively. "I'd like to
think I played *some* small part in it."

Appalled, and highly embarrassed, Winston cleared
his throat. "I'm sorry, Archer, I didn't know you were
busy."

He made a move to back out, but Blackwood waved
him into the office. "That's quite all right. We have no
secrets, do we, McLeod? It might be an education for Sher-

iff Masterson to see how bad men function in the big city under the guise of respectable businessmen."

"How dare you?" McLeod growled. "These people you're smearing are friends of ours. People of influence. They can help not only your paper, but your career as well. Why, with their backing—with *our* backing—you could be senator!"

"And end up in your back pockets? Your concern for your friends wouldn't by chance stem from the rumors regarding your own railroads? That you bribed three separate members of your friend Grant's Cabinet? That you talked them into selling you public lands for pennies on the—"

Sander leaned across the desk. "I don't have to listen to these lies!"

"Archer, maybe—"

Without bothering to listen to Winston's warning, Blackwood met McLeod's angry gaze head-on. "Have you ever, Mr. McLeod, been so poor you don't know where your next meal is? Have you ever thought what it's like for a child of seven working in a factory? Seven days a week, never feeling the sun on his face, never seeing the stars at night. Never playing, never dreaming. Just trudging home from work so beaten down, he can barely keep his eyes open long enough to fall onto his filthy pallet on the floor?"

"Yes," Sander hissed, as if hating the memory.

"Then *you* tell *me*. How does he survive, McLeod? Where in the name of God does he find hope?"

It seemed, as he spoke, that no one breathed. His presence and the rhythm of his words were so powerful, so hypnotic, they lost all sense of what he was saying, so caught up were they in his presentation. Bat looked around him at the captivated faces and paused at Saranda's. He'd never seen such an arrested look on her face in all the years he'd known her.

"The *Globe-Journal*, Mr. McLeod," Blackwood continued, "is a well-fueled torch that's going to shine a beacon of hope into all the dark and stinking corners of this miserable city. I made this paper what it is today. Me, with more hard work than you and your friends will do in a lifetime. So you mark me well, McLeod. I'm going to blaze a trail, goddammit, and I'm not looking back. I'm going to pound away at this forest of greed and corruption with a ruddy sword if I have to. Because your friends, with their double-talk and dirty dealings, are wrong. And sooner or later, if I have anything to say about it, they're going to be brought to their knees."

"We'll just see about that," shouted McLeod before he stormed out of the room, fairly knocking them aside as he shoved his bulk out through the door.

Blackwood turned to them as the fury in his eyes receded. In an ironic tone, he said, "Welcome to the *Globe-Journal*, Sheriff Masterson."

Then his eyes raked over Saranda in a sweepingly intimate look before lifting to Winston's face.

"Thanks," said Bat warily. "I reckon I've learned a thing or two."

Winston, clearly embarrassed and at a loss, glanced from Bat and Saranda and back to Blackwood with a pleading look, the light streaming in through the wooden shades glinting off his spectacles. All too aware that she'd promised to meet Blackwood later in the Park, Saranda wasn't eager to stay. "Winny, perhaps Mr. Masterson and I should continue with the tour," she suggested with a smile. "You join us presently."

He gave her a grateful look. "Would you mind? I think I should talk to Archer about this."

"Not at all, dear. Take your time."

As she was closing the door, they heard Winston say

in a tentative tone, "Archer, I'm not sure it's wise to antagonize a powerful man like Sander."

"Don't waste your time worrying about McLeod," came Blackwood's dismissive reply. "He's next, and he knows it."

Bat let out a low whistle once the door was safely closed. "I don't know if he means it, but that Blackwood's good. I never saw anyone that good."

"I never said he wasn't good," Saranda answered, irritated by his obvious admiration. "Good enough to pawn himself off as this selfless character who cares for the poor and the underdog. It's the biggest joke of all."

Bat was watching her closely as they moved away. The hallway was empty, so he pulled her up short, a frown creasing his brow, his thick mustache moving as he pursed his lips.

"I'm leaving," he told her abruptly.

"Leaving? What do you mean?"

"Going back to Dodge."

"But, Bat, you can't. I arranged for you to come so you could be at the wedding."

"Your wedding, sugar, is the last place I want to be. Even if it is part of your big shuck."

She lowered her voice. "It may have started out as a con, but it *is* my wedding. The only one I shall ever have. I was hoping you could act as my family. There's no one else."

His eyes softened, but he shook his head. "Honey, I'm sorry, but I can't stay and watch you do this."

Something in his tone alerted her to a deeper significance. "What do you mean?"

"I mean you're playing with fire."

"Don't be silly. It's the most brilliant job I've ever pulled. And my last. When it's over, I shall settle down to being Mrs. Winston Van Slyke, and Mace Blackwood will have received the retribution he deserves."

"While you hog-tie yourself to a man you don't give a hoot for, for all the rest of your life?"

"I'm extremely fond of Winny. I may even grow to love him in time."

"You'll love him when hell freezes over."

"Why, Bat—"

His hand tightened on her arm. "I know you, honey, as much as anyone can. And I'm telling you, you've met your match in Blackwood."

"Are you doubting my abilities?"

"I'm not talking about your abilities. I'm talking about your feelings. This fellow has his rope on you."

She flushed, remembering her helplessness and her response the night before when he'd bound her wrists above her head.

"Blackwood? Don't be absurd!"

Someone appeared then in the hall, so Bat waited impatiently until the coast was clear.

"I've always known the kind of man you'd fall for," he insisted in a low tone. "Someone who's a better shuck artist than you are."

"He is *not* better!"

Bat shook his head sadly. "You've never been up against anyone like him before. I've seen you make a lot of plays, some of them so sticky I figured you'd never get out of them. But I never saw you look at a man the way you look at Blackwood. Or even the way you look when you say his name."

"What utter nonsense."

"You don't know what you're getting yourself into. Honey, I'm sorry, but I got instincts of my own. And something tells me you're getting in over your head."

She jerked her chin at him. "You're wrong, Bat. I

despise the very name of Blackwood. More than you'll ever know."

"That may be. But you're falling in love with *this* Blackwood. And I'd just as soon not be around to see what becomes of it."

True to his word, Bat cut his visit short and left that very afternoon. Winston and Jackson accompanied them to the train, disappointed that he was leaving so soon. But their disappointment was nothing compared to Saranda's. After a life of being on the run, she considered Bat her only real friend.

At the station, standing amid the whirling steam as his train prepared to depart, Bat kissed Saranda's hand and, for the benefit of her new family, wished her a long and happy life.

"Be careful," he warned, for her ears alone. "And wire me if you need help. As long as I'm alive, you'll have someone to turn to." With a last word of thanks to the Van Slykes, he tipped his derby, chucked her chin with the gold knob of his cane, and boarded the westbound train.

She watched the caboose chug off into the distance, feeling a sense of loss she hadn't felt in years. She was alone now, facing her enemy with nothing but her wits. Turning away, with Bat's words of warning ringing in her ears, she readied herself for her meeting with Blackwood.

CHAPTER 6

It was an unseasonably warm afternoon in Central Park, but Saranda was unaware of her surroundings. In a smoky blue camel's hair and silk walking suit with pleated train, she'd arrived in a state of trembling anticipation, wondering what Blackwood had in mind, what threat he posed. There were only a few days left until the wedding. Having been interrupted in his crusade the night before, he was likely to redouble his attack. Tense and jumpy, she'd spent a sleepless night provisioning herself against his next move. Bat's words kept swimming through her mind. In matters of the intellect, she was unsurpassed. She could pretend any artifice and win anyone over in its execution. But in plays of the heart—where her emotions were involved—she sensed the truth of Bat's admonition. She might very well be in over her head.

Blackwood arrived late, looking, she had to admit, rather dashing in his afternoon finery, his hat slanted at a rakish angle, his watch chain gleaming a rich, heavy gold in the afternoon sun. It looked old and dreadfully expensive. She wondered fleetingly if he'd stolen it. Or seduced some woman into giving it to him.

They strolled away from the carriage road, where the four o'clock throng was still assembling. There, practicing their daily ritual, was a steady procession of the wealthy, the aristocratic, and the notorious of New York society in their various conveyances, waving to one another and calling greetings above the din of horses' hooves and wheels. It was a splendid array. All the city's elite turned out to see and be seen amid the cool green oasis. Saranda recognized the broughams of the Jays, the Livingstons, the Van Rensselaers, and the Stuyvesants. Jim Fisk and other financiers flaunted themselves and their affluence in gleaming barouches and victorias, pulled by sleek steeds. The Beautiful Young dashed along in phaetons, waving scarves and silk fans to draw attention to their fleeting beauty.

Saranda looked around her, at the carriages, the clothes, the money flaunted with such ease, the houses flanking the elm-shaded perimeter of the Park. All of this —the blooded horses, the mansion on Fifth Avenue, the respectability, the permanence—all this was going to be hers.

It was a timely reminder. She was well aware that Blackwood had brought her here to convince her to call off the wedding. She had only to look at him to detect his reckless confidence that he'd accomplish his task. He walked with determined strides, his long legs moving so swiftly at times, she was hard-pressed to keep up. Just the way he carried himself gave her the impression he loved being in his own body—that there was nothing more glorious than being Mace Blackwood. It made men want to be like him, made women want to . . .

She shook herself, bringing her thoughts back to the present. After last night, she was determined to be on her guard. She'd spent the morning sharpening her wits so even he wouldn't find a chink in her armor.

"I hear your friend the sheriff left on the afternoon train," he said, breaking the expectant silence she'd maintained in awaiting his first move.

She angled him a cautious look. "Friend? I met Mr. Masterson only this weekend. What would possess you to call him my friend?"

"It's my business to read people, Miss Voors."

"Your business. As a newsman, you mean."

"Naturally. Which brings us back to the question at hand. Don't think I didn't notice your sidestepping. It has occurred to me, in fact, that it was *your* suggestion to bring Masterson to town—and not Winston's at all."

She was wondering how to answer when she was saved the burden of an awkward reply. A man walking toward them suddenly tripped and grabbed onto Mace to right himself. "I'm *so* sorry!" he cried, apparently aghast at his clumsiness. He was elderly, with a hat pulled down to conceal most of his face, wearing clothes that had seen better days. He brushed heartily at Blackwood's impeccable spring suit. "Do forgive me. I don't know what came over me. You aren't hurt?"

"I'm quite all right," he replied stiffly.

With a last apology, the man wandered off. Astonished, Saranda realized the old man had lifted Blackwood's billfold!

Mace Blackwood, the reigning prince of the Blackwood clan, had had his wallet stolen in broad daylight, in the middle of Central Park—the safest, most patrolled area of the city! For three hundred years, the Blackwoods had been masters of pickpocketry and sleight of hand. It was so incredible, she wanted to laugh.

She didn't care that he'd had his money stolen. She was even tempted to leave it alone, chalking it up as punishment for the liberties he'd taken the night before. But her professional pride was so outraged, she couldn't resist the urge for retribution. No street filcher was going to get away with such a clumsy heist. Not with her around.

The trick would be to retrieve his property without Blackwood's knowledge. But what an achievement if she succeeded!

The challenge conquered her earlier reticence. Her fingers tingled as her pulse accelerated and her mouth went dry. She felt the old love of the hunt surging through her veins. She'd never cared about possessions. It had always been the thrill of the sport, the shiver of excitement that set her on fire and made her feel alive. The danger, the uncertainty, the recklessness of the risk, all combined to stimulate her in a way no man on earth ever had.

Until last night.

But last night—and its inherent uncertainties—could be forgotten in the venture ahead. This was familiar territory. This was something she could do with her eyes closed.

As Blackwood stared darkly after the retreating figure of the thief, Saranda slipped an earring off one of her lobes and pocketed it. "Why, Mr. Archer, my earbob! The one Winny gave me! I do believe I've dropped it! Could it have happened when that man bumped us?"

Let him think what he would. It wasn't important. She needed a reason to follow the man, and this was as good as any.

"I doubt you're going to find it out here," he said.

She laughed. "Nonsense. I'm an optimist, Mr. Archer. I believe we all get what we deserve in the end."

She smiled with secret delight as she took his arm and headed off at a purposeful pace to follow the smug thief. While pretending to comb the ground for her jewelry, she kept a sharp eye on the figure ahead, waiting for her opening. She didn't worry about him getting away. Experience had taught her that sooner or later the perfect opportunity always presented itself.

Once she saw him stop, take out the wallet, count its contents, and give a startled jerk. Because he saw to much of the business of running the *Globe-Journal*, Blackwood often carried large sums of cash. She guessed there was as much as a thousand dollars in the billfold. Watching as the loafer pocketed it once again with a supreme air of satisfaction, she renewed her determination that he wouldn't spend a penny of it.

They walked along the elm-ridged Mall and came out upon the Esplanade with its stately stone staircases leading to the Bethesda Fountain below. There were people everywhere, enjoying the breeze off the lake, the afternoon sun, the melodies of the brass band drifting from the bandstand. Out across the lake, rowboats with striped awning covers made their way lazily across the water. People strolled along the banks, the men mostly in dark suits, the women in muted walking suits as befitted afternoon. Swans glided over the surface of the lake. Children squealed with laughter from the carousel, from goat wagons or saddle donkeys. A camel pulled a lawn mower across a distant patch of green.

And still she awaited her chance.

Finally, it presented itself. They descended the stone staircase, hot on Shabby Suit's heels. While craftily—so he thought—casing his next victim, the pickpocket wandered over to the black iron water fountain that offered drinking water cooled by blocks of ice in a pit below.

"Ah!" she cried. "Here's my earring! Didn't I tell you I'd find it? My, but I'm thirsty after that brisk walk. Do wait, won't you, Mr. Archer? I won't be a minute."

Arching a questioning brow, he watched her go.

This, she knew, was the tricky part. Blackwood was

watching her like a hawk. If she made one obvious move, he'd detect it. The challenge was not so much in returning the wallet to his pocket, but in doing so undetected.

They had to wait as a nanny with a group of children held each one up to the cascading flow of water. As the man finally bent to drink, she moved up behind him, waiting her turn in line. He was so distractedly pleased with himself that he didn't even bother to look behind him. He walked off, and she drank from the fountain, then returned to Blackwood with her hands behind her back and a smile of triumph on her face.

"Thank you for waiting, Mr. Archer. I'm so happy to have found the earbob. I should have died if I'd really lost it. It means so much to me because Winny gave it to me." Slyly, she slipped the billfold into the pocket of her skirt. She was certain from the bored look in his eyes that he hadn't seen her. When the opportunity presented itself, she'd replace it without his knowledge.

"Then I'm happy to oblige."

"But you wanted to talk to me, Mr. Archer. Did you perchance have something—pressing you wanted to say?"

She smiled her most dazzling smile. Her eyes were alight with the knowledge of what she'd just done. It never ceased to thrill her—to make her pulse drum in her ears, to send the blood rushing through her veins. Her mind was racing, already plotting ways of replacing the wallet in his coat pocket.

He looked at her a moment, saw the seductive triumph gleaming in her eyes. Unexpectedly, he took her hand and pulled her back behind a tree. Winston, with his interest in horticulture, would have known what kind of tree it was. All she knew was that her heart was pounding a vicious rhythm, and that Blackwood, pressing into her, was hard against her thigh. The unexpectedness of it warmed her like whiskey flowing through her veins.

"You're sensational," he rasped. Taking her lips with sudden ruthless abandon, he kissed her deeply, shoving her back against the tree. "Christ, what you do to me. You're like a melody pounding in my head, like someone I've known all my life. You're the last woman on earth I'd ever want. But I think sometimes, if I can't have you, I shall go out of my bloody mind."

He was frighteningly convincing. As if the pretense was abandoned, and he was speaking from his heart. His hands moved over her with unquestioned skill, wrenching her mind from her plot as his mouth nibbled her cheek, her ear, her neck. His blatant masculinity overpowered her. She felt her breath leave her in little gasps as she closed her eyes and began to float beneath his touch. He dipped his dark head and kissed her with unchecked passion, plunging his tongue into her mouth until she, breathless now, kissed him back with a rashness of her own.

Then, her body on fire, she opened her eyes and saw his face. The hated Blackwood face with the swarthy features, the heavy black brows, the piercing midnight eyes above a mouth so blatantly sexual, it should have been against the law. But she was never one to revere lawful commandments. The obscure, the forbidden, those were the realms of her soul. She was as undeniably drawn to that illicit mouth as she would be to a priceless necklace locked in the most impenetrable vault. Not for any wish to possess it. Just for the fun of knowing she could.

That's all it was, she told herself. The danger. The reckless flaunting of all she'd held dear. But Bat's words came back to haunt her. *You're falling in love with this Blackwood . . . this Blackwood. . . .*

"Unhand me," she cried, shoving against the hard-muscled planes of his massive chest. Slipping past him, she hurried away from the nearby crowd. It wouldn't do to be seen kissing Winston's best friend in a public park. But then, she realized belatedly, that was what Blackwood wanted. So the story would get back to Winston, the wedding called off. And Blackwood free to steal the *Globe-Journal* from under Winston's unsuspecting nose.

He joined her, easily matching her frantic pace with a leisurely, long-legged stride. "You surprise me. Blushing protestations?" His voice dipped lower. "After last night?"

"This is highly unorthodox, Mr. Archer," she said stiffly, clinging to the safety of her role.

He threw back his head and laughed. "*Unorthodox?* Since when does a woman like you care about conventions?"

"You presume too much in assuming you know what a *woman like me* does or doesn't care for. You, don't, after all, know much about me, do you?"

"Don't I?"

It was times like this when she thought he knew it all. She stopped walking. They were in a grove of secluded trees, off the main path. It was cool and shady in the leafy hideaway. She wondered what deviltry had brought her to this spot, far away from prying eyes. Was it to shield herself from his manipulations? Or was it because she hoped, in the sequestered thicket, that he'd take her in his arms and make her feel all the wondrous sensations she was trying so hard to deny?

"I know a woman like you can't be happy with a commonplace life," he told her, speaking to her back. "I know that deep inside, you chafe against conventions and man-made laws just as I do. That you have a restless, wandering soul and an appetite for adventure that no mediocre existence can fulfill. That the thought of presiding over afternoon teas and charitable bazaars is enough to send cold shivers down your spine."

He traced a solitary finger from the base of her neck

down the length of her spine. She did shiver, but not because she was thinking of bazaars.

"I know you're a rebel." He put his mouth to her ear, where she could feel the warm intemperance of his breath. "That you were born more clever than all the rest. That you're a woman who'd rather make love in a barn than a bed. That you haven't met the man who can take you in his arms and make you forget all you're after in the sovereignty of his kiss." He drew her closer, so her back was pressed against him, and slid an arm around her waist.

She swallowed hard. She felt weak and trembly as she leaned back against him. His erection swelled as her bottom brushed against it, making her loins tingle with unwonted need. Yet her mind savored his words the way a dying man might relish his last drink. How did he know all that? He'd touched at the secrets of her soul, the very fringes of the thoughts that haunted her at night, when she thought about a life with Winston. Then she chastised herself for being such a fool. He'd said it himself, in language cloaked by his disguise. It was a con artist's job to read people, to understand their strengths and weaknesses. The best of the breed could discover truths in a single conversation that a person's friends might never learn in a lifetime. Oh, he was good. There was no doubt about it. Words were his weapons, and he wielded them like a well-honed sword. She'd have to keep on her toes to remain ahead of him. But she had armaments the others didn't. She knew his words for what they were.

"A pretty speech," she retorted in a shivery voice. "Do you deliver it to all the women you're trying to seduce?"

He stilled. She thought for a moment that he might move away. Instead, he slowly slid his large, possessive hands up to her breasts and asked, very softly, "If you wanted to know what I was like in bed, why didn't you just ask?"

A jolt of excitement shot through her body and settled in the moist, steamy heat between her legs. She could feel the danger of her situation. But that, of course, was the pleasure of it. On the heels of an afternoon of playing society hostess, she felt blissfully alive.

"You can hardly blame me for being curious," she replied as casually as she could manage. "I wondered, if you must know, if your protestations were genuine. If a man like you ever really means what he says."

The greatest lover in Europe, she thought. *Why wouldn't I be curious?*

"Does this feel real?" He took her hand and brought it behind her, held it against his crotch. He bulged beneath her palm, straining against his trousers like a demon battling for release. The size of him was intoxicating. This prince of darkness she'd hungered after the night before, this god of the underworld who had haunted her dreams so she could no longer decipher, in the dead of a sleepless night, if she'd experienced or imagined the terrible beauty —this unholy serpent, was not, after all, the stuff of legend. He was real. He was human. And he was hers for the taking.

His other hand left her breast and brushed the curve of her mouth. Her lips parted, and he thrust his thumb inside.

"What do you want from me . . . *Sarah?*"

She closed her eyes. What did she want? She wanted to drop to her knees and free him from the prison of his clothing—to take him on her tongue and pull him deep inside. To fill her mouth with him and feel him swell against her moist flesh . . . Her throat was so dry, she knew if she spoke, her voice would come out in a croak.

His thumb was moving in her mouth, so she abandoned the effort and sucked on it instead.

"Tell me," he commanded softly.

The temptation was overwhelming.

Since she didn't, he took charge. Crushing her hand against him with one hand, inserting his thumb slowly in and out of her mouth with the other, he spoke in a harsh whisper.

"Do you want me to keep playing this game? Or would you prefer that I strip away your defenses as I could so easily rip away your clothes? To take you in my arms and make you admit that—in spite of everything—in spite of who we are and what we're after—you want me every bit as much as I want you?"

"What do you think I want?" she gasped.

"I think you want me to lift up your skirts—and come inside you—and haul you up against that tree—and make you scream—"

She was insensible to his movements. Without her realizing how, he'd dropped his hands and worked her skirt up her legs, sliding it up her thighs. As he spoke, his hands sought the waistband of her silk drawers and slipped inside. He found the curls between her legs and sank his finger into the moist, welcoming heat.

"So I was right." His finger moved inside her with such skillfully probing penetration that she felt her breath burning her lungs. His other hand grasped her neck and pressed, keeping her from collapsing completely. She was overcome by a heavy, somnolent, simmering yearning, his voice and the drift of his words as hypnotically seductive as his fingers playing with her control. Her mouth, parted now with the urgency of her breath, hungered to answer him in kind. "Do you like my finger inside you? What about two? Or three? What if I rub you with my thumb, like so?"

She moaned aloud. Her juices soaked his hand. She wanted him so badly, she could easily have wrenched off her clothes and taken him, in the middle of a public park, wrapping her legs around him and inviting him with hot words to slam her up against the nearest tree.

"Does Winston make you wet the way I do?" he growled.

Winston's name on his lips made her stiffen in his arms. She'd forgotten all about Winston. She'd forgotten about Sarah Voors and Archer. She'd forgotten all she was after. Who this man was and what he represented. She'd forgotten everything in the rapturous torture of his touch.

As she stilled, his fingers ceased their probing. He lifted his mouth from her ear and rested his forehead heavily against the back of her head. As if looking at her was too much, as if it might weaken him beyond his facility to cope.

Collecting himself, he heaved a ragged breath. "I can't do this," he said as his fingers slid out of her and left her aching with unquenched desire. Slowly, reluctantly, he skimmed her skirt back over her trembling thighs. She heard it swish as the hem fell to her ankles. "I can't be with you, wanting you, needing you, never knowing where I stand. I know you're marrying Winston. I *know* it, dammit. But something—some distant voice inside—keeps whispering that you belong to me. That no man alive can understand you, accept you, the way I can. That at Winston's side, you'd be shackled to an impossible existence. But in my arms, you'd be set free."

"Don't say that," she cried. "I don't want to believe that. I *can't* believe it."

She had to remember who he was. He was her enemy. The brother of the man who . . . The son, the grandson, the *great*-grandson, of all the Blackwood enemies before him. He wasn't just a man. He was a symbol. He was something to conquer. To vanquish, just as she must banish his words from her brain. She had to remain strong. Because the truth was, he was making her feel things no man ever had. He was opening a core of emotion that she'd clamped tight years ago. With his persuasions, with the uncanny gospel of his words, he was piercing secret corners of her purposely sealed heart.

Putting his hands to her shoulders, he spun her around with such force that her head swayed precariously. Reaching around her, he cupped her backside and hauled her fiercely close. "If you don't want me, goddammit, say so," he demanded. "But if there's hope . . . If you think of me at night, when no one's around to know—"

She must remember her role. She had to string him along until the wedding. "Even if that were true, I wouldn't tell you," she whispered, more honestly than she'd intended.

He pulled her into his arms and held her close, as if savoring the sound of the words.

Suddenly, she remembered the wallet she'd secreted in her pocket. This was the perfect opportunity to replace it. She went to reach for it, but he caught her hand and brought it to his lips.

"Then at least I can feel free to hope."

His lips against her palm were warm, persuasive, sending electrical shocks up her arm. Then, just as abruptly as he'd taken her, he let go and allowed her to fall back against the tree. She felt so shaken, she struggled to take deep breaths, desperate to calm her throbbing nerves.

She waited until he was heading toward the exit of the Park before sliding her hand into her pocket. Empty! She tried the other one. Again, nothing. A white rage blinded her. He'd known all along. All this time, while making her feel that he'd slipped and confessed inner truths, he'd been stealthily lifting the billfold from her pocket. Without her even feeling it!

Her rage subsided, to be replaced by a strange sense of kinship. He was a master, there was no doubt about it. And he was as reckless as she. If she'd risked tipping her hand by purloining his billfold, he'd been equally improvident in recovering it. They had, that afternoon, effectively laid their cards on the table, as much as admitting, in their folly, who they were. Because at the finish, it was the game that counted, and not the end result. No one but a Blackwood could understand a Sherwin.

But what did he really know, and how much was intuition, guesswork? More important, what would be his next move?

CHAPTER 7

For three days, Saranda awaited Blackwood's next move. Every time someone walked into a room, she jumped, thinking it might be him. At all the balls held in Winston's and her honor, she studied the guests in vain, hoping to catch a glimpse of his familiar figure looming over the crowd. Yet, in spite of her vigilance, he was noticeably absent from the festivities. As he continued to stay away, the suspense made her edgy; she wondered if she would find him around the next corner, or if the next voice she heard would be his. Others attributed it to pre-wedding jitters. But she knew different. Remarkably, as her tension mounted, she found herself missing him. She'd been looking forward to a bit of sport before the wedding, when her real campaign to destroy him would begin. She felt strangely let down by his confounding refusal to play the game.

But female intuition told her there was more to it. That he was feeling as battered by the game as she. That he was disconcerted by the same maelstrom that had confused her own senses since the night of the masked ball. The night he'd thrust her wrists above her head and, roping them tight, had staked his claim on her trembling body, and taught her what it was like to feel helpless desire. Flam artist he might be, but she'd felt in him the same unchecked passion, the same doubts, that kept her tossing at night in sweat-dampened sheets.

She wished Bat were still here. It would be a comfort to have someone to talk to—to help her put things in perspective. Because if Blackwood *was* feeling the same desperate longing for her that she was for him . . . where did they go from here?

The night before the wedding, there was yet another prenuptial ball. Saranda adorned herself in pale pink off-the-shoulder satin in a studied departure from the dark gowns that dominated the fashion scene. At the last minute, she removed her satin drawers and tossed them tempestuously aside. With one night left, Blackwood would no doubt choose tonight to make his final move. If he did, he'd find no impediment to his wild, roving hands. This time, she decided, she'd shock *him*!

The conspicuous lack of lingerie made her feel dangerously, deliciously aware of herself as a woman. She could feel her thighs brush against each other as she walked, creating an irresistible friction that recalled Mace's hands toying with the tangled wet curls. She knew from the looks in others' eyes that they sensed her sharpened awareness. With her blond hair pinned high in a riot of tumbling curls, she was a vision of saucy sophistication, carefully tailored for Blackwood's benefit.

Except that he never made an appearance.

She waited the entire evening, wondering what surprise he had in store. She'd prepared herself for every conceivable situation, not the least of which was full-blown seduction. If Blackwood could get her into bed tonight, he'd have the ammunition he needed to stop the wedding.

But he never showed up.

Neither did the father of the groom. It was much remarked upon, as it wasn't like Jackson to miss such an important evening. He was devoted to his only son and never missed an opportunity to play the doting father. But when Winston explained there was a crisis at the paper that his father was helping "Archer" handle, talk turned to other matters.

Saranda spent the evening trying to concentrate on mindless conversations as she danced with every man present. Winston, she noted, was glowing with a rare excitement. With everyone slapping him on the back and congratulating him, he seemed to have swollen up like a proud peacock.

When at last he was able to claim a dance with his bride-to-be, he seemed nearly drunk with happiness. Yet he held her gingerly, at arm's length, as befitted a public occasion. His embrace felt tepid, unimaginative, after the rugged ferocity of Blackwood's possession. Stepping to his lead, she felt a momentary panic. She tried to imagine Winston running his hands up her thighs, tried to visualize his face as he discovered the bare skin, touched the moist warmth that even now throbbed with unrequited need.

She was marrying this man tomorrow. She might be a confidence artist, but she believed in loyalty. Once she said her vows, she intended to spend her life being a good and faithful wife. It was, after all, the least she could give Winston. But dancing with him, remembering the fierce splendor of Blackwood's seduction, she began to realize just what this covenant meant. To her. To her life. She thought of the price she would be paying to win a victory, and questioned for the first time in her life whether it would be worth it.

"I feel," Winston told her, cutting into her thoughts, "like the luckiest man in the world. To have you, dearest Sarah, for my own. It's more than I've ever imagined."

She'd have to pretend to be Sarah for the rest of her life. Never again would anyone call her by her own name. Never again to answer the call of her own nature, to break free from the constraints of society.

Distractedly, she touched his cheek. "I shall be good to you, Winston," she vowed. "I shall make it all worthwhile."

His eyes, beneath his spectacles, shone like the sea on a sunny day. "I wish my mother were alive. It would mean so much to me to have her here. She'd like you, you know. You're so much like her. So good and kind. Charming, witty, lighthearted . . . You're everything I'm not and wish I could be. You're like Archer in a way. You both embrace life fearlessly. Yet you've both been so good to Father and me. Wherever my mother is, I think she must be very happy."

Saranda doubted that, but his words gave her the courage she needed. They anchored her, reminding her of her reasons for marrying Winston. The emotional reasons, beyond her lust for vengeance against the Blackwoods. Why, she'd marry him anyway, even if Blackwood bowed out of the scene. His statement reminded her of her father, and all he'd hoped for her. She suddenly felt his presence like a warm embrace, and she knew in that moment that she was doing the right thing. This was what her father had wanted for her. If she'd let him down unforgivably once before, she could make up for it by going through with this wedding. It was the only gift she could give him. The only thing she had left to give.

"My father would like you too, Winny," she told him honestly. "You're everything he hoped I'd marry, and more."

Around midnight, when Blackwood still hadn't appeared, a servant brought Winston a note on a silver tray.

"Father wants to see us at home," he told Saranda. "At once."

"That sounds ominous. What could it be?"

"Perhaps the problem at the paper is more serious than we'd thought."

Unbidden, Saranda felt a prickle at the back of her neck. Intuition warned her to beware.

Jackson was in the study when they arrived. "Winston. Sarah. Come in, please."

He seemed like a different man. His voice sounded weary, and he looked old. The skin on his face seemed to hang, his blue eyes dimmed of their usual sympathetic light. The jacket he'd been wearing had been removed and his tie opened. She'd never seen him less than formally attired in all the months she'd known him. Even at the dinner table, he was dressed as if going to a ball. What had happened here that would cause this change? Was it her imagination, or was he gazing at her coldly?

She looked around, searching for clues. The cheery fire was a sharp contrast to the mood. It roared in the grate, illuminating the portrait of Lalita above it.

Suddenly, Saranda understood. *Jackson knew.* She could read it in his eyes. Blackwood had done his dirty work. But how much did they really know?

Jackson fixed her with a steady gaze. "What can you tell us about a young woman named Saranda Sherwin?"

CHAPTER 8

So Blackwood had known all along. Damn him! Not only had he turned her in, he'd twice proved her a fool. He'd obviously felt nothing for her, bluffing her into believing he cared. It was clear what he'd done. He wasn't trying to convince her to call off the wedding, after all. He was just throwing her off-track so he could expose her when she least expected it. But she'd be damned if she'd give up without a fight. As dark as the situation appeared, she refused to give up hope. Her fury made her strong. There had to be a way to salvage this. She hadn't worked this hard to have it fall to pieces now. *Not because Mace Blackwood had outwitted her!*

She knew she had to think fast. Her mind assessed the situation and weighed the options with lightning speed. Then, in a bold move, she said the only thing she could say.

"I'm Saranda Sherwin."

"What?" cried Winston.

"Then it's true," Jackson stated, ignoring his son. "You are a—confidence woman . . . an adventuress."

"Father!"

Saranda touched Winston's sleeve to silence him. "Don't, Winny. It's the truth."

Stunned, Winston fumbled behind him and slumped into a nearby chair.

"Do you mind?" Without awaiting permission, she went to the sideboard and poured herself a healthy dose of brandy, which she drank in several gulps. She imagined they'd be shocked, but what did it matter now? It gave her a moment to compose her thoughts, to decide the best course of action.

When she turned around, they were staring at her. "Would you care for some?"

Numbly, they shook their heads. She waved Jackson into a seat, which he took with utter exhaustion.

"The story, if told, wants telling from the beginning."

The two men exchanged startled glances. Belatedly, she realized she'd lapsed into her own accent. It altered her voice, giving a breezy, sophisticated quality to the words she spoke, her enunciation as fine as that of any duchess.

"First, as you've no doubt guessed, I'm not Sarah Voors. Not the American-born daughter of an old Dutch family. There *was* a Frederick Voors, and he died, just as I've told you. Had a daughter educated in England, at that. The real Sarah died years ago. I met her shortly before her death, which is how I acquired the idea of using her in the first place."

She took another sip of the brandy, smaller this time, as she was beginning to feel its effects.

"This is unbelievable," Winston muttered. "What did you say your real name is? *Saran*—"

"Sa-*ran*-da," she corrected Winston's pronunciation.

"Rather like Miranda. The truth of the matter is, my family have been confidence artists for generations. Almost three hundred years, to be exact," she added, with an unconscious pride in her tone. "We started off small, as cockney pickpockets scrapping for a bit of bread. Then, because that was the only sort we came in contact with, the tradition continued. We were poor, but we certainly weren't stupid. Each successive generation added new skills to the family's repertoire of tricks. One married a cat burglar, another a carnival performer, another a cardsharp, and so on along the line. The parents passed down the skills to the subsequent generation. So by the time I was thirteen, I knew how to do it all. I'm quite good at it, you see."

"Indeed," murmured Jackson grimly.

She took another breath. "My father," she continued in a softer tone, "was a master at the con. In all the generations of our family, it was he who excelled. He was so remarkable, he could fool even me. But good as he was, he was always aware that he was still a member of the lower classes. That no matter how he succeeded, it would always be them against us. Don't misunderstand me. He loved being a confidence artist. And artist he truly was. He wasn't fully alive unless he was using his skills to pull the wool over someone's eyes. It wasn't the money he relished —it was the challenge, the sheer effrontery of the game."

Jackson glanced about the study at the expensive bric-a-brac, as if wondering what might be missing. She chose to ignore the implication.

"Love the profession as he did, my father led a hard life because of it. He'd been kicked about considerably, even been in prison a time or two. Suffered rather badly, I'm afraid, as did my mother. In the underworld," she added with a slight raise of her chin, "my father was considered the king of the con. Aristocracy in his own way.

But he was still looked down on and defiled by the true aristocracy."

"He wasn't surprised?" Jackson asked incredulously.

"Of course not. We had a long tradition of such discrimination in our family. As I grew older, though, it haunted him. He cherished me, you see, as any ordinary father would. He wanted more for me than a life of uncertainty, of constantly being on the go. He worried that I'd suffer as my parents had. He despised the class system of England and wanted me to rise above it. To be a lady. To become one of the aristocracy."

"You mean he was willing to sell you to the highest bidder."

She felt a flash of anger. "I don't expect you to understand. You can't conceive of what it was like to come from such a background. By conventional standards, I concede my father's thinking was twisted. But he wanted nothing more for me than other fathers desire for their children. A better life. So he began early, planning the most elaborate hoax of his career. When I was just a child, he began grooming me to marry into the aristocracy. Taught me how to speak properly, how to dress, how to dance and converse so no one would ever guess where I'd come from. It became so ingrained in me that as I grew, it was second nature. I became as focused as he. I knew from an early age that I was slated for something special. He even called me Princess, as if to remind me. 'You're better than this,' he'd tell me. 'You were born for royalty.' The tragedy was, I believed him."

"Tragedy?" Winston asked.

"I might as well be honest. While my father was grooming me to marry a prince, I was learning other things as well. He tried not to teach me the tricks of his trade. But I was clever, you see. I could see the joy he took in his work. And I wanted to share that with him. When I asked how he'd perpetrated some gambit, he'd gruffly refuse to tell me. But I'd sit on his lap"—her lips turned up in a tender smile—"and beg prettily, and soon he couldn't refuse. I found I was more my father's daughter than he wanted to admit." She gave a small sigh. "You may well imagine my dilemma. I loved my father tremendously. He was, quite simply, everything to me. But resigned as I was to the path he'd chosen for me, I loved the life as well."

Winston was clearly in shock as he stared at her. Jackson, shifting in his seat, said, "You spoke of a tragedy."

She stared into the fire, standing with her back to them. "My parents were murdered. Horribly, when I was thirteen. I tried to help them, but I was,"—her voice cracked—"I was *prevented*," she finished bitterly. She could see it all again in her mind's eye. The flames, the screams, the wretched laughter as Lance Blackwood . . .

She shook her head to clear it and returned, with some effort, to her story. "It took me years to recover from the—consequences of my parents' death. When I finally did, I did the only thing I could do: traveled about Europe, perfecting my technique. My father's dream for me had quite literally gone up in flames. I had nothing with which to make a living except the wits I'd been born with and what my father had taught me."

"Why didn't you marry as your father wanted?"

A stab of pain caused her stomach to churn. She grabbed hold of the mantel and took a deep breath. She hadn't allowed herself to think about this in years. After all this time, it was still too raw to remember now.

"I had all I could do to recover. Don't forget, I was only thirteen."

"Go on," said Winston softly.

"I came to this country three years ago. Traveled extensively, pulling various scams as a means of making a living, before deciding on New York as a base. I shan't sugarcoat this. When I arrived in the city, and heard about you, I thought—well, I suppose I thought it was an opportunity to make my father's dream come true."

It wasn't the truth, not completely. But professional pride had been bred into her. She wouldn't expose Blackwood to save herself. Not if there was any other way.

"And you chose us because of Lalita?" Jackson asked, glancing at the portrait of his beloved wife. "You made yourself over to resemble her."

"Yes. I read everything I could about her. She was, as you recall, prominently displayed in the newspapers of the time. Lalita skating on the lake. Lalita attending the opera. Lalita winning prizes for her flowers. I began to study her. Spent six months learning to ice-skate to perfection so I could happen upon Winny skating on the lake and make his acquaintance. Studied the Dutch customs Lalita was known to hold dear. It took eight months of grueling work to come up with the right approach, to perfect my credentials. It had to be perfect, you see, because with any luck it would be the last time. Then, through a stroke of fortune, I discovered how much you both missed her. And I knew I could use that."

"Did your conscience never bother you?" Jackson asked in an uncharacteristically acid tone.

"I never thought about it, to be honest. It was, if anything, the crowning glory in a spectacular career."

Winston was turning progressively more pale. He rose and went to the sideboard, muttering, "I think I *will* have that drink." She watched him, the slump of his shoulders, the deliberation of movement that spoke of his shock. She waited for him to turn back around, then fixed him with a sorrowful gaze.

"You weren't people to me in the beginning," she

explained. "You were simply suckers to be had. What I didn't count on was your decency."

"Forgive me," Jackson interjected, "but that strikes me as an odd thing to say, considering all that's come before it."

"You must remember, I grew up pilfering from British aristocracy. I was taught, and truly believed, that those who had money either took possession of it through illegal means or inherited it from those who had. If, through my wits, I could purloin some of it for my family, why shouldn't I? The wealthy stole their wealth in much the same manner we did, only they were hypocritical enough not to admit it. That, I was taught, was why they spent so much of their money on charitable pursuits. To assuage their guilt over the manner in which the money was made in the first place. So, naturally, I had a certain contempt for the moneyed classes as a whole. It seemed to me that I was somehow more honest in my dealings. At least I made people happy while I was with them."

"I can vouch for that," said Winston, draining his brandy.

"We didn't have many rules when I was growing up. What few there were pertained to not fraternizing with those outside the family, that sort of thing. But one tenet was strictly adhered to. Suckers deserved what they got. The premise being that anyone stupid enough to be suckered in the first place was going to be taken advantage of by someone, somewhere along the line. So it might just as well be us. Do you see the sense in it?"

Winston set his glass down on the table and dropped back into his seat. "Not particularly," he said, growing gloomier by the moment.

"I don't say this to be unkind. Only to help you understand my state of mind on meeting you. I suspected your goodness as the same sort of act that mine was. But it wasn't long before I realized you *seemed* good because you *were*. No one has ever been so monstrously kind to me." She paused a beat, then played her trump card. "Because of that, I knew I couldn't go through with it. You deserve better than a baggage like me. So, I was planning to tell you the truth this evening. In fact, I'd already written out a confession. If you'll have one of the servants look in the top drawer of the room I occupied this weekend, you'll see I'm telling the truth."

A servant was summoned, and Saranda told him where to find the letter. As they waited, she had time to reflect on her good fortune at having thought of such a ploy ahead of time—in case of just such an occurrence. The servant returned and handed the confession to Jackson, who read it before passing it on to his son.

"I suppose," she said when they'd finished, "when all is said and done, I'd already decided to sacrifice my own happiness and set you free."

She began to walk dejectedly toward the door. "What do you intend doing?" Jackson asked.

"I shall—return to the old life, I suppose. There's nothing left to do. I'm so terribly sorry, Winny . . . Jackson. It never occurred to me that I would come to care for you both the way I do. I only hope, in the lonely years ahead . . . when you remember me . . . that you can find it in your heart to forgive me."

"Father, surely—"

Whether she was an adventuress or not, Winston was madly in love with his fiancée. She was like no woman he'd ever known. Now he knew why. He found it oddly exciting, knowing the truth. It was intriguing. It was glamourous. *His* intended wife—a woman of mystery? Yet he'd never disobeyed his father in all his life. If something could keep her from leaving, it would have to be with Jackson's blessing.

Jackson waved his son to silence. "I told the man who informed me of this that he was wrong. That if you were involved in such a thing, you'd changed. That you were a loving and decent woman and wouldn't be able to bring yourself to coldly—" He flushed. "Well, I knew you couldn't go through with it, that's all that counts."

"You couldn't have pretended to—care for me, could you?" Winston asked shakily, hoping against hope that this glorious woman had been sincere in her feelings, at least.

She turned to look at him, at the dark and light shadings of his salt-and-pepper hair, at the sincerity of his trusting aqua eyes. She saw, too, what this discovery had done to him. That arrested look of heightened interest. Winston Van Slyke, who considered himself too dull to woo a woman, wanted to know if he was really loved by this bad girl. She'd learned long ago never to be surprised by anything.

"I care for both of you more than you'll ever know," she said sincerely. *And that's why I can't let Blackwood get away with fleecing you.* She turned to Jackson.

"I assume Archer—with his great investigative abilities—was the one who told you."

Sadly, Jackson nodded his head. "Of course Archer's dead set against this marriage. He's of the opinion that charges should be pressed against you, the police called—"

"Arrested?" cried Winston.

Her anger choked her. *Bloody Blackwood!* Just like his hateful brother—and all the other Blackwood scourges down through the generations. How could she have been so blind? Hadn't her father warned her? It wouldn't be the first time the Blackwoods had broken the professional code of honor. It was just like one of them to resort to this sort of despicable tactic. . . .

It was for that very reason that she couldn't retreat and leave him free access to the Van Slyke fortune and power. She had to fight him with all she had available. And she had within her arsenal weapons she'd never even dusted off.

CHAPTER 9

Saranda crossed the city room at a fast clip, endeavoring to be as inconspicuous as a lone woman could be in such surroundings. Several reporters were putting the finishing touches on stories for the morning edition, their typewriter keys clicking irregularly. Editors were calling for copy. Everywhere, desks were piled high with books, magazines, stacks of paper, galley proofs, and half-empty coffee cups. Ashtrays overflowed, and the air was thick with smoke. Everything seemed to be smeared with ink. It was all she could do to get through the room without ruining her costume.

The men stopped to look at her, sweeping along in her pink satin gown. She paid them no mind. If she stopped to explain, she'd be delayed again, and Blackwood —if he was here at all—might slip through her fingers. It was bad enough that she'd had to argue her way past the guard at the front door. He'd let her pass only because she'd reminded him of her marriage to Winston the follow-

ing day—a marriage that would make her part-owner of
the *Globe-Journal*.

Blackwood's office was in a far corner, away from the
city room. The corridors leading to his office were dark,
since this part of the building wasn't generally used at
night. But she thought she saw a faint flickering light below the closed door. She paused to take a steadying breath,
warning herself that it might be no more than her imagination. When she felt ready, she threw open the door.

The room was lighted with a single gas lamp, turned
down low to offer the meagerest illumination. Blackwood
stood behind his desk, a cigarette dangling from his lips,
going over a list with a man she recognized as Morgan, the
assistant managing editor. The lamp threw their shadows
up the wall and across the ceiling, so they loomed eerily
across the room like imagined monsters in the shadows of a
child's room. The men looked up in surprise. She saw
Blackwood's eyes flick over her, then harden as his lip
curled in a sneer.

"Miss Voors," Morgan greeted her. "It's a pleasure to
see you again. I'm so looking forward to the wedding tomorrow."

"Thank you," she murmured automatically. It was
clear from the look on his face that he couldn't fathom
why she was there. But Blackwood knew.

"That's all, Morgan," he said, dismissing him. "I
don't care how you do it, just get it done. Don't bother me
with details."

"Yes sir, Mr. Archer." He paused, looking back at
Saranda uncertainly. "Well, I'll see you tomorrow, I guess,
Miss Voors."

"Will he?" Blackwood asked when Morgan had
closed the door behind him.

She stepped forward so her shadow leapt upward and

entwined with his. His devil's face was hard, wary in the half-light.

"You bloody, double-dealing—*Blackwood!*" She didn't bother to maintain her American accent.

He ground his cigarette into the ashtray and exhaled a last stream of smoke. "You didn't really think you could get the better of me?" he said softly. His accent, too, was suddenly more pronounced, less cultivated—as if, faced with his opponent on equal footing, he no longer needed the facade.

"I might have known you'd stoop to something as low as turning me in. You and your family always took the easy way out. There's a code about such matters, Blackwood, or haven't you heard of it? I must be out of my mind even to *ask* such a question. Look whom I'm talking to!"

"The Sherwins, I take it, are shining examples of humanity."

"At least we Sherwins lived within the boundaries of the accepted rules of operation. I could just as easily have told the Van Slykes who you were. I knew from the beginning. But that would have been too easy. And not much ripping fun, at that. I chose to play the game. To use my brains and abilities to outsmart you every step of the way. But then, you Blackwoods always fall back on dishonorable tactics when your wits fail you."

He came around his desk with angry strides. "You call your family turning mine over to the authorities *fair play?* We were exposed to the worst kind of public ridicule because of you—humiliated in every corner of England."

"You deserved it! You stepped over the line. It wasn't enough for you to kidnap that American, and plan for your brother to take his place. We couldn't blame you for that. Why not give it a go? The most spectacular assemblage of wealth and jewels on a single ship? A leisurely cruise down the Nile? It was just the sort of con we'd have played to perfection. That's where you made your first mistake. The aristocracy was ours. You had the arrogance to invade our territory, without the ingenuity to back it up."

"And you couldn't stand the thought of someone elbowing you aside."

"You'd think that, naturally. If you'd done it with grace, with finesse, with something approximating *planning*, we might have applauded your success."

"Since when did a Sherwin applaud anything a Blackwood did? You've looked down your noses at us for two hundred years."

"With good reason, I might add. Look at the mess you made of that con. It was in motion. You'd kidnapped the American. Your brother, Lance, was to take his place on the ship and relieve the passengers of their no doubt ill-gotten gains. But you couldn't stop there. You had to kill the man. You broke the code before we ever stepped in. *Confidence artists don't resort to murder.* If you're any good, you don't have to."

"You're so bloody superior, you and your whole family. Informing the authorities and having my parents arrested before they could pull the job. My mother was ill —did you know that? She hadn't flammed anyone in years. But they dragged her to the gallows and hanged her in front of that pack of wolves that passes for polite society. You know nothing of what that meant to us, *nothing* about what really happened."

"Tell me, by all means. I enjoy a good fairy tale as well as the next woman."

She saw in his eyes a deep and abiding hatred that mirrored her own. "I owe you nothing, *Princess*, least of all an explanation."

His derisive use of her father's pet name turned her cold. She balled her hands into fists of rage, her arms shaking with the effort to keep from swinging at his smug, conspicuous jaw. "That's where you're wrong. You owe me more, Mace Blackwood, than you can ever hope to repay. That lunatic brother of yours didn't stop with the American. He killed my parents. Listed an advertisement in the personals stating that the Blackwoods *respectfully* announced they would have their revenge on the sixth of June. Did you help him word the ad? It possessed just the ring of reckless insolence that appeals to you."

"I had nothing to do with it."

"We stayed home that night, thinking it best to play it safe. *Home.* A tiny cottage in the country we'd just moved into. My mother excited because, in all her life, she'd never had a house of her own."

He turned away. "I don't want to hear this."

"Somehow, your illustrious brother found out where we lived. He blocked the doors and set fire to the house. I crawled out the chimney, but it was too small for them to fit through. He wouldn't let me help them. He held me down and *laughed* while my parents burned to death right before us."

Her words reverberated in the silence as he absorbed them. Then, tonelessly, he said, "That's not the brother I knew."

Saranda cocked her head impertinently. "Surely, Mace Blackwood—consummate con artist that you are—wasn't fooled by someone as inept as his late brother?"

He turned back to her, with all the furies of hell burning in his eyes. "And how did *you* escape?" he asked cruelly. "If what you say is true, I can't imagine my *illustrious brother* passing up a morsel like you."

She slapped him then, with all the wrath she'd been denied through the years, hit him so hard, her hand felt broken. The sound of it rumbled like thunder through the room. "I was *thirteen years old.*" Her voice broke. She couldn't go on. She couldn't even tell him what his brother had done. "Don't talk to me about shining examples of humanity. You Blackwoods are the very scum of the earth."

"I don't answer for my family," he ground out through tightly clenched teeth.

"If I came from your family, neither would I."

He caught her arms and jerked her up against him. His power, unleashed, enveloped her sensibilities like a gale at sea. She could feel his ferocity in every line of his hard body as he slammed her against him with a passion that had nothing to do with tenderness or caring or love.

"All my life, I knew you as an enemy to be crushed."

Even as her mind reviled him, her body leapt at the contact. The animosity between them clashed like swords, throwing sparks of emotions that surpassed their rage. Like flint on steel, there struck a recognition that the rivalry between them was more erotic, more primal in nature, than any caress could ever be.

"But it's you who'll be crushed," she warned, breathing heavily, backing up a step. "Because I've defeated you at your own game. Do you know what the Van Slykes said to me when they learned the truth?"

"That they love you. That you've brought a breath of fresh air into their stale lives. That they don't care who or what you've been. They believe in you and want you for their own."

"Practically *verbatim*."

He narrowed his gaze. "I assume you spared them the shock of my true identity."

"I told you, if I'd wanted to expose you, I'd have done so. I shall have a much grander time establishing a position of power for myself that will eventually surpass your own. As Winny's wife and Jackson's daughter-in-law, I'll be in a position to manipulate your every move. Step by step, I shall take a hand in the running of the business. I shall—subtly, of course—turn them so sour on you, they'll wonder they ever trusted you. In the end, you'll be humiliated and—ultimately, publicly—kicked out on your ear. And I shall have the great pleasure of watching it happen, and of knowing it was my doing. You've wasted your time here, Blackwood. You might as well pack your bags now."

"Then I suppose I've lost." He took another step forward, forcing her backward so she came up abruptly against the desk at her back. "Still, it doesn't have to be a total defeat."

The timbre of his voice had changed. It was hushed and silky, deceptively smooth. She could read his intentions in the gleam of his midnight eyes. "Stay away from me," she gasped.

"Surely, you're not afraid of me? I've already admitted defeat."

"As if I'd trust anything you'd say."

He raised a brow. "Trust? No, sweetheart, it's not about trust between us."

"You're right. It's about a battle between our families that has finally come to an end. The Sherwins have won, Blackwood. You have no further hand to play."

Even as she said it, she knew it wasn't true. Despite the bad blood between them, they had unfinished business. Because the game, this time, had gone too far.

"That's separate. The feud, the competition—that has nothing to do with what's happening between you and me."

"You must think I'm the rankest kind of amateur. Do you think I don't know what you're up to?"

He put his hand to her cheek and stroked the softly shadowed contours of her face. "What am I up to?"

He was so close, she could feel the muscles of his chest toying with her breasts. Against all sense, she hungered to be touched.

"If you can succeed in seducing me, you can run to Winston with the news and effect a last-minute cancellation—"

His hand drifted from her cheek down the naked column of her neck, to softly caress the slope of her gleaming shoulder. "I could tell them you slept with me whether you do or not. But you know as well as I do they wouldn't believe me."

"That argument won't work either, Blackwood," she said in a dangerously breathy tone.

"Very well, Miss Sherwin. Why don't we just lay our cards on the table?"

"Why not indeed?"

"Then here it is. I don't like you any more than you like me. In fact, I can't think of a woman I'd be less likely to covet. My family cared for yours no more than yours cared for mine. But I find myself in the unfortunate circumstance of wanting you to distraction. My—body wants you." He took her hand and pressed it against him. He was enormous, straining for release. He leapt like a tiger beneath her hand. So she'd been right, she thought euphorically. He *did* want her! "For some reason I can't even fathom, I can't look at you without wondering what you'd look like panting in my arms. Without wanting to feel your naked skin beneath my hands. Or taste your sweat on my tongue. Without needing to come inside you and make you cry out in passion and lose some of that *goddamned* control." A faint moan escaped her throat. "You're all I think about. You're like a fever in my brain. I keep thinking if I took you *just once*, I might finally expel you from my mind. So I don't suppose either of us is leaving this office before we've had what you came for."

"I came to tell you—"

"You could have done that any time. You could have left me wondering for the rest of the night if the wedding would take place. But you didn't wait. You knew if this was going to happen, it had to be tonight. Because once you're Winston's wife, I won't come near you. The minute you say 'I do,' you and I take off the gloves, darling, and the real battle begins. So it's now or never." He lowered his mouth to her shoulder, and her breath left her in a sigh.

"Now or never," she repeated in a daze.

"One night to forget who we are and what it all means. You're so confident of winning. Surely, you wouldn't deny me the spoils of the game. Or more to the point . . . deny yourself."

She looked up and met his sweltering gaze. After three days of not seeing him, she'd forgotten how devastatingly handsome he was. "I shan't fall in love with you, if that's what you're thinking. This will give you no advantage over me. I'm still going after you with both barrels loaded."

"Stop trying so hard to figure it out. I don't give a hang what you think of me. And I don't need your tender mercy. I tell you point-blank, if you think you've won, you may be in for a surprise. But that's beside the point." He wrapped a curl around his finger. Then, taking the pins from her hair, one by one, he dropped them to the floor. She felt her taut nerves jump as each pin clicked against the tile.

He ran both hands through the silvery hair, fluffing it with his fingers, dragging them slowly through the length as he watched the play of light on the silky strands. It spilled like moonlight over her shoulders. "Did you have to be so beautiful?" he rasped.

"Do you have to look so much like a Blackwood?"

He looked at her for a moment, his eyes piercing hers, his hands tangled in her hair. "Tell me what you want."

She couldn't look at him. It brought back memories

of his brother she'd rather not relive. As it was, she couldn't believe she was doing this. But she had to have him. It was as elemental as food for her body and air to breathe. Her eyes dropped to his mouth—that blatant, sexual mouth that could make her wild with a grin or wet with a word.

She closed her eyes. If she didn't look at him, maybe she could separate this moment from the past. From what his brother had done. Her voice was a mere whisper when she spoke. "I want you to stop wasting time," she told him, "and make love to me."

He let go of her hair and took her naked shoulders in his hands. Bending her backward, he brought his mouth to hers with a kiss so searing, it scalded her heart. So rapacious, she was disabled by the white heat of her own desire. The scattered passions of the evening all flowed together in a flame that destroyed like wildfire, consuming all other emotions and leaving her shattered in its wake. Her blood boiling like lava in her veins, she heard a strangled cry and realized it had come from her own throat. The hands that had lashed out at him earlier now gripped his broad shoulders as she lost her balance and fell against his desk.

He reached behind her and swept his arm across it. The contents crashed to the floor, but the sound of it was muffled by the roaring in her head. Lowering her onto the clean surface, he pinned her to it so she arched beneath him, his erection thrusting against her, the neckline of her gown slipping below her shoulders so she was open and exposed beneath his weight. His lips never left hers. Searching, probing, crushing hers beneath his own, he lashed her with a blinding kiss.

It was never meant to be more. A hurried tumble with a bewitching temptress who'd haunted his dreams. But somewhere along the way, he relinquished his delusions to the soft, parted folds of her lips, to the clean, female scent of her skin. He lingered and tasted where he'd thought to hit and run. The hand that held hers pinned to the desk left it to clutch at her breast instead. Prohibited by pink satin, he nudged it aside with his stubbled jaw, exposing the hard nipple before his mouth clamped with moist succor upon it. He sucked at her greedily, nipping with his teeth, as if, having dropped the pretenses, he was free to feast on her at will.

Never could she have imagined the sweet agony of his mouth. It sought to take all of her, mowing down any lingering hesitation with a driving will that recognized no barriers to its goal.

His hand, meanwhile, was busy rucking up the yardage of her skirt—a tedious, seemingly endless, task. Transfixed by the swelling of her nipple beneath his tongue, she was nonetheless aware of the rustle of satin as he sought its end. She knew what he was seeking, felt strangely suspended between the delicious sensations of his mouth at her breast and the agonizing anticipation of him forcing aside her skirts and finding her at last.

More satin . . . and more . . . and more . . . Then layer upon layer of lacy petticoats barring his way. She held her breath as she waited. And then—at last—at last—he touched her.

"So you didn't come for this?" he murmured when he found no drawers to impede him.

His hand was so hot, it seemed to sizzle in the juices of her desire. He inserted a finger, and it came out wet, sticky. Another plunge—two fingers this time—and he was drenched with her. She moved so that he went deeper, as far as his fingers would allow, forgetting everything but the need to be filled and stretched and dominated by the man she—

"You want me that badly, do you?" he growled at her ear, taking feral satisfaction in the all-too-evident fact. He pulled his hand away and, to show her, smeared the sticky juices across her breast.

"I want you so badly, I'll die if you don't take me."

He lapped up the juices, groaning deep in his throat.

In the process, her skirts fell back to the floor. Reaching for her, he swore viciously, then took hold of her arms and pulled her to her feet. She swayed before him, awash with wanting him, her eyes unfocused and her mouth dry. He shoved her up against the wall so she fell face-forward, her hand clutching at the wooden blinds that hid the windows from view. As he pinned her there with the flat of one hand, her breasts thrust hard against the wall, he unfastened the back of her gown with the other. She recalled, with some losing portion of her brain that still struggled for sanity, that the door was unlocked. In his haste, in his need, he hadn't bothered with privacy. Anyone could walk in at any time.

She wondered if he'd even stop. And then, as her dress slid to the floor and his hand found her once again between her thighs, she knew it was too late. Anyone who happened in would get an eyeful. She couldn't stop herself now if she tried.

"Step out of that dress," he commanded, his voice a soft, warm breath at her ear.

She did so, and he kicked it away. She stood now, her back to him, clad in nothing but an ice-pink corset and matching pale stockings and shoes.

"Now spread your legs for me."

She stepped apart.

"Wider."

In doing so, she was forced to lean her cheek against the wall.

"That's it," he coaxed, his hand exploring her from behind. He kissed her bare shoulder and the slender angles of her back. "Christ, you're more lovely than I'd imagined."

She smiled for the first time, glorying in her power to arouse the beast in him. "Why don't you stop imagining and do something about it?" She wiggled her hips, encouraging him to take her. She was breathing rashly now, the fiery blast of it parching her throat.

"What do you want?" he insisted.

"I want what you promised. Come inside and make me scream."

Even as she said it, she only half believed. No man had ever made her so crazy that she'd lost her dominion and screamed out loud. But then, she remembered, he was the greatest lover in all of Europe. By accounts, he'd made *comtesses* scream in Paris and *baronesas* fall to their knees and beg in Madrid. Maybe . . . just maybe . . .

For a moment, his breath, expelled from his lungs, mingled with hers. Like a prizefighter readying himself for the battle ahead.

He left her, and she heard the faint whisper of clothing. She clung to the wall as if by moving, she'd collapse. Even her fingertips tingled in anticipation, much as they did before a heist. She couldn't help remembering the size of him, couldn't wait to discover what it felt like to be so thoroughly filled by a man. . . .

Then his hands were at her thighs. He lifted her and plunged into her from behind. She was so wet, he shot in like a ramrod, even as she—remarkably—cried aloud. Her arms flung wide, she grasped the wall and leaned her forehead against it as he slammed into her. He pulled her back against him, cupping her breasts with his hands, then shoved her back to the partition, seeking purchase. His hands kneaded her nipples as he thrust, sending spirals of escalating hunger inside and through her until all she could feel was her need for him.

She'd never imagined anything so delicious. She clung to him, stretching to accommodate him as if she'd been born for this moment. So attuned was she to his every thrust that her body, her nerves, even the blood in her veins, leapt to life with each rocking jolt. He was so deep inside her—so large and demanding, making no concessions for his size—that the contact bordered on torment. Yet when he pulled back, she missed it, needing the agony and the subsequent delectable relief from it as she needed the breath that was hurled from her with every mighty plunge.

"I've never had anyone as big as you," she told him over her shoulder.

"How does it feel?" he demanded.

"Oh, God!"

Her body burned, and a thin sheen of sweat gleamed in the flickering light. She could feel her own sweat on her breasts beneath his palms. She reached back and brushed him with her fingers as he plundered her, felt the chiseled, corded length of him plunge in and out.

"But I should warn you," she gasped, still fighting him. *"No man* has ever made me lose control."

He paused for a heartbeat. The statement challenged him, fueled his ferocious need to best her. He dropped one hand in front and found the triangle of curling hair soaked with her own juices, warm, open, throbbing with yearning. His fingers found a slick rhythm, urging her on. His breath beat a cadence in her ear. He began to whisper to her— hot, senseless words that were so utterly intoxicating, they made her mouth go slack. She gasped aloud and would have screamed her exaltation except that his other hand flew to her mouth. He crushed her to silence, then ground out, in a husky, panting voice, "Taste yourself on me." And he thrust his fingers into her mouth.

Lost to him completely, she licked them, sucked them, tasting her own lust.

"That's it," he whispered. "Give yourself to me. Give me what you've given no other man. Turn yourself over to me. That's it, darling. Be mine . . . *mine* . . . just this one time."

She lost control. Biting his hand, she surrendered herself to the shudders that shook her and carried her to a completion that, moments later, only served to further her need and leave her more ravenous than before.

"That's right," he murmured. "Show me how much you want me."

She did want him. God, how she wanted him! Like she'd wanted nothing and no one. He was devouring her, absorbing her, drawing her into himself and leaving nothing behind but her need. She let go of her mind and exploded beneath him, blinded by white stars and spasm upon spasm of unbelievable pleasure that surged through her and made her pray it would never end.

She'd barely finished spinning when he withdrew from her, turned her to face him, and kissed her slack, parched lips. Lifting her so she was forced to wrap her legs around him, he brought himself to her, rubbing himself in her wetness for a moment before heaving himself back inside. This time he moved with the more determined purpose of sating his own mad desires. He slammed her back against the wall with such ferocity that she had to cling to him to keep from being hurled like a rag doll. Kissing her deeply, he pounded away, splitting her in two, making her gasp aloud. Her mind began to swirl again as he thrust his tongue into her mouth and muffled his own growl of release with her lips.

They clung to each other for moments, damp with sweat, panting as their hearts gradually slowed in tempo. Still supporting her, he reached up with his hand and ran it, like a blind man, across her face. As he did so, he slid out of her and buried his face in her breasts. "Oh, Christ," he gasped, gathering her to him and kissing her moist skin. His mouth traveled, reverently, to her rib cage, her navel, the soft round of her belly. Like a dying man seeking water, he licked her sweat, drank of her flesh. "Good God!"

She'd never felt so sated, so replete, in all her life. It was a staggering revelation. They'd made a bargain. Lust for the sake of lust. One rollicking romp, born of curiosity, one professional to another, discovering the secrets of their trades. Nothing more, nothing less.

Except that she felt so much a part of him, she couldn't drag herself away. She wanted to stay just so, clinging to his damp head, clutching him to her breast, holding him for life. No man had ever moved her so completely. No man had made her feel more whole.

In the aftermath, she was left with a shattering truth. *It wasn't enough.*

CHAPTER 10

If he were any other man, she'd call off the wedding and abandon the con. But he was *Mace Blackwood,* her sworn enemy—a man whose family had sought the destruction of her own for generations.

Saranda was the last of the Sherwins, the keeper of the family flame. She had a responsibility, not only to her father, but to all the Sherwins stretching back through time. The Blackwoods had been their nemesis for three hundred years! She couldn't forget that. More personally, she couldn't ignore what *Lance* Blackwood had done. Willfully, vengefully, giving no thought to her as a person in her own right. Yet she couldn't escape from the one glaring truth that was more demoralizing—and more exhilarating —than all the rest.

She was in love with the man who'd betrayed her. So desperately in love, she didn't know what to do.

She was faced with a dilemma that forced her to question the very nature of her existence. What did it mean—*to her*—to be a Sherwin? All her life she'd been torn between what she was naturally and what her father had wanted for her. The Sherwins, by their very nature, were bluffsters of the highest order. Nobility in the singular realms of the underworld, notorious throughout England not just for their sense of style, but for the integrity with which they plied their trade. They didn't steal from those who would be hurt. They didn't con anyone except those people crooked enough that they were willing to risk anything in the hopes of a quick return. Yet her father had decreed that *she* would break the ranks. She'd be the first Sherwin to crash into, and become one with, the respectable world. She had a sacred mission.

But instead, what was she? A shuckster who'd been denied, and was denying herself, the glory of the con. Denying her birthright as a Sherwin in exchange for elevating the family to a higher plane. She could do so by marrying Winston that night. The foundation had been laid. All she had to do was walk into that church and say good-bye to her old existence. The trouble was, for the first time in her life, she'd come up against an obstacle that her father, in all his thorough training, hadn't prepared her for.

She wanted Mace Blackwood more than life itself.

But how could she have him? Aside from the fact that she was marrying another man, there were other, more pressing, considerations. Every time she looked at him, she'd wonder if it was *she* he wanted, or the winning of the game. She'd never be able to trust him. Never touch him without recalling what his brother, Lance, had done. How it had ruined her life. How she still carried scars from that night that refused to heal.

The fact that she wanted him was a betrayal of all she'd held dear. Of the one goal that had helped her survive that awful time in London after her parents' death. To the one thought that had kept her alive.

Revenge against the Blackwoods.

It was within her grasp, if only she had the courage to go through with it. Personal feelings must be set aside. It helped harden her to realize she was experiencing what he'd wanted her to feel. Having devastated her with his lovemaking, he'd anticipated the confusion that would mar this day of triumph. *But how had he known?* She'd never been moved by any other man.

He'd known, of course, because he was a chameleon, just as she was. He became, for each person, what was wanted of him. It was simply a role. He was not to be trusted, *never* to be believed. So what if he'd seemed as moved—as surprised—as she by what had transpired the night before? *He wanted her to believe it.* He wanted her to believe that no woman on earth had ever brought to the surface such punishing emotions. That no romp in bed had ever made him feel as alive, as potent, as serene within himself, as this fusing of bodies—*of minds, of souls*—had been with her.

He wanted her to believe it because it would give him the edge. And when she least expected it, he'd yank the rug from under her and leave her with nothing.

The worst of it was, some small part of her *did* believe. Believed that in the aftermath of passion—*of love*—such as she'd never dreamed existed, he was as stunned and newly awakened as she. Believed that, knowing what they'd shared, he couldn't let her go. That, impossible and daring as it might be to confess it, having each other was worth the risk.

Believed that he'd show up at the church, break up the proceedings, sweep her into his arms, and boldly carry her away.

That he'd rescue her from her own madness in marrying a man she didn't love, now that she knew—wretchedly—that she *could* love.

It meant the end of her father's dream. But in the throes of newfound love, she didn't care. As Winston's wife, she'd be respectable. But her instincts told her that with Mace Blackwood, she could be that most precious of all things: *herself*.

The knowledge that he could have deceived her the night before—that his seeming wonder at their union could have been a facade—made him, perversely, all the more appealing. Mace was so much like her father that being with him was like returning to a long-lost home. No one but her father had been able to outwit her. No one had ever been that good. If she'd been conned, Blackwood was an even greater artist than her father. It was more intriguing than maddening.

Because the truth was, she wasn't a society matron. At heart, she loved the bluff. That Blackwood excelled at it, that he relished it as much as she, made her love him all the more. He was the embodiment of all she'd been forbidden, the very essence of her true self. Even if he was a Blackwood.

Her father might understand. But he wouldn't like it one bloody bit.

THE WEDDING OF the year was a dazzling affair, resplendent with the grandeur expected of society nuptials. Saranda played fairy princess to a crowd who wanted to believe it was true. The beautiful, enchanting Sarah Voors, who'd appeared from nowhere to capture the heart of one of society's most elusive bachelors, heir apparent to the city's most powerful and sought after newspaper, the *Globe-Journal*. She knew her role. She wasn't marrying a man so much as she was marrying into an empire whose influence could be felt around the world. She conducted herself with the requisite dignity and grace. All the while praying desperately, *Come to me, Blackwood. Steal me away.*

The fervency of her emotions was reflected in her face. Everyone commented on it, the whispers sweeping the room as she made her appearance. In Winston's mother's iridescent satin-and-pearl gown, she was a vision. Her silver hair framed her face in soft curls, intertwined with diamonds and pearls. They shimmered as she glided down the aisle amid hundreds of white candles and pale rose petals that led a softly illuminated, headily scented path to the altar. Her face, a shattered canvas that morning, radiated a lustrous sheen of freshly blooming hope that was the envy of every marriageable young lady, and made every man there want to protect her from harm.

And all the while she was wondering, Where was Blackwood? Would he come for her? Could he possibly, after all that had happened, let her go through with this charade?

His words haunted her with every step she took. *Once you're Winston's wife, I won't come near you.* Each step brought her closer to a fate she'd wanted, even manipulated and fought for, but that she knew now she could never endure.

But she hadn't been born a chameleon for nothing. With her unique talent, she appeared different to each and every guest. They saw, as she made that slow walk down the aisle, what they wanted to see. She was the picture of the blushing bride. Yet her lips, sensually parted and glistening in the candlelight, offered unconscious promises of delight that caused those same protective gentlemen to squirm in their pews against the sudden tightening of their trousers. Beneath the grace of her gown, her body seemed ripe with possibilities. Her breasts, spilling out of her satin bodice, managed, through her carriage, through the feline undulations of her walk down the aisle, to convey, along with her virginal aloofness, a hint of scandalous titillation. Combined with the show of silky shoulders and bare, diamond-braceleted arms, she'd created an image of expensive, highly prized, voluptuously offered flesh. She was, without a doubt, the most exquisite, lushly promising bride they'd ever seen. No man present could watch her walk down that aisle without wondering what it would be like to slip the gown from her sumptuous body and bury his face in the softness of her breasts.

Every man, that is, except the one the show was meant for. Mace Blackwood didn't even bother to show up.

CHAPTER 11

"I was so afraid you wouldn't go through with it," Winston admitted. "After what Archer said, I could only guess what you might do. I could forgive what happened, easily, but if you left me—" He shrugged, as if incapable of finding the words.

They were alone in Winston's bedroom in the Van Slyke mansion, a dark-paneled bedroom with a nautical theme. The rug, the curtains, the covers on the bed, were a soft steel blue. It was decorated with a Dutch flag, models of clippers, and an old tintype of Lalita Van Slyke. The bed was a four-poster, each of the posts carved to resemble figureheads on a ship. Wood was piled neatly in the fireplace, waiting to be lighted. It had been decided that they'd spend the night there before departing for Niagara Falls in the morning.

"I shan't leave you, Winston," she vowed. Not now. Not having realized an awful truth. That Blackwood had conned her, after all. That he *hadn't* cared.

Winston smiled sheepishly. "I sort of like it when you call me Winny."

"Winny," she repeated.

"And I guess I'll have to call you Saranda from now on. It might take some getting used to—"

"It might be easier if you just called me Sarah. But I must warn you, Winny. I may speak in my real voice with you and Jackson, but no one else. It may become a burden to you, keeping such a secret the rest of our lives."

"Burden," he cried. "It's the most exciting thing that's ever happened to me!"

He gazed at her earnestly, reverently, but with a new light in his eyes. Having discovered his bride was an adventuress, he didn't know what to expect. The realization seemed to heighten his awareness of her. While he'd never so much as kissed her before today, he now looked as if he couldn't wait to get his hands on her. There was a curious glint in his eyes, as if wondering what such a woman would be like in bed.

"I want to thank you, Winny, for being so good to me. I want to—be a proper wife to you."

"Sarah—*Saranda*—do you think—"

"What, Winny?"

"Well, I know you say you care about me. But do you think, in time, you might learn to—love me?"

With an effort, she smiled at him. "I think a woman would be balmy not to love you. And I promise you, I shall do everything in my power to make you happy. Now run along and have a drink with your father. Allow me some time to ready myself for you."

WHEN HE'D LEFT, she walked over to the mirror, set in a nautical chest of drawers. She studied her face critically. The huge, dazed eyes, the high cheekbones that cast angular shadows in the hollows of her cheeks. The pouty lips that Winston would be kissing in just a matter of time. Unbidden, memories of her night with Blackwood stirred like mist in her mind.

His words came back to her as if he were behind her, murmuring in her ear. *I know you're marrying Winston. . . . But something . . . keeps whispering that you belong to me. That no man alive can understand you, accept you, the way I can. That at Winston's side, you'd be shackled to an impossible existence. But in my arms, you'd be set free.*

She couldn't listen to these mad ravings. Because he hadn't meant a word he'd said. It had all been part of his endless scheming. A merciless game in which besting her was the objective. How could she have expected anything else? How could she have been such a fool?

Yesterday she'd have consummated her marriage to Winston without a thought. But that was before she'd known the miracle of Blackwood's lovemaking. Before he'd stolen a small part of her that she'd given no one and taken it with him. Like a thief in the night.

It was too late now for regrets. She'd made a commitment to Winston, and she intended to honor it. She must give him something in return for his kindness. She must make him believe she wanted him every bit as much—

As she wanted Blackwood.

She was reaching up to remove the pearls from her hair when she heard the shot. It was so unexpected, she held her breath, waiting to be sure. It could have been something crashing downstairs, she thought, trying to deny her suspicions. But no—there it was again. Another gunshot, shattering the stillness of the mansion.

Wrenching the door open, she ran down the grand stairs. Halfway down, she caught sight of a figure running out the front door. A tall, athletic man with curling black hair. Something shriveled up and died inside her.

I tell you point-blank, if you think you've won, you may be in for a surprise.

Spurred to action, she flew down the stairs, searching the rooms frantically, calling Winston's name. In the doorway of the study, she lurched to a stop as an acid taste rushed to her throat.

They'd been drinking brandy. The glasses were overturned on the floor, one of them broken, spilling the contents on the Netherland rug. Winston and Jackson lay among the broken glass and spilled liquor, both shot through the head.

With a strangled cry, she fell on Winston, hoping desperately, against all reason, that he was still alive. She lifted him in her arms. He was too heavy to hold up, and he fell back to the floor at her feet. Dropping to her knees, she fumbled for a pulse. There was none. Winston lay on his back with blood seeping from his head, his spectacles askew, his aqua eyes open, staring lifelessly at the ceiling. She began pounding at his chest.

"Winny . . . no . . . oh, no . . ."

But she knew in her heart it was too late.

"No . . . no . . . no!" The voice seemed to come from a distant tunnel, sounding like the whimpering of a wounded beast. She rocked beside him, wailing her denial of this tragedy.

Distraught, she looked around. It was then that she noticed the gun lying, as if discarded, on the far side of Jackson's body, on the way out of the study. She went to it, picked it up, and stared at it. It was Jackson's own.

Slowly, as if in a trance, she walked back to Winston. *She'd* caused this. By playing God with this dear man's life, she'd brought about his death. She knelt beside him once again and brushed his hair back from his face.

She was leaning over him when someone entered the room. She looked up to see the massive bulk and red-fringed whiskers of Sander McLeod. "I was in the washroom when I heard—" He stopped short, horror registering on his face.

"Help me," she pleaded.

"God in heaven. What have you done?"

She stood slowly on trembling legs. "Done? I didn't—"

"You've killed them!"

"No. You're wrong." She looked down at the gun dangling from her hand. Her fingers convulsed open, and it clattered to the floor. *"No!"*

McLeod, clutching his burgeoning girth, stuck his head out the door and yelled for the butler. There was no answer. Jackson had dismissed the servants for the evening. He turned back to her. "Don't move, you—"

He was heading out the door. "Where are you going?" she cried in a panic.

"Where do you think?"

Before she could stop him, he was charging down the hall. She heard the door open, and before she had time to think, he was bellowing for the police at the top of his lungs. Though she was numbed with shock, paralyzed in her alarm, her predicament nonetheless began to penetrate the fuzziness in her head. She had to move fast. There was no time now to grieve. She didn't know why McLeod was here. But it was possible that, being a trusting sort, Jackson had told him her story. If so, she knew she'd be found guilty even before the trial. McLeod was a frighteningly influential man. Against his testimony, no amount of explanation would convince the police that a clip artist who'd set out to marry into one of New York's first families hadn't shot them when they'd found out what she was up to.

Blind panic clouded her brain. She flew up the stairs to Winston's room and grabbed the valise that lay packed and waiting for their honeymoon in Niagara. She looked around for any money on the dresser, but there was none. And there was no time to explore further. She could hear McLeod's frantic calls all the way up the street. In the heart of Fifth Avenue, it wouldn't be long before a policeman heeded the call.

She slipped down the stairs, raced through the house, and rattled the back door. It was locked. She fumbled with the latch. She could hear voices in the front hall. Her hands shook at the lock, but she refused to give up. Her instinct for survival was too strong, too deeply ingrained by generations of perilous getaways. As the footsteps sounded throughout the house, the latch finally opened beneath her quaking hands. She ran out, just in time, into the cold dark refuge of the harboring night.

CHAPTER 12

At any hour, the Bowery seemed to breathe and pulsate its own peculiar brand of life. A haven for bargain-hunters during the day, it transformed itself into a wicked, pleasure-laden quarter after dark. Saranda passed barrooms, hotels, beer halls, music halls, cheap theaters, restaurants, and an assortment of small and offbeat museums.

Violence was no stranger to the district. Illegal prizefights were staged nightly by the rowdies, vagabonds, and drunken thugs who populated the area. Frustration was the mother of these pugilists. While the city attracted men of unusual strength and physical vitality, their intelligence and ambition were often squandered by their limited resources. Often, the only path of employment open to them was by the brutal exploitation of their fists.

As much as anything, though, it was an area that flaunted its disrespect of the law. Justice, being blind, was a danger to immigrants shoved like rats in a crate into the slums of a teeming city. Laws threatened the very activities that made existence bearable. Temperance men were continually threatening to close down saloons on Sundays, the only time when a working man could drink in an area where social clubs were almost nonexistent. Tavern keepers and hackmen were required to have public licenses but had to be citizens to apply. While the uptown reformers decried the vice, violence, and evasion of law, the Bowery closed its ranks and protected its own.

In short, it was the perfect place to hide.

THE BEER HALL was thick with smoke, rank with the smells of stale brew and unwashed male bodies. The men, drinking from tankards at long wooden tables, glanced up as she came in. She was bound to cause a commotion, dressed as she was in her wedding gown. She squirmed uncomfortably beneath their gaze. She'd have preferred to blend in less conspicuously. But there was little she could do at the moment. There'd been no time to change, and her first order of business was finding a place to hide.

She finally spotted the man she was looking for laughing and slamming tankards on the table with some of his friends. She made her way to him as swiftly as possible, wanting nothing more than to become invisible.

"Stubbs, I have to talk to you."

He was called Stubbs because he had thick stubs for fingers. But he was the best safecracker in the business and knew more about New York's underworld than anyone else on the Lower East Side.

The men were outdoing each other by bragging about their exploits. Stubbs looked up at her in the middle of a guffaw, and his leering face quickly changed to one of respect. "Why, hello," he greeted her, obviously surprised to see this vision, glowing in white satin and diamonds and tumbling, pearl-strewn hair, looking like an angel sent from heaven. Recovering himself, he said, "Boys, we're in the company of royalty. Meet the best damn—"

She cut Stubbs off before he could go too far. "I need your help," she said urgently.

He sensed her agitation and, with a parting nod to the boys, stood and led her to a back table as ribald comments floated in their wake. Ignoring them, Saranda sat with her back to the room, feeling the safety of darkness swallow and comfort her, even as her heart continued to pound.

"I'm in trouble," she began without preamble, keeping her voice low.

"*You're* in trouble?"

"They think I killed the Van Slykes."

He grew serious. "Who thinks?" Like her, he spoke in little more than a whisper.

"The police."

"What makes them think so?"

"They were murdered earlier tonight. I was upstairs. I was bending over Winston when Sander McLeod came in the room. I believe he said he was in the washroom. In any event, he leapt to conclusions and yelled for the police. I came here as quickly as I could."

"Sander McLeod, Jesus. What was he doing there?"

"I don't know. I didn't know he *was* there. He must have come to toast the marriage with Jackson, or some such thing."

"Could he have killed them?"

"No. I saw who did it."

"Then who?"

She put her face in her hands. Even now, she didn't want to believe it. She knew the Blackwoods had resorted to murder before. But that was Lance. She'd found no evidence that Mace had been involved. After last night, she'd wanted to believe—

What?

In spite of what she'd told him, she'd never thought of him as a murderer. Lance Blackwood had been an incompetent con man, and consequently had been forced into desperate measures. But Mace was good. In fact, he was the best she'd ever seen. She would never have thought him capable of coldbloodedly gunning down people who'd trusted their hearts to him.

But he had. She'd seen him running away. There could be no mistake.

Dear God! How could she have been so wrong? The only man she could ever love—and he'd done a thing like this!

She rubbed her aching forehead. "I was set up by a clipper named Blackwood. It's a long story. The streets are already crawling with police. Stubbs, I need a place to hide. Just until the smoke clears."

"Done. You can use my room upstairs. I'll bunk with a pal."

"Thank you. And I need some clothes. Something plain and unnoticeable. Gingham. No, better yet, brown muslin. Or grey. Something to blend in with the surroundings. I can't walk about in Worth gowns and diamonds. Speaking of diamonds, see what you can get me for these." She removed the diamond bracelets from her wrists and handed them over. They'd belonged to Winston's mother, Lalita, and had been part of Winston's wedding present to her. "I need the money."

He inspected the jeweled cuffs with a practiced eye. "Shame to part with these. They're old Dutch diamonds. Eighteenth century's my guess. Damn near priceless. You won't get five percent on them, in these parts."

She thought regretfully of the blue diamonds in the

Van Slyke safe. "They're all I have. Oh, except these." Reaching up, she unfastened the pearls and pulled them from her hair.

"Don't you want to hold on to them?"

"I don't care about the jewels. I just want to stay alive long enough to let Blackwood know what I think of his handiwork."

Stubbs pocketed the gems and heaved a sigh. "I won't lie to you, Saranda. I'll do what I can. I'll hide you out, get you clothes, and even see what I can find out. I owe it to you. Professional courtesy, you might say, and I know you'd do the same for me. But killing the Van Slykes, for Chrissake—"

"I told you, I didn't."

"I know, and I believe you. But I have to tell you straight. Sander McLeod's about the biggest man in this town, next to Jackson Van Slyke himself. With him pointing the finger . . . you don't have a prayer."

"That," said Saranda, "is what I'm afraid of."

THREE DAYS LATER, Saranda was beginning to realize she was in more trouble than she'd first imagined. The newspapers Stubbs brought her were filled with sensational front-page stories exploiting the murder and decrying her name. Worse, Sander McLeod had brought startling and inexplicable accusations. He'd not only accused her of murdering the Van Slykes, he'd disclosed the fact that she was a known criminal, that her real name was Saranda Sherwin, and that she'd killed Jackson and Winston because they'd discovered her identity after the wedding and ordered her to leave. He claimed Jackson had confessed all of this just moments before he'd died.

"It isn't true!" she told Stubbs, tossing the paper

aside. "Jackson and Winston did know the truth. But they knew *before* the wedding, not after. They forgave me and still wanted me in the family. Jackson couldn't have told McLeod he was throwing me out. He's lying."

"Then how'd he find out the rest of it?"

There was only one way he could have.

The *Globe-Journal* was the worst offender. Outraged by the death of their beloved publisher and his son, the *Globe-Journal*'s employees vowed Saranda would hang before she'd live to inherit the paper. Under normal circumstances, under the terms of Jackson's newly drawn will, the paper would already be hers. To prevent what it called a travesty of justice, the *Globe-Journal* blasted her in print, offered a ten-thousand-dollar reward for her capture, and called for a citywide offensive to hunt her down. It ran under the headline PRINCESS OF THIEVES. The next day every other paper dubbed her the same. An old photograph of Lalita accompanied the articles, with Saranda's resemblance to the woman—and her blatant exploitation of it in her con—outlined in detail. In one masterstroke, her own newspaper destroyed her anonymity.

Only Blackwood could have supplied those details. After killing them, what better way out of it than to have her arrested and convicted? But what did he want out of it? Would he really go to this much trouble to blow her con?

There was only one possible answer. *The newspaper.*

A horrible thought occurred to her. Had he been planning the murders all along, as a safeguard in case she succeeded with the marriage? If she was convicted of the murder, the *Globe-Journal* would go into receivership, and if he could raise the money, Blackwood could snap it up. Jackson had spoken openly about his earlier intentions of leaving the paper to "Archer" when he died. As gifted as Blackwood was with words, he could easily make a case for himself. Any number of wealthy, lonely, lovesick women would likely *give* him the money he needed. And no one would ever suspect the truth.

No one but Saranda.

If this was true, he needed her captured at the first opportunity. Hence, the all-out attack.

But that didn't explain Sander McLeod. What possible reason could *he* have to lie to the police? He'd been outspoken in his criticism of the paper's "bleeding heart" editorials. Was it possible he was working with Blackwood in some way? They'd argued at the paper the day of Bat's tour. But that, like everything else in Blackwood's life, could easily have been faked. Knowing Winston would bring Bat by his office, he and Sander could have timed the altercation accordingly.

There was no time to investigate. Once the reward was announced, she became the most-wanted woman in New York. The *Globe-Journal* announced publicly it was hiring Pinkerton detectives to track her down. Everyone else in the city, it seemed, was joining the chase.

Police were everywhere. When she saw a group of thugs with their heads together behind a copy of the *Globe-Journal*, Saranda knew it was time to move on. It was too dangerous where she was, surrounded by pickpockets, whores, and thieves. The phrase "no honor among thieves" hadn't been coined for nothing. Any one of the lowlifes haunting the Bowery could turn her in at any time.

When she came downstairs on the third day to find a policeman questioning the bartender, she knew she could wait no longer. Racing back up the steps, she grabbed her packed valise and headed for Stubbs's temporary room.

"Where will you be?" he asked when he heard she was leaving.

She thought frantically. She had to leave the city. Her heart cried out for revenge, but she knew she must not indulge it. She'd been thoroughly outmaneuvered, and the only thing she could do was get away. If she stayed even another day, she risked capture and certain conviction. There was no one in the city she could count on. Where could she go?

Bat. Bat would offer her sanctuary while she figured out what to do. Bat, who'd said on parting, *As long as I'm alive, you'll have someone to turn to.*

"Kansas," she said, brightening for the first time since the murders. "I'm going back to Dodge."

CHAPTER 13

Dodge City. Like everyone else living in New York, Saranda had heard the wild tales coming from the western Kansas town. Spawned from the military post of Fort Dodge, it quickly became a booming camp of buffalo hunters, where the hides of the slaughtered beasts were bought and sold by the thousands. Bullwhackers launched their wagons from Dodge, carrying freight to all the forts, ranches, and camps within two hundred miles. But it was cattle and the cowmen that had put the town on the map. Hundreds of thousands of head of livestock were herded up the dusty trails from Texas to be shipped from Dodge on the railroad east, or to continue on through to Ogallala.

Tales had spread far and wide of Texas cowboys "hurrahing" the town, of gunfights on the streets, of murders that had resulted in hurried burials on the now-infamous Boot Hill. Indian scares were still rampant. Dodge had a reputation as the wickedest little city in America, where bad men consorted with loose women in the seventeen

saloons, three dance halls, and assorted brothels that ser-
viced the population of a thousand. Where con men, horse
thieves, bank robbers, and gunmen were as common as
grasshoppers on the surrounding plains.

Saranda had spent time in Kansas back in the days
when Bat was hunting buffalo and scouting for the army,
but Dodge had never impressed her. Wichita was the wild
and woolly Kansas town then, and it was there that she'd
made her headquarters before leaving with Bat for Sweet-
water, Texas. It was there, too, that she'd met Wyatt Earp,
who'd been marshal at the time. Wichita had, along with
Ellsworth, Hays City, and Abilene, a reputation for being
the most unrestrainable burg in the country, but apparently
these brief flashes of splendor had simply been rehearsals
for the wickedness of Dodge. In comparing the other
cowtowns, a Kansas paper had printed the headline:

DODGE CITY. A DEN OF THIEVES
AND CUT THROATS—THE WHOLE
TOWN IN LEAGUE TO ROB THE
UNWARY STRANGER.

She knew newspapers tended to exaggerate. But if
Dodge was wilder than Wichita had been, she knew they
hadn't exaggerated much.

She folded the paper she'd been reading and used it
to fan herself. The train was stifling, smelling of unwashed
bodies, witch hazel, and hair oil. She wore a plain traveling
suit and a hat the color of sand, designed to render her
invisible as she moved from town to town. A mousy-brown
wig covered the shimmer of her moonlight hair. Now she
found it heavy and cloying in the heat. It was too hot to
keep the windows closed and too dusty to open them. Ev-

eryone was suffering, fanning themselves and complaining about the oppressive temperature.

She'd never thought she'd have to return. The West, while offering ripe opportunities to ply her trade, had never appealed to her. The dust, the heat, the uncouth men who reminded her of the lean times on the streets of London's East End. The smell of poverty and desperation. Too many people running from the law, old lives, themselves. Her travels had provided an opportunity to search the country for Blackwood, ferreting out the corners con artists were known to inhabit. When she'd learned of his presence in New York, she'd set out with high hopes and soaring spirits. But everything had changed. It was no longer a wild adventure, a game. Suddenly, it was too real. Because of her, two decent men had been killed—men who'd loved her, men she'd sworn to protect. Coming back to the western plains brought home to her how bitterly she'd failed.

She closed her eyes. The rhythmic chugging of the train should have soothed her. But she was beyond soothing at this point. For three months now, after her escape from New York, she'd been hotly pursued by the law, bounty hunters, Pinkerton men, and U.S. marshals, all determined to return her to justice and collect the reward.

The journey west was never easy. Every town she turned up in offered another close call. There was never a moment to rest, never an opportunity to feel safe. Never even time to properly mourn the Van Slykes' death. She'd had to vary her route, backtracking, heading north or south when she wanted to go west, just to throw off her pursuers. She took stages, rode horseback, even talked her way onto a hunting expedition—no small feat in a country dominated by stubborn men—in an attempt to break the predictability of her route. But no matter what she did or where she went, she came so close to being caught time after time that she began to wonder if someone was reading her mind.

The train began to slow as they meandered through herds of bawling longhorn cattle tended by ragged cowboys and drew into town. She looked out the window and saw horrendous piles of bleached white bones stacked along the side of the tracks.

The passengers in her car strained their necks or stood by their seats to get a glimpse of the infamous Dodge City.

"Boot Hill be damned," said a fresh-faced young greenhorn with a whistle. "They just chuck their dead alongside the road!"

Some gentlemen in the back chuckled. One of them kindly leaned forward and explained, "Them's buffalo bones, son. Our ruffians fare a tad better."

The tracks ran parallel to the main street of town, which she remembered was called Front Street. The town hadn't changed a lot in two years. To the right was a collection of wooden buildings, most of them saloons. There was a crowd of people gathered at the depot. Only one train from the East came through town each day, and its arrival was still a great event. Most townspeople came out to greet it.

There was quite an assortment of swaggering humanity assembled about the small depot. Tall-hatted Texans mingled with merchants in boiled shirts, buffalo hunters in bloodstained buckskin, slick-haired gamblers in broadcloth and silk hats with carefully tended mustaches and diamonds underplaying their air of measured gentility. Bullwhackers drove their wagons with cracks of their bullwhips, crying out to their teams of oxen, nearly knocking pedestrians off the boardwalks as they rattled through town, but pulling their teams to a sudden halt in the middle of the road to view the proceedings. Frontiersmen, scouts, mule skinners, railroaders, and gunfighters all turned out to see who might step off the train.

The few women were dressed in gingham and cheap prints, but most had the used look about them of whores and actresses of one variety or another. There was dust everywhere, and everyone's clothes seemed to have a fine smattering.

Saranda stepped out into the summer carnival atmosphere, wondering instinctively how she might use it to her advantage.

Her first order of business was to locate Bat. At the sheriff's office, she was told he was out in the county but was due back by evening. She didn't leave a message. With wanted posters of her flooding the country, some hotshot deputy was likely to wire New York before Bat returned.

Her second task was deciding on a cover. She knew from experience that often the best hiding places were the most conspicuous. Anyone looking for her would be seeking a woman hiding in dark corners from the forces of the law. They'd never expect her to flaunt her presence in town. Thanks to Jackson's generosity, she had a valise full of the best clothes money could buy. Such attire would appear suspicious if she didn't have a cover worthy of them. Deciding that she might as well put them to use, she donned her finest New York clothes, kept the brown wig, topped it with a hat only a woman of supreme confidence would dare be seen in, placed wire-rimmed spectacles upon her nose, and marched into the Dodge House to announce herself, in ringing English tones, as the Countess of Lynderfield.

"C-Countess?" stuttered the proprietor. "Why, we've never had—well, we've had our share of visitors, don't get me wrong. President Hayes rolled into town just last year. Didn't get off the train, but he was here. But we ain't never had no royalty before."

She didn't bother to correct him. Peering at the hand-lettered sign that promised to "change the bedlinens every ten days whether they need it or not," she decided the deception was expedient. If he thought her royalty, perhaps she'd be afforded clean sheets.

Dodge House was the best hotel in town. Like the rest of the buildings on Front Street, it was a long, narrow, rustic wooden building. It had a gabled roof, boasted two stories, had a porch out front with a balcony running across the front of the upper floor, and was attached to the billiard hall next door. Mr. Cox, one of the proprietors, bragged that it contained twenty-eight rooms, a restaurant, and bar, and could accommodate ninety persons. Having traveled about the West for longer than she cared to remember, Saranda was accustomed to such boasts.

She spent the next few hours exploring the town, reading newspapers, learning everything she could about her surroundings. Dodge House was crammed full of cattle barons and businessmen, all more than eager to discuss the merits of the town with a titled, if somewhat dowdy, Englishwoman. She was treated with the greatest deference and clumsy gallantry. She could easily have lived off the offers for dinner that she received on an hourly basis.

But it was costly, keeping up the pretense of nobility. The money she'd received for the bracelets was all but gone. She had fifteen dollars left. So as she explored the town, she began to plan the best way of making a living.

Dodge was a minuscule town, consisting of six main streets running east and west, and four bisecting them. Front Street fronted the railroad, and it was in the Plaza around Front and Bridge streets that the primary businesses were congregated. The streets were little more than wide dirt paths continually churning dust into the air. As most of the buildings were made of wood, barrels of water were dispersed at periodic intervals in case of fire.

The railroad tracks were known as the Deadline. North of the Deadline, firearms were prohibited and were —at least in theory—required to be checked in special gun racks provided in hotels, corrals, gambling establishments, and saloons. The first thing anyone saw when coming into town from the west was a hand-painted sign, crudely scrawled, that stated: THE CARRYING OF FIREARMS STRICTLY PROHIBITED, and under that another suggesting: TRY PRICKLY ASH BITTERS.

South of the Deadline was another story. While the law was enforced only when necessary north of the line, it was rarely enforced in the south end. There, brothels, dance halls, variety theaters, and saloons thrived at all hours of the day and night, with drunken cowboys shooting in the streets and zigzagging from one establishment to the other, looking for trouble.

Bridge Street continued south to the toll bridge spanning the brawling Arkansas River. South of that, cattlemen grazed their herds, waiting for shipment east or fattening them up for the continuation on the trail north. At the northeast end of town was a bold, treeless hill dotted with makeshift graves—the Boot Hill for which all other such renegade cemeteries were named. There, euphemisms for being shot to death included such epitaphs as *killed by lightning* and *too many irons in the fire*.

If she'd thought it would be difficult to ferret out the local society of confidence men, she was mistaken. Most of them plied their trade openly in the form of showcase games on the wooden sidewalks of Front Street. There, they set up glass cases displaying counterfeit jewelry and baubles, hoping to entice youths fresh off the trails. After months of eighteen-hour days in the saddle, suffering meager provisions, the ravages of weather, and assorted accidents and perils along the seemingly endless trail from Texas, the cowboys rode into Dodge ready and willing to spend their hard-earned wages on one brief but memorable hurrah. They were lured to the cases of jewelry, convinced they'd been offered the best deal in town, and often stayed to participate in games of three-card monte or the pea-and-shell ruse. It would have been the easiest thing in the world to walk over and fleece the fleecers of their easily won cash, but she didn't know yet how much assistance she'd require from them. She decided to keep a low profile. Besides, she had her cover to consider.

Soon enough, though, she had to face the prospect of making some money. Waiting until dark, she donned a simple grey frock, let her own hair flow loose, and snuck out the back way of the hotel, heading south of the Deadline. There she saw firsthand the ruckus that had inspired Dodge's reputation.

The din was astonishing. In New York and London, the noises of the cities sounded like a constant hum—the streetcars, the trains, the clopping of horses' hooves on cobblestones, the honking of horns on the thoroughfares, the calling of hawkers in the streets. Nothing unusual, and readily taken for granted. Here, the racket was irregular, even dangerous. Loud, tinny music drifted from behind saloon doors. The streets were full of Texans, swaggering their arrogance, determined to show these Kansas Yankees that they'd stand for none of their northern laws and even less of their guff. They rode their horses up on the boardwalks and into saloons where they brandished sixguns and ordered another drink. Gunfire sounded regularly as some of the "hurray gangs" shot out lights or mirrors or windows, or anyone who happened to get in their way. They seemed to thrive on annoying other citizens, shoving their way to and fro with booming voices that carried an equal measure of curses and threats. Saranda jumped as a bullet whizzed by her head to strike an object uncomfortably close by.

She was grabbed a time or two and twirled about the

street in a high-spirited jig, mistaken for a dance-hall girl on the make. These men had been on the trail for as long as six months and hadn't seen a woman in all that time. They reeked of the excesses of alcohol and carried firearms they weren't shy about using. It was a perilous situation at best. She quickly realized she could be accidentally killed just crossing the street.

She was rescued from a particularly insistent cowboy by the unannounced arrival of Bat Masterson. Amid the filthy cowmen, he was a welcome sight. Unlike a lot of westerners, he took pains with his appearance. His mustache was neatly trimmed, showing a bit of lip underneath. He was dressed for evening in a black suit and white shirt with a string tie fastened below the stiff collar. His derby was set at a jaunty tilt. He walked with a slight limp, but it was such a loose-hipped, cocky walk that it belied the impediment and didn't slow him down. The tip of his cane gleamed gold in the light of the gas lamps.

In the ensuing scuffle, the story came out. One cowhand, turning mean after losing his money at the faro table, had shot the dealer in the arm, then bolted into the street, brandishing his weapon and threatening to finish off the customers if he wasn't repaid what he lost. Someone had run for the sheriff, and he arrived amid the bedlam like the eye of a hurricane passing through the storm. Coolly, twirling his cane like a baton, he approached the ruffian, talking to him in a tough yet strangely soothing voice, as one might talk to a balking colt.

"I'll have that canister," he said, referring to the man's gun. "Maybe you haven't heard, but we have a law prohibiting the carrying of firearms. Since you're new in town, I'll give you the benefit of the doubt."

The cowboy gazed wildly about him at the dozens of armed men still swarming in and out of doorways along the street. Taking advantage of the distraction, Bat lunged for-

ward and hit the offender soundly on the head with the
end of his cane, knocking him cold. This now-famous maneuver was called "buffaloing." The use of buffalo as a verb
had originated with Saranda's old acquaintance Wyatt
Earp, and his unique way of bringing prisoners to heel.
Except that while Bat used his cane, Wyatt found it hand-
ier to use the butt of his Colt.

Another man ran forward and gathered the limp
body into his arms.

"Take him to the calaboose," Bat ordered. "When he
comes to, fine him. And let the doc know he's got some
business."

He left without seeming to make a dent in the surrounding activities.

Saranda didn't call to him, preferring a more private
reunion. But using the incident as a distraction of her own,
she wiggled free from the cowboy who had her in his grip
and ran around the nearest building to a relatively quieter
street behind. The sight of the volatile Texans convinced
her she wanted nothing to do with them—at least not in
the dark, with so little promise of protection. She decided
for the time being to look for a more suitable victim, a
businessman perhaps, who might take pity on a lone
woman without being drunk enough to molest her.

She found a likely-looking man coming out of a
cathouse. With that satisfied look on his face, he might just
be feeling generous enough to compensate yet another
woman, but for a different reason. Reaching beneath her
skirts, she unpinned a cheap cameo locket from her petticoat, assumed a panicked look, and ran up to the gentleman, breathlessly calling to him in a semblance of her
newly reacquired Kansas accent, which she'd been pri-
vately working on for the better part of the afternoon.

"Sir! Oh, thank goodness I found someone! I'm desperate for help, and I don't know where to turn."

He jumped a little when she touched his arm, but the tearful face she presented relaxed his features. "Why, my dear, what is it?"

"My brother was just murdered," she sobbed. "Up the street. You must have heard the gunfire."

"Well, my dear, I mean—" There was gunfire even as they spoke. It was as common as the squeal of streetcars in New York.

"Of course, how silly. I'm not thinking clearly. You understand. It's just that he was my only living relative. I came all the way from Topeka to meet him, when he wrote telling me he was bringing cattle this way. And now, because of some silly misunderstanding, he's—he's dead. And I don't even have the fare for the train home!"

She put her head to his shoulder in a trusting sort of way as he fumbled about his coat pocket in search of a handkerchief.

"Young lady, I don't know what I can do for you. . . ."

"Oh, thank you," she said quickly, taking him up on an offer he hadn't made. "The only thing I have left in the world is this"—she lifted it from around her neck—"my mother's locket. I don't see how I can part with it, but I have to get my brother home, don't I? If you might buy it from me, it would be so helpful." She moved closer, stroking the muscles of his arm beneath his coat in a show of unconscious supplication. "I'd be so terribly grateful, if only you could help. I just—" She began to cry once again. "I just don't know what else I can do."

He'd found his handkerchief and was attempting in a fumbling manner to dry her eyes. When he wasn't forthcoming with the cash, she cried harder. Some of the whores peered out from the window in various stages of undress.

He was beginning to realize they were making a

scene in a way that a shooting wouldn't. "All right, my dear, please don't cry. How much do you want for the necklace?"

"Fifty dollars would help so much. I could get my brother back to—"

"Fifty dollars!" She began to wail. "Yes, yes. Well, here you are. Fifty dollars, you said?"

Reluctantly, she parted with the necklace. "You will take care of it, won't you? It's all that's left of my beloved mother." With a last heartfelt sob, she turned and headed down an alley, as if it was all too much to bear.

Halfway down, as she was happily tucking her money into the bosom of her dress, she was startled by a flare of light as a match was struck against a wall. A man stood in the shadows, his hat covering his face, which was turned from her as he lit the cigarette at his lips. "Have you another locket?" he asked in a deep, hushed voice. "I'd rather fancy helping a damsel in distress."

He turned to face her, and her heart froze. The light reflected on his face for just an instant before he shook the match and extinguished it. Time enough to recognize Blackwood, and to catch his cocksure grin.

CHAPTER 14

Practical questions flooded her mind, penetrating the panic. How had he found her? What was he doing here? Was he aware she knew he'd killed the Van Slykes? Had he come to silence her?

If so, she suspected she wouldn't get out of this alley alive.

"There was a time when you looked happier to see me," he said, greeting her in that whispery voice that sent a shiver down her spine. She'd always thought his voice unbearably sensual, with its deep timbre, its polished pronunciation, its hushed and intimate tone. Now she perceived a note of menace that, until the night of her seduction in his office, hadn't made itself known. She heard a derisive chuckle coming from his direction and saw the faint red glow of the cigarette tip as he inhaled.

It reminded her who she was. She wasn't some simpering female who'd simply been spurned by her lover. She was a professional. Somehow, he'd outrivaled her at her own game. But she wasn't without resources. She'd match her wits, her reflexes, with his any day of the week. She had to think, and she had to do it now.

Pictures of the events of the evening flashed through her mind. Bat knocking the rowdy senseless. The gentleman who'd given her the fifty dollars. Propelled by instinct, she picked up her skirts and wheeled around, racing for the street she'd just left behind. She heard him hot on her heels, felt the boardwalk shudder as he leapt onto it in pursuit. Searching the street frantically, she spotted the man she was looking for walking a hundred yards away.

"Hey, mister!" she called out to him. She felt Blackwood lurch to a halt behind her. Running toward the gentleman she'd just fleeced, she called to him in a taunting tone.

"You've just been robbed, mister! There *is* no brother, and that locket's a fake." She lifted her skirt high to reveal a petticoat underneath with six or seven lockets pinned to its folds. "Maybe you won't be so trusting next time," she goaded.

She laughed raucously and moved as if to run away. But the gentleman was on her in a flash, grabbing hold of her and shaking her in his wrath. "That so?" he cried. "We'll just see who has the last laugh."

He dragged her off, leaving her just enough time to look back at her pursuer and pantomime a triumphant laugh. The thrill of besting him churned euphorically through her veins. Now who was feeling smug? she wanted to ask him. She saw him toss his cigarette aside in a gesture of frustration as she was hauled away and out of sight.

The jail house consisted of two-by-six planks with peepholes, laid flat and spiked together with iron rods at either end. A second story had been added as a city clerk's office and police court. Inside, it was full to bursting with rough, dirty men, swearing and kicking their aggravation at the bars of their cells. Some spat tobacco juice across the room. The cowboy Bat had buffaloed earlier still lay unconscious on the floor. A young deputy watched over the mob from a cluttered desk.

The place stank of horses, whiskey, cigars, stale bodies, and various forms of carnage from the trail. Most of them hadn't stopped to bathe before plunging into their pleasures south of the Deadline.

"I want to see the marshal," her gentleman announced, shoving her inside. At the sight of a woman, the noise and spitting ceased, and the men stared, wondering if they'd imagined her in their drunken delirium.

"The marshal's gone," the deputy said uncertainly, sitting up straighter in his chair. "I ain't jest sure where he is."

"P'robly dealin' faro at the Long Branch," cracked a cowboy as his cohorts snickered.

"Then get the sheriff. I don't care who you bring. Just get someone in here now. I've been robbed, and I demand satisfaction."

It was a few minutes before the deputy returned. During that time, the gentleman never let go of Saranda, and the prisoners never stopped staring. No one said a word, for which Saranda was grateful. She was too busy trying to keep her relief from showing. Even if Blackwood followed her in here, she knew Bat would never let him take her away.

Finally, the deputy returned with Sheriff Masterson in tow. He seemed annoyed at having been so unceremoniously summoned from whatever he'd been doing.

But the moment he saw her, his stance changed from brisk aggravation to a steely, watchful calm. His light grey eyes, so startling against the sun-darkened skin and short black hair, rested on her thoughtfully, assessing his options.

"What's the trouble?" he asked cautiously. He looked every inch the lawman.

"I'll tell you what the trouble is," the gentleman replied. "I was robbed by this woman. And afterward, she had the temerity to *laugh* in my face."

A sort of cheer arose from the prisoners, most of whom were drunk enough that, in spite of their incarceration, the prospect of trouble was still appealing.

Masterson's eyes flicked to the deputy. "Take the prisoners upstairs and fine 'em, then turn 'em loose."

"What about him?" the deputy asked, gesturing toward the unconscious man on the floor.

"Let him be. I'll deal with him when he comes to."

The cells were cleared out as the delighted cowboys hooted their way up the stairs, their high-heeled boots stomping like thunder on the wood.

As the gentleman told his story, Bat's hard gaze rested on her face. "Let's have the money," he said, holding out his hand when the man finished.

She reached into her bodice and withdrew the fifty dollars. When he jerked his head, she walked into the empty cell and watched silently as he locked the door behind. "The money stays put," he informed the gentleman.

"What do you mean, stays put?"

"Evidence."

"But I'm just passing through town. My train leaves in the morning."

"Leave an address, and we'll forward it in due time."

The man's chest swelled indignantly. "Well, I never heard of such a thing!"

Masterson, rummaging through the desk for a pencil and paper, paused, fixed the man with a deadly gaze, and said, "There's an ordinance in town against carrying firearms. You want to end up in the same cell?"

The man's hand went to the gun he carried beneath his coat. "You'd arrest *me*? I'm the victim!"

"Then fill out your name and address and be on that train in the morning."

"But can't we settle this before then? Won't I be needed as a witness?"

"I reckon my word'll be enough."

He fixed the man with such a challenging look that he didn't dare protest further. It was clear that no one, seeing that look in the sheriff's eyes, would question his word. The deputy came down the stairs then, and Masterson said, "See the gentleman gets back safely to his hotel. And make sure he's on the morning train."

Confused, the man grumbled, "The laws seem pretty one-sided in this town," as he was led away.

The room was expectantly quiet in the aftermath as they stood, alone together. Bat turned to look at her, the fifty dollars still in his hand. Simultaneously, they burst into laughter.

Shaking his head in amusement, he handed the money to her. She took half of it and passed the rest back through the bars. "Your share," she told him, reverting to her English accent. "I should work with you more often."

He pocketed the cash. "Thanks, I'll take it." She'd never known him to turn down money. He removed his derby and placed it carefully on the desk.

"I was wondering when you'd show up."

"Then you've heard."

"Seems like it's *all* I hear about. You okay?"

"Aside from a few close calls."

He sat on the edge of his desk. "Want to tell me why you got yourself caught tonight?"

"I just ran into Blackwood. He killed the Van Slykes. I think he might be here to add me to the list."

"This the first time you've seen him?"

"No. He's been following me. But I've always seen him in time to leave town before he could come close. This time was *too* close. I came knowing you'd keep him from me."

He was looking at her thoughtfully. "That's a powerful reward they have offered for you. It ever occur to you I might turn you in and collect on it?"

"It occurred to me."

"And . . . ?"

"I decided it wasn't much of a risk. Not after all we've been through."

Bat smiled tenderly. "I reckon you're right. A shame, though. Ten thousand dollars is quite a stake."

"You didn't save my life just to turn me in for ten thousand pieces of silver."

"I didn't at that."

"Do you recall when we met?"

"How could I forget? Was it two or three years ago now?"

"You and Wyatt, and that dreadful Dr. Holliday, were pulling that pathetic sham."

"The one where Doc painted the brick gold and sold it at a discount to people on the train."

"And he had the audacity—not to mention lack of judgment—to attempt to sell it to *me*!"

"And you told him you couldn't afford it, but—"

"—If he *did* manage to sell it, he might split the profits with me. Such indignation!"

He was chuckling softly. "So he sold it to some greenhorn. When the sucker got off the train, Wyatt and I flashed phony badges, confiscated the brick *and* the money, and sent him off with a warning never to show his face again."

"And when he asked about the money—"

"We told him we needed it for evidence. Then you

showed up and demanded your share for keeping quiet. By God, you were something. I never saw anyone as good as you."

They smiled wistfully at each other for a moment, letting the memories bond them.

"Of course," he admitted, "we weren't in the same league with *your* cons. But those days are long gone. Now we're real lawmen. We've gone respectable."

"Which, you must admit, is the most outrageous con of all. Oh, Bat, things were so much simpler then. What happened to complicate them?"

"We both took a turn at respectability, I reckon. Now you're on the dodge, and I'm too damn busy for my own good." He locked the front door. "The only problem with being a peace officer is they expect you to keep the peace."

"I saw you buffalo that scamp tonight. A pretty piece of work, I must say. Although I thought a sheriff wasn't supposed to handle town problems."

"Well, I let it be known if Wyatt couldn't be found, I'd help things along."

"That's because you're nicer than Wyatt."

It was an ongoing battle. Bat revered Wyatt Earp and Saranda berated him for the sanctimonious way he treated Bat.

"I just want to stay alive, same as everyone. But right now, the first order of business is keeping *you* alive."

She reached into her petticoats, removed a small file, applied it to the lock of her cell, and let herself out. The bars squealed as they swung open, capturing his attention.

"Away from Blackwood, you mean," she said.

"Which reminds me, I've got a bone to pick with that Blackwood. Ever since those stories he did on me, I've become some kind of dadblamed hero. Every jackrabbit with a gun is pouring into town, wanting to test my reputation. I'm having a helluva time getting any gambling done."

"That's why we have to take care of him. Your gambling may be suffering, but he's interfering with my ability to stay in one piece."

"Blackwood's just part of the bigger problem. What we have to figure out is, what are we going to do with you?"

"If we can take care of Blackwood, I shall disappear—"

"It's not that simple. There've already been a stream of Pinkertons and bounty hunters asking around."

"Here? Already?"

"I steered 'em wrong. You can stay here for a while. I'll do what I can to protect you. But those men are smart, and they're determined. They'll be back."

The man on the cell floor rolled over, snorted some air into his lungs, then was still. Bat and Saranda looked at each other, visibly relaxing.

"You're jumpy," he observed. "Not that I blame you. You're practically the most wanted woman in America. I reckon I'd be jumpy too."

"I've never been so visible before. It's as if they know my every move before I make it. Do you think Blackwood's tipping them off? Setting a trap I can't get out of?"

"Could be. If he wants to kill you, he might be a bit more private about it. But there are ways of arranging things once the Pinkertons get you."

She felt the world closing in around her.

"What do you want?" he asked. "Tell me, and I'll do what I can to help."

"I want Blackwood—"

"Christ, Saranda! Can't you think of anything else?" She looked up at him, startled by the outburst. "Honey, listen to me. If you don't take care of yourself, they're going to get you. If worse comes to worst, I can use my authority and say I've got you in custody and will turn you over myself. But I can't protect you for long. Sooner or later, a U.S. marshal's going to show up with a warrant. Now, by God, what do you want? Do you want to prove your innocence?"

"I don't care about that. I just want to go somewhere where they don't know my face."

"What about the Van Slyke money?"

"I didn't get in it for the money. I can always make money."

She'd done it to pay Blackwood back. And now here she was, running from him and half the lawmen in the country. It rankled so her teeth ached from clenching them.

He slumped down in his chair. "Okay. We might have to get you out of the country. Down to Mexico. Lay low until the fuss dies down."

"It won't do me any good to be in Mexico if Blackwood meets me in some alley and slits my throat."

"It won't do you any good to be dead."

Every time she thought of Blackwood, she felt bottled up with frustrated rage. How could she have been such a fool? How could she have allowed her emotions to interfere with her judgment? And how, in God's name, had she allowed herself to be conned—by a *Blackwood, no less!*— who could coldbloodedly gun down men who'd been so good to him, without so much as a qualm? She looked up at Bat, her battling emotions showing all too vulnerably in her enormous eyes. "Blackwood gunned down two people who really loved me. Would you have me forget all that to save myself?"

Bat could read the deeper meaning in her eyes. She loved Blackwood, and he'd betrayed her. He sighed, exasperated. "Okay. You won't cooperate till Blackwood's taken care of; let's take care of him."

"I knew I could count on you." She sat atop the desk with her legs crossed Indian fashion and leaned forward in her enthusiasm. "What do you have planned?"

He stroked his mustache as he considered. "We'll just have to put a scare into him he'll never forget."

CHAPTER 15

Saranda spent the night locked in the cell with Bat dozing in his chair, watching over her. The next morning he brought breakfast, then went out on what he called a "hunting spree." He returned late in the afternoon with some men's clothes in his hands and a mischievous look in his eyes.

"I found him," he informed her. "Watching the calaboose, no doubt waiting for your exit. Don't worry. I fixed him good."

"Fixed him? How?"

"Spread it around town he's one of them eastern dandies too set on himself. Told the boys he's one with a Fifth Avenue swagger and strut. Goes around bad-mouthing cowboys. That should do it."

"Do what?"

"You'll see. Here." He tossed her the bundle of clothes. "Get into these. We'll go watch the fun."

She dressed hurriedly as he kept his back turned. The

pants were too long, so she rolled them up and cinched the waist in folds beneath the belt. The jacket fit a little better. With her hair piled up beneath a sombrero, she could pass for a boy at a distance. When she was ready, he put his derby on his head, took up his cane, and grandly offered her his arm.

"I'd better not," she declined, indicating her clothes. "The boys might start wondering about *you*."

They were just in time. Out on Front Street, amid the congestion of horses, oxen, and mules jamming the wide thoroughfare, a large group of Dodgers were wrestling Blackwood to the ground. They tied his hands behind his back with a kerchief, but in the struggle he pulled free. Bat removed a pair of handcuffs from his back pocket and tossed them over, following them with the keys. The stranger's hands were then jerked behind his back and his wrists snapped together in the steel restraints. None too gently, they lowered a rope around his neck, heaved him up onto the back of a horse, mounted their own animals, and rode off with him in tow.

Saranda's heart lurched at the brutal display. "They're going to hang him?" she cried. "For putting on airs?" It was just this sort of senseless cruelty that had soured her on the West.

Bat was smiling. "You wanted him out of your hair, didn't you? Let's go see what happens."

He'd thought to provide horses, which they mounted, following at a distance. The crowd stopped at one of the few big trees by the river. There, they hoisted the rope over a branch and set their victim in place.

Amid a barrage of razzing, Blackwood sat straight and tall in the saddle. They'd removed his hat, and his black hair curled wildly about his head. His strong jaw set, his eyes revealing nothing, he sat with such placid self-possession that he might have arranged the spectacle himself.

But she noticed he watched them closely the whole time. She could almost feel his brain working as the hour of his death drew near.

Appalled, she gawked at the scene. There, by a river, under a lone tree, with more spectators flocking by the minute to witness the sight, these ruffians were going to hang a man because he was different. They didn't know that he was pursuing Saranda. They didn't know her life might hang in the balance, dependent on their whims. They knew only what they'd been told, and *that* had been a fabrication. As always, they'd been easily fooled.

She'd never witnessed such a shocking indifference for the sanctity of life. This treatment, afforded a stranger, would have shocked her. But this wasn't some impersonal criminal whose retribution she was witnessing. This was Mace Blackwood. The only man she'd ever truly made love to. Looking at his handsome face, she knew that in spite of everything, she loved him still.

Loathing herself for her weakness, she nevertheless reached across her horse and clutched Bat's hand. "Bat, stop this. Now."

"Too late, sugar."

The rope was tightened about Blackwood's neck. The sun beat down mercilessly. Saranda felt the sweat trickling from her breasts and down her sides. Even as the rope was jerked tight, cutting into his windpipe, Blackwood sat stubbornly composed, determined not to show the terror that any sane person would feel.

"All right, boys," one of them cried out. "Let's get on with it."

"Got any last words, mister?" another queried.

It was a moment before he spoke. Then, in a voice made hoarse for the rope around his neck, he said with an air of supreme confidence, "I could say them better at the nearest saloon."

The boys laughed then, some of them slapping each other on the backs or nudging their neighbors with their elbows.

"Yer a cool customer, mister, fer a dude. What do you wanta be called? I reckon anyone cool as you deserves a tombstone fer his pains."

"You want my name?" Blackwood asked.

An expectant hush settled on the plains, broken only by the rushing river. By some odd twist of fate, the stranger held them all in the palm of his hand. Then he uttered the deciding words.

"Luke McGlue's my name, gentlemen. But, by all means, call me Luke."

It was too much even for the most seasoned pranksters. The roar from the riverbank was so deafening, it seemed even the residents of Boot Hill must have heard. Men fell down in the grass, rolling as they howled. All around, there was a rollicking cheer. Some of them came up to the stranger and slapped him on the back so hard, his horse threatened to bolt and hang him by default. Eventually, the rope was removed from his neck, his hands were freed, and the cuffs proffered to him as a souvenir. It was agreed that, for once, the drinks would be on the Dodgers.

As Saranda stared disbelievingly after them, they carted him off toward the Long Branch and a good stiff round of drinks.

Eventually, Bat and Saranda were the only two left. She was so shaken by the experience that she sat still in her saddle, staring vacantly at the now-deserted tree.

"What happened?"

Bat shook his head admiringly. "I gotta hand it to that Blackwood."

"I don't understand. What did he do?"

"You might recall the Dodgers are fond of a good

joke. As hard as life is in these parts, any excuse for levity is welcomed."

"Yes, yes, but what—"

"Luke McGlue doesn't exist. The boys made him up and blame every hoax perpetuated in town on him. When the preacher's horse was stolen, they told him Luke McGlue'd done it. When a cigar drummer's wares were passed around and smoked behind his back, it was Luke McGlue who did it. Last week, they put a notice in the paper addressing Luke McGlue, mayor. That Blackwood's quick, I'll grant you that. Picked up on the joke his first day in town."

Saranda's heart was still racing dangerously. "I must say, when you offer to fix someone, you keep your word. Isn't hanging a bit extreme?"

"Oh, they wouldn't have hanged him," Bat assured her with a shrug. "Just put a scare into him."

"A fine job they did of scaring him! Nothing's changed. If anything, he's won the hearts of your townspeople with this ridiculous charade. There's no telling what he might try next, with the aid of his new chums."

"You got to admire his cool," he said resentfully.

"I certainly do not." But she did. In a lifetime of associating with grifters, she'd never seen anyone as cool under pressure as Blackwood had been just now. "Now what? Any more brilliant ideas?"

"I reckon we bring Wyatt in on this."

"No. I never knew Wyatt to come up with a decent idea—unless, of course, he stole it and took credit for it himself. His idea of taking care of someone is to have that awful Holliday slit his throat with a knife."

But Bat wouldn't be swayed where his friend and hero was concerned. "Let's just hear what he has to say."

CHAPTER 16

Wyatt met them at the jailhouse, a relatively quiet place during the day. He was tall with golden hair and a full drooping mustache, looking like a gruff and shaggy lion. Eight years older than Bat, he radiated a hard-edged aura of danger and unflappability. He wasn't a man to talk without cause. He wasn't even particularly well liked. On the western plains, Wyatt was considered an educated man, and this, compounded by his tough silences, afforded him few friends. When he pushed too hard and offended someone, Bat stepped in with his easy smile and smoothed the way. Saranda's problem with Earp stemmed from the fact that Wyatt never seemed to appreciate the contribution Bat made to the great Wyatt Earp's reputation.

Wyatt listened to the story quietly, then sneered, twisting his mustache. "You pups!" he spat. It was another of Saranda's grievances against the man. Being older, and having introduced Bat to much of life on the frontier, he never ceased to talk down to him as a teacher might a wayward pupil. But in all her years with Bat, she'd never heard him say one uncomplimentary thing about Wyatt.

"Don't start with us, Wyatt," she warned.

"Start with you? I ought to finish the two of you off. As usual, you're looking at the situation from a cockeyed point of view."

"And just how do you suggest we look at it?" she challenged.

"Logically. You've got to get the man to confess, so you can hold your head up. Then you won't *have* to run."

"I'm a shuck artist," she pointed out. "I don't stay and fight."

"You'll be a dead shuck artist if you don't."

"That's beside the point. You don't know Blackwood. He talks people into doing things they'd never *dream* of doing. Frankly, he's more clever than the two of you put together. You can't expect a man like him to volunteer the information you're after—"

Wyatt gave a sour smile. "I have yet to meet the man who could argue with a pair of fists. Me and Bat'll just beat all Hades out of him until he gives us a confession."

"Oh, that's just like you! You think you can brutalize everyone into submission."

"Saranda—"

"Bat, you know it's true. He either clubs someone with his gun or brawls in the street with his fists. Everyone exclaims over what a great fighter he is. But they forget to mention he always makes sure he's got you and your handy sixgun to back his play."

"Do you want my help or don't you?" Wyatt growled.

"Not that way."

"You got a better idea?"

Reluctantly, she exchanged looks with Bat. "No," she admitted.

"Good," said Wyatt, grinning in anticipation. "You'd

best stay clear. We may be hard-pressed not to kill the sonofabitch."

"I want his confession," she insisted, "not his death."

Wyatt gave her a keen look. "Sweet on him, are you? In that case, I reckon Bat will enjoy getting in a few extra licks."

THOUGH SHE'D BEEN warned to stay away, Saranda followed at a distance. She watched as Bat and Wyatt dragged the unsuspecting Blackwood from the jubilation of the Long Branch Saloon. As they carted him, struggling the whole way, to the livery. As Ham Bell was expelled from his barn and the door bolted closed. Creeping closer, she cringed as the sound of a fist hitting flesh echoed through the structure.

Sickened, she reeled back to the jail house, torn between her emotions and her good sense. She knew what Wyatt was capable of. She'd seen a man's face turned to pulp under the merciless assault of his hamlike fists. She couldn't bear to think of Blackwood's handsome features bloodied and rearranged. Yet something had to be done. He wasn't going to get away with killing the Van Slykes. The Blackwood string of murders must end here.

Still, she couldn't help shuddering at what Wyatt and Bat might do to him. Why did she have to feel this way about him? Why couldn't she happily wish him dead?

On her way, she spotted a man in an eastern suit whom she recognized instantly as a Pinkerton agent. He was smoking a cigar with a thoughtful look on his face, gazing up and down the street as if wondering where she might hide. Flattening herself back against the wall of the closest building, she backtracked and took another route. The trap was closing around her. If she didn't leave Dodge soon, she risked being caught. If only Bat and Wyatt could get the confession she needed!

THEY HADN'T YET returned an hour later, after she'd nearly worn a groove in the floor with her pacing. She couldn't stay waiting any longer. She had to go see what was happening. It was dangerous, with the Pinkerton man out on the streets. But a glance out the window told her it was growing dark. Slipping into her boy's outfit, piling her hair beneath the hat, she stealthily made her way to the livery by use of the back roads.

The area was deserted. Which meant people on the streets knew something was going on. It was too quiet. Afraid they'd killed him, she raced to the barn and put her ear to the outside wall. There wasn't a sound.

Suddenly, the bolt slid back. Saranda leapt around the side of the structure just in time to see Blackwood walk out. As he passed under a lantern, she could see that his face, far from being mashed to pulp, was absolutely intact. There was some sort of scratch around his mouth, but otherwise he looked perfect. As he walked away, without the slightest trace of a limp, Saranda caught the slight, smug tuggings of a smile.

When he'd disappeared into the night, Bat and Wyatt walked through the door. They looked abnormally cheerful, which, if she hadn't seen him, she'd suspect didn't bode well for Blackwood. With intentional sarcasm, she asked, "You didn't hurt him *too* much, I hope?"

"Naw," said Bat. "He's fine."

"He's a sight better than fine," stated Wyatt. "He's innocent."

She couldn't believe what she was hearing. "What are you talking about?"

"He didn't kill them. He told us."

"He—*told* you?"

"You'll never guess who did it."

"Oh, please. Tell me."

"His brother."

She was quiet for a long time, her features hardening. "His brother, Lance?"

"That's it. He wants him caught as much as you do. A helluva man, that Blackwood. Makes me sorry I had to throw that first punch."

Saranda put her hand to her aching head. "Let me understand this. You hit him *once*—"

"In the mouth."

"And he told you he didn't do it, so you *stopped?*"

Wyatt, looking satisfied, nodded. "That's about the size of it."

"Fools! Did you forget you're dealing with a supreme confidence man? He conned you!"

"Now look. I consider myself a decent judge of character. That Blackwood's a fine fellow. And he didn't kill those easterners."

"You mean he convinced you he didn't."

Bat, who'd been quiet all this time, spoke sheepishly. "I think he may be telling the truth."

"Bat, Lance Blackwood is dead. Now Mace has convinced you clowns that a dead man committed those murders."

"He says he's alive."

"I don't believe I'm hearing this. For an hour, I've been pacing that floor praying you weren't killing the man. And all this time, he was suckering you."

"He says he wants to clear your name. Says he has evidence that'll do it."

"Did he show you the evidence?"

"No."

"Of course not. There *is* no evidence. If he wants to do anything, it's dispose of me where the body won't be found."

"He wants to take you back to New York and prove—"

"Bat, Blackwood is the most gifted bluff artist since —me! You can't believe a thing this man says. If he does want to take me back, it's to turn me over to the police so I can be tried for murder. If that happens, you know as well as I that I shall hang."

"He seemed sincere to me," Wyatt said stubbornly.

"Of course he did. That's his job." She heaved a sigh. "Never mind. Thank you for your help. But I can see I'll have to take care of him myself."

CHAPTER 17

She had to think of something. The Pinkertons knew she was in Dodge. It wouldn't be long before others followed, bent on her capture and conviction. But of all these threats, Blackwood was the most immediate. He'd proven himself adept at trailing her, and even more skilled at talking his way out of difficulties. She had to think of a way to put him out of commission once and for all.

All she could do was use his strengths against him. If he was so hot on her trail, she might be able to lure him up to Canada. There, it would be a simple matter to notify authorities of his presence in the country. Back home, he was still a wanted man. In a British commonwealth, he could be extradicted and sent back to England.

If she was lucky, he'd be so intent on trailing her, he wouldn't guess her plan. He'd assume she was heading for Canada as a way of avoiding United States officials herself. Once Blackwood was in custody, she could take some time and figure out what to do next. It might well be, as Bat had suggested, that her days in America were over.

She slipped in the back door of the Dodge House and packed her bag. She left the money for her room on the dresser, not wanting to be seen entering or leaving the hotel. The fewer people who knew about her plans, the more chance she had of sneaking out of town under the Pinkerton's nose.

She crept down the hall toward the back stairs. Most of the guests were either in the dining room having their dollar meals or had already drifted up the street to toss down some drinks or try their hand at faro or chuck-a-luck. Once she'd maneuvered the hallways successfully, she paused outside to breathe a sigh of relief.

Already, Dodge was in full swing. Music and laughter drifted up the street, and an occasional round of gunfire. She felt safer in the dark, the evening clatter assuring her that life continued as always, and her escape was of no consequence to anyone but herself. Still, she couldn't shake the feeling she was being watched. Blackwood, no doubt. Good, she decided. He wouldn't have a horse handy. If she hurried, she could leave with enough of a head start that he couldn't harm her yet could easily follow her trail. Let him track her, she gloated. All the way to Canada.

She flattened herself against the wall as some groups of cowboys drifted past. Poking her head around the corner of the building, she saw the horse she'd ordered waiting in the alley beside the billiard hall, pawing impatiently at the ground. When the coast was clear, she edged around the corner and made a run for it. She hooked her bag over the saddle horn, untied the reins, and put her foot in the stirrup.

Before she could mount, she was grabbed from

behind. A hand clamped itself over her mouth, and she was yanked back so forcefully, the air left her lungs. On the brink of freedom, she found herself pinned back against a masculine frame as hard and unyielding as stone.

CHAPTER 18

"Nice of the sheriff to provide transportation," Blackwood said in her ear.

She felt something cold close over her wrist. He pulled it behind her and grappled for the other arm. Her fear made her strong, and she yanked it from his grasp, only to be hauled around so he could reach in front. Cold metal clamped over the other wrist, binding the two together before her. Struggling to free herself, she realized with a sick feeling that he'd used Bat's handcuffs to restrain her.

She broke into a sweat. Fear shot up her spine. This was the man who'd coldbloodedly killed Winston and his father as they'd sat drinking brandy. He'd already shown himself to be a clever opponent. She fought down the panic, endeavoring to think. She didn't doubt she could escape, given an opportunity. Her main concern was he wouldn't keep her alive long enough for her to outsmart him.

He settled her back against him again, fighting to

keep her still. She could feel his massive body against her back. An arm like steel held her pinned to him, angling across her shoulders so it grazed her breasts. His other hand crushed the soft corners of her mouth.

Bedlam reined over the surrounding town, yet she felt for an instant that they were in their own quiet pocket, the air hushed and expectant as she waited for him to speak. He held her patiently, giving her time to stop kicking and squirming, to settle down before he conveyed his demands. The quiet, deadly calm was more frightening than the inescapable grip of his arms, or any threat he might make. It showed him to be a man of infinite forbearance, a man who would bide his time until he achieved his objective.

On the verge of surrender, she gave a rebellious jerk in his arms. He put his mouth to her ear, so close she could feel him smile. "Go ahead," he whispered. "Struggle. If it isn't a challenge, it isn't worth the trouble."

Inflamed by his bloated superiority, by the arrogant assumption that he'd already won this game of wits, she kicked backward and landed a wicked blow to his shin. She heard the slight intake of his breath before he chuckled in her ear.

"You disappoint me. I expected something more imaginative from a woman of your talents." Her professional pride insulted, she struggled harder as his arms tightened, hugging her close. "That's it. Vent your frustration. I have all the time in the world. I've waited a long time to get you like this. If I have to, I can wait a lifetime."

His voice, as caressing as a lover's, lent a chilling note to his words. The smell of him, that clean, male scent devoid of any telltale colognes, overwhelmed her. She cautioned herself to keep her head. She must play to his weakness. If he assumed he'd beaten her, by all means play up the delusion. It could only work to her favor in the end.

She slumped back against him.

"Giving up so soon? Just when I was beginning to enjoy myself."

She felt like a mouse being toyed with by a cat who knew he was stronger, smarter, and fleeter of foot. How best to defeat a cat? With his curiosity. Make him wonder. Throw him off-guard. Make *him* do the work.

She recalled his hot words as he'd slammed her up against his office wall and taken her from behind. The way his anger had turned to tenderness against his will. The melding of their bodies that was like a mating of souls. It was beyond lovemaking. It was as if they'd heard the same chord of music, the one no one else could hear. She knew she could use that to her advantage. His protests notwithstanding, there wasn't a man alive who could escape her charms, once she'd set her sights on him. She just had to take it slowly, one carefully planned step at a time. She'd seek out his weak spots and play to them.

Slowly, she dropped her head back against his shoulder in a gesture of resignation.

"Oh, you're good," he murmured. "But I feel it's only fair to warn you: I'm more clever than I look. Play with me, and you'll get burned. Is that clear?"

She nodded.

"Good girl. Now, I'm going to take my hand away. If you scream, no one will pay the slightest bit of attention. They'll think you're a whore playing it rough. But *I'll* know. And I'll be close to you. So close, you'll think I'm under your skin."

When he removed his hand from her mouth, one cautious fraction at a time, she licked dry lips and made her first move. "Too late," she told him in a purposely husky voice. "You got under my skin a long time ago."

Still behind her, he brought a large hand to her face, cupped her cheek, and ran it down the length of her throat. "Careful, sweetheart," he warned. "I might believe you."

He heaved her up into the saddle and mounted behind her. Gripping his arm like a vise across her chest, he pulled her back into him so closely, she could feel the buttons of his coat cutting into her back. A shudder of apprehension swept through her as he took up the reins and kicked the horse through the back roads of town and off across the prairie.

They rode hard, putting distance between them and Dodge as the twilight darkened to night. Still they rode, the thundering of the horse's hooves the only sound out on the starlit prairie. She settled back, plotting her next move, watching the stars, keeping track of their direction so she could make her way back. There was no hope of rescue. As usual, she could depend on no one. If she was going to escape, she'd have to do it on her own.

Still, while she coolly ticked off possible ploys in her head, she couldn't help the erratic thump of her heart against his enslaving arm. She felt strangely alone with him, riding through the endless prairie, with the stars and the moon as their only witness. She'd never been in such peril.

If only her heart weren't so at war with her head. If only being held in his arms didn't feel like destiny come to call. If only it didn't make her want to forget the danger, her anger, her tenuous position, and simply enjoy the feel of him one last time.

This realization shocked her more than anything that had passed before it. What had happened to her since meeting Blackwood? Was she so stupid, so despicably *female*, that she'd ignore everything else, just for the feel of his arms about her? She didn't want to love him. Couldn't afford to. Certainly didn't trust him. But her body, fitting so snugly against his, betrayed the angry thoughts in her head. Her body rejoiced at the contact.

An hour or so later, in the silence and emptiness of the desolate plains, they spotted a tree spreading its branches in silhouette by a trickling silver creek. Saranda thought it was an oak, but it didn't matter. One way or another, that tree spelled trouble. She didn't know if he intended to hang her, or just shoot her and leave her to rot beneath its branches. But in a prairie full of nothing but tall grasses, snakes, and insects, that tree offered a blatant invitation for their journey to end.

He reined up, as she knew he would. Dismounting, he pulled her down after him. Grabbing the cuffs and pulling her along with him, he tied the reins to a low-hanging branch. He put her back to the tree and said, "Don't move," as he began unbuckling his belt.

She backed against the trunk, feeling the bark bite into her, snagging her clothes. She could smell the sap of the tree, feel the gentle breeze as it rustled faintly through the leaves. His belt buckle flashed in the moonlight as he pulled it loose. Her mouth went dry. She tried to swallow and couldn't.

She was trying to think of something to say to forestall his intentions, but the horrid realization that she didn't really want him to stop numbed her tongue. He looked up and paused. In that light, her hair was the color of moonbeams, her eyes wide and blazing like sapphires. He read her thoughts in them and lifted a corner of his mouth. The moonlight played against his teeth, gaudily white against the darkness, flashing like his buckle.

"Don't flatter yourself," he told her in a harsh tone. "I just want you indisposed while I make a fire."

He pulled the belt free, bent low, and fastened it tightly around her ankles. She didn't struggle. Without knowing it, he'd just aided and abetted her plan.

"Sit down," he commanded. She did so, settling herself in grass that rose to her shoulders. She looked around her, wondering what else might be crawling around in the surrounding jungle.

"You're safe," he assured her. "The only thing you have to worry about is me."

He walked in a widening circle, bending occasionally, picking up an assortment of sticks, cow chips, and dead grasses. Carefully, easing her skirt up an inch at a time to avoid being spotted, she reached into her petticoat and retracted a small file. He looked at her, and she stilled. To distract him, she called, "I don't suppose you brought a last meal of sorts."

"I don't suppose I did."

He returned to his scavenging, and she inserted the file into the lock. She only bothered to open one of the cuffs. She'd have time enough to free the other wrist later.

As he bent to start the fire, she stretched her arms down and worked the belt loose by degrees. He struck a match, but the breeze extinguished it. She stepped out of the belt as he tried again. By the third match, she was crawling around the horse, which he'd left conveniently close by. She had to hurry. In a moment, the fire would catch, and he'd look her way.

She never knew what happened after that. One moment he was stooped over the fire, the next he was before her, shoving her back against the trunk of the tree with a force that knocked the wind from her. He put a hand at her throat to keep her still, unwrapped the horse's reins, and shooed him away. The animal ran a few yards, then stopped to graze. He didn't watch. He turned to her, took her hand in his, and wrested the file from her fingers.

Softly, he swore at himself. "I should've known."

His anger gave him an overpowering strength. Her struggles were like puffs of breath against the mighty oak at her back. With hardly an effort, he dragged both arms backward around the tree and fastened the handcuffs at the back. Cold steel against warm flesh. The tree trunk was wide enough that her arms were stretched taut, straining in their sockets.

"You're hurting me," she told him, but he didn't care. He began to pat down her clothes with rough, insistent hands. Raising her skirts, he discovered the many lockets, baubles, and tools of her trade, all pinned or tucked away in their protective pockets so they wouldn't jingle when she walked. He yanked at the ties, thrust the petticoat down, and pulled at her legs so she was forced to step out of it. Impaled against the tree as she was, she had little choice.

When he'd tossed the petticoats out of reach, he stepped back and studied her with narrowed eyes. "Now . . . if I were a woman," he mused, "where would I hide my—devices?"

The fire had flared up during this time, casting an eerie vermilion glow on their features. He looked devilish in the odd light, the shadows stretching across his face to add menace to the angular lines. The thick brows seemed to shoot up his forehead, and his eyes seemed to glow red with lust. His gaze came to rest on her bosom, invitingly thrust out before her, riding high beneath the strain of her back-stretched arms.

"You wouldn't!" she gasped.

"Normally, I'm a man of words," he replied in a conversational tone. "But I can always resort to brute force when pushed." He gazed at her breasts and clucked an imitation of regret. "Too bad, Princess. It's just too tempting to pass up."

Without the slightest reluctance, he unfastened the buttons of her short, fitted jacket, then, with both hands, parted the material as if parting a curtain and revealing some concealed treasure. Under her jacket, she wore a blouse especially made for her. With a false buttoned front, it had a carefully concealed slit underneath so she could get into it in emergencies. He fingered it, found the slit, and grinned. "Console yourself with the thought that this pains me as much as it does you," he said, lingering over her breasts.

"I hope they burn you."

"Don't forget," he said in an intimate tone, "they've burned me once before."

Her breasts weren't large, but they were full and firm, supported by a specially outfitted corset. He fingered them appreciatively, then moved lower as she snarled at him.

"If you wanted to touch me, you could say so honestly, instead of hiding behind this ridiculous charade—"

"Charade?" His hand came out holding two other files of different sizes. These he tossed aside. Plunging his hand back between her breasts, he brought it out time and again, with a fistful of money, some high-ranking cards, and a pair of ivory dice. These he shook around the palm of his hand, studying her reflectively. "Shall we wager your virtue on the outcome of these dice? I'll take a wild guess. If I can hit sevens—say, three times in a row—I win the prize, and you lose whatever tender virtue you might have left. Oh, let's be generous, Princess. Ten times. Would you chance it?" She jerked her chin up defiantly. "I thought not." The dice went the way of all her other tools.

"What do you want from me?" she cried in frustration. If he was going to rape her, why didn't he just get on with it? Why did he have to toy with her this way? Her breath was coming fast and hard, her heart constricting in her throat.

He moved so close that his body pressed against hers. Taking her face in his hands, he tipped it so he could look down into her eyes. The light shifted, and he lost that ghoulish quality. The last detached part of her mind noted that he was darkly handsome, and that her body was responding wretchedly to his proximity.

"What do I want from you?" he whispered in that singularly intimate tone. "I want every last secret of yours out in the open. I want you bared before me like the day you were born. Nothing to hide, and nothing hidden that might jump out and sting me in the dead of night."

As he spoke, his other hand had been creeping down her thigh. He took the material of her skirt in his fingers. To her horror, she felt cool air on her legs as her skirt bunched up, inch by agonizing inch, into his hand. With a start, she realized what he was doing.

"No, please," she gasped. "There's nothing there. I'll swear to you on my father's grave. You can trust me."

"*Trust* you? Surely, you've heard the saying 'Fool me once, shame on you. Fool me twice, shame on me.'" He gathered the skirt about her hips, used his leg to pin it there, then moved his hand around the outside of her underclothing, roving like a bloodhound on the hunt. "I'm nobody's fool, Princess. Not the second time." Discovering nothing from the outside, he found the waist of her drawers and shoved his hand inside.

He grazed her backside, gliding across the taut skin, then rounded her thigh and found the crisp, curling hair in front. More gently now, his firm fingers probed, then parted the folds and slipped easily inside.

His gaze flew to hers, and their eyes locked—his astonished, hers bright with humiliation. For the moment his fingers entered her, she grew wet to his touch.

She caught the flash of arousal in his eyes.

"I shan't give myself to you voluntarily," she warned. "Never again. You'll have to keep me tied to this tree."

"Is that what it takes to excite you? Being chained to a tree? Has anyone ever tied you up and taken you like a stallion masters a mare? And made you love it so much, you begged for more?"

"That's just what you'll have to do. But I vow to you, I shall fight you every step of the way."

"You do that," he said, lowering his head. "But don't forget I'm a gamester. The battle's half the fun."

CHAPTER 19

When she jerked her head away, avoiding his mouth, he contented himself with nibbling at her neck. She felt her knees weaken as a jolt of excitement rocked her head back against the tree. His hand rounded her backside, squeezing her buttocks as his fingers continued to probe, long since abandoning the notion of hidden instruments, bent only on the enflaming of her desire.

She felt torn between that desire and a stark terror that curled from the pit of her stomach and settled in her heart. The night of the masked ball, when he'd bound her hands with ropes, her excitement at her helplessness had been predicated on the knowledge that she was safe. A single scream would bring someone running to her rescue. It was like a game she could control, in part, by her knowledge of the presence of others. But here, in the dark, lonely emptiness of the Kansas plains, she was completely at his mercy. As much as her body betrayed her—wanting him beyond bearing even now—her mind was distinctly aware of her danger at his hands. The exaltation of his touch warred with the sight of his face, with memories he was loosing from carefully erected strongholds of her heart. He was a killer. Out here, miles away from deliverance, there was no telling what he might do.

Her breath was coming in gasps. Panic surfaced as he moved the menace of his body close against her own. She threw back her head to scream. It wouldn't do any good, she knew. But the sensations stampeded through her with such raw ferocity, she felt on the verge of hysterics for the second time in her life—at risk of detonating beneath his rapacious hands, her formidable longing blasting through her like dynamite demolishing a mountain of stone. It seemed the only thing to do was scream her anguish to the night.

He saw her intention and, with the reflexes of a rattler, pulled a hand free and clamped it hard over her mouth. "Not yet, sweetheart. You scream in passion, or you don't scream at all."

His hand, gagging her, began to move across her mouth as still his fingers inside her ignited tremors she couldn't control. As her breath escaped in frightened gasps, he explored her lips with his fingers, then thrust them into her mouth. Torn between fright and longing, she was seized by a mad desire to bite them in two. But even as her teeth closed down, she was rattled by his nearness, and she gave up and sucked on them instead.

"That's it, Princess," he murmured. He pulled his hand away. Unbidden, her mouth reached for his fingers. But he was busy brushing the hair from her face, her shoulders, his fingers caressing her skin along the way. He was so gentle, it scared her all the more. She knew at any moment, he could turn violent, using his hand in her hair to yank back her head and slit her throat.

She began to whimper softly. "Please," she whispered.

"Please, what? Please take my fingers out of you?" He did so, and to her utter shame, she found herself thrusting her hips forward, seeking his touch. He shoved his leg between her thighs, giving her something to rub against. "Or please put them back in?"

She could hear her own desperate lamentation. Fury mingled with her other emotions to aggravate her unwanted arousal. No man had ever had such power over her. No one had ever possessed the sorcery to make her weak with need just from the whisper of his voice against her ear. She hated herself for wanting him—hated him for making her want him.

"Tell me," he insisted. Turning her to face him, he saw her desire in the glitter of her eyes, in the parting of her lips. But he saw something else. The terror when she looked into his face. The flash of fear as his hand found her breast and squeezed. He'd never seen such a wounded look of foreboding and pleading in his life.

He tipped her chin up and looked deeper into her eyes. His hand fell from her breast as if he'd been burned. He studied her a moment, watching as her fright usurped her longing, and she began to shake.

"Did someone hurt you once?" he asked.

It was so unexpected, so tenderly uttered, that tears sprang to her eyes. She didn't cry easily. To do so before him would be to expose herself in a way she hadn't by showing him the depth of her physical need. Mortified, she turned her face away.

All was quiet for many moments. A slight breeze rustled the grass. The fire crackled and sparked. The horse blew, rattled its bridle, pawed the ground. Still Saranda kept her eyes closed, fighting not to reveal to him any more than she already had.

She felt a strong finger trail her cheek and hardened herself to what would come. Why should he care about her pain? Why should he care about the conflict that was tearing her apart? He could have her, kill her, do anything he wanted.

She didn't hear him move, but the next thing she knew, the key was turning in the lock, and her arms fell free. She looked back in time to see him remove the other handcuff. He didn't see the look of surprise she gave him because he was taking her wrists, one at a time, and rubbing them where the cuffs had chafed. Her fingers throbbed as the blood began to move.

"I owe you an apology," he said softly, his voice barely carrying in the expanse of the starry night. "I only meant to keep you from fleeing till you'd heard me out."

She was so astonished, she could think of nothing to say. She didn't believe him. She'd been deceived by him once before. But she couldn't guess at his intentions. She'd never before felt so off-balance.

"It would make things easier if you promised not to run off. At least for tonight. I ask no more than that."

Too choked up to speak, she simply nodded her head. Still, the instincts of her profession died hard. If she could lull him into trusting her tonight, she could more easily escape in the morning.

"You needn't worry," he said gently. "I won't hurt you. I suspect you've been hurt enough."

It was the most threatening thing he could have said. If he'd raped her, she could have hated him, but her hatred would make her strong. This sudden compassion disarmed her, made her weak. If he faked passion, that was one thing. But tender care . . .

She turned and ran suddenly, from the words he'd spoken, from the emotions he'd unleashed, from the ugly pictures he'd expelled from her mind. But even in her delirium, she remembered her promise not to run away. She stopped a few feet off, with her back to him, and stood with her face in her hands, shaking violently, fighting desperately to keep from crying.

She heard the crunch of his footsteps as he followed her. He came up behind and put hands on her arms. She was stiff, unyielding.

"It's all right," he soothed. "You don't have to tell me. You're shivering. Come over by the fire."

He led her back toward the beckoning warmth. She didn't say a word. Her face was burning with an embarrassment more acute than if he'd stripped her and exposed her to his roving eyes. All she could think was, *He guesses all my secrets. How long before he stumbles upon the worst one of all?*

CHAPTER 20

She awoke the next morning, stiff from sleeping on the ground, shivering in the postdawn chill. The sky was a pale alabaster blue, but pink lights splashed soft hues of color to the endless horizon. The air, fresh, clean, invigorating, smelled sweetly of sage. She stretched her cramped muscles, rolled onto her stomach, and stopped short, her breath suspended in her lungs.

He was gloriously naked. Standing in the stream, he rose from the water like some pagan god, his body gleaming in the early morning sun.

He was a grand specimen, his body athletic, beautifully defined. The broad shoulders above a delectably hairy chest, the narrow waistline, the sleek, chiseled buttocks, the hard thighs and muscled calves. With cupped palms, he covered himself with the icy water, whistling softly to himself as if relishing the feel of it, clean and resurrected under the open sky. The shock of it, the absolute beauty of him, was a jolt to her senses. He raised a perfectly coiled arm.

Even the dark hair underneath was an inducement to further exploration. She'd known the Blackwoods were acrobats at one time. She'd been aware of their renown as great physical creatures. Hadn't she even been contemptuous of it? Boorish ruffians? All brawn and no brains? But seeing the proof of the rumors was a revelation. His forearms alone were enough to stop a woman's heart. Commandingly developed, flexing with muscles when he moved, strong and hairy with sleek, tapered wrists. She couldn't swallow. She couldn't breathe. Watching him—so totally and unashamedly unaware of her prying eyes—was like watching a stallion careening in the wild. She'd never seen such heartrending male magnificence in all her life.

He turned then, and she saw the root of that bold, reckless confidence. He was Olympian in stature. So large, she wondered how in the world he could possibly . . .

She could well imagine that women were thunderstruck at first sight of him. She wondered if it was possible to become so familiar with him that they could see him unsheathed without feeling awestruck.

Belatedly, she realized he was now watching *her*, noting her reaction. She flushed and averted her eyes. Because he was a stranger. He wasn't the man she'd loved. The man she'd been intimate with, come close to giving herself wholeheartedly to, didn't exist. She didn't even know who this man really was.

He reached for his shirt, dried himself off with masculine efficiency, and pulled on his pants with a minimum of fuss. She allowed herself a sigh of relief. He'd been the one naked, but *she'd* felt exposed.

"Good morning," he greeted her in a pleasant tone, as if she hadn't just been gawking at his naked form. "I was beginning to think you'd sleep all day. I suppose we can get down to business—that is, of course, unless you'd like to bathe first."

The hand holding the shirt gestured toward the stream.

"With you watching?"

"Well . . ." His voice was hushed, his eyes piercing. "It's hardly fair that you should have all the fun."

She said nothing. She couldn't afford to be distracted. Instinct told her he was about to make his play, and she would need all her wits to convince him she believed him long enough to escape.

He came to squat across the ruins of the fire from her. "I've a proposition, Miss Sherwin—"

"It seems a bit formal, after what's transpired, to call me Miss Sherwin. Besides which, they know who I am—no doubt thanks to you. If someone should overhear you—"

"You're wrong. I didn't tell them."

"You expect me to believe that? No one knew but you."

"If you'll allow me to continue, we might come to some satisfaction."

She waved a hand in the air. "By all means."

"If Miss Sherwin is too risky—and I agree it is—I suppose Saranda is equally so."

Her heart, unbidden, leapt at the sound of her name on his tongue. "No," she agreed. "Not Saranda."

"What *shall* I call you, then?"

"I couldn't care less what you call me. I've gone by many names. One is the same as any other."

He leaned back on his elbow and narrowed an eye as he surveyed her. "What do you think of Dusty?" he asked.

"Dusty? As in, the furniture *is* . . . dusty?"

"Dusty. As in the dusty coloring of your hair." Reaching over, he fingered one of the tumbling silky locks. When she flinched, he let the hair slip from his fingers, slapped her on the back, and sent a goodly amount of dust flying. "Also, as in you *are* . . . dusty."

She jerked away from him, suddenly caring very much what he called her. "It's not very complimentary. You might as well call me Dirty."

"Very well—"

"Don't you dare!"

He chuckled. "I thought you didn't care what I called you."

"Kindly remind me if you meant to *talk* business—or *give me* the business."

"Very well. I shall be perfectly frank. We have a pretty good idea by now who we are and what we want. I want the *Globe-Journal*, and you want to be cleared of charges that will invariably lead to your execution."

"Well, that's certainly frank."

"The way I see it, the only way I can get the newspaper is through you."

"Correction. The only way for you to get that newspaper is over my dead body."

"Look, Miss Sherwin. I don't like this any more than you. Given the opportunity, I'd just as soon never see you again. But I need you as much as you need me. Which means we must work together."

"How—exactly—do I need you?" *Aside from the obvious*, she wanted to add.

"Because you're the most-wanted woman in America. And because I can prove your innocence."

"How?"

"I know McLeod's story to be the farce it is. We both know I told Jackson the truth before the wedding. And that he had no intention of throwing you out on your ear —much as I tried to convince him to do just that."

"Knowing it and proving it—"

He waved her to silence. Standing, he went to retrieve his coat and returned holding an envelope in the Van Slykes' distinctive color of Delftware blue. He held it out to her. She stared at it without touching it, at the small, upright handwriting she recognized as Jackson's, addressing the envelope to Archer at his hotel.

Because she didn't move, he took the letter from the envelope and held it out for her to read.

"My dear Archer," it read. "Never have we faced a difference as serious as the one we face now. I've always considered you more of a son than an employee. In fact, under different circumstances, I would happily and without pause leave the paper in your more than capable hands. But you must understand. Winston loves Sarah, as do I. We've weighed carefully your warnings, that an adventuress rarely changes, that she may merely want from us all she can take. We simply don't believe it. We know Sarah to be good of heart, just as we know the goodness in you. It is our wish that she marry Winston as planned, and become a proud member of our family. We've told her as much. This need go no further. For it is my express wish that you forget what you know and treat my future daughter-in-law with the same respect, kindness, and consideration with which I've treated you. I would consider this a great kindness to an old man who cares deeply for you."

It was signed simply, "Jackson."

It saddened her to read the proof of his devotion— not just to her, but to Blackwood. He'd been taken in by not one sham artist, but two. He'd paid a terrible price for his goodness.

She dropped her hands into her lap and lowered her head.

He replaced the letter in the pocket of his coat and sank down once again beside her. "That letter was dated the night *before* the wedding. Proving McLeod is lying, and negating the motive. If Jackson accepted you so—*lovingly*" —as if he choked on the word—"into his family, you had no reason to kill him."

"Why is McLeod lying?"

"Because he wants the paper, naturally. He's opposed to everything it stands for. The fight to break the stronghold of the robber barons, the championing of the plight of the immigrants . . . All of it threatens not only *his* existence, but that of his chums. He's been outspoken against the Van Slykes for years, using everything but brute force to dismantle the paper and its growing power. Nothing worked, until now."

"Are you saying he had the Van Slykes killed so he could get hold of the newspaper?"

"That's precisely what I'm saying."

"But Sander McLeod is one of the most respectable men in New York—"

"Surely, you're not so naïve as to believe the trappings of respectability. You should know as well as anyone that looks, even actions, often have little to do with one's real designs. Have you asked yourself why he was at the mansion that night, just as the murders were committed?"

"If the two of you were in it together—"

"McLeod hates me. I'm a threat to all he holds dear. He knows that once I go after him in print, he stands to lose everything he's worked to build. He'd never join forces with me, and I think you know it."

"But it's too unbelievable—"

"Easier to believe a con artist killed them when his flam went awry?"

"Yes."

"Then you have a dilemma."

She thought for a minute while he watched her closely. Then she looked up, straight into his deep blue eyes. "Why do you want the paper?"

He leaned back on one elbow. "I could tell you I want it to continue the work of the Van Slykes—to continue the fight for the rights of the underdog—but you wouldn't believe that, would you?"

"Not bloody likely."

"Very well . . . I want it for the power it has—and will continue to have under my management."

"Now *that* I believe."

"So this is the arrangement. I shall get you safely back to New York and clear your name, and you, in return, are to sign exclusive ownership of the *Globe-Journal* over to me." Reaching into his pocket once again, he withdrew a legal document and handed it to her. Astonished, she took it from him, opened it, and read the first lines.

"This *gives* you the paper, lock, stock, and barrel, for *nothing*."

"Clever girl. Oh, don't worry. It's all perfectly legal. Contingent on your name being cleared, of course, and coming into your inheritance."

"You had this drawn up before you left New York? What did you do, stop at the barristers' on your way out of town?"

"That's my offer. . . . Take it or leave it."

She tossed the paper aside. "I shall leave it, thank you." She stood, went to the horse, retrieved a brush from her valise, and returned, brushing out her hair. As far as she was concerned, the discussion was over.

"Would it interest you to know how McLeod had them killed?"

"I know how you *claim* they were killed. But I saw something that night you hadn't counted on. I saw you leaving the scene of the crime."

"If you saw someone leaving the scene of the crime, it wasn't me. It was Lance."

She wheeled on him, angry now. *"Lance is dead."*

"I know you believe it. But he isn't. He's visited me in New York on a number of occasions."

"His ship went down at sea."

"He wasn't on that ship. It just seemed the expedient thing to let everyone believe he was."

"Your brother wasn't clever enough to fake his own death. Not and get away with it for so many years."

"Why are you shaking?"

She hadn't realized she was. She gripped the brush to keep her hands from trembling. "Because I hate your brother even more than I despise you. If I thought he *was* alive—" Alive . . . after all this time . . . It was impossible!

"You expect me to believe you'd turn in your own brother?"

"To save my own neck? Would you doubt it?"

She turned and looked at him. "You're despicable. All you Blackwoods."

His tone hardened. "Your objection is noted. Do we have a deal or don't we?"

She refused to believe Lance Blackwood was alive. No doubt Mace was hoping to lure her back to the city under false pretenses, turn her over to the authorities, and have her tried and convicted for murder. Even the letter from Jackson was questionable. A man like Mace Blackwood would have no trouble finding an expert forger to do the job.

"I shall have to think it over," she said.

"You do that, Princess."

She knew from the twist of his mouth that he understood her motives. She had to time this just right. She must catch him totally off-guard. A man like Blackwood would be watching her every move. He'd expect some elaborate skulking attempt. Therefore, she must make it simple.

An hour later, while replacing her brush in her bag, she simply stepped into the stirrup, settled herself in the saddle, and without so much as a fuss, rode away. When she'd ridden some distance, she turned, waved, and noted his frustration as he stared off after her. He'd be left alone on an empty prairie without so much as a horse. But she had no doubt he'd find a way to follow her before long.

Putting her heels to the horse, she headed back to Dodge.

CHAPTER 21

"Are you out of your mind?" Bat ranted when she returned. "This place is swarming with men looking for you, and sooner or later every one of them ends up in this office. I want you out of here. Now."

"You'll protect me. Just tell them I'm your sister."

"Things are too hot. I've been asking around. Officially, their job is to bring you in to trial. But I took one of the Pinkertons out for a drink. Seems someone suggested that if you happen to get shot escaping, their fee is doubled. I can't keep you alive if they're gunning for you. What I *can* do is take you to Mexico myself, to make sure you get there."

"I'm not going to Mexico. I'm going to Canada."

"Mexico's closer."

"I'm going to lure Blackwood into a trap. Once we're in Canada, the authorities can take him into custody and ship him back to England in chains. And I shall be standing on the dock, waving good-bye."

He was quiet for a moment, brushing his mustache. "I did some checking."

"On Blackwood?"

"Wired New York. Seems he quit the paper."

"He didn't mention it. Why did he quit?"

"Wouldn't go along with the reward for you. Defended you publicly. Stormed out of the place. It made all the New York papers. All but the *Globe-Journal*, that is."

"He *defended* me?"

"That's what I'm told."

"Don't look so sanctimonious. If it's true—"

"I told you it made the papers."

"—he had a good reason for doing so. Part of the master plan."

He looked at her thoughtfully. "I believe him. And you know I wouldn't say so if I thought you were in danger. Why not give him a chance, honey? Isn't it about time you trusted someone?"

She turned from him, stunned by the treason of his words. "Trust a Blackwood? I'd rather stake my life on a rattler."

"Even rattlers shed their skin."

"You don't know the Blackwoods like I do. They're like me, but without any conscience. They take what they want, and they don't care who gets hurt. Well, I *care*. I've had my eyes opened. The deaths of two wonderful men are on my head because I didn't stop Blackwood sooner. I was the only one who knew what he really was, and I did nothing but play games with him. *No more*. It seems I'm still the only one who knows what he really is. And it's up to me to stop him."

"Even if you get yourself killed by the law in the process?"

"I won't."

"You've been too lucky. Winning streaks don't last forever."

"It just has to last me to Canada. That's all I ask."

She had her hand on the doorknob when his soft voice stalled her. "He's in love with you."

She turned, slowly. "You think everyone's in love with me."

He looked sad, resigned. "He doesn't know it, but he is."

Saranda raised a brow. "Enough to kill two men to get at me?" she asked sarcastically.

But on her way to the hotel she was finally proved wrong. Shoved aside by a group of rowdy cowboys swarming out of a saloon, she stopped dead in her tracks. For there, heading away from her, was a dead man. Lance Blackwood, the physical embodiment of evil.

As he cocked his head, laughing at his companion's crude joke, she recognized him with a sick convulsion of her stomach. Appallingly reminiscent of his brother, Mace, he was tall with curly black hair and deep blue eyes. But one of those eyes was creased by scar tissue, looking sideways in its socket in a lifeless leer. There were other, more subtle differences. Lance was leaner, tougher, more transparent than Mace. Like a true master, Mace could make his face display any emotion he wanted to convey. Lance had always shown that brittle anger that made him seem to vibrate even when standing still. He presented the cocksure bravado of a peacock in full plumage. But she could see in his one good eye the defiance of a man who knew he wasn't up to snuff. The pretense had worn on him over the years. Younger than Mace by two years, he looked infinitely older.

"Come along, blokes," he called with a drunken fling of his arm. "The next round's on me."

She knew that voice. The coarse cockney accent he'd never been able to lose. The hard, sneering tone.

She was shaking uncontrollably. Without knowing it, she clutched the front of her skirt in a tight-fisted ball. She couldn't tell if she was breathing. Sweat beaded her upper lip. The impulse to be sick was overwhelming. She stood, trembling, reeling dizzily, recalling that pitiless, jeering face as the flames licked around them and he—laughing—

The memories paralyzed her. Scalding, bitter memories rushed out of that dark corner of her mind where she'd fought to keep them buried. Tears filled her eyes as she recalled the helplessness, the brutal anger, and finally the consequences that had changed her life and made her despise and fear herself.

Isn't it about time you trusted someone?

Thanks to Lance Blackwood, she couldn't even trust herself.

She wasn't a killer, but she had murder in her heart. In a trance, she staggered toward the closest water barrel along the street. Bat had told her Wyatt Earp secretly kept several rifles stashed behind the water barrels around town in case of emergencies. If ever there was an emergency, this was it. Reaching behind the wooden barrel, her hand came in contact with the cold steel muzzle of a Sharps 50—the preferred rifle of buffalo hunters along the plains.

It was a monstrous gun that would no doubt knock her down when she fired. But she wasn't thinking rationally. Lance Blackwood was alive—that was all she needed to know. Laughing with his lowlife chums as if he hadn't single-handedly stolen all the hope, all the goodness, in her life.

Stalking him with her rifle in hand, she found him south of the Deadline, in front of the Lady Gay Saloon. He was just about to enter with his group of disorderly compatriots when her trembling voice stopped him.

"Lance . . ."

He turned. It took him a moment to focus his good eye on her face. Recognition altered his features. "Go on in, lads. I'll be along directly."

Eyeing the rifle, one of them asked, "Need any help?"

"Don't bother, mate," Lance said contemptuously. "I can tyke care of this snippet meself."

When they'd departed, he swaggered toward her, his thumbs stuck in his pants pockets, his elbows at an angle from his body. "Well, well. If it ain't little Saranda Sherwin. Ye've turned into a ruddy beauty."

The rifle trembled in her hands. "I thought you were dead."

He grinned, showing strong white teeth in a wolfish mouth. A stab of pain shot through her as she thought of Mace. "I scuttled ye right enough, eh?"

He was coming closer.

"What are ye goin' to do with that rifle, eh, luv? Have me head?"

"I'm going to kill you for what you did to me."

"Wot did I do, eh? Nothin' any red-blooded bloke wouldn't want fer himself. But, darlin', ye didn't look in them days like wot ye do now. If ye put away that rifle, I might be persuaded—"

Enraged, her heart pounding in her head, she raised the rifle and aimed.

Lance just laughed. The same wretched, cackling laugh that haunted her dreams. "Ye can't do it, Sherwin. Yer no killer. Ain't that wot you bloody Sherwins say? Gloatin' about yer bloomin' principles. Go on, then, if it makes you happy. Pull the ruddy trigger. Prove to yerself yer just like me."

His chest came up against the rifle. All she had to do

was pull the trigger, and she'd put a hole through him the size of country squash. Her finger squeezed. She could feel revenge on her tongue. But at the last minute, she couldn't do it. Because she wasn't like him at all.

He chortled low in his throat. Taking the rifle from her, he ran the muzzle tauntingly along her cheek. "I'm tyking ye back, luv. But who knows what might happen along the way?"

She blanched with horror. She'd rather die than go anywhere with him.

"Ye haven't changed, Sherwin. Still afraid of yer own shadow."

It wasn't true. The only person she'd ever feared was him. But he made her feel so brutalized, so utterly helpless, that in that moment she believed him. She felt all at once like that girl of thirteen, being cowed by an enemy with no compunction or mercy.

Why hadn't she had the guts to kill him?

She couldn't face him. The instinct to flee, to get as far from him as she possibly could, clouded her good sense. She could have conned anyone else. But Lance Blackwood wasn't just anyone. In his own way, he held her in his power every bit as much as his brother did—but for different reasons altogether. She was so jumbled, she couldn't think straight. She knew only one thing. Lance Blackwood wasn't taking her alive.

He watched her, arrogantly certain of his ability to overpower her. Hadn't he done so once before? But instinct told her that could work for her. Catching him off-guard, she seized the rifle and swung hard, cracking it across his head. He howled, stumbled back, tottered to his knees. Sputtering, he swore viciously as he struggled for consciousness.

Saranda turned and ran. Racing for her horse, she

mounted in one swift leap and galloped through town. Her plans forgotten, her life shattered once again, she headed with all speed to the one safe haven that, incredibly, leapt to mind.

Mace.

CHAPTER 22

A storm was brewing, one of those sudden prairie storms that come from nowhere. Dark clouds eclipsed the sky, and there was the tang of rain in the air. Yet the wind was balmy, as caressing as a lover's breath.

Saranda came upon him walking across the grassy plains. His coat, thrown over his shoulder, was flapping in the breeze. He carried the bag she'd forgotten in his hand. His mop of curls was wild from the wind. From a distance, he looked small, dejected, like a boy who'd lost his pony and had no hope of getting home to supper.

She'd ridden so furiously that the horse was dripping foam. Yet, on the threshold of her destination, she walked the gasping animal to him cautiously, anticipating his next move. He looked up at her dispassionately, as if he'd expected her all along. If he was angry, nothing in his features gave it away.

She drew rein and waited for him to come to her. Her hair blew about her face like a shield. When he came even with her, he kept on walking, passing by. She sat there, her back to him, listening to the rhythmic crunch of his footsteps in the dry grass.

"I didn't believe you," she said without turning.

"I didn't expect you to."

"I saw Lance."

He heard the tremor in her voice. The crunching stopped. Only the moaning of the gale remained.

"McLeod hired him to bring you in."

"To kill me, you mean."

"He wouldn't do that."

"You'll forgive me, I'm sure, if I choose not to believe that. I know your brother better than you think." She dismounted. "I've decided to take you up on your proposition."

"Which proposition was that, Princess?"

"If those papers are handy, I'm ready to sign."

Slowly, he bent and laid the bag on the ground. It disappeared in the sea of grass.

He struggled to control his coat, took the papers from the pocket, and brought forth a pen. She dipped it in the inkwell he provided and put it to the fluttering paper. On the verge of signing, she hesitated. "What name should I use?"

"Saranda Van Slyke."

He was watching her closely. Taking a deep breath, she scrawled the unaccustomed signature. Her hand shook, and the pen scratched like a witch's fingernail across the paper.

When she was done, the pen fell from her hand and blew away. She bent to retrieve it, but his hand, large and warm, took hers and held it fast.

"Why are you shaking?"

"It isn't every day I see a man return from the grave."

"And having seen my brother, you decided I was the —lesser of two evils. Is that it?"

She looked up into his eyes. They were piercing, dark as a moonless night. In their depths, she thought she saw a certain vulnerability. A question he wouldn't ask. *He's in love with you. But he doesn't know it.* Could it possibly be true?

"How do I know when the path grows rocky, you won't choose Lance over me?"

His gaze searched her face. "I can protect you without harming my brother."

"And if you're forced to choose?"

"I won't be." He said it adamantly, as if believing it hard enough would make it come true.

"I need a guarantee," she said softly. "Promise me you won't let Lance take me."

His eyes narrowed at her choice of words. After the slightest of pauses, he said, "I promise."

She looked at him intently, trying to read his thoughts in his face. "Who are you?" she asked.

"You know who I am."

"I doubt anyone's ever known who you really are."

Looking up at the sky, he considered his response. It was slate grey by now, uncharacteristically close. A droplet of rain splashed across his cheek. "I'm your only hope. In a battle against my brother, I'm all you have."

"Don't say that," she said, snatching her hand away.

"Why shouldn't I say it? If it's the truth."

"Because you—"

What? Because he made her hope for the first time in her irremediable life? Hope that he'd rise from the ashes of his family flames, reborn as her personal avenging angel? That he hated his own kind as much as she did? That together they could join forces and put an end to the Blackwood tyranny for all time?

"What did Lance do to you?"

She turned away.

"What did he do to make you shake at the sight of him? At the very mention of his name?"

She took a step away, but he caught her fingers once again. The touch of his hand stopped her. "Whatever it was—"

She turned and looked at him. The sympathy she saw in his eyes was real. She had to believe it. Just for now. Just for this one intolerable night. That someone cared. That someone would protect her. *That someone would fix it.*

"Tell me what you want."

His voice, uttering the old familiar words, gave her an exquisite sense of peace. He still held her hand, although the length of their arms separated them. What she really wanted was to cry. To pour out the whole tragic story —the truth of what had happened with Lance—to someone who would listen without judgment, and understand. For someone to reassure her that she'd done the best she could. That it *wasn't* her fault. That the outcome would have been the same no matter what.

But she knew that was a lie.

Of course, she'd never tell him. Not him, of all people. She couldn't confess that for the first time since that horrible time, she wanted someone else to carry the burden of her guilt. That she wanted his strength, his protection. That she'd never wanted—never needed—anything more.

Images flashed through her mind that were too painful to face.

"I want you to love me," she said in a trembling voice. Then amended hastily, "*Make* love to me. I want to stop seeing Lance's face."

Wordlessly, he urged her closer and brought her hand to his lips.

"This doesn't mean I'm going to trust you," she warned.

He pulled her to him so her breasts were crushed against his chest.

"I wouldn't expect you to."

"I do need you. To help me out of this. I shall accept that. But no more."

Except that, tonight, she needed him more than he'd ever know.

"No more than I need you."

She couldn't tell how he meant that. He bent his head and ever so gently pressed his lips to her temple. She felt the contact all the way down to her toes.

"It's—a business proposition," she insisted.

"Business. Naturally."

Her blouse seemed to open magically beneath his hands. When he let go of it, it sailed some distance on the wind. She felt the strangely warm air circle her, making her aware that he was stripping her clothes from her beneath a rain-heavy sky, in the middle of nowhere.

"Two professionals," she continued breathlessly, "joining forces for a common goal."

"I should hardly call what we're doing *common*."

"I just want us to understand each other."

He took the waistband of her skirt in his hands and opened the fastenings with a tug.

"I suspect we understand each other just fine."

The skirt fell to her feet.

By the time he was naked, the rain began to fall. Like the wind, it was warm, bathing them like a cleansing tonic. As one, they fell to their knees. Her hair, wet now, whipped his face. He took it in both hands and drew her closer, kissing her with a tenderness that put to flames the images in her mind. "Forget," he murmured against her lips, holding her head close. "All that exists is this."

His lips against hers, he lowered her to the ground. The grass was high around them, covering them from view. It scratched at her back, her shoulders, but squandered against the onslaught of emotions, she barely noticed it. For he was kissing her with all the tender devotion any woman could ever want. For once, he didn't speak. He stroked her face, kissed her cheeks, her eyelids, her hair. His hands gentled her, stroking, soothing, then igniting a passion that flowed so effortlessly, one emotion into another, that it was a seamless trek. He palmed her breasts, grazed her thighs, and became one with her with such flawless ease that a sort of radiance seemed to emanate from them. Coming together was like discovering the true and hidden self. Moving over her, his skin anointing hers, he held her like a treasure, conveying, with his lips, with his hands, with a body like a citadel, that she was safe from harm. That nothing and no one could touch her while she lay in his arms.

Bathed in spring rain, rising to meet him as he offered his power and his strength, she'd never felt more cherished in all her life.

Even if she knew it wasn't real . . .

CHAPTER 23

Saranda lay contentedly in Mace's arms, more relaxed than she could ever remember feeling. Their lovemaking, like the rain, had washed away her fears. Her heart beat a slumbering rhythm. Her mind floated in a dreamy sea of colorful mist. Without emotions. Without thoughts. *Without words*.

It was a rare occasion when her mind was silent, and she could just *be*.

"Ready to face the dragons, Countess?"

She raised up on her elbows, looking down into eyes that twinkled like a starry sky. "How did you know?"

But it was useless to ask. He just knew. He knew where she was going, what she was planning, even as she planned it. As if he had a direct link to her brain. Was it any surprise that he knew she'd donned the disguise of a countess?

"We should go," she said, rising to her feet. "Bat says Dodge is swarming with badges. The sooner we leave—"

"Not so fast. We have unfinished business."

For an instant, she thought he intended to make love to her again. "Unfinished *business?*"

He must have read her thoughts, for his mouth crooked in a knowing smile. "In Dodge."

He rose, too, and she stared at him in disbelief. "You don't mean we're returning?"

He winked at her. "I always did admire a clever woman."

"Didn't you hear what I said? It's too dangerous— there are lawmen everywhere."

He reached for his shirt, which was strewn, like the rest of his clothes, in the surrounding grass. "All the more reason to go back."

"Tell me you haven't lost your mind."

"You tell *me* something. What is it you're afraid of? Being detected by a badge? Or running into Lance?"

It wasn't a question she cared to answer. "Why is it necessary?"

"Because there's one last thing I have to do. We'll check into the hotel under your established disguise—"

"Am I to understand that you're giving me orders?"

He turned and fixed her with a steely gaze. "Let's get one thing straight, shall we? There can only be one leader."

"I agree. And it's me."

"You?"

"Naturally. I've been on my own for years. As successfully, I might add, as you. I have no intention of having some Harry-come-lately waltz into my life at this late stage and tell me how to conduct my business."

"*Your* business? I'm the one saving your bloody neck!"

"Surely you're not suggesting I take orders from a

Blackwood? One of the same Blackwoods who so poorly botched their last big con that they—"

He lunged at her, taking her neck in his fist and pressing his thumb into her throat. "Don't you—*ever*—talk to me like that again. Do you hear me?"

She wrenched his hand from her throat. "And don't you ever presume to make a fool of me. I shall be watching you, Mace Blackwood. And if I get so much as an inkling that you're lying to me, tricking me, or duping me in *any* way, you'll regret it."

He dropped his hand. "So much for the truce."

"What do you expect?"

His gaze met hers. "I expect you to do what I say *when* I say. Or you may get us both killed."

"Oh, why didn't you say so? You expect me to *trust* you. Aren't you forgetting one minor detail? It's not part of the deal."

BACK IN TOWN, they plunged across the muddy street and entered the lobby of the Dodge House. Saranda had thought to replace her brown wig, but her clothing, like Mace's, was soaking wet. The proprietor eyed their bedraggled state in surprise, but only said, "Why, Countess Lynderfield, we figured you left us."

"I did, Mr. Cox," she said in her best aristocratic accent, "but I've returned, as you can see. I shall require my old room back." An impulse seized her, born of her annoyance with Blackwood. So he expected her to take orders, did he? "And a room for my—steward," she added with a vicious smile.

She caught the flash in Mace's eyes as they locked with hers.

"Your what?" asked Mr. Cox.

"A sort of valet, if you will," she explained a bit too sweetly. "Except, of course, that he's not a gentleman's gentleman, but rather a lady's."

By the time the proprietor had turned wide eyes to him, Mace had already masked his reaction. So smoothly no one but a professional could detect it, his face altered into the subservient lines of one born to serve. A corner of his mouth turning up was the only sign of his sarcasm as he gave a slight bow and introduced himself. "Jenkins—at her lady's service." She almost laughed. He was quick, she'd give him that. Then his next words showed her she couldn't put him down as easily as she'd imagined. "We shall require adjoining rooms, my good man," he announced in an excellent imitation of a majordomo's stuffy English tones. "In case the countess should need me to draw her a bath."

"There's a bathhouse up the street," Mr. Cox offered. "Two bits for a bath that's been used not more'n three times. A dollar if—"

Assuming the imperious look of an outraged attendant, Mace looked down his nose at the man and sneered, "You wouldn't expect her ladyship to bathe in a common bathhouse, surely!"

"Well, no, course not. I didn't mean no offense."

"The rooms, if you please."

He held out his hand, and Cox jumped to oblige, dropping two keys into his waiting palm. "Thank you, sir," Mace said crisply. "You are most kind."

"If you need anything—"

"Please don't trouble yourself. I shall discharge the requirements of her ladyship myself."

He took the keys and headed for the stairs. Amused by his performance, and by her choice of roles for him, Saranda stood her ground and called, "Oh, Jenkins."

He turned.

"The bag, if you please."

There was a moment, when he looked from her face to the bag on the floor and back again, when she held her breath. Something in his manner warned her not to push him. But she couldn't help herself. Suddenly, she was having a marvelous time.

"Of course, my lady." With a bow worthy of the humblest servant, he picked up the bag with exaggerated dignity, as if the picking up of such bags down through the years had been his supreme source of pride.

She cast a sly look at the proprietor. "He's a treasure, really. I don't know what I should have done without him."

"Well"—Mr. Cox cleared the obstruction in his throat—"enjoy your stay—again—Your Highness."

Once inside her room, she fell onto the bed, laughing. "I rather fancy being called 'Highness.'"

He glowered at her, tossing the bag aside. "You rather fancy getting the better of me. Would her ladyship like me to unpack? May I attend you in any way? Perhaps you'd like me to help you undress."

He yanked her from the bed, unbuttoned her jacket, and pulled it from her savagely, thrusting it aside. Then, looking down at her startled face, he dropped her arm and turned from her with an air of defeat.

His reaction piqued her curiosity. Obviously, she'd hit a nerve. "If I'd known it would bother you so, I might have—"

"What?"

She gave a saucy smile. "Enjoyed it all the more, I daresay. I had to tell him *something*, didn't I?"

"Did it occur to you to tell him I was the earl?"

"Did you see the look on his face? He probably thinks I keep you along just to—how would a countess put it?—satisfy the tender cravings of my flesh." He wasn't amused. "Oh, do buck up. Unless, of course, there's some reason you're not telling me? You haven't been abused by the aristocracy or anything like that?"

For just an instant, the look he gave her was stark with pain. It vanished as quickly as it had appeared. "Don't be absurd."

She'd seen something in that look that softened her heart. He'd been hurt somewhere along the way, so deeply injured he couldn't even admit it. She knew about that sort of pain.

"Would you care to talk about it?" she offered more kindly.

"There's nothing to talk about. And if there were, *Countess*—"

He broke off abruptly.

"Let me finish it for you. I should be the last person you'd tell. Is that it?"

He went to the window, parted the gingham curtains, and peered out on the rainy street below. She had the feeling she'd wounded him, but she couldn't know why. After the tenderness he'd shown her, it seemed a sorry reward. Yet he'd touched a chord in her that no one had ever known existed. He'd caught a glimpse of a wound so raw that, even after all these years, it refused to heal. She didn't know how to react to that. She wasn't accustomed to having someone perceive her pain. So she'd acted heartlessly, to punish him for seeing through the act.

She wanted to apologize, wanted to help. But she didn't trust him. She didn't even know if this was real or an act. If she went to him and offered succor, would he—like the child who'd faked an injury—jump up with a laugh and claim he'd fooled her?

"I'd intended to compliment you. I've rarely seen anyone as speedy on the uptake as you were downstairs. You're quite the artist, aren't you?"

He turned after a moment and gave her a pitiless stare.

"Oh, *do* stop pouting," she persisted. "I was merely having a spot of fun."

"It's getting dark," he announced abruptly. "I'm going out."

"Out? Where?"

"To play poker."

"Poker? Do you mean to tell me you brought us back here to play poker?"

"That's exactly what I mean to tell you."

"You could have played poker with me."

"Ah," he said, putting his hat on his head, "but you forget one thing."

"What's that?"

"You don't play fair."

He left her feeling as if he'd just slapped her in the face.

Suddenly, she realized he'd intended this reaction. To numb her. To distract her from what he was doing. It made no sense that he'd come all the way back to Dodge just to sit in on a game of poker.

What *was* he doing?

There was only one thing to do—follow him and find out.

CHAPTER 24

Once on Front Street, she had to weave her way through a wave of cowboys in order to keep Mace in sight. He walked purposefully westward, as if he knew where he was going. As they passed the boot shop, the bakery, the butcher, and a handful of saloons, the wide wooden sidewalks creaked beneath the crush of humanity.

Mace stopped once along the way in front of a pair of brightly painted wagons parked along the street. Pausing to look them up and down, he continued on his way. When she came alongside of them, she saw painted on them, in flourishing red script, HAVERSTAM'S AMAZING TRAVELING TROUPE. No doubt, she guessed, he was recalling memories of his acrobatic past.

They crossed First Avenue, and to her surprise, Blackwood passed the dry goods and the Alhambra and turned into the Lone Star—the saloon owned in part by Bat Masterson.

She stood outside a moment as a throng of bullwhackers pushed by her through the front doors. Peeking inside, she could see Bat dealing faro at the long green table. A sign outside, bearing the likeness of the tiger, advertised that faro was played on the premises. Playing against the faro bank was consequently known as bucking the tiger, she remembered.

Saranda grabbed one of the men as he was about to enter—a blood-smeared hunter who wasn't likely to run into her in her guise as the countess. "Sir," she asked in her Kansas accent, "would you be so kind as to ask Sheriff Masterson to step outside for a moment?"

He agreed, no doubt assuming she was too shy to go inside, and went in to find Bat. As she waited, she saw Mace through the smoke, settling himself down at a round wooden table where a group of men were involved in a game of draw poker.

It was clear, from the expression on Bat's face, that he was annoyed with her. "I thought I told you to get out of town."

"I'd be only too happy. Except when we should be running for our lives, your new best friend, Mr. Blackwood, is possessed of a sudden hankering for a game of poker."

"So you reconciled."

"Reconciled seems to be a matter of opinion. I found out he was telling the truth. At least about Lance."

"I figured he was. Remember that Pinkerton I told you about?"

"The one you took for a drink?"

"That's the one. He came in here last night feeling talkative. They're not just after you, honey. They want Blackwood, too."

"The Pinkertons?"

"Of course they don't know he's Blackwood. They're after Archer—and get this. The orders are dead or alive."

"But why?"

"Ask him. This Pink says they nearly got him once. Except he outsmarted them and got away. I'd say that puts the two of you on the same side."

"Still . . . He's hiding something. I don't know what it is, but I should like to keep an eye on him. You can help, if you would."

A reluctant smile turned up the corners of his mustache as he sensed the wheels turning in her brain. "All right," he said grudgingly. "What now?"

IN THE CRAMPED back office, she dressed in the clothes Bat had brought her. The dress was short, a goldish-yellow satin that showed her trim legs and laid bare her shoulders and half her bosom. She wore a black wig, darkened her eyebrows, and reddened her lips so she looked every inch the sultry and exotic dance-hall girl. Except that most of the soiled doves were plain, quarrelsome creatures. In her dark wig, Saranda possessed a cool, elegant beauty that was sure to turn heads.

She came out into the saloon to a burst of noise. True to form, two of the girls were fighting over some minor slight, rolling on the floor and pulling each other's hair. Some nearby men were placing bets on the outcome, but most were too busy to pay much mind. Even among the women, fights were such a commonplace occurrence that they rarely elicited much comment, unless one of the participants was killed.

She spotted Wyatt Earp, playing monte and winning. But she was distracted by some raised voices coming from Blackwood's table. One of the gamblers, a border ruffian from the looks of him, had just accused Mace of cheating. He did, in fact, have a stack of chips in front of him, while his fellow gamblers were getting poorer by the minute. The tension was thick. Saranda, from her vantage point, could see the ruffian's hand balling into a fist. He wasn't carrying a gun, but his face was strained, and clearly he was itching for a fight.

"I've always wanted to learn to play poker, gentlemen," she interceded in her Kansas accent. "You wouldn't mind if I sat in on a few rounds, would you?"

Their surprise broke the tension as they looked askance at one another. Mace was peering at her closely, as if trying to decide if his suspicions were true. A hint of a smile curled the corner of his mouth.

"By all means," he said in the exaggerated tones of the manservant. "Perhaps if you were to win a hand or two, it would convince our companion that it's lack of skill on his part, and not the manipulation of it on mine, that accounts for his poor luck."

"I never had *this* kind of poor luck," the ruffian grumbled.

"Then I appoint *you* to tell me the rules of the game," Saranda said, smiling sweetly. "Maybe we can show this foreigner a thing or two."

Thus encouraged, the ruffian swallowed his irritation and hurriedly, embarrassedly, explained the game. They began to play. After losing two rounds to Mace, she suddenly showed three queens, and the deal passed to her. Blackwood, handing over the cards, gave her a wry look.

She shuffled, making it appear awkward, then let the ruffian cut the deck. Asking ignorant questions the whole way, affecting a believable innocence, she allowed each man at the table a few wins to soothe their ruffled sensibilities. When she offered to pass the deal, they declined. They were doing far better under her awkward ministrations than they'd done under the dealership of the Englishman.

When she'd pacified them to her satisfaction, she began to win. Then, to her amazement, Mace showed two aces she hadn't dealt him, and won the hand. Supremely confident of his abilities, he allowed her the deal.

It soon became a contest of wills. She'd deal Mace a hand, knowing full well every card she'd passed him, and he'd turn over a completely different hand. It challenged her to think ahead, to decide what cards he might choose, and to better him without making anyone suspicious. She began to enjoy herself. It was like a masterfully played chess game, the give-and-take flowing smoothly, the thrill of the challenge making it difficult to keep a straight face. She began to crow every time she won, disguising it in the feminine nonsense of clapping hands and statements like, "I can't believe I won *again*!"

She won, in fact, round after round, until she'd not only cleaned out everyone else's money, she'd systematically taken every last dollar from Mace.

A crowd had gathered to watch the spectacle. While the men losing at the table weren't happy about relinquishing their money, they took the philosophical attitude that it was better to lose to a beautiful woman than to a suspected cardsharp who wasn't even an American.

Meanwhile, she'd heard a number of comments and questions thrown at Bat regarding his "new girl." When she heard him taking appointments, she knew it was time to disappear. Bat knew he was doing it in jest, but these hardened warriors, wanderers, and explorers of the harsh Kansas plains didn't look like men who easily took no for an answer.

She was about to excuse herself when Blackwood said, "What say you, my man, to one last round?"

Saranda suddenly noticed something she'd missed in her absorption with beating him at his own game. He was here for a reason. She looked around the table and noted the man he'd spoken to. A middle-aged chap with slicked-back hair, a checked jacket, and colorful bow tie, he ruminatively chewed his cigar. She recognized the look in his eyes at once and cursed herself for a fool. Mace had known all along what she was belatedly just discovering: that this man would gamble anything, just to play the game.

Looking at Blackwood, she understood something else. That her interference had caused just the diversion he needed to maneuver his mark where he wanted him.

"I'm dead broke, mister."

"Cash poor, perhaps. Who at this table isn't, with the exception of the young—lady. But I should wager you have something of value that you might put up. Against, say, a thousand dollars' worth of mining stock?"

Mace retrieved some documents from his coat pocket and tossed them onto the table.

Bow Tie's eyes narrowed shrewdly. "How do I know—"

Mace shrugged, sitting back comfortably in his chair. "Inspect them for yourself."

Bow Tie did and, when he was satisfied, let out a pent-up breath. "I got me a little traveling troupe."

"Of what use would such a fortune be to me?"

"Well, there's three fine wagons, complete with stoves. You could sell 'em. Or, hell, you could take over the show. I got some mighty pretty girls, go along with the deal."

Mace allowed himself a smile. "In that case—" He broke off with a shrug while the men chuckled and Saranda fumed.

What did he think he was doing?

Saranda dealt. Bow Tie held two tens, and when he turned in his cards, she made sure he got a third. To Mace she dealt a mixed hand, nothing significant. He called. Bow Tie laid out his three tens. Mace spread out a hand containing three smiling jacks.

Saranda slumped back in her chair.

"Well," said the ex-showman philosophically, "I had a good run. Treat the girls right, and they'll make you a pretty penny in return."

Outside, Saranda asked through clenched teeth, "What are we going to do with three wagons full of showgirls?"

"You wanted to get out of Dodge, didn't you?"

"Yes . . ."

"Don't forget we've a purpose now. Take a look at this." He passed her a telegram. "From my people in New York."

She read it through once, then went over it again. "Six months! Isn't that an awfully short amount of time?"

"It is. Normally, the court might allow up to a year to prove just cause before a venture such as the *Globe-Journal* goes into receivership. Which means our friend Sander McLeod has used his influence with the judge."

"But the date was set—"

"Three months ago. Leaving us less than three months to make it back to New York in one piece, prove your innocence, and stop the paper from being bought out from under us by McLeod."

"Then we should be on our way!"

"Tell me something. What do you think our chances would be if we simply boarded a train headed for New York?"

She hated to admit he was right. "Still, who knows what delays we might encounter en route?"

"I've made allowances for that."

"Forgive my ignorance, but this brings us back to the question at hand."

"Why the traveling troupe?" He grinned and chucked her chin. "Why else? To throw the bloodhounds off the trail."

Once again, he'd had it planned all along.

CHAPTER 25

"English or American?" Mace asked.

"For our identities?" She thought a moment. "They know you're English. So American would seem the wiser course. But then, in terms of showmanship, Americans are always keen on an English accent. Connotes a certain glamour that might work well for us."

"English it is. Oxford or cockney?"

"Oh, cockney, by all means. Much more circus-like."

They were in their own rooms with the adjoining door open. While she'd been packing, he'd been fiddling with his appearance in the mirror. When he turned around, his thick, curling hair had been slicked back with oil so it was perfectly straight. He had a new pencil-thin black mustache that gave him a rough-and-tumble appearance, lent him an aura of rakish street-smarts instead of elegant sophistication. He wriggled it experimentally. "What do you think?"

"It makes you look quite the boor."

"Perfect. Wait till you see the rest of it."

He slipped into a checked jacket and bow tie. Clamping an Irish cap upon his head, he looked every inch the swaggering showman who might travel the country with a passel of scantily clad girls. He swept the cap from his head, gathered it to his heart, and gave a bow worthy of a cut-rate impresario.

"Tommy Ward, me lie-dy, at yer service." Straightening up, he added, "Incidentally, that frock you were wearing—that sand-colored thing—"

"My traveling outfit?"

"That's it, the dusty one. Leave that out. We shall have need of it."

"Oh, shall we?"

"I've asked the sheriff to spread it around that you'll be wearing it when we make our dash for it."

"Have you, indeed? Shall I place a target on it as well? So they don't miss me when they aim?"

"Are you always this suspicious?"

"I have reason, I should think. Bat just told me he's been ordered by a U.S. marshal to turn me over if he happens upon me. He's promised to wire us with any news. Incidentally, you didn't tell me they were after you as well."

"McLeod is clever enough to realize my only chance of acquiring the paper is through you. He knows what we're planning, and he knows how much time we have to do it in. With us separated, he had an even chance. If his men couldn't track you, they might run across me. With us together, we lessen the odds somewhat. Particularly, if we can make a convincing go of this traveling troupe."

There was a knock on his door. He went to answer it, and ushered in a man and a woman who looked as much like Mace and Saranda as anyone could. She could see the woman was wearing a wig, no doubt picked out by Black-wood.

Mace took the travel suit from Saranda and closed his door on the woman while she changed, using the time to give last-minute instructions to the man.

"Remember, if you're detained, you don't know who hired you. We shall be headed for Canada, but you don't know that either. All you do know is you were paid rather handsomely to board a train and ride for as long as possible."

As he spoke, he rattled a leather bag full of coins before dropping it into the man's palm.

When they'd left, Saranda stared at him, wondering if he'd guessed yet another of her secrets. "Canada? Is that where we're off to?"

"Of course not. But they're bound to say something, once they're caught. They might as well earn their money and divert the onward marching forces of the law for as long as is humanly possible."

"Downright clever, hiring look-alikes."

He raised a startled brow. "Is that a compliment, Miss Sherwin?"

AFTER TELLING BAT their plans and saying good-bye, they went out to meet the girls in the secluded back lot where Mace had arranged to have the wagons moved. There were four of them. Abby and Anna were twins, fresh-faced lovelies who looked no older than eighteen, but who claimed to be the finest sharpshooters this side of the Mississippi. Lucy was a redhead with full, luscious lips capable of distracting any man alive. She ran a sleight-of-hand booth, and Saranda could see at once what an asset her looks were. No man could fully concentrate on finding the pea in the shell when Lucy pursed her lips in seeming concentration. The last of them, Flying Dove, was a tall, stately half-breed Indian with loose-flowing black hair, prominent cheekbones, and a come-and-get-it look in her eyes that contrasted starkly with the hauteur of her manner. From the way she examined Mace with a gleam in her half-lowered eyes, Saranda knew instinctively she was a whore.

"And what do *you* do?" she asked the Indian woman, because she hadn't volunteered. "In the show, I mean."

Mace's eyes flicked to Saranda's face and lingered a moment before blinking away.

"Acrobatics," said the woman with exaggerated dignity.

Mace's grin split his face. "Do ye now? I've a bit of the talent meself, so I 'ave." Speaking flawless cockney, he sounded uncomfortably like Lance. "I've" came out "Oy've," and the inflections were without equal. But it was the implication in his words that galled Saranda.

Picking up on it, Flying Dove gave him an enigmatic smile. "Then we should get together to—discuss it sometime. We might have a partnership in the works."

Saranda flashed her a look that said in no uncertain terms this man was *her* partner. But the woman wasn't aware of it. She was still smiling suggestively into Blackwood's amused eyes.

"Could be, darlin', could right well be," he said. "Well, lydies, I'll introduce meself. Tommy Ward, lately of the Ward and Powell Traveling Extravaganza in London, across the great wide sea. And this is me fine assistant— Dusty DeVille. Have ye been told why we're here?"

"Benny told us he lost us to you in a poker game," said Lucy bitterly.

"Splendid. Then there's no need fer explanations, is there now, which, if ye must know, suits me fine. I've won ye, and I want to set ye straight 'ere and now. I'll not be taking advantage of ye. If ye'll put yerselves in me hands, we'll fashion a show that'll turn the suckers' heads and have 'em beggin' to put money in the plates."

He walked around them, thumb scratching his chin, looking them up and down. "Now, ladies, show me what it is each of ye does best."

Saranda didn't even want to hazard a guess.

AFTER A DEMONSTRATION of their talents, the girls gave them a tour of the wagons. Each was equipped with a stove and storage for food so they could cook meals along the way. The first wagon belonged to the men—the drivers and the showmaster. The second, equipped with four bunk beds like the first, carried the women. The third was stuffed with costumes, tents, and the various accoutrements that enabled them to put on a show. "Benny wasn't the most organized of managers," the girls told them. "There's a lot of stuff in here we don't even use."

Mace dug through some of it and pulled out a bar suspended by ropes. "What about this?"

"The trapeze?" asked Lucy. "Naw. I think someone used it a long time ago. Like I said, Benny never threw anything away."

Fingering it briefly, Mace's wide mouth curved into a secretive grin.

While they were inspecting the ladies' wagon, Flying Dove motioned him outside. When they'd left, Lucy, who seemed to be the oldest of the group, let out an exasperated snort. "Did you see the way she looked at him? He'll be under her spell before you know it, and we'll be sweeping out her tent for a living."

"One thing you can say about Benny, he treated us all fair."

"He shouldn't have hired her in the first place. Gives us a bad name. She goes off with the cowboys, and they expect us to do the same." Lucy turned to Saranda. "I'd keep an eye on that man of mine if I was you. Before that whore gets her paws on him."

"He ain't my man, luv," Saranda protested. "I just work with the chap."

"You mean he's up for grabs?" cried the twins together. Saranda groaned, and left.

Alone with Blackwood in the prop wagon, she fingered the gauzy costumes. "Some disguise you've picked for us. Just where do I fit in?"

"I was just wondering that myself. What can you do?"

"You mean you want me to work? In this—rolling excuse for a whorehouse?"

"Darling, look what we're working with," he said, keeping his voice low lest the girls hear his real accent. "Twin cherubs, an incompetent cardsharp who no doubt couldn't make it on the outside, and a half-breed whore. I'm counting on you to be my star attraction."

"This is nothing but a skin show!"

"All the better. We shall need money to get to New York. Or had you forgotten our goal?"

"I was just wondering the same about you. You seem unduly sidetracked by your—good fortune."

He moved closer and took her face in his hands. His thumbs stroked her cheeks as he fixed her with an oddly penetrating gaze. "Mark me well, Princess. I'm never side-tracked when it comes to something I want."

"Just so you don't forget what *I* want in the process."

CHAPTER 26

The first challenge came when Mace dismissed the drivers and informed the girls they'd be driving themselves.

"Us?" they cried.

"Drive these wagons?"

"That's about the size of it, luv."

"But—we don't do those kind of things!" Lucy informed him.

Saranda knew what the girls couldn't—the fewer people along to learn their true identities, the better. If the girls guessed, they could handle themselves. But with three hulking men along, who knew what danger they might be inviting? The suspicion the move was likely to garner made it worth the added margin of safety.

So they started out across the toll bridge—three brightly painted wagons each with two show ponies tied behind—in the shank of day, heading south. Somewhere, their look-alikes were riding the rails, leaving them free, for the moment, to plan ahead.

Saranda was exempt from driving duty, a fact that caused the girls to close ranks. She rode in the lead wagon, bumping along as the caravan slowly crawled across the plains.

They plodded along until sunset, when they pulled up and made camp. Saranda was stiff from riding in the wagon all day, while the girls were complaining about the aches in their shoulders from holding the reins. Still, their complaining was less bitter than in the beginning. Mace had spent the day riding with each of the three girls who were driving, giving suggestions and worming his way into their good graces. Before they'd left Dodge, he'd bought them each a pair of buttery-soft kid gloves to protect their hands. This, of course, softened the blow of having to drive, and touched them with his thoughtfulness for their comfort.

While the other women started supper, Flying Dove followed Mace out onto the surrounding plains. Saranda watched as he spoke to her, noting the way the woman moved her body, enticing him with an invitation. She could tell from his stance that he was amused, but she wondered how long he could hold out against such a blatant offering. The Indian was darkly beautiful, sultry, exotic—everything Saranda wasn't.

As she watched, the Indian began to show Mace some of her routine. There was no doubt she was talented. Lithe as a puma, she could stretch her form into contortions that seemed impossible, balancing this way and that before effecting multiple flips in the air. Mace watched for a time, then, with lips moving, took her waist in his hands. The pang in Saranda's heart was so sharp, she clutched it. A venomous rage filled her as she watched his hands move along the brunette's limber body. He twisted her, bent her, then lifted her high so she could use him as leverage and add yet another flip to her routine.

The worst of it was how well they looked together. Both dark and tall, both with the sleek bodies of acrobats, they moved together with enviable grace. With an inborn instinct, Flying Dove caught onto Mace's ideas at once, moving her body with and against his so they seemed to dance together in a ballet whose music only they could hear.

Saranda had never been jealous in her life. Yet she was so eaten up by the force of her emotions, watching his hands travel over that woman's body, recalling the magic they'd performed on her own, that she could no longer stand to watch. Taking a strong cup of tea in with her, she secreted herself back in the wagon.

When it was dark, Mace came in carrying a plate of corn bread and beans.

"Has she been sufficiently schooled for one day?" she asked caustically.

He gave her a grin as he placed the food before her, then dropped onto one of the bunks. "What's the matter? Feeling neglected?"

"Hardly. I was just reflecting on the hardships of the job you've taken to hand."

"Strictly business, I assure you."

"The chat is, her acrobatics extend beyond the show ring."

"Indeed?" He raised a teasing brow. "You've intrigued me."

Belatedly, she cursed herself. She recalled her father's words in the early days of her training: *Be wary of making a suggestion you'd just as soon not plant in their minds. Often, the other person hasn't thought of the idea. Once you've placed it in their heads, they can think of little else.* She abruptly changed the subject. "Where are we headed?"

He pulled out a map and showed her. "If we head due east, there's more likelihood of being detected. So, I thought we'd throw them offtrack. Head south, hitting the smaller towns across Oklahoma, part of Arkansas, and down to New Orleans. From there, we can catch a steamer for New York and make up for lost time. It's a circuitous route, but they won't be expecting us to take the long way back. Although it will no doubt rob us of precious time, it may also enable us to travel unimpeded."

She had to agree it made sense, even if she was anxious about the upcoming ordeal. In spite of her protestations to the contrary, she was trusting him with a great deal. Never before had she returned to face the music. Always, her prime concern after the completion of a con was to disappear. It was in her nature to run away. It made her nervous to think of facing charges that might well end in her being hanged for murder. Mace had assured her he'd rescue her from such a fate. But how did she know she could trust him? A suspicious inner voice kept nagging her: *What if he's leading you into a trap?*

"You seem to have it all planned," she commented as she sampled the beans.

His face lighted up, then, on the verge of some glib remark, settled into suspicious lines. "What have I neglected?"

"Oh, I was just wondering what accommodations you'd made for the more practical aspects of this venture. The sleeping arrangements, for instance."

"Well, now. I hadn't thought of it."

"There are three wagons. The one is full to bursting with women already. None of whom, I might add, seem too awfully fond of *me*. The costume wagon is so jammed full of paraphernalia that there's no room for a body. That leaves only one other possibility."

"And what's that, Princess?" he asked in a tone that set her toes to tingling.

"You know bloody well what that is."

"I suppose it means you'll have to share this wagon with me."

"Actually, I was thinking more along the lines of sleeping here by myself."

"And where, pray tell, am I supposed to sleep?"

"It's a lovely warm night. I should think sleeping under the stars would suit you."

His flash of temper seared her as he stood and towered over her. "It doesn't suit me. You can sleep across the room if you're so bloody shy all of a sudden."

"Now, darling, you know yourself that won't do. For strictly business reasons, naturally. Already, the women are exhibiting signs of jealousy. I shouldn't want them to hate me unduly, thinking I was being granted favors they weren't allowed."

He glowered at her, rankled by her cool, taunting tone.

"You're an impresario now," she added. "You must think of your cover. And speaking of covers, here's yours."

She handed him a blanket and pillow.

"You're a coldhearted wench," he grumbled.

"That," she said with a smile, "is what I've been told."

CHAPTER 27

The first town they came to, Mace hired some men for the day and set to hoisting the tents with their help, spending most of his time keeping the hired men from halting and gaping at the girls. It was good business, he explained, to show the men a peek at what they might expect. That way, they'd brag later in the saloons; it was the best publicity the show could receive. After they were finished, he went into town and proceeded to drum up business, letting the citizens know a carnival had come to town.

That night, he took his place as hawker for the show, but he allowed the girls to work their acts as usual. In the big tent, the twins performed on their ponies, standing on the animals' backs and leaping through the air to change places. Later, they performed feats of marksmanship that were truly impressive, first from the ground, then from the backs of running horses. The crowd was small but responded enthusiastically to the twins.

In between, Flying Dove came on in her flimsy costume and performed her contortions to wild applause. On the way out, Lucy ran her pea-and-shell game, in hopes of picking up some extra cash for the troupe. But she was so bumbling that a good number of men, in spite of her pretty pout, guessed and won the pot.

Saranda and Mace watched without comment. Once, their eyes met, and the understanding that flowed between them was electric. This was a small-time operation that could be a hundred times more lucrative than it was.

That night, after the crowd had departed, he called a meeting in the big tent and announced some changes would be made.

"The twins are fine as they are," he announced, causing them to giggle appreciatively. "But I'm after something different. More variety. More—" He sought the word.

"Heart," Saranda provided. "We've enough flesh to tantalize the most contented of men. But ye've forgotten the most important thing. Men living a life away from home are lonely not just for the sight of women, but for the sentiment. Something to remind them of days gone by. To soften them up for the touch to come."

"What do you suggest?" Lucy asked, looking at Mace.

"For one, darlin'—and don't take this personally— you're off the shell game. Ye might as well pay them to play." Her face crumbled as she turned a bright, embarrassed red. It was her only role in the show, and she'd just been fired. "Fret not, darlin', we'll find you a job more suited to yer talents. Dusty will take over out front."

Lucy shot Saranda a look that needed no interpretation. But Mace continued as if nothing were amiss.

"I'll let Dusty tell you herself what her further contributions will be."

Without hesitation, she said, "I shall sing songs that

remind the gents of 'ome. Then, if you'll allow me one of the tents, I shall disguise meself as a Gypsy and read fortunes."

"Excellent. And I shall join Flying Dove and show them some feats worth writing home about. What d'ye say, lydies? Shall we join together and take these lonely men fer all they're worth?"

"So long as you leave them a little pocket change," said Flying Dove, drifting off toward the tent's exit and town. "For *after* the show."

IN THE NEXT town, they tried out the new act. At first, Mace put Lucy in charge of announcing, but her voice was too small, and after the first few lines, she could think of nothing to say. So he took over and offered such a litany of praises for his women that the men were salivating, virtually fighting one another to get inside.

That night, Mace and Flying Dove worked together for the first time. He'd spent the afternoon limbering up and rehearsing with the beautiful Indian. The result was a stunning display of acrobatics that nearly brought down the roof. Dressed in a black outfit that hugged his muscular body like a second skin, Mace looked as sleek and deadly as a panther. In her jeweled black sheer costume, with her straight, gleaming hair hanging down her back, the half-breed was the perfect foil. Together they moved with such grace, such suggestive rhythm, that it brought a hot flush to Saranda's cheeks. Like two jungle cats, they pranced and stretched and leapt into each other's arms with a beauty that was spellbinding. The thrill of watching them was almost carnal. She felt as if she'd been afforded an intimate view of some exotic bedroom ritual.

The act was unbearably sensual, and as such had

Saranda quivering with rage. In her own blond hair, fixed in innocent curls, she sang her one song so sweetly, so purely, with such a brokenhearted tremor in her voice, that it brought tears to men's eyes. But her mind was so consumed with visions of Mace's hands gliding over the Indian's body that she barely noticed the applause.

EVERY NIGHT, AFTER the long wagon ride, Mace and Flying Dove would practice their routine. He fashioned the needed equipment to expand their repertoire, and that night he suspended the Indian into the air on the edge of a long pole, where she performed gymnastics as the muscles in his arms strained to hold her aloft. It was a big success, and he immediately made plans to add the abandoned trapeze to the act.

But he knew a good thing when he saw it, and he'd noted the applause—and the money thrown her way—when Saranda had sung. Passing by her one day, he informed her she'd be singing two more songs—this time in a skimpier costume. When she rebelled, her eyes spitting fire, he simply tossed her the outfit he wanted her to wear and went back to his practice with Flying Dove.

It was a pink gauzy concoction that perfectly suited her coloring but showed far more of her body than she cared to. She put it on and marched out to the tent to show him it was impossible.

A single lantern offered a meager golden glow. There in the soft light, Mace and his partner were practicing swinging on the trapeze, high above a net. Mace swung with a powerful grace, every muscle in his virile form rippling as he moved. Saranda stopped and watched, a lump forming in her throat that she couldn't quite comprehend.

All her life, she'd been contemptuous of the Blackwoods'
affiliation with the circus. It was something that had been
bred into her family for generations. Yet, standing far below, looking up at him with her heart in her throat, she
thought she'd never seen anything more beautiful. His
body seemed made for movement, for action, for sleek undulations. It was a body to thrill the senses.

Flying Dove waited on a bar across the tent. At the
precise moment when Mace was well-positioned, hanging
upside down from his calves, she hurled herself into the air
and was caught in his powerful hands. Saranda felt dizzy,
looking on. Her fear of heights enveloped her. Just watching them was terrifying. She couldn't imagine how they
could fly through the air with such confidence, such ease.
She knew she couldn't so much as climb the *ladder*—not if
her life depended on it.

Again, she felt consumed by jealousy. She envied the
Indian her ability. She shared something with Mace that
Saranda never could. She was a part of his world, of his
past.

The concentration with which Mace performed his
act, the time he spent practicing, spoke of his devotion to
an art form Saranda could never understand and could certainly never share.

Or was she imagining his devotion? Was it time
spent with the Indian he relished—and not the routine?

She looked down at her skimpy costume and saw
herself for the first time. She was a woman who used sex—
or at least the promise of it—to lure men into loosening
their pockets so her clever fingers could remove the contents. Yet here she was, behaving like some indignant
matron with offended sensibilities because Mace had demanded she do more of the same. Why did it bother her,
when it never had before?

Then she knew. Somewhere along the way, her potent sexuality had become something she gave to him alone. The fact that he wanted to exploit her sensual charms for money shattered her confidence. Was what she offered him so meaningless that he could, without conscience, barter it to others?

The acrobats positioned themselves once again, Mace flexing his long fingers in preparation for the catch. Saranda moved into the light below, catching his eye. He glanced at her dismissively, then, noting her costume, turned as if mesmerized, and stared. His partner jumped when she was supposed to, only to be ignored by the man she'd relied on to catch her. With a startled cry, she was hurled to the net below.

He slipped from the trapeze so that he, too, fell to the net, bouncing high several times. Distractedly, he made certain the Indian was all right. But she could see his mind was elsewhere, and she angrily brushed him off. Unfazed, he turned back to Saranda, climbed from the net, and walked toward her as if walking in his sleep.

She knew she was lovely because she'd looked in the mirror. She knew the pink costume hugged her curves, accented her breasts, and made her thighs look like an invitation to delicious intimacies. With her blond hair tumbling to her shoulders, she looked like some enchanted fairy come to life. She was ripe and curvaceous, a vision of sumptuous female flesh. All this she knew. But she hadn't expected this reaction from such a calculating man.

Suddenly feeling rather cheerful, she turned as if exhibiting her costume so he could catch a healthy glimpse of her backside. It was so tightly clad in the gold-trimmed hip band that each softly rounded arc was visible. She walked forward a few steps and heard him catch his breath.

"Perhaps we should reconsider this," he said, as inti-

mately as if his lips were at her ear. Her heart thrilled at
the possessiveness of his tone. It was clear he'd underesti-
mated her effect in the ensemble.

She decided then and there to wear the ruddy costume if it killed her.

CHAPTER 28

In the next town, they began to hit their stride. Saranda sang the added songs and was rewarded as the audience tossed coins at her feet. As the twins were hanging upside down from ponies and shooting at stuffed birds, she disguised herself in dark wig and bright colors as a Gypsy fortune-teller and told prophecies to lonely pioneer men. She'd learned the art from her mother, using a combination of tarot, astrology, and the ancient runes, along with a smattering of a science her mother had developed analyzing peoples' names. It would have been easy enough to slide by, telling them the usual things lonely men wanted to hear. But she was a perfectionist. Without having planned it, she gave genuine readings that left each patron more astonished than the last, and a growing collection of coins in the silk pouch in her bosom.

After the crowds had left, she was getting ready to dismantle her operation, when the tent flap opened and Mace walked in. The tent was small, and he seemed to fill it with his presence. Even exhausted from the show, he radiated more charisma than any man she'd ever known.

She took the money from her bodice and handed it over. He dumped the gleaming contents into his palm and gave a low whistle. "Quite a tidy little haul."

"Gypsies, it would seem, are irresistible."

Their eyes met.

"This Gypsy, it seems, has an uncanny ability to read a man's most secret thoughts. I've been hearing about you all evening," he said.

She assumed her Gypsy accent and the manner of intrigue, and said in a husky voice, "No man's secrets are safe vith me."

"What's this I hear about you reading names?"

"Oh, that. Mother taught me. She believed a person's name could tell a great deal about the person. It's tricky, though, out here. One never knows if the name one's given is real. But the pseudonyms people choose can be quite telling."

"I'm intrigued. What, for instance, would you say to Tommy Ward?"

"Officially?"

He shrugged.

"Have a seat."

He sat across the table from her. A single kerosene lantern lighted the tent, throwing pointed shadows about the room. She turned it lower, as was her custom with a reading. "I warn you. This will cost you."

His eyes never left hers. They both knew she wasn't speaking of money. Fascinated, he gestured for her to go on.

"Very well. Ward means a guardian, or watchdog, which is interesting since you're in essence guarding me. But Tommy—that's the truly interesting choice. Thomas means twin. I should say it speaks to your awareness of being a person of many faces. You were named for a weapon. Yet in a pinch, you choose the identity of a man of multiple facets. In short, a con man."

"What else do you know?"

"That your mother was undoubtedly an admirer of medieval literature."

"How did you—"

"Oh, that's easy. She named her sons Mace and Lance. Medieval weapons. What else would you like to know?"

His mouth twitched. With an amused, patronizing smile, he settled back in his chair, brought one foot to rest on his other knee, and settled back. "By all means. Tell me my secrets."

"I shall need the tarot for that. And your cooperation."

"Anything you say."

"Shuffle the cards for me."

He took them and shuffled them like a cardsharp, fanning them from hand to hand. Obviously, he intended to make a joke of it.

"Lay them in three piles."

With a mockingly serious frown, he obeyed. Stacking them, she laid out a center card.

"Aha," she said in her husky Gypsy voice, "the guides varn you to stay avay from Indian maidens."

He looked up from the table and laughed. "You phony."

"Is that a challenge?"

"Just show me the tricks of the trade."

"I'm not sure I care to."

"Afraid?"

"Perhaps."

"Because I might spot the weaknesses?"

"No. By now, I should expect you to."

"Ah, a compliment. What, then?"

"I'm afraid of finding out something I don't want to know."

"You're telling me this works?"

"I don't know how it works. But sometimes I see things—*understand* things—I wouldn't normally."

They were silent, staring into each other's eyes. She caught the flash of hesitation as his narrowed in assessment. "I say we risk it," he said finally.

"Which means you don't believe me."

"Does it?"

"If you really thought I could discover your secrets, you wouldn't touch those cards."

He grinned. "Very well. I confess to doubts."

She took a deep breath and let it out slowly. Replacing the card, she handed the deck back to him. "Take these in your hands and think of your deepest secret."

He took them, but his grin widened as he allowed his gaze to travel the line of her breasts.

"That's no secret," she snapped. "Concentrate. Bring it all back to you. Transfer it from your mind into the cards."

He held her gaze for another moment. She caught the change of expression, saw the moment when he decided to rise to the challenge. He closed his eyes. The vein in his temple throbbed. She felt the atmosphere in the tent settle and focus.

"Done," he said.

"Shuffle them again until they feel right. The whole time, concentrate on the one thought. Then, when you're ready, replace them in three piles."

With the cards back in her hand, she laid one faceup. "That's you," she said, pointing to the Chariot. He studied it intently. "It speaks of having a balance, but perhaps not realizing it. See how he's holding the reins and balancing two worlds—the spiritual and the material."

She laid down more cards, facedown this time, making a pattern. Then, slowly, she turned over the ten of Wands.

"Well, this is no surprise. You're searching for an identity. You're in the process of changing, but there are so many identities from which to choose, that you—you're looking for the right one, the *real* one. Who you really are."

"A fine reading to give a flimflam man."

"This is your past." She turned the card over and flinched. Thoughtfully, she turned over another card. Turbulent pictures whirled through her mind, like memories she'd had no part of. "The cards say you're a deeply tortured man. You hide it behind a mask, yet there's a part of you that's like a beaten animal licking his wounds. It's murky—dark—I feel that you're grieving for the family you lost. It's confusing. I think this is your brother. He caused the loss of your family, which would point to his botching of the job that led to your parents' death. But this indicates something I don't understand. It implies the loss of a child. Says the loss devastated you, never stopped haunting you. That you suffer every day of your—"

His fist slammed down on the cards, scattering them. She jumped. She'd become so engrossed in the reading, she'd almost forgotten he was there. She looked up to see etched in his face the same black torment that had screamed at her from the cards. The intensity of it frightened her. But she'd seen something in the cards that had touched the bleakest corners of her heart. "You had a child," she whispered.

His mouth quivered. He rose and stood with his back to her. The air in the room was so charged with pain that she wept for him inside.

"I'm sorry," she said, feeling wretched. "I wish I'd never started this."

He turned. "By all means, finish it," he said bitterly. "Dredge up the rest."

There were still a few cards lying facedown on the table. With a shaking hand, she gathered them up.

"I don't want to know," she said softly. Then, lifting her eyes to his, she corrected herself. "That isn't true. I want more than anything to know. I want to know everything about you. What you hope for, what you dream about, why you suffer. But not this way."

"If you're so curious—not to mention so *talented* at telling fortunes—why do you care how you find out?"

She stood and went to him, taking his hand in hers.

"I want to know because you trust me enough to tell me."

He gave a harsh sound that passed for a bark of laughter. "Trust. A charming word, between the likes of us."

He tried to pull his hand away, but she held it tight. "Just tell me one thing."

The pain in his eyes was receding, replaced by a guarded shield. "What's that?"

"Is it true Lance ruined *your* life, as well?"

"If you mean that job, you have to understand. Lance was . . . ill. He wasn't responsible for his actions. He thought he was helping—"

He broke off suddenly. She didn't need him to continue. His justification told her more than she wanted to know. As long as he lived, Lance Blackwood would have a protector in his brother, Mace.

"You're wrong," she told him. "I don't have to understand anything. Your brother is a reprehensible wretch, undeserving of your loyalty or your protection. I only pray God my life doesn't hang in the balance."

"Don't be ridiculous."

"Tell me, Mace. Given the choice between my life and your brother's . . . which would you choose?"

CHAPTER 29

Several days later, they realized they were lost. They hadn't come to a town in days, and they were running short of water. They rode for hours in the unrelenting blaze of the desert sun, hoping to find a new supply—a river, a stream, anything. Somehow they'd strayed off-course.

AFTER TWO DAYS of wandering without water, with the women on the verge of mutiny, they ran into Indians. There were ten of them, young, virile braves, painted for war.

As they reined up, Flying Dove moved to Mace's side. "They're Pawnee," she told him softly. "Looking for trouble. You must kill them, or they will kill you and take the women."

The braves began circling the wagons.

"Can you speak the language?"

"Enough."

"Get inside," Mace ordered the other women. Then he turned to Flying Dove. "You come with me."

Abby handed him the rifle she'd retrieved from her wagon. But he merely shook his head.

From inside the wagon, the women looked out on the scene. Mace and Flying Dove walked forward slowly toward an older brave who was apparently the leader.

"He's going to try and talk to them!" Abby marveled.

"He's going to get us all killed," grumbled Lucy. "Or worse."

Saranda watched as the braves dismounted and took hold of Mace, holding him spread-eagle as Flying Dove spoke hurriedly. "Do you have a pistol?" she asked Abby.

"Yes."

"Give it to me."

She put the gun in her pocket and stepped out into the heat. Shading her eyes with one hand to distract them from the other hand in her pocket, she walked slowly to Mace's side. The braves paused and stared at her.

"I told you to stay inside," Mace snapped, still held pinned by the Indians.

"Do they speak English?"

"No," said Flying Dove.

"I have a gun in my pocket. Take it and use it, before it's too late."

"I don't want it," he insisted.

The braves who weren't holding Mace began to circle her. One touched her golden hair, another pinched the material of her dress. They made a tight circle, their mouths widening in appreciative grins.

"These men haven't had a woman in some time," Mace warned. "Unless you want—"

"I want you to take this gun and use it."

One of the braves grabbed the hair at the nape of her neck and roughly pulled it back so that her face tipped up toward his.

Mace's face hardened, and his voice cracked out like a bullwhip. *"Saranda, get in the goddamned wagon."*

Flying Dove registered surprise at his use of the strange name. But she spoke sharply to the braves, and they moved away.

"Why be so stubborn—"

His eyes narrowed, and he growled at her, "Get out of here. *Now.*"

One of the braves spoke. "He says they'll leave us—in exchange for a woman," Flying Dove whispered.

"Tell him no deal."

She touched his arm. "I'll go with them. I'll—"

"Tell him my women aren't worth my life. Tell him they're useless. They're weak. They can't cook, they can't take care of a man. Tell him I spit on my women. My ponies are of more value. But I give those ponies to no one."

She translated as he spoke.

As one, the braves looked back at the wagons, noting the sleek ponies. The men who were holding on to him let him go as they moved off to inspect the horses. Freed, Mace grabbed Saranda's arm with such force that she felt his fingers bite like brands into her flesh. He jerked her to him furiously.

"You could have a *little* faith in me."

"You could be killed—"

"If I get killed, it's because of you."

She stared at him, horrified.

He shook her. "Goddammit, don't you know what you do to a man?"

She looked into his eyes, which were as cold and hard as stone. Terrified for him, she murmured, "Mace—"

But he wasn't interested. His eyes flicked over to the Indians, who were inspecting the horses' teeth. "Get the hell back in that wagon before you find out."

Reluctantly, she returned to the wagon. The air inside was thick with fear. "Did he take it?" Abby asked.

"No." Saranda took the pistol from her pocket and laid it on the bunk.

"They're leaving," Lucy shouted out.

The twins ran for the window. "With our ponies!"

They tripped over their skirts in an attempt to get outside. "Wait!" Abby called after the retreating braves. "Come back!"

Mace grabbed her and put his hand to her mouth to silence her. "Fool! Do you want them to come back for you?"

She wrenched her mouth free. "You gave away our horses. How are we supposed to perform our act?"

"Would you prefer I gave them you?"

The women stared at him. He'd forgotten himself and used his real voice. The silence that followed was oppressive. They kept staring at him as if he'd betrayed them.

"They took the horses in exchange for water."

He held out a skin full of water, and one by one, the women drank, but sullenly, as if he'd put a gun to their heads.

"We had those ponies for years," Abby said in a little-girl voice. "We trained them ourselves. You should have killed those Indians before you let anyone take them away."

When the twins and Lucy returned to the wagon, Flying Dove turned back to Mace. "They have no understanding of the danger they were in."

In her eyes was the promise that she did.

.   .   .   .

THEY SPENT THE day traveling south, trying to
put as much distance between themselves and the Indians
in case they decided to return. Flying Dove assured him the
ponies were fine enough that the braves would feel satisfied. But the air was so stagnant and bitter that Mace
pushed them ever southward, hoping to dispel the mood.

That night, the tension was so thick, Saranda decided to go out for some fresh air. Lucy and the twins
stayed in their wagons. But as Saranda passed by the fire,
she heard a woman's voice. It was Flying Dove, sitting
across the fire from Mace.

"You saved me today from a very bad fate," she said.

"I did nothing. Only offered them some horses in
exchange for water."

He didn't bother with the cockney accent.

"You did much more than you'll ever know. It would
have killed me to go with them. A half-breed is not treated
well. It's why I became what I am. Selling my body in your
world seemed preferable to what I left behind."

"You don't have to worry. No one's taking you anywhere."

"I believe you. I wanted to—thank you. For your
kindness."

Pulling him to his feet, she put her arms about his
waist and kissed him.

Saranda's heart lurched in her breast. The impulse to
rush forward and yank the woman away was so strong, she
had to clench her fists to keep rooted in the shadows. Because, much as she longed to claim him, she didn't have
the right. Mace was free to dally with whomever he
pleased.

The Indian's hands crept up and spanned the broad

expanse of his back as she deepened the kiss. Her jealousy festering, her fingers hungering to thrash the predator, Saranda turned away.

She was stopped by the Indian's disappointed sigh. "Please," the woman said, "allow me to thank you."

Saranda turned back in time to see Mace take the woman's hand in his and kiss it tenderly but dismissively. "There's nothing to thank me for," he insisted.

It was gently put, but the woman understood. Wistfully, she gazed up at him a moment, then withdrew her hand and left.

Saranda stood as she was for a moment, watching as Mace squatted down by the fire and clenched his hands together.

"Poor Mace," she said, moving into the light. He looked up, startled out of his thoughts. "The other women won't speak to you. And that one can't keep her hands off you. Your life has become rather complicated, since taking me on."

His devilish mouth lifted in a wry smile. "In the old days, it would have been simple," he agreed.

She sat down across the fire from him. "In the old days, you'd have slept with them all and used your charms to keep them in line."

"Something like that."

"And now?"

His gaze lifted to her face. She caught a certain sadness as he studied her. "Now I have you to consider."

"What does that mean?" Her voice had become breathy with hope.

He held her gaze for a full minute, and she felt herself drawn into the dark magic of his eyes. Then, as she watched and waited, she saw him harden himself against the promise he read in her eyes. His hands balled into fists, and he became a Blackwood once again.

"It means if I want that paper, I have to keep my mind on business."

She dropped her eyes. "I see," she said quietly. "I had thought, at this late date, we might have moved beyond playing games with one another."

"But in the end, love, there's nothing left but the game. We're both damned good at what we do. You can make any man on earth do your bidding—"

"Any man?"

"And I can talk a war party out of killing us and raping the women. Sometimes it's so easy, I find myself trying to talk people into outrageous things, just to see if it can be done."

"And it always can."

A look of disgust flashed across his face. "Always. But never forget one thing: we're great at the illusions because we have to be. Because there's nothing else inside."

She sat for a moment, watching the firelight play across his face. For a moment, she saw a trace of the torment she'd witnessed during the tarot reading that had pained her as much as it had him.

"Are you certain?" she asked. "That's there's nothing inside?"

He looked up, and she knew she'd never seen a more haunted look in a man's eyes. "There can't be," he told her. "It's too late."

CHAPTER 30

As they approached the Arkansas line, resentment was running high. To replace the pony act, Mace and Saranda —dressed in her Gypsy attire—went out into the audience with a mind-reading act. Mace didn't have to teach Saranda the code. She'd known it from the age of six.

The surprise was how well they worked together. Once they decided they were on the same team, there was no hesitation, no resistance. The words flowed between them like poetry. They began to lose sight of the audience, to gaze into each other's eyes, as the energy crackled between them. Never had Saranda worked with anyone as good. Even her father, whom she'd thought to be the best in the business, couldn't hold a candle to Mace Blackwood. The thrill of it was intoxicating, the verbal exchange as titillating as the most languid foreplay. It was so highly charged, it was like making love in public.

They weren't the only ones to feel it. The act was wildly successful. They made more money that night than they ever had. There was a long line waiting for readings after the show. The twins, deprived of half their livelihood, and Flying Dove, sensing the chemistry between Mace and Saranda, sulked and complained that Mace was featuring Saranda to the exclusion of everyone else.

"I'll bet you got rid of our horses purposely," Abby accused, "so she could take our place!"

It was just the beginning of his problems. After the show, a frantic mother rushed up to Mace with the news that her small son was missing. Saranda had disappeared, so the others banded together, searching the grounds for the boy. Half an hour later, with the mother dissolved in helpless tears, Mace ordered the women to stay with her while he made a more thorough search.

His exploration of the premises turned up nothing. As a final resort, he thought to check the wagons. The first two were empty. But a small light flickered in Saranda's. He climbed the steps, opened the door, and stopped in his tracks.

Saranda sat on the floor with her back to the door, rocking the four-year-old boy in her arms. A single candle sat beside them on the floor, casting a quivering glow. But what arrested him was the sound of Saranda's voice. Rocking the child, staring off into space, she sang a lullaby so sweetly, so lovingly, that it all but broke his heart. He had to clutch the doorknob to steady himself.

As she sang, she unconsciously lowered her head and kissed the child's dark hair. Her lips lingered in the shining locks, as if she couldn't bear to pull away. She presented such a picture of cherished devotion that Mace, feeling like an intruder, began to back away.

Through her fog, she felt the wagon move. She turned and saw him there, staring at her with tears in his eyes. His face was so shattered, she thought for a moment she was staring into a mirror. Some sane part of her brain told her why he was there. But she'd been so deeply entrenched in memories that she couldn't distinguish, in that moment, what was real and what was remembered. Standing awkwardly, with the child still clutched in her arms, she gave him a last kiss and handed him forth.

"Take him," she said in a gasping voice. "I can't take care of him."

Alarmed, Mace took the child.

The boy looked from one to another. "Why is that lady crying?" he asked.

She hadn't realized the tears were streaming down her face. Putting a hand to her cheek, she turned away and leaned her head against the rail of the top bunk.

"She's crying because she likes you," Mace told him.

"I like her singing."

"So do I. Come along, little tiger. I shall take you to your mum."

The walls of the wagon seemed to close in on Saranda in the silence they left behind. It all came back to her in a rush—the dreaded memory. How it felt to return to that bitter-cold room, with the rats and the smells, without her child in her arms. The hollow, aching loneliness of knowing she'd done the right thing. The realization that she couldn't do anything else. The racking guilt that came from knowing the insufficient coldness of her own heart.

She shoved her way out of the wagon and went to hide herself away in her tent. He'd be back. He'd come to find her. And what could she say? What could she tell him? How could she tell anyone that she'd caused her own child's death?

MACE FOUND HER eventually, after he'd returned the child to the hysterical mother. Saranda was standing by her little reading table, staring down at it. When she looked up and saw him, she turned away. As she leaned her head against the center pole of the tent, her shoulders began to shake with her sobs.

He came up slowly behind her. "Saranda," he whispered.

He put his hand to her shoulders. The touch was warm, comforting. It made her feel lonelier than before he'd come.

He turned her, tilting her head up to face him. Slowly, and with infinite care, he used the back of his knuckles to wipe the tears from her cheeks. Looking up, she saw such compassion, such empathy, in his eyes that she began to sob again.

"Tell me," he coaxed.

She'd kept it secret for so long. The words burned in her brain, tasting on her tongue. But she shook her head. How could she tell him, of all people?

"Would you do something for me?" she asked softly.

"Anything."

"Kiss me. Make me forget what I can't bear to remember."

He contemplated her a moment, then stepped closer and took her in his arms. They were strong and warm. Arms a woman could lose herself in. Arms that could keep away the cares of the world, make her feel safe and protected. He bent his head and took her lips with his.

For an instant, she thrilled at the familiar soaring inside. Her head spun, and she molded herself to him, losing herself in the pleasure of his kiss. She'd put it all aside, she vowed, never to be thought of again.

But when she opened her eyes, she saw Lance's face. Strangling with panic, she made a mewing sound deep in her throat and thrust Mace away.

"Forgive me," she gasped, crying once again. "I can't kiss you without seeing your brother."

"What does he have to do with anything?"

"I wish to God he was never born."

"Tell me, Saranda. What did Lance do to you?"

"I can't. Mace, please—"

He pulled her close, holding her protectively in his arms. "Tell me, Princess."

Where once he'd used the nickname to taunt her, it was now a tender endearment. But self-preservation was an instinct too strong to easily ignore. The fear she'd felt for twelve long years engulfed her now. She knew what he'd think of her if he knew the truth. She knew, too, that loving him as she did, she couldn't bear to see that look on his face.

Better to hurt him over something trivial than to destroy him completely.

She pulled away. "Is this another experiment? To see what you can talk someone into *this* time? Can you make the secretive adventuress spill the dark secrets of her soul?"

She'd wounded him. In his anguish, he didn't even bother to hide it. The look in his eyes at the undeserved attack pierced her heart and shamed her. She began to cry again. "I'm sorry. I'm so tired of hurting people. But I don't know how to do anything else."

He was unrelenting. Slowly, patiently, he took her in his arms and pulled her close one more time. "Tell me," he insisted.

"You don't want to know."

"I want to help you."

"Help me? There *is* no help for me."

His lips were at her hair. "Whatever it is, I shall understand."

"Understand?" She pushed away. "*I* don't even understand!"

He could see she was growing hysterical. In her eyes was the wild look of a trapped animal willing to risk even death to be free. He shook her so that her silver hair flew about her head.

"Tell me."

She wrenched away from him and screamed, "I killed my own child!"

He was so shocked, he didn't even bother to reach for her. He stood frozen, looking at her as if he couldn't believe what he was hearing. In the back of her brain, she realized he wasn't looking at her as she'd expected. There was something more personal in the stunned expression. But she wasn't thinking rationally, and it slipped from her before it could register.

"I might as well tell you," she said in a small, defeated voice.

He didn't move. He didn't alter his expression. He merely waited, numbly, for her to explain.

She put a hand to her eyes, covering them as she recalled the twisted memory.

"I—had a child at fourteen. A boy. I named him— well, that doesn't matter, does it? He wasn't wanted. I was raped, and he was the result. The whole time I was pregnant, I hated this growing intrusion. I couldn't think about the child without remembering the circumstances—why I was having him. My parents were dead. I had no one to turn to. I was so shocked, I think, over the way my parents died, that I couldn't seem to think. It was as if all the training I'd had died with them. I didn't know what to do."

She looked up at him. He hadn't moved. He looked as haunted as it was possible for a man to be. *He hates me now*, she thought. And why not? Hadn't she spent these many years secretly hating herself?

"I had the child by myself in a dingy room I'd managed to scrape enough shillings together to let. A horrible place. He was *all* I had. Before his birth, I'd been able to get enough money together to keep a roof over my head. But afterward—well, a baby's rather a hindrance to a bluff artist. No man wants to take on the burden of another man's child. Certainly not the sort of men I was doing business with. I used to think of the irony of it all. My father had groomed me to be a bride of the aristocracy. And there I was, begging for food to keep alive a child I'd never wanted and—and—"

She couldn't say it.

"And couldn't love," he supplied.

She glanced at him. In his eyes was a pity she hadn't expected. It hurt her more than the accusation she'd thought to see. She'd seen that look in the eyes of so many people on the streets of London. Everyone pitied, and no one helped.

She sighed. She might as well confess as much as she dared.

"I wanted to love him. God knows, he was so lovely, with his curly black—" She put her hand to her mouth. *Spare him what you can. Isn't it bad enough?* "I did everything I could to care for him. But he'd look up at me with those blue eyes, and all I could see was—the man who'd raped me. He was so like him. Yet he wasn't, because he was small and helpless, and needed a mother's love. I tried and tried, but I couldn't give him what he needed."

She began to cry again. She went to rest her cheek against the tent pole.

"I kept him for over three years. Every day I'd wake up and think, *Today is the day I shall find a way to make this work. Today I shall open my heart to him without remembering my hatred of his father.* But I never could. Eventually, it became too difficult to support him. We were dressed in rags, half-starving. I wasn't eating enough to keep my milk flowing. The baby cried all night from hunger. I felt like such a failure. Any cow in the fields could give birth, could care for its young in a way I couldn't. I've never felt so inadequate in all my life. I began to think if only I were free to operate, I could pull a con that was worthy of my heritage—build a stake for us, and get us out of the punishing poverty we'd been living in for nearly four years. So that's what I decided to—"

"Did my brother harm your child?" Mace asked with a piercing glare.

"Mace, please—"

In the act of turning away, she was grabbed by a hand of granite and whirled around to face a pair of uncompromising deep blue eyes.

"Tell me, dammit. Did Lance hurt your child?"

"No. I did that myself."

"What then?" He took hold of her other arm and shook her. "What did he do to you?"

She saw in his eyes that he'd already guessed the truth. What difference did it make anymore?

She gave up and said the awful words.

"He was the baby's father. Lance raped me after he set fire to my parents' house. As they were screaming their agony, he pinned me down and raped me, laughing all the while."

CHAPTER 31

His hands dropped from her.

"The son of a *bitch*!" he raged. Looking around, he took her reading table in his hands, raised it high above his head, and flung it to the ground, smashing it to slivers. He was looking around as if for someone to strangle when he met her startled gaze. Wide-eyed, bewildered, frightened by the intensity of his unleashed emotions, she backed away.

He rushed to her and caught her arms in his punishing grip. "Don't look at me like that!" he commanded. "I'm not Lance. I'm not like him, I tell you!"

She swallowed hard, because in this light, with the madness in his eyes, he looked very much like the brother who'd willfully destroyed her.

"Jesus. You really think I am."

"I don't know what to think. I only know it was a Blackwood who found out where we were living. Who put an advertisement in the *Times* stating the date of our destruction. Who came at night and blocked the doors so we couldn't get out, and set fire to our house. I was small enough that I climbed up through the chimney. But as I was struggling to free my parents from the outside, it was a Blackwood who grabbed me—like you're doing now. Who flung me to the ground and took me against my will as my parents burned to death, screaming, before my eyes."

He took his hands from her and looked at them as if he'd never seen them before.

"My brother wasn't—responsible for himself."

"Your *brother* was a bloody maniac. I was thirteen years old. I'd never so much as *kissed* a man. He didn't care that he was hurting me, or that he was killing me inside by keeping me from saving my parents. He just kept laughing and laughing and *laughing*—"

She lashed out at him, beating at his chest, slapping his face with the same wild, ineffective swings she'd used on Lance that fateful night.

He fought her. Taking her wrists in his hands, he shoved her back against the tent pole, then brought her wrists high above her head to press them against the wooden beam. With his body, he pinned her there, lowering his forehead to rest on the top of her head. "Christ, I'm sorry," he murmured, almost incoherent himself. "Jesus, God—if only I could—"

"Take it away? No one can ever take it away. Your brother was the cruelest man I ever came across in a lifetime of consorting with criminals. It's your fault, dammit! You and your ruddy family—protecting him, pretending he wasn't the lunatic he was. That's the reason our family turned him in after he killed that American boy. We knew if someone didn't stop him, he'd— They had him in custody. He was going to hang along with your parents. But *you* had to break him out. So he could return and wreak his revenge."

"He was my *brother*. He was young, and ambitious,

but he could never live up to the family's expectations. He worshiped me, wanted to be like me. But every time he was involved, something went wrong. I kept trying to help him. If we suspected there was something wrong with him, we kept thinking time would take care of it. He begged for a chance to prove himself. So we gave him the flam. He was to kidnap the American, take his place on the ship, get what jewels he could, then return the American to his family. But, through Lance's carelessness, the American saw me. Lance killed him thinking he was doing me a favor. A *favor*! I nearly killed him when I found out."

"I wish to God you had."

His hands tightened on her wrists. "I'm not a killer. I told you."

"You're a Blackwood, aren't you?"

Like a deflated balloon, the air seemed to leave him. He sagged against her, then let her go and moved away. Her body felt cold and strangely bereft without his crushing warmth. She brought her hands down and clenched them together to keep them from shaking.

"So you had the baby. My—"

"Nephew. Yes."

"Then what happened?"

"When B—when the baby was almost four, I heard Lance had been killed. They said the ship he was escaping on sank at sea. Did you know he was alive?"

"I was the one who pulled him from the ship."

She was sorry she'd asked. If only he'd let well enough alone . . .

"I thought he was dead. I thought at last I could be free of his vile memory. All I needed was some time to gather my resources, to plan a con big enough that I could support the baby. So I turned him over to an orphanage."

He shuddered at the agony in her eyes.

"It was meant to be temporary. I told them I'd be

back to retrieve him. I asked them to take good care of him till I returned. But I had no money to give. I suppose they didn't believe me. When I returned, with money in my pocket at last, they told me he'd died. Pneumonia, they said. But I know what really killed him. It was my neglect."

"Don't."

"Don't what? Don't face the truth? I've spent my life running away from the truth. But the fact is, I killed that child. I wasn't capable of giving him what he needed. A tiny, innocent boy, and I couldn't find it in me to love him, or to care for him, as he deserved. I've paid for it a thousand times over. But what of him? When I think of him, dying alone, without comfort or—" She broke into sobs. "In the end, I'm as much of a monster as your brother."

"Don't say that."

"Not saying it doesn't make it less the truth."

"You were a child. Growing up the way you did, what did you know of love?"

"Don't. I don't want to hear this. I can't justify what I did."

"Why not? Because you might find it in your heart to forgive?"

"I shall never forgive him. Do you hear me? *Never!*"

He was silent for a moment. Then, very softly, he said, "I meant that you might forgive yourself."

The thought of it terrified her more than the threat of punishment for her crimes. "I can't forgive anyone," she told him. "After I learned to live with the baby's death, all I could think of was revenge. I decided to embrace the traditions of my family. To be the best confidence woman this world had ever seen. I spent a few years in Europe, honing my skills and keeping track of your whereabouts. When you came to America, I followed, determined to destroy you in whatever way I could. If I couldn't have

Lance, I'd have the last living Blackwood's head on a plate. I didn't realize until I saw him again how much I hate him still."

He said nothing. There was a great sadness in his eyes.

"I've been toying with you as a form of revenge. Every time I came near you, it was thrilling. Because it was like having Lance Blackwood under my thumb. No longer was he attacking me against my will. This time, I was controlling the game."

She'd never seen him flinch, not from danger, not from a challenge, not from pain. But he flinched now, and her heart shattered at the futility of it all.

"What is it you're not saying?" he croaked, with a con man's instincts.

"Now that you know, I'm not certain I can look at you again without thinking of Lance."

CHAPTER 32

The next few weeks passed in a fog. Confessions that might have brought them closer together instead built a wall between them that neither could surmount. The confrontation had unsettled Mace in a way Saranda couldn't fathom. She had the feeling she'd never seen him when he wasn't playing a role. Yet in those weeks following their face-off, he became moody and remote. Saranda could only guess at the depth of his despair at learning the truth about the brother he'd loved and protected most of his life. But it puzzled her that he'd given up so completely. He seemed strangely defeated, as if beaten by some force she couldn't comprehend. She'd spent her life hating his family. She'd openly sought revenge. Looking at his ravaged face, she knew that in some measure, she'd won it. The surprise was how deeply hurt she was by his defeat. His illusions crushed, he seemed stripped of the pride, the confidence, that had made him the man he was. He was a con man without a con, the saddest circumstance of all.

He seemed to her like a man who'd looked inside and found nothing there. In spite of her own deep pain, she wanted desperately to help him. But what could she do? It was the travesty of her life that she'd learned an ugly truth at a tender age: She was a woman incapable of love. Those in pain were better off without her insufficient care.

SHE WENT TO the wagon one night to find him sitting on the bunk, his elbows resting on his knees, a bottle dangling in his hand. He looked up when she entered and closed his eyes, as if the light was too sharp. "Saranda, go away."

She closed the door behind her. "I was just wondering how long it would take you to stop feeling sorry for yourself."

He took a liberal sip from the bottle. "How long did it take you?" he sneered.

"I'm sure I can't understand your behavior. If anything, I should be the one—"

"I'm sure you can't," he slurred. "Understand."

"Then help me. Tell me what's troubling you so much that you'd forget why we're here."

"I shall ask you again. Get the hell out of here before I—" He stopped and took a long drink from the bottle.

"What have I done to you?" she whispered, alarmed now by the depth of his torment.

"What have you done?" He gave a laughing snort. "You've held up a mirror. It doesn't matter where you go or what you do. That mirror just keeps following you around."

"Have you forgotten? We have a job to do."

"A job. Always another job—"

"Mace, you're scaring me."

He stood up slowly and tossed the bottle aside. It

slammed against the wall, shattering and spilling the remains on the wagon floor. She glanced at it and back to him as he came toward her, towering above her, forced to lean slightly beneath the low roof.

"I'm scaring *you*. That's a laugh. That's nothing, sweetheart, to how you scare me." He reached out and took her silvery hair in his hand, yanking her to him so that she came up breathless against his chest. "Christ, you're so desirable. Everything a man like me should want in a woman. My brother—damn his soul—took one look at you and wanted you above all things. Do you think I don't know what that's like? Do you think I can look at you, smell you, without wanting to see you panting beneath me?" He kissed her fiercely. His breath, reeking of whiskey, mingled with hers as his tongue plundered her mouth. He held her so tightly, she thought she'd suffocate in his arms.

He crushed her breast in his palm, took both hands, and ran them down the length of her slender back to cup and squeeze the generous buttocks and pull her into his groin. He was so hard, it was like coming up against a shaft of steel. She whimpered, because in spite of it all, she wanted this man more than she wanted to live.

But she wanted more than his body. She wanted to heal him. She desired his heart, freely given. She craved his soul. *If only he weren't a Blackwood . . .*

"I'd like to take you right here and now," he rasped against her ear. "Slip inside and make you crazy. Crush you to me and make you forget every man you've ever known."

"Oh, yes," she whispered. She was aching with desire. His hands at her buttocks kneaded with a demanding rhythm, parting the cheeks as he thrust her up against the swollen armor of his lust.

"I want to feel your skin beneath my hands. Taste your nipples on my tongue. Shove myself up inside you and feel you quiver beneath me." He withdrew a hand and ruminatively smoothed the backs of his knuckles across her lips. "I want to come in your mouth."

She opened her lips and took his fingers in.

He jerked them from her mouth, took her chin in his hand, and raised it so he was glaring viciously into her eyes. "But I'd be proving myself a Blackwood, wouldn't I?"

"You're wrong," she panted. "It wasn't the same. It wasn't that way at all."

"Well . . ." His eyes took in her mouth as she parted it beneath the cruel grip of his hand at her chin. "You always were a good liar." Leaning, he gave her a chaste parting kiss. "Don't fret, darling. You haven't done a thing. You're not, after all, responsible for the accident of my birth."

He turned, dismissing her. She stood for a long time, watching him, breathing hard.

When he spoke, it was in a cautious, clipped tone, as if leashing some inner fury. "Now do as I say and get the hell out of this wagon. Before another Blackwood brother forgets himself and rapes you too."

CHAPTER 33

Lucy was driving the lead wagon one afternoon when she was stopped by a trio of riders. They were Mexicans, heavily armed and loaded down with ammunition. Expecting trouble, Lucy pulled rein.

The other wagons came to a halt behind her. Since Mace had taken over the lead wagon, Saranda had been forced to share the second with the other women—a situation that was uncomfortable at best. Now, as the wagons lurched to a halt, she looked out the small window and saw the men talking to Lucy. Bandits! As one of them motioned with his rifle, Lucy cast a hesitant glance back at her own wagon where she knew Mace was and stepped to the ground.

Another bandit pounded on the lead wagon's door. After a moment, the door swung open and Mace stepped down, his hair rumpled, his jaw stubbled with black beard, making him look nearly as disreputable as the intruders.

The twins, who'd been driving the other wagons,

were rousted from their perches and forced to the ground. While the leader held them all at rifle point, the others made their way back to the women's wagon. Their boot-steps crunched in the dry terrain, heralding their approach.

Flying Dove joined Saranda at the window. "I do not think they came to rob us," she whispered.

"To kill us, then? But why?"

The Indian turned and gave her a steady gaze. "Perhaps you know better than I."

There was banging on their door then, and one man yelling for them to come outside.

"Have you ever shot a man?" Flying Dove asked in the same hushed tone.

"No."

"Nor I. Could you?"

Saranda shook her head. She hadn't been able to kill Lance Blackwood, even when she'd had the chance.

"Then I will take the gun and pray for strength."

At that moment, the door opened and one bandit reached inside. Swearing in Spanish, he caught Saranda's arm and jerked her out of the wagon. While he was distracted, Flying Dove took the gun and thrust it into the back waistband of her skirt.

They were shoved out into the glaring sun. The heat was still and oppressive, the sun so bright it hurt the eyes.

Mace was speaking drunkenly to the head bandit in fluent Spanish. Since she didn't speak the language, Saranda couldn't understand the words. But his tone was clear. Swaying slightly on his feet, Mace was attempting to con the bandit.

She looked at the twins and saw the terror in their faces. Obviously, they feared what she did: that Mace, drunk and self-destructive, would be of no help in this fight.

She could smell the danger. The bandit's eyes were

cold, unfeeling, the look of a man who has no intention of being swayed. He barked an order at Lucy.

"He wants you to get the money," Mace told her. He turned back to the Mexican and began a litany in persuasive Spanish. For a few moments, the bandit seemed to listen, his gaze hungry. Then, with a stained-tooth grin, he spoke again.

As the women held their breaths, Mace shrugged expansively, as if to say, *Well, I tried*. He jerked his head toward the wagon, bidding Lucy to do as she was told.

"I'm not going to just hand this louse the money we worked so hard for," Lucy protested.

Mace turned and gave her a level look. "Do you want him to kill you?"

"If you were any kind of a man, you wouldn't let them do this."

The bandit interceded. In Spanish, Mace told him what Lucy had said. Amused, the bandit dropped his head back and roared with laughter. As Lucy went into the wagon to retrieve the money box, Mace offered the robber a drink from his bottle. Dropping his arm companionably over Mace's shoulders, the Mexican drank heartily.

Meanwhile, the other bandits were eyeing the women. One called to his boss as he moved close to Abby.

The leader disengaged himself from Mace and went to join his fellow outlaws. Abby began whimpering as the man trailed a hand along her arm. She shot Mace a look of fury that blasted his betrayal for allowing this to happen. Desperately, she shrank away from the Mexican's foul breath.

Together, the three men surveyed the women one by one, making obviously crude comments and laughing as they went to each, stroking their faces and fingering their hair. When they came to Flying Dove, she turned to the side so they couldn't see the gun. But Mace saw it. His eyes flicked to it, then quickly away.

The Mexicans apparently had no use for a half-breed. The leader made a great show of sneering and spat at her feet.

Lucy came forth with the money box and handed it resentfully to the leader. The men circled her, nodding their heads as they noted her red hair and pouty lips. One bandit made it clear he wouldn't mind having her.

Then the leader turned and spotted Saranda. He stood rooted for a moment, staring. She met his suddenly heated gaze with a rebellious tilt of her chin. But she knew with a sinking heart that there would be no help for her. She'd seen that same look in Lance Blackwood's eyes, just before he'd raped her. Now that the bandit had noticed her, she knew this man wouldn't be turned away.

Mace saw it, too. He put his arm about the bandit's shoulders as he'd done earlier, and in jovial tones offered him another drink. The Mexican didn't even look his way. As though in a trance, he shrugged Mace off, handed the money box to his partner, and walked toward Saranda.

His eyes took in her every curve, lingering on the full breasts, taking in the rounded arch of her hips. He grabbed her arm, turned her around as if inspecting a horse, and caught his breath. His hand, caked with dirt, molded itself to her backside as the breath choked in her throat.

He began to speak to her in a low tone. The words were unintelligible, but she recognized the sound of a lust-crazed man when she heard it. When he turned her back to face him, she saw the awful glitter in his hooded eyes.

She looked over at Mace. For an instant, their eyes met, hers registering panic, his genuine despair. Was he going to stand there and let these men take her, out here on the desert like some spoils of war?

The bandit spoke to his partner, who gave an appreciative snort, came around behind her, and cruelly twisted her arms behind her back, forcing her breasts to rise. Holding his rifle halfway up the barrel, the leader circled the outthrust globes with the muzzle. His lips curled in a sneer as he reached over, grabbed the neckline of her dress in his hand, and yanked it open. Saranda struggled, but could do nothing. She stood bared to the waist in front of these brutal strangers, with the sun beating down on her exposed breasts.

Mace said something in a low voice. The bandit shrugged him off, reaching forth to touch her flesh. She gritted her teeth to keep from vomiting as the twins burst into tears.

Again, Mace spoke in a low, persuasive tone. Angry now, squeezing her breast possessively, the bandit turned on him and growled out a command. With a shrug, Mace retreated, leaving Saranda staring an awful reality in the face. Once again, she was going to be brutalized. But this time it was different, worse. Because the man she loved would stand by and watch, and do nothing to help her.

She looked desperately at him as the Mexican lowered his cracked lips to her skin. "Mace . . ." she moaned in soft entreaty.

He stopped next to Flying Dove. His shoulders slumped, his back to Saranda, he muttered, "Some people are just too stupid to con."

Then, with lightning reflexes, he grabbed the gun from the Indian's skirt and whirled. At Mace's harsh words, the leader had lifted his head, and the next thing Saranda knew, Mace was firing the gun. The Mexican's face exploded before her eyes.

In the horror of it, time seemed to grind to a halt. As if in slow motion, the bandit fell before her, his face blown clean away. The man pinning her arms shoved her forward, so she fell on the dead body. When she looked up, both remaining bandits were running for their horses. One leapt over the backside and into the saddle and, taking the money box with him, raced with his partner across the desert at full speed, scattering clouds of dust behind.

Mace raised his arm and aimed at the fleeing men. The bandits had ridden some distance off by then, but he tracked one coldly and pulled the trigger. It was an impossible shot. Yet, a split second after it rang out, the fugitive fell to the ground. Mace fired a third shot and missed, the outlaw with the money box already too far away.

As the smoke cleared, a tremendous silence settled over the land. Saranda stared up at Mace, shock and terror mingling in her gaze, as in the other's. He stood there, dead sober, looking with horror at the faceless bandit who'd only moments before been a living man.

The women watched in stunned silence as he stood, the smoking gun dangling at his side as if it were suddenly too heavy to carry. They watched as this man who'd just saved them dropped to his knees in the dust and stared at the body before him as if belatedly praying for the dead man's soul. They watched in horror, in hushed reverence, for still they couldn't believe what they'd just witnessed.

Oblivious to them, Mace sat, knees apart, crouched over the body, the gun—still in his hand—dragging on the ground at his side. He never moved, seemed unaware they stood there.

Saranda rose in a daze, her bare skin splattered with blood and bits of the bandit's remains. She barely noticed as Abby retrieved a shawl from the wagon and wrapped it around her. She had eyes only for Mace. She'd never seen such remorse, such torment, such self-recrimination, in all her life.

"Now I'm like Lance," he said, almost too softly for her to hear.

"He was evil, Mace. He would have killed me. After they *all* raped me."

"Saranda, there hasn't been a man alive I couldn't flam. I could have done it. But I got scared. I lost my head."

He dropped the gun, as if belatedly realizing he still held it, then sat staring at his hand as if he'd never seen it before.

"You saved our lives. There's no way those men were going to let us go."

"I'm not a killer, dammit," he snarled. Then, calmer, he added, "I can't say that anymore, can I? Just like Lance. What was it you said? Once a Blackwood . . ."

She grabbed his arm and turned him to face her. "No," she cried, fighting to get through the punishing black mist in his brain. "You're not like Lance. If anything, this proves it."

"That I killed two men because it was easier than talking them out of their intentions?"

"No. You killed them to save my life. Lance kills because he's full of hate. You killed because you love me."

He looked into her eyes and recognized the truth of her words. With a lunge, he caught her waist and pulled her to him, clutching her to his chest as he realized what he'd almost lost. His head buried in her hair, he allowed her to sob into his neck as he lowered his head and his tears mingled with hers.

One by one, the women retreated to the wagons and left them alone.

CHAPTER 34

Never before had each allowed another human being to see so sharply to the very core of them—the secret emotions, fears, and vulnerabilities they'd become masters at shielding from—and using against—an unforgiving world.

In each others' arms, they'd finally felt safe. Perhaps for the first time in their lives. Yet the truth of the situation began to penetrate, to make the revelations seem unreal, where only moments before they'd seemed the only reality in a lifetime of fabrications.

For the fact was, they clutched each other over the body of a dead man—a man who had sought to destroy them both.

They separated slowly, as if the effort was too great. Saranda felt like a woman who'd awakened in a stranger's bed—not knowing what to say, or what to expect. Uncertain if a promise was implied, and unwilling to broach a subject that might spoil the tender mood.

But this gift of being able to reveal their true selves

was too precious to return unopened and with regrets. So Mace took her face in his large hands and wiped away her tears with his thumbs.

"We've things to talk about," he said in a tone that promised further intimacies. "But now we've more pressing business."

Greatly relieved, she nodded. Reaching up, she used the tips of her fingers to wipe the remaining traces of his own tears. Then, putting her fingers to her mouth, she tasted their salty moisture, relishing the emotion they represented.

"I think those bandits knew we'd be here," she told him. "Though I can't say why I think so. Instinct, only."

"Let's find out."

He glanced down at the dead body distastefully, then rolled it over and made a thorough search of the man's pockets. "Nothing here."

Standing stiffly, he made his way to the bandit's horse. A search of the saddlebags brought forth a fistful of paper. She saw Mace's shoulders slump. Wondering at his discouragement, she pulled the shawl tighter about her and went to put a tentative hand on his arm.

"What is it?"

Without words, he handed her the papers. She took them curiously. One was a clipping from the *Globe-Journal* with the picture of Lalita Van Slyke, used to help identify Saranda. The other was a drawing that looked very much like a younger Mace.

"How did they get this?" she asked.

"There's only one way they could have." He turned, and she saw in his eyes the same tortured longing for denial she'd seen when she'd told him about the baby. "From Lance."

If Lance had supplied the picture, he was willingly

sacrificing his own brother to a gunman's bullet, which didn't surprise her. "How do you know?"

"That's a copy of a picture my mother used to carry in a locket. There was a picture of Lance on one side and me on the other. After her death, Lance was so distraught, I let him keep it. He still had it when I saw him in New York."

She had a vague memory of a golden locket cold against her skin the night Lance raped her. The urge to say "I told you so" was so strong, she had to bite down to keep silent. Mingling with it was a rage that the wretch could so coldbloodedly throw his own brother to the wolves. From the little Mace had told her, Lance had worshiped his older brother. Why now would he sacrifice him to the highest bidder without a qualm?

"You're right, of course." She could see his relief. "If those bandits were sent, it means they know where we are. Or Lance knows, in any case. Whom he's told—I should like to think he's told no one—"

"Mace, he sent someone to kill you."

"We don't know that."

"Do you honestly believe those men were merely after our money, and our virtue?"

The tension rose between them once again. "I don't know what to believe. We can only go by what we know. If Lance knows where we are, and what our cover is, it's become too dangerous for us to continue. We shall have to abandon the troupe at the next town and head for New Orleans."

"Why wait for the next town? For all we know, your brother will be waiting for us there. One of the bandits got away. He's likely to go flying to Lance with the news of their failure. Why not leave now?"

"Because aside from the Mexican's horse, we have

only those that pull the wagons. We'd have to leave one wagon behind."

"So leave them all behind. Pile the women into one wagon, for that matter."

"And leave them without their livelihood?"

She felt more chastened than annoyed. "Very well. Whatever you say."

He gave her the faintest trace of a smile, looking once again like the Mace of old. "Are you telling me you trust me?"

"We'll talk about that later." But the smile she gave him was kind. In truth, she was touched by his concern for women who meant so little to him, in the scheme of things, and whose care could only place him in more danger.

He looked about him, sniffing the air as if becoming aware of their surroundings for the first time. "You'd better change," he reminded her gently, pulling the torn edges of her bodice together so his warm knuckles grazed her breasts. "It's late. We must make some progress before the storm hits."

She hadn't noticed signs of a storm, but now, gazing across the plains, she saw dark thunderclouds gathering in the Southwest.

She went in the wagon to change, using a little of their precious water to sponge herself where the bandit had pawed her. It felt cool and healing on her fevered skin, gave her a moment of respite from the terrible events of the day. As she pulled on the plain calico dress, the memory of Mace's eyes—eyes that brimmed with tears of love for her, warmed her, washed away the pain of confrontation with the bandits as no prairie water ever could.

Then she heard Mace's voice calling the women outside. She stilled, detecting a note of panic that startled her. She'd never heard that tone in his voice before. One of the women—Lucy?—gave a stark screech of terror. Had the bandit returned? Had he brought more men? She looked out the window but saw nothing except Mace and the women staring as if transfixed across the dark distant plains. She hastily buttoned her bodice, then stepped out into a scorching gust of wind. And saw at once what the panic was about.

Worse than bandits. More terrifying than the threat of violent men. It wasn't just a storm approaching. It was a tornado.

CHAPTER 35

It approached as if from out of nowhere at an alarming speed, a great swirling, monstrous wind, dark and menacing, hurling dust and debris in its wake. She'd seen twisters before, seen the awesome devastation they could wreak.

There was no time to think. In a panic, the women ran blindly in different directions, irrationally seeking to outrun a force that mowed down everything in its path with incredible speed. Only Lucy dived beneath a wagon, clutching at its wheel. Unthinking, Saranda moved to follow, only to be grabbed by a hand that bit into her flesh and wrenched her away. The fierce wind whipped at her hair, flinging dust and rocks at her face and body. The noise was deafening, descending on them like some demon unleashed from hell. Dragging her, Mace headed for a cluster of cottonwoods, tossing her down before diving over her and flattening himself to the ground. Following suit, Saranda clung to the thickest trunk she could. The wind kept blowing her off the ground, forcing her to grip the tree with arms and legs to keep from being blown away.

Suddenly, she heard a faint scream above the roar of the wind. Forcing her eyes open, she saw the twister lift one of the wagons, horse and all, and fling it, like a toy, hundreds of feet in the air. Clinging to the spinning wheel, Lucy was cast to the ground where she fell broken, then was blown like a human tumbleweed across the rough terrain. Then, beside Saranda, a slender tree was sucked from the earth with a crack, the branches scratching her face and barely missing her eye as it whirled away.

Shutting her eyes against the onslaught of dust and rocks and splinters of wood, Saranda clung to the tree, terrified she was going to die. Fighting by instinct alone to stay rooted to safety, she struggled against the power and majesty of nature, which blackened the earth and rendered her like a stalk of straw in the storm.

Then it was over, as abruptly as it had begun. The wind died down, and the noise receded to a low, distant roar. Saranda had so much dust in her eyes that for long moments she couldn't focus. When at last they cleared, she saw Mace beside her, raising himself from the ground, as filthy and scratched as she was. Relieved, she glanced behind to see the twister moving in a northeasterly direction, but dwindling now to a smaller, swirling column that diminished rapidly as it swept away.

She felt his hands at her shoulders. "Are you all right?" Mace asked.

She turned to him. He looked as shaken as she felt but appeared otherwise unhurt. He wiped a hand across her cheek, and she saw the streak of blood from her face where the branches had scratched her. She felt battered and sore, covered with dust, and her cheek stung. But otherwise she was fine. They were alive. It was a miracle. Gratefully, she nodded.

"Then I'd better see to the women."

Saranda looked out over the plains as Mace walked with determined strides to where Lucy's body lay twisted and broken hundreds of yards away. All about them was strewn the wreckage of the gale. Horses and wagons had been flung wide, the wagons crashing on the animals, who lay on their sides, one still, one writhing in grunting agony. The wagons themselves had been reduced to shards of wood, their contents hurled across the prairie. For hundreds of yards, she could see bright bits of material that had once been costumes or tents but were now tattered beyond recognition. Aside from poor Lucy, she could see none of the other women. Had they been blown too far away for Mace to find them?

She headed in the opposite direction, moving rigidly, feeling weighted down by the heaviness of her muscles. The plains were eerily silent now in the aftermath of destruction. Yet as she trudged off past the rubble in search of bodies, she could hear traces of thunder in the distance.

She caught sight of a mound that might well be a body some yards off. As she hurried closer, the thunder seemed to draw nearer. Suddenly, she stopped in her tracks. It wasn't thunder. The roar came closer, an unbroken crescendo. With her heart in her throat, she turned to look. Was it another tornado? Not after—

Then she saw it. A long line of cattle, running at full tilt, dashing, blind with terror, this way and that, but ever forward in an unending mass. They came and they came and they came . . . more cattle than she'd ever seen, thundering across the bleak landscape—directly in Mace's path.

She screamed to him, but he didn't seem to hear her, only the onrushing beasts. He began running toward the trees to escape the horrible onslaught of hooves and pounding flesh descending on him in a deadly arc. But they were coming too fast! As he ran, he waved his arms to try to ward them off, but instead they veered in his direction, charging at him as if following his lead. Saranda had just enough time to let out a scream of horror before the steers trampled him in a charging mass, and she saw him vanish beneath them.

CHAPTER 36

Never had time seemed to stop like this. Breathless, she was forced to stand and watch as wave after wave of the horde descended upon Mace, surely crushing her lover's body beneath its hooves. She might have screamed the entire time—she didn't know. Certainly, her hands were clutched over her mouth as if to quell the awful sounds coming from her throat. Too horrified to cry, too petrified for rational thought, she felt her body jerk toward him in spasms as the spooked livestock swerved and jumped and balked at the spot where Mace had fallen to the ground.

It seemed a lifetime before they finally passed and she could run, as senseless as the cattle, across the parched prairie to his side. She stopped just before she got to him, letting out a cry at the sight of him. He'd been ripped to pieces! His clothes were in shreds, his body cut and bleeding and oddly twisted. His arms were encased around his head, protecting it, but she could see red gashes where blood matted the black curls. For one awful moment, she was afraid to touch him—afraid of the cold, dead feel of his beloved body beneath her hands. Then he moved slightly with a strangled, muffled groan. Wild with relief, she threw herself on him, shielding him with her body as if to protect him from any more devastation.

At her touch, he let out another gurgling cry and convulsed onto his back. At once she saw why the sounds coming from him were so strange. His throat had been cut by a wayward hoof. Blood gushed from the wound.

Even as she moved to help him, she burst into tears. Wadding her skirt, she pressed it to his throat in a futile effort to stanch the flow of blood. As she did, she heard again the pounding of hooves and looked up to see a handful of cowmen galloping across the horizon in breakneck pursuit of their cattle. Dropping her skirt, she leapt up and frantically waved to them, screaming for help. But they passed her by as if she were part of a landscape too familiar to glance at twice, racing past in a swirl of dust. She wasn't even sure they'd seen her. Within minutes, they were out of sight.

She returned to Mace, dropping to her knees beside him, pressing her skirt once again to cover his mangled throat. He'd passed out by this time and was barely breathing, dangerously pale, so badly beaten and losing so much blood. It was a wonder he was still alive. She knew if he didn't have help, he wouldn't live for long. What could she do? She had no water, no supplies, no knowledge of medicine. Alone in this terrible place, she was helpless and desperate.

Taking his face in her hands, she rested her forehead gently on his and let her tears bathe his battered face. Her helplessness choked her, making it difficult to breathe. She couldn't even move him. The horses were dead, the wagons destroyed. She didn't even know where the nearest town might be. For all she knew, it could be a hundred miles away. Frustration churned in her heart, and with it an anger that blinded her to the landscape. She was a woman who could think her way out of any situation with a fellow human being. But against the forces of nature—against so ravaging a circumstance as this—she felt small, insignificant, defenselessly female in a vast and brutal world.

Then a small hope soothed the terror in her heart. Perhaps the cowboys, having recovered their runaway herd, would pass this way again. It was a bleak hope. The cattle had run too many miles east off the trail to Dodge. Likely, the men would steer them north and west and meet the rest of their party along the trail. Still, it was possible that someone—the chuckwagon, the scout, the trail boss—would ride by. It *was* possible, wasn't it? She looked up at the sky. It was already late in the day. Soon it would be dark. Too little time to scour the countryside for what might be left of their supplies. If someone *did* come by, they might easily miss Mace lying alone in the endless terrain. She had to stay with him and wait for someone to come, to comfort him the best she could.

Unbidden, a traitorous thought flashed through her mind. Nothing she could do would silence it, stamp it out. No matter what she did, Mace would probably die. And if she left him now, he would die alone, untended, in a strange land with no comforting hand on his brow. *Just like her son.*

A chill of terror clutched her. Carefully, she eased him into her arms and, mindless of the blood, held him close. If Mace was to die, she vowed, he'd do so in the arms of someone who loved him with all her heart and soul.

.   .   .

SHE DIDN'T SLEEP. There were too many ter-
rors to keep her awake. The howl of a coyote—or was it a
wolf? The eerie blackness of the night, the slither of some
nocturnal creature in the dry grasses that surrounded them
like a sea of unknown dangers. The thought, unbidden,
that the visitor she was praying for might prove the greatest peril of all. *Lance knew where they were.* What if he
came upon them, alone and helpless in this endless night,
and, hearing the death rattle in his brother's ruptured
throat, decided to finish the job?

As the night wore on, and Mace's breathing grew
more shallow with each breath, as he almost choked several times on his own blood, she began to wonder if death
mightn't be a mercy after all. As his shock wore off, he
began to feel his pain. She couldn't touch him without his
flesh convulsing in agony. He wove in and out of consciousness, trying to speak at times, but collapsing finally
from the frustrations of his efforts. She couldn't seem to
stop the flow of blood from his throat, though the pressure
of a bandage torn from her skirt had slowed it down. Even
if he survived, she wondered if he'd ever be able to talk
again.

What would a man like Mace be without a voice?
Without the power of a golden tongue?

She chided herself through the long night for thinking such things. If he lived at all, it would be a miracle. If
he lived, she'd be so grateful, she wouldn't care if he ever
spoke again. She'd do anything, sacrifice all she had and
more, just to know he wasn't going to die.

By the time the first light of dawn began to color the
eastern sky, she was so weary, she could barely keep her
eyes open. But she mustn't sleep. She could scarcely hear
his breathing now. She had to put her ear to his chest just
to make certain he was still alive. She'd cursed herself all
night for not going out immediately in search of water. Her

tongue felt thick and parched in her mouth. If she was suffering, how must Mace feel? But could he swallow? Perhaps a strip of her petticoat soaked in water would help ease his suffering. Maybe if she was able to bathe his throat, it would stop oozing blood, stop the painful gurgling when he tried to draw a deeper breath.

She'd lied, cheated, and stolen for everything she'd wanted in life. But now, in the middle of nowhere, a cup full of water seemed the most precious, most unattainable, treasure on earth.

As the sky lightened, she eased him from her arms to lie prone on the hard ground. Looking at him brought a helpless sob to her throat. His body, once so beautiful, so strong, looked as if someone had taken a razor and slashed it indiscriminately. He was bruised and swollen beyond recognition, little more than food for the coyotes and the buzzards already circling overhead.

She removed her bloodstained petticoat and gently laid it over Mace to keep the sun from burning him while she was gone. Then, with her heart aching at leaving him, she kissed his cheek and slowly, painfully, stood. Her legs had fallen asleep beneath his punishing weight, so it was an agony to walk. Sharp needles prickled her muscles as the circulation began painfully to flow. But she pushed on, thinking of Mace's need, hoping to find something—anything—in the wagons' far-flung debris that might give her lover a fighting chance.

She stumbled along, stooping to inspect a shattered box here, a ragged piece of material there. She found Lucy's body being fed on by birds of prey and, sickened, screamed at them, waving her arms. She should bury her, she knew. But the living came first. She had to help Mace before he, too, became food for the vultures.

In her weakened state, it took her most of the morning to scour the countryside. The water barrels had been shattered along with the wagons. She could locate none of the food they'd brought along. Likely they'd been blown farther along the path of the tornado. She did find one large piece of canvas tent that would shield Mace from the scorching sun, so she draped the heavy material over her arm and dragged it behind her. Then she recognized a tin box that had been Flying Dove's. Inside, she found some unfamiliar herbs and salves. She had no idea what the ointments contained. Some bottles had been broken in the crash, but others had survived, and she hoped they contained something that would help Mace heal. Hugging the box to her, she began to feel hopeful for the first time. If only she could find some water.

After another hour of searching, she came at last upon a trampled canteen half-filled with water. Wrenching open the top, she drank several greedy sips of the warm water before forcing herself to stop. If this was all the water they had, Mace would need every drop.

Satisfied with her quest, she began the long walk back. The vultures had moved to the horses now, flapping their wings as she passed and cawing their dominion in the still noon heat. She'd wandered so far off, she could no longer see the spot where Mace lay. Perspiration dripped from her face and down her back as her stomach churned, reminding her she hadn't eaten for two days. Still, she hurried along, concerned for Mace and fearful that he might have succumbed during her long search.

At last she spotted the petticoat she'd left behind to shield him. Dropping her supplies, she ran toward it with a burst of adrenaline, then stopped in shock. Her heart rushed to her throat as she stared, unseeing, at the petticoat lying flat on the ground.

Mace was gone!

CHAPTER 37

Saranda didn't know what to do. She began wandering in frantic circles, asking the same desperate questions. What could have happened to him? Where could he be? He *couldn't* have just walked away.

She was in such a blind panic that she couldn't breathe. She had to force herself to stop, to take measured breaths, to think this through. Could some wild animal have dragged him away? No, it would have devoured him where he lay. That meant someone must have taken him. But who?

Then she thought of Lance. Could he, or some hired gun, have stumbled upon Mace while she was gone and carried him away? She fought down her terror and tried to remember what Bat had told her about tracking. He'd excelled at tracking horse thieves others had given up for lost. Maybe if she concentrated, she could use what little she remembered to her advantage.

But where could he be? He'd been on the threshold of

death. How could he survive being thrown over a saddle and carried off?

Would she ever see him again? Would he die without her ever knowing what had become of him?

She couldn't stand it. She had to stay sane. Because she was so close to losing her mind, any small indulgence into self-pity would push her over the edge. She couldn't think about the fact that she was alone in a wilderness she knew next to nothing about, without food or means of travel. Mace could already be dead. And if he wasn't, he was likely suffering more cruelly than he had when the cattle had trampled him and left him crushed and unconscious.

She hadn't felt this helpless desperation since the time she'd known she must give up her child. It reminded her of how painful it was to love someone so deeply. To want to shield herself from those emotions, to deny their existence, because it hurt too much to carry them in her heart.

She must do something, must face the terror, but it was a reality she couldn't bear to live with: that the one she loved had died because she'd left him alone.

Trembling, she forced herself to scour the dry land for signs. At first she could see nothing; the earth swam beneath the welling up of tears. But eventually, by force of will, she focused on the barren land and saw a chilling sight: Hoof prints.

Someone had taken him.

But who? Why would anyone want to throw such a wounded man over the back of a horse and carry him away? The thought was horrifying. Under such rough treatment, Mace would bleed to death in an hour.

She had to find him, to save him from such a fate.

Numbly, she slipped the strap of the canteen over her shoulder, and set out to follow the tracks. The sun was high and hot, beating down in a pitiless glare. She walked and walked as her skin began to burn and the path ahead blurred before her eyes. She didn't know how long she walked, losing the trail and picking it up again as she traversed rocks and grasses and dry river beds. When her stomach growled, she ignored it. When she was so tired she fell to her knees in the dust, she picked herself up and walked again. Only when she felt she couldn't take another breath of the arid air did she allow herself a sip of water. She had no way of knowing how long her journey would take. She must ration the water with care.

Eventually, as the sun began to sink in the west, she fell and couldn't bring herself to rise. Without sleep or sustenance, with barely enough water to keep her alive, she was too weak to continue. Even as she cursed her feebleness, she clung to the thought that somewhere, at the end of this trail, Mace was alive. Her cheek hit a smooth, warm rock, and she fell instantly asleep, too fatigued even to worry about what might be lurking in the desert night.

For three days she trudged, one step after the other, following a trail she was certain, with the passing of each minute, would lead to disaster. It was madness. Without a horse, she'd never catch up to them. She didn't even have the strength. Her skin was so badly burned, it hurt to touch it. She had two swallows of water left. And her legs, weakened by lack of food and the endless motion, wobbled now when she walked.

Finally, it was over. She couldn't coax another step out of her burning feet. In a delirium, she kept imagining different fates that might have befallen Mace along the way—each more harrowing than the last. She shuddered at the tortured pictures that flashed through her mind. More than water, more than food, she needed rest.

But how could she give up? How could she not do all

she could to find him, discover his fate, no matter how horrible it might be?

But she couldn't. Without knowing how it happened, she found herself on the ground. No matter how she struggled, she couldn't rise. She tried dragging herself a few feet before falling back with a sob. Pressing her face into the dirt, she cried racking, mournful tears for what might have been. It was so unfair. Just when she and Mace had found each other, had declared their love, to be separated like this. To die alone, never knowing what had become of the other. She would gladly give her life if she could save Mace. But to surrender like this—helpless, defeated, without even a chance to try . . .

Her sparse tears mingled with the dust, and soon she was losing consciousness, waiting with a shattered heart to die.

SHE HAD TO be dreaming, or dead. Saranda thought she smelled the salve Flying Dove had used on burns and scrapes—its stink of bear grease and some herbs she couldn't name was unmistakable. But what kind of tricks was her mind playing?

Then she felt gentle hands brushing her arms and legs, massaging her skin with delicate pressure. Saranda struggled to rouse herself, moving with difficulty. Everything hurt, every muscle ached. *If I hurt this much, I must still be alive*, she thought wildly.

With determination she forced her eyelids to open, but she could see only shadows. She was in some kind of enclosure—a tent? "Where—" she whispered, but her voice was barely audible.

"You are safe," a woman's voice murmured. "But you must rest."

Saranda was grateful to hear the comforting words. Her eyes were used to the darkness now, and she could see the face of the Indian woman nursing her.

"Where is Mace? Is he alive?" Saranda's voice was stronger now, but still scratchy and harsh.

The woman touched her hand to Saranda's lips. "Sleep now," she said. "You are badly burned, but you will live."

Then she rose to her feet, and slipped from the tepee without responding to the desperate questions of her patient. Saranda felt tears welling up in her eyes. Mace must be dead if they would tell her nothing. The tears slid down her cheeks as she mourned her lost love. In moments she had fallen asleep.

SHAKILY, SARANDA STOOD up and moved to the opening in the tepee. Peering out, she saw that the sun had nearly set. How long had she been here? And, oh God, what had become of Mace?

She watched for long minutes as the Indian camp bustled with activity. Suddenly her heart froze. Flying Dove stood only yards away. She hadn't perished in the storm, but somehow had survived! Maybe she knew what had become of Mace . . .

She was dressed in a soft doeskin beaded dress, her hair flowing free. She looked astonishingly beautiful among her own kind. When she saw Saranda, she walked slowly toward her and said, somewhat grudgingly, "I see you made it, Miss Sherwin."

Saranda's mind struggled to grasp what she was hearing. She felt hopelessly muddled. She couldn't guess why Flying Dove was alive, or how she'd come to be here. She had no idea how she knew her real name.

Unless . . .

Unless Mace had told her.

"Where is he?" she breathed, afraid to voice the question aloud, afraid to hope.

She saw the hesitation in the woman's eyes, as if she were deciding whether or not to reveal the truth. Then, reluctantly, she answered, "Come with me."

Flying Dove turned and walked away, like a specter in some ghastly dream. Saranda put one foot in front of the other, impelling herself to follow, not sure if the woman was leading her to a man or a grave. It was too much to hope that he was alive.

Such miracles didn't happen to her.

At one of the tepees, the Indian woman pulled back the flap and stepped aside. She stood, looking resentfully at Saranda, who approached the opening the way she would a burrow of snakes. Then she stopped, a heavy sick dread gripping her heart. He was alive, surely. But what would she find? A mangled face, a swollen, twisted form? A broken man without a voice—where once that voice had been the key to his dominion?

A monster to replace a specimen of such masculine power and beauty?

She'd never seen a man more beaten than he'd been. How could he have survived?

"Take care not to upset him," Flying Dove said. She was behaving so strangely, Saranda knew she must assume the worst. It was as if, by her very reluctance to reveal him, Flying Dove was telling her it would have been better if she'd never come.

On the threshold of reunion, Saranda lost her nerve. She'd braved the wilderness alone. She'd slept on the hard ground, ignoring nightcrawlers and wolves, turning her face from the ravages of wind and sun and sand. She'd done without food and water that she might find the man she loved.

But now, after so much searching, hoping, praying, of denying her despair . . . now she was afraid to walk inside and behold him.

She looked at Flying Dove. Her fear must have shown in her eyes, for the half-breed gestured with a lift of her chin for her to walk inside. Swallowing hard, clutching her tattered skirts in sweaty hands, Saranda stepped through the flap of buffalo skin.

CHAPTER 38

He sat cross-legged before a cold fire pit, wearing fringed buckskin leggings but no shirt. His chest, as virile as she remembered, with that thick smattering of rich black hair, bore scars, but appeared to her startled eyes to be nearly healed. His left arm was wrapped tightly in a splint. But the body, the face, all of him was as she remembered before the accident. Except for the splint and the scar at his throat, she'd never guess he'd been so terribly injured.

With him was an ancient Indian who, because of his haughty glare at her intrusion, Saranda guessed was the chief. A young maiden, very pretty with a flat brown face, was kneeling beside Mace, giggling as she popped dried berries into his mouth. Mace had been about to hand the chief a long, smoking pipe when Saranda stepped inside and he halted mid-motion.

"Saranda! My God, I thought you were dead."

She was so startled by the pleasant atmosphere inside that anger—long denied for the necessity of survival—bubbled to the surface. "Is this what you've been doing while I was braving the wilds to find you? While I tortured myself with visions of the horrors that had befallen you? While I prayed you weren't dead, then—thinking of the alternatives—hoped you were? While I trudged through this God-forsaken desert without food or water, just to see if you were alive? And all this time you were holed up like some sort of bloody sultan, being pampered by fair maids and—"

He'd risen, his head nearly touching the roof of the tepee. He was walking toward her as she spoke, but the closer he came, the farther away he seemed. He was so stunning, he took her breath away. It was as if he were walking through a mist toward her. She could see on his face his shock at seeing her, his joy at knowing she was alive, his surprise at her attack. And then he was standing before her, and she couldn't tell if he was real. In mid-sentence, she stopped her tirade and crumpled to his feet.

SHE CAME TO some time later to the smell of herbs and bear grease again. Someone was rubbing something into her hands, something soothing that took away the sting of the sun. She opened her eyes to see Flying Dove reaching into a jar of salve. When she saw Saranda's gaze on her, she lowered her eyes and moved away.

Then she saw Mace's face. "They told me you were dead," he said in a voice that sounded different from the one she'd remembered—more rasping, more whispery, and ultimately more appealing. "If I'd known, I swear I'd have come for you—"

She raised burnt hands and ran them wonderingly along the vast expanse of chest, feeling the warm flesh, the taut muscles, the crisp mass of hair. With a finger, she gently stroked the healed line at his throat. "You're real," she whispered, still not believing it was true. "Oh, Mace, I thought I'd killed you."

With his good arm, he lifted her shoulders so she was propelled toward him, her arms going by instinct about his neck to hold him tightly against her. He felt so unbelievably good in her arms, so warm, so *alive*. She still didn't understand it all. But she didn't care. It was enough to hold him, to breathe in his clean scent, to run her fingers through the hair at the back of his neck and pull his head down to hers. She raised her lips and met his with a cry, tasting his kiss with a wildness that was all tangled up with gratitude and passion and disbelief.

"You're all right?" she asked, still trying to reassure herself this wasn't a dream.

"I'm fine," he murmured into her hair. "With the exception of some scars and a dislocated shoulder, which is nicely healed. The splint comes off in the morning. Their medicine man has potent remedies. Had me fixed up in a remarkable amount of time."

"Then I owe him a great deal," she said, leaning back and once again tracing the scar on his throat. "You're a fortunate cur, I must say."

"I didn't think so till now. Try as he might, the medicine man couldn't heal the emptiness of my spirit when I thought you were lost to me."

"Yes, I could see how you were grieving when I came in," she retorted.

"What? Little Turtle? She's the chief's daughter. I could hardly offend him, after he offered me sanctuary—"

She was laughing. It felt so remarkable to laugh, to look up and see his handsome face. He grinned then, and she thought of Lance. The smile fell from her face. How, after all she'd been through, could she still look at him and see his brother? She shoved the thought aside.

"Why did you think I was dead? Don't you remember I was with you after the stampede?"

"I thought so, but I couldn't recall. Flying Dove said they sent braves out to look for you. She said you were dead. I thought, in my delirium, that she'd been the one with me."

Saranda looked at Flying Dove, who was kneeling close by. Apparently, they'd be allowed no privacy. "Flying Dove, why didn't you tell Mace?"

"I didn't want to raise his hopes. You were unconscious. What if you had died?"

She said it so harshly, Saranda thought Flying Dove had been hoping she would.

"Perhaps we should count our blessings at such a miracle," Mace suggested in his new voice, with its tantalizing aura of mystery.

Saranda looked from the Indian to her lover and knew he was right. It didn't matter that Flying Dove was hoping to keep Mace for herself. It was in the past. Everything was behind them. All the old goals, the old desires. Nothing mattered now but that they were together. The rest would take care of itself.

For three days, Saranda rested and recuperated while Mace continued to build up his strength with acrobatic exercises that tested the limits of his body. She was content to lie back and watch him, sipping the nasty herb concoctions she was given to replenish her own energy and allowing the magical salve to cool her skin and heal her burn. If there was no privacy for more intimate reacquaintances, she told herself she could wait. They had all the time in the world.

They spoke guardedly of loving, yet after the initial overjoyed kiss, neither ever made another move. On the odd occasion when she found herself alone with him, she'd look into his eyes and want to go into his arms, but something would stop her, some old demon that wouldn't let loose its hold on her mind. In spite of all they'd been through, in spite of their newly discovered love, the emotional barriers were still in place.

It was a devastating discovery.

She tried her best to ignore it. Given time and distance, she told herself, the barriers would drop away. They felt awkward now because the relationship was newly defined. They hadn't yet erected signposts to help them along the way. Soon, she thought . . . when they left this place where disaster had almost robbed them of one another. When they could forget the pain of the past.

But how, she agonized, after all this, could they hesitate? What was it that kept them from unreservedly opening themselves to one another, and giving freely of the love they'd both felt for each other while they were apart? Strangely enough, she'd felt closer to Mace when she'd been searching for him than she did when he was by her side.

Then, on the third day, scouts came back with alarming news. A posse was moving into Indian Territory, looking for Saranda. Saranda's heart froze. An idea had been forming in her mind—a way of escaping from the past altogether. But she hesitated to tell Mace, waiting for him to broach the subject, sensing that he would disagree.

Mace came to her that night. "It seems we've had a decision forced upon us," he began. She could see his hesitation, as if he hadn't wanted to face this moment any more than she.

"I want to go to Mexico," she told him. "We'll find a place and live in peace. I've just found you again, after believing I'd lost you. In all this time, I learned one thing: that nothing is as important as us being together. I don't care about the past, McLeod, the paper, any of it. I just want to be free to love you." She didn't mention Lance's name. She didn't dare.

He took her hand in his and ran his thumb along the back of it, seeking the physical closeness to bridge the emotion gap that seemed to widen with each passing day. "I feel the same. But if we run to Mexico, you'll always have this cloud hanging over you. The threat of someone around the corner wanting to turn you in for the reward. It's silly to be looking back over our shoulders for the rest of our lives. Once we get back to New York, I know I can clear your name."

"I can't risk losing you again."

He looked into her eyes, and she felt herself swallowed up in the dark depths. "We shall never be able to stay in one place again. You only think so now. But sooner or later someone will show up with an old wanted poster, and we'll have to move on. I know what I'm saying. Don't forget, I can't set foot in my homeland ever again. I don't want that for you, for us. Not when we have it in our grasp to change things. If I ever imagined that we could escape the past, this posse has shown me the folly of such thinking. There's too much money at stake. They'll never give up while we live."

"But to face all that again. I'm afraid—"

"Of the posse? Or of what's between us?"

She lowered her eyes. She'd forgotten his uncanny ability to read the secrets of her soul.

"I know you're afraid. So am I. But if we don't face this, we shall never resolve it."

"We will if we try. Mace, don't you see? I don't care about this fight. I just want us to be happy. I just want to—"

"Escape?" She looked up to find his eyes piercing

hers. "We can't escape from ourselves, Saranda. I know you want to go to Mexico because you feel by avoiding the past, we can forget all that's kept us apart. But you're wrong. If this separation has taught me anything, it's that neither time nor distance nor outside forces threaten us. I never felt as close to you as I did while you were away."

"You, too?" she whispered.

A spark of truth passed between them. She felt raw suddenly, as if in that moment, for the first time, they'd communicated honestly and from their hearts.

He smiled. "You see? The past will be between us no matter where we go, until we face it."

"But the danger if we go back to New York. . . ." The very name tasted bitter on her tongue. New York, at this juncture, seemed like another world. She couldn't see herself in the city again, couldn't imagine resuming a journey that had lost meaning for her in the frantic race for life and death. To risk his life on something so meaningless . . . To risk whatever happiness they might have by resurrecting the nightmare of the past.

"Do you think I want to lose you anymore than you want to lose me? But neither do I want to wake up one morning and find you shot on the way to the market for a ten thousand dollar reward. Saranda, we can do this, love. We just have to be brave."

She knew he was right. Swallowing nervously, she nodded.

He squeezed her hand tighter. "That's my girl. Can you travel?"

She wanted this to work more than she'd ever wanted anything in her life. She wanted to feel in his presence the overwhelming willingness to sacrifice herself for his happiness—the way she had felt when they'd been apart. She wanted to feel so close to him that nothing on earth could ever pry them apart.

With a valiant smile, she said, "I can do anything if it means being with you."

She hoped it was true.

CHAPTER 39

Finally, they reached the sweltering, humid swampland bordering New Orleans. After months of crossing the plains, stopping only in small towns along the way, it felt odd to be in a city again. New Orleans was particularly disorienting because of its European flavor. The narrow streets and ancient buildings, the foreign lilt to the voices, served as reminders of a continent they'd long ago left behind. People of varied races and colors strolled the avenues, the women shaded beneath parasols to shield their skin from the tropical sun, the servants in colorful turbans, with baskets of fish or fresh fruit carried upon their heads. As they wove their way through the crowds, Mace and Saranda heard French spoken more often than English.

They sold their horses, bought new clothes, and, dressed as tourists, headed straight for the ticket office. Saranda wore a dark wig, wrapped with a long white silk scarf that she'd thrown over her shoulder and across the lower half of her face. Mace slanted his fedora down to cover his eyes. Dressed in a white linen suit to escape the stifling bayou heat, he looked cool and distinguished, a far cry from Tommy Ward of the traveling troupe. Saranda envied him. In the heat, the wig felt heavy and oppressive. She couldn't wait to find a hotel room and yank it off. To run her hands through her own freshly washed hair, relishing the feel of freedom from restraint. To lie naked on cool sheets behind shutters that kept out the glare, the insects, the heat.

The shipping office swarmed with people. "Good, it's busy," Mace said quietly. "Less opportunity to be noticed."

"Let's accomplish this with a minimum of fuss, shall we? I can't wait to get out of these clothes."

He angled his head and looked at her through shaded eyes. "Is that a proposition?"

She could feel the heat of his gaze spark in her loins. All the way to New Orleans, both had become keenly aware of the change in their relationship. The next time they touched, it would be with a new awareness, a new emotional intimacy. At last they would come together as lovers, vowed to heal the ravages of their souls. Yet each time they looked at one another, there was an awareness of what hadn't been spoken. Lance still stood between them. Nothing regarding him had really changed. So they kept putting it off, embracing action as a way of avoiding the inevitable.

"A proposition? That depends on how well you perform today," she replied lightly.

"An interesting choice of words." He smiled. "I assure you, I can perform equally well—day or night."

"You might want to keep your mind on the job at hand. I should hate to be killed before—"

"Before . . . ?"

"Before we're afforded an opportunity to test your boasts."

He grinned. "I assure you, love. I have no intention of allowing anything to interfere with that. As to boasts—"

"You're mighty bold, all of a sudden, I must say."

He was looking at her with a gentle gleam in his eyes. "Perhaps it's the thought of not having to run anymore. Of being alone with you on a ship bound for New York—locked in a cabin with nothing else to do."

She shivered at the thought of it. It was what she'd wanted for so long. Yet . . .

"We'd better get those tickets or the ship will sail without us," she threatened, her voice teasing.

She took his arm, slapped it when his hand circled her waist and dropped lower for a quick caress of her backside, then settled her face in respectable lines and walked inside with him.

There was a line of ten or more people purchasing tickets for a riverboat sailing up the Mississippi that afternoon. Saranda took the opportunity to look around her. There were a number of men at the counters lining the windows, most of them dressed like Mace in light linen suits, some reading newspapers, some checking schedules, one or two writing out what looked like bank drafts with the pen and inkwell provided. No one looked suspicious, no one seemed to be paying undue attention to her or anyone else. Yet she felt Mace stiffen beside her. When she looked up at him, she noticed he was frowning thoughtfully.

"What is it?" she asked.

"I don't know," he muttered as if he hadn't truly heard her but was still lost in thought. She watched as he casually glanced about the room. On the surface, everything appeared quiet. Nothing suspicious. Nothing out of the ordinary. Yet she could feel his muscles tighten beneath her hand, as if he was readying himself for flight.

He's just being cautious, she told herself. There's nothing to fear.

Yet her pulse was racing by the time they stepped up to the window. The ticket agent looked from one to the other questioningly. Mace nudged her with his elbow, encouraging her to speak.

"We'd like two tickets to New York, please," she said in her best mid-Atlantic accent. "Day after tomorrow."

"New York, you say?"

There was nothing overt in the agent's eyes. Just the slightest hesitation as he glanced toward the far windows. Instantly, Mace's hand tightened on her arm. "Let's go," he whispered.

Before she could blink, he'd jerked her away and was running, dragging her behind, to the door.

In the surprise of it, she barely had time to glance around. In doing so, she caught a flash of one of the white-suited men drawing a pistol from his breast pocket and aiming it at them while two other men leapt from their stations in pursuit.

As Mace slammed the door behind them, the instinct for survival flooded her veins. He dropped her arm and took hold of her hand in one swift motion. Held with an unrelenting grip, spurred on by the power of his stride, she flew across the wide boulevard and into the nearby street, her feet barely seeming to touch the pavement.

Strangers to the city, they ran blindly. Moving into the Vieux Carré, they skirted narrow streets lined with old brick buildings and balconies of wrought-iron lace. Heavy scents of food and something more earthy spiced the air. Walls of aging stucco rolled by them as they headed through alley after alley, hearing the voices of men in hot pursuit. Once, as they reached the end of a street, a gunshot rang out and pieces of brick shattered inches from

Saranda's head. Catching sight of the gunman in a nearby entryway, Mace glanced at a stone wall twelve feet high.

"Get over it," he ordered.

She looked up at the wall, choking with the knowledge that she could never climb it. Her fear of heights froze her in place, even as the man raised his gun to fire again.

Mace, however, didn't pause. He shoved her up from the knees so she was forced to clutch the top of the barrier or fall. Scrambling to keep her legs beneath her, she closed her eyes as the ground began to spin. In spite of the danger, she was paralyzed.

"Move!" he called to her. "Jump down on the other side."

"I can't."

"What do you mean, you can't?"

She looked back at him, and he saw her panic. "*I can't!*"

Crouching, he took an acrobatic leap into the air that landed him nicely on top of the enclosure just as a bullet put a hole in the bricks six inches below. In a single motion, he put his hands to the top and swung himself down to land, as easily as a cat, on his feet below.

"Jump into my arms," he called.

"Are you daft?"

Another bullet sounded closer, this one catching her skirt and ricocheting off the wall. She knew she had only two choices: Jump and be saved—or stay there and die. She wanted to live, yet she was so petrified, she couldn't bring herself to move.

"What is it?" he shouted.

"I'm scared of heights."

He looked at her for a moment as if he couldn't comprehend what he was hearing. "A fine time to tell me," he grumbled.

The gunman was moving closer. She glanced back to

see him approaching, raising his gun again. "You might as well give yourself up, Miss Sherwin," he called out as he carefully took aim. "We have you surrounded. You'll never make it out of here alive."

She knew, in that moment, that it was true. "Go on without me," she told Mace over her shoulder. "I can't do it."

Then she felt a whoosh of air beside her. Turning, she saw Mace crouching next to her as if he'd flown on to the top of the wall. He turned his back to her. "Get on."

"What?"

"Get on and hold tight."

"I ca—"

He grabbed her arms, jerked them around his neck, and settled her on his back. Then, without so much as an instant of preparation, he leapt into the air as their pursuer was taking aim just below.

Her arms convulsed around him. The ground rushed up to meet them. The sensation of floating through air terrified her, yet morbidly she couldn't close her eyes. To do so would mean some loss of control. Instead, she clutched him so tightly about the neck that by the time they'd landed, he was choking. He had to pry her hands loose from his throat and slide her down his back.

For a moment, her legs wobbled so she couldn't stand. Gripping his arm to find her balance, she slapped at it with all her might. "Don't ever do that again!" she screamed, panting and clutching her stomach.

"Would you prefer a bullet in your back?"

It was beginning to dawn on her that she was safely on the ground, that their pursuer was a very high wall away. She looked back at the rampart, fighting to breathe. Clammy perspiration caused her stays to cling damply to her ribs, cutting off her breath.

"We're safe?" she cried.

"For the moment. Remind me, though, never to save your life again."

Her panic was receding. "Did I give you the impression I was ungrateful?"

"I have the bruises to show it."

He was looking about them. They stood now in an equally short, narrow street, with only one exit straight ahead. Another street bisected it, forming a dead end. If someone were to block it, they'd be surrounded front and back, with tall buildings on either side. They could hear footsteps all around, and the angry shouts of the man they'd just left behind. Lucky for them, Saranda thought, he wasn't the athlete Mace Blackwood was. *No man was.*

Just then, a closed black carriage drew up, blocking the exit. Mace caught her hand, stilling her. The shades were drawn, hiding the person inside. It could be anyone.

He looked around again. Alone, he might scale the side buildings. But with Saranda, it was impossible. They were caught in a trap, boxed in from all sides.

The carriage door opened. They could see a masculine hand and part of an arm, but nothing else. "There's no time," said a low voice. "Get in."

CHAPTER 40

Mace guided Saranda behind him, shielding her with the mass of his body, as they cautiously approached the carriage. She could almost feel the wheels in his brain working, anticipating ways of extricating them from a threatening situation. Trying to figure out who might be lurking in the shadows of the closed coach.

"Hurry up, for Chrissakes. They're on my tail as it is."

Mace and Saranda exchanged puzzled glances. Impatiently, the man stuck his head out the door.

"Bat!" cried Saranda, dropping Mace's hand and running to him. "What are you doing here?"

"I figured you'd be in New Orleans by now, and I thought you might need some help."

He gestured them inside. Saranda took the empty seat, and Mace sank in beside her. The gesture wasn't lost on Bat.

"How long have you been here?"

"A week or so. They've been watching the shipping office all that time. I staked it out myself, hoping you'd come along. I had to warn you. They're looking for you everywhere. There isn't a safe way out of town."

"Any word from New York?"

"The pressure's building. The closer he comes to this deadline, the bigger the reward offered and the more men this McLeod sends out to find you. I'd watch my back."

"We will. Thanks."

Bat noticed her casual use of the word "we" and exhaled heavily.

"I took the liberty of getting you some tickets. They're expecting you to head for New York. There's a riverboat leaving today for St. Louis. You can't board in town—they'll be watching for you. This carriage will take you upriver to where you'll board. I'd change costumes in case they've wired ahead what you're wearing."

He rapped on the roof of the carriage with his cane, and the driver pulled to a halt. Opening the door, he stepped down. Saranda followed, closing the door behind them and moving a few steps away.

"How can I thank you for coming?"

He took her hand. "I don't suppose you'd run off to Mexico with me?"

He said it half-jokingly, but she sensed the serious-ness of his proposal. "Bat—"

He caught the way she glanced back at the carriage, back at Blackwood.

"I have to help Mace now."

Mace. No longer *that bloody Blackwood.* "I see." He peered at her closely. "What about Lance? Have you thought about that?"

"Lance . . . is something we shall have to work out in our own time."

"I know how much you hate him. How long you've hated all the Blackwoods. I just hope you *can* work it out."

"I'm sorry," she said, feeling helpless. "About Mexico. About everything—"

"Well, I tried." He handed her the tickets. "You just call me if you need me, promise?"

It was clear he thought her chances with Mace were minimal. Not that she could blame him. Too often, she still thought so herself.

He opened the door and handed her inside, then watched as she gave the tickets to Mace.

"How can we thank you?" Mace asked. Again, Bat flinched at the use of "we."

"Don't ever let me hear about you hurting her," he said. Then he closed the door, and the carriage lurched away.

CHAPTER 41

The riverboat cabin was gaudily luxurious. Decorated in gold with accents in bright jewel tones of ruby, emerald, and sapphire, it looked to Saranda's eyes like the captain's quarters on a pirate ship. The walls were papered in watered silk. The four-poster bed was curtained in brocade and fringed in gold silk rope. Thick Persian rugs warmed the wood floor. To the side was a small sitting room with a camelback gold settee and matching chairs with an assortment of needlework pillows so colorful they gave the impression of artfully strewn gems.

From their portholes came the lulling wash of the river as it churned and cascaded over the wheel. The rhythm of the boat was soothing, a creeping along of such grace and elegance, it seemed to belong to days gone by. Saranda felt she'd been transported back in time, as if she were hovering in some enchanted world where reality wouldn't dare intrude.

Mace seemed to feel it, too. Stripped of his jacket,

looking sleek and predatory in white shirt and pants that molded themselves to his athletic frame, he came to her and pulled the wig from her head. His strong fingers tangled in the silver hair beneath, reminding her of the night in his office—in Archer's office—when he'd done the same after removing her hairpins and dropping them to the floor. That night, he'd shown her, for the first time in her life, that she could respond to a man as powerfully as a woman could—as long as she didn't look him in the face.

"No sultan ever had it so good," he said, his gaze sweeping over the decor.

"I don't know about that. From what I hear, sultans have their pick of women," she teased.

"If that's so, call me sovereign of all I survey," he parried back.

"Careful, darling. I might take that to mean you'd choose me above all others."

"I would choose you," he said, rubbing his thumb along her lip, "were I the only man alive, with all the women of the earth at my feet."

"*All* women? Even Pilar?"

She didn't know what it was that made her say it. What goaded her to spoil the mood by bringing up his past? The instant she said it, she knew it was a dreadful mistake. His eyes clouded over, his hands fell from her, and he turned from her so abruptly, she stumbled a little when he suddenly wasn't there.

"What do you know of that?" he asked quietly.

"I know you were posing as a British earl in Italy—wooing some Italian *contessa*, wasn't it? When you were spirited away by Pilar and her men. I know you disappeared for months after that. Rumor was, Pilar's charms were more distracting than even the *contessa*'s jewels." She paused, then pressed on. She had to know. "I can understand the *contessa*, Mace, but what kind of con did Pilar fit into?"

Slowly, he turned around and looked at her as if he'd never seen her before. As if she were the most heartless creature he'd ever known. "Pilar was part of no con. I loved her with all my heart and soul."

It was the last thing she'd expected, and the last she wanted to hear. The pain of it made her feel alone in a world she suddenly couldn't comprehend. Anger gripped her heart. But she wasn't angry with Mace. Rather, she felt consumed by self-loathing. She'd purposely hurt him, and she didn't know why.

"Never mind, Mace. You don't have to tell me. I didn't bring it up to hurt you. Or perhaps I did. I'm ashamed of having done so. In fact, I'm rather sorry I brought it up at all," she confessed shakily.

"Nevertheless, having brought it up, you shall hear the entire story."

He spoke bitterly, but there was no malice in his voice, no forceful intonation. He spoke as a man who'd been so deeply saddened by this part of his life that he seemed apart from it—as if relating a tale he'd heard of someone else.

"As you've said, I was passing myself off as one of the aristocracy. Something I'd done with great success throughout Europe."

"I remember." *The greatest lover in all of Europe. Made the ladies of the aristocracy swoon and beg for more.*

He clenched his hands behind his back and began to pace the room.

"One day we were attacked by what we assumed to be bandits, but who, it turned out, were actually revolutionaries. I was wounded in the scuffle. Badly. While I lay unconscious, they took me—with the intention of holding me for ransom. I think I was out for several days. It's difficult to recall. All I know is, one night I opened my eyes, and there before me was the most—" He paused, savoring the memory. Then, shaking his head as if to clear it, he continued. "The most amazing woman. The fiercest-looking woman I'd ever seen, but engagingly so. All wild black hair and flashing eyes. Half-Spanish, half-Italian, she had —something. An air about her that said, beautiful as she was, *this* was a woman of immeasurable substance. A little slip of a thing, she was, but she could command men with a single insolent lift of her brow."

"I'm not sure I want to hear this."

He gave her a hard look. "Correct me if I'm wrong. Weren't you the one who forced the issue?" When she sighed and sank into a chair, he went on. "Her name was Pilar, I soon learned. She was the leader of this band of revolutionaries. She spat abuse at me day and night, calling me an aristocratic swine and worse. I finally told her that the joke was on her. Told her who I really was. When she didn't believe me, I sat back and laughed and waited for her to discover it on her own. She did discover it, in time. That I was no more blue-blooded than she was. Although I was complimented that she believed the act."

"Naturally," Saranda murmured.

"When they discovered I was telling the truth, they didn't know what to do with me. There was little point in killing me, since I wasn't part of the class they were fighting. It left them in rather a quandary. But as I'd recuperated, I had ample time to observe them, to question their goals. I began to admire their dedication to their cause, their desire to aid the underdog, and most of all, their ideals. I came to see that they genuinely wanted to help the poor people of their country and were willing to risk their lives daily that others might find a better existence. I'd never met anyone like them before."

"So you fell in love with Pilar."

"Yes," he said softly. "I loved her and saw for the first time what a sham my life had been. That I'd been wasting my talents on selfish pursuits when I could have channeled them into something that, like Pilar and her revolutionaries, would help others. So I joined forces with them. I suggested we ask the *contessa* for the planned ransom—she'd pay generously, I knew—then sent out the word that I'd been killed trying to escape, once the money was procured. I knew Chiara—the *contessa*—would assume I'd escaped trying to get back to her arms. She'd always wanted romance above all else, so what better to bestow on her as a parting gift than a romantic fantasy she could cherish for the rest of her days?"

"Indeed." She stood up, moved to a side table, and picked up a small yellow vase, studying it intently so she didn't have to look him in the face. "So you—the world's greatest flimflam artist, who'd spent years comfortably gracing the beds of aristocratic women—joined forces with those who fought against the very class that had supported you all those years."

"Something like that. It changed me. Because of Pilar, I began to see the world through different eyes. She was a passionate warrior, but also the most compassionate person I'd ever encountered. She taught me—" He stumbled, caught himself, and forced out the words. "She taught me to care about people, and about what happened to them."

The pieces were beginning to fall into place. "It must have been a wonderful time for you."

"It was," he said simply, "the happiest time of my life."

"What happened? Why didn't you stay?"

He took a harsh breath, struggling to coax air into his lungs. "I stayed as long as I could. We were happy, we had a mission, a purpose. We were very much in love. Then, one day, Pilar told me I was going to be a father."

The small vase in her hand broke beneath the sudden pressure of her grip. She began to tremble so badly, she didn't notice the blood on her palm where she'd cut herself.

He looked at her with eyes still shocked by the memory of the night of her tarot reading. "You *knew* it had to do with a child. How did you know?"

Helplessly, she shook her head. She heard in his voice the sorrow that already told her what she needed to know. What she suddenly didn't want to know.

"What happened?" she asked again, her voice choked.

"Someone turned us in. We were surprised in the middle of the night by soldiers. They burst into the camp, blasting away. Pilar was killed, along with some of her men. I wanted to stay so they could kill me as well, but the others dragged me away. The next day we went back and found Pilar's body. They'd raped and abused—" His voice broke and he turned away.

Saranda went to him, put her hands on his shoulders, and rested her head on his back. "I'm so sorry. So terribly, terribly sorry."

She held him for several minutes in silence, willing her compassion to warm and soothe him. "Did you ever find out who betrayed you?" she asked.

"No. When I was coherent enough to ask questions, I was satisfied that it was no one in camp. Unless, of course, it was someone who'd been killed."

"What did you do after that?"

"Stayed with them and fought like a demon. A few months later, the revolution was over. Most of the men had been captured or killed. Pilar and the baby were dead. There was no longer any reason to stay. But I was never the same after that. I came to see myself as an enemy to the upper classes everywhere. I was haunted by the idea that there must be something I could do—something that would be of lasting value. That wouldn't just fade into distant memory like Pilar and her men."

It could have been her father talking. Mace despised the inhumanity of the world as much as her father ever had. All her life, she'd thought of the Blackwoods as enemies of the Sherwins. Yet *this* Blackwood was more like her beloved father than anyone she'd ever met.

"Is that why you were conning the Van Slykes? Because they were the American equivalent of aristocracy?"

He turned and looked at her as if she were crazy. "Who says I was conning the Van Slykes?"

She didn't understand what he was saying. "I assumed—you used the name Archer—I just—"

"At first, yes, it started out as a flam of sorts. When I arrived in New York, still grieving over Pilar, I heard the Van Slykes owned a newspaper that claimed to stand up for the poor and downtrodden. I thought this must be the biggest hoax of all. They were no doubt stuffy rich gents pretending to care as a means of stuffing their already bulging pockets. So I decided to infiltrate their ranks as Archer and work diligently to see that they actually carried out their phony aims. The surprise, of course, was how genuine they were. That they really cared. I was, you could say, as seduced by their dedication as I was by Pilar's—but in a different manner. Somewhere along the way, I became not just a part of the team but the driving force that pushed the paper into exposing wrongs it might never have dared. The Van Slykes were humanitarians, but they were sometimes not quite bold enough in their actions. I managed to change all that. And found a family of sorts in the bargain."

"Until I came along," she whispered.

"Until you came along. I knew who you were, naturally. I knew you'd been trailing me across two continents.

And I vowed not to let you take the Van Slyke money without a fight."

She stared at him. "Let me get this straight. *You* were protecting the Van Slykes from *me?*"

"Naturally. What did you think I was doing?"

Suddenly, she began to laugh. "*I* was protecting them from *you!*"

He smiled then. "It seems there have been some serious misunderstandings all around. Have you a suggestion as to how we might set things right?"

His eyes, so tormented moments ago, softened tenderly as he looked into hers. She stretched up and kissed him. "Thank you for telling me. I knew there were depths to you I hadn't begun to explore, but I had no idea you were so—"

"So what?"

"So wonderful."

He grinned. "I'm delighted you think so."

"Only—" She hesitated.

"What, Princess?"

"Must I worry? About Pilar, I mean?"

"That I pine for her and the child?"

"Yes."

He was quiet. "I think a part of me grieves for them still," he began. "Just as a part of you grieves for your child. I spent years in self-recrimination, thinking I could have done something to prevent her death. But if you're asking me if my loving Pilar affects the way I feel for you . . ."

"That is exactly what I'm asking."

He took her face in both hands. "Ah, sweetheart, you're the first happy thing that's happened to me since."

She felt surrounded by a lovely warmth as she went into his arms, as if she were snuggling into a soft blanket on a bitter-cold day. She didn't want to spoil what they'd found. She wanted to cherish this feeling of acceptance, of love. But she believed she had to say something. If they were ever truly going to trust each other, she had to bring it out in the open once and for all. "If only all my questions could be answered so readily," she murmured.

It was a moment before he spoke. She felt the muscles in his arms tense and knew she was treading dangerous waters. But she couldn't stop now. Something compelled her to seek the truth.

"Questions," he asked, "or doubts?"

"Doubts." Her voice was barely audible.

"What doubts, Princess?"

She swallowed hard. "Mace, have you ever considered that it may have been Lance who betrayed you? Who told the soldiers where you were? Who was responsible for the death of your child and the woman you loved?"

CHAPTER 42

He stiffened as if she'd thrust a knife into his back. "Never!" He shoved her away from him.

She was startled by his stubbornness. "How can you know for sure? You *knew* he was alive. Failure as a bluff man that he was, it couldn't have pleased him that you were abandoning the con. I should imagine he came to think of you as his bread and butter. Tell me, what did he say when you told him you were giving up the life to fight with a band of idealistic revolutionaries?"

He refused to answer.

"Mace, remember the night I gave you that tarot reading? Remember my confusion? The cards told me Lance was responsible for the loss of your child. I thought I had to be mistaken."

"Fortune-telling," he scoffed.

"Then you tell me," she persisted. "Who else could it have been? Who coveted you enough to want to keep you with him? Who needed you to cover his messy mistakes? Who would have felt the most threatened by Pilar?"

"I don't believe it. I *can't* believe it."

"Because you don't want to?" she asked quietly.

"Because I know he wouldn't do it. You don't know him the way I do. You don't know what he did for me."

It was torture, asking him. She didn't care what Lance had suffered. She didn't care what had made him the monster he was. But she *did* care about Mace. "Tell me." When he turned and gave her a questioning look, she went to him and gently touched his arm. "I love you, Mace. I need to know everything, if we have any hope at all of—"

"Very well. It happened in London, when we were quite young. I was teaching Lance to pick pockets. I saw a man and thought I recognized him as someone likely to have enough cash to make it worthwhile. I sent Lance out to pick his pocket. It turned out the man was the high inspector—the toughest constable in London. A man famous for his cruelty. The one man you'd never want to get caught by. And I sent my kid brother out to pick his pocket."

He began to pace again, filling the cabin with his size. "It was a two-man deal. I was to bump into him, and Lance was to pick his pocket while he was distracted. But of course the inspector knew at once what was happening. I recognized that fact and took off, but Lance was always slow on the uptake. The inspector hauled him off to the police station. I followed and listened from outside the window."

He raked a hand across his jaw. Saranda said nothing. She was afraid if she said anything that he'd stop talking.

"They began to beat him, badgering him between blows. 'Tell me who put you up to it,' they kept saying. I pressed myself against the wall and willed Lance to use his head. Remember what I taught you, I reminded him. Tell them anything. *Flam them, for Chrissake.* But Lance was so stubborn, he wouldn't tell them anything. Even when they promised to let him go."

By now, he couldn't stand still. He stalked about the cabin like a caged tiger. Still, Saranda listened.

"They beat him for *hours.* I kept thinking I should turn myself in, but I knew it wouldn't do any good. They were lying when they said they'd let Lance go. As long as I was on the outside, I had a chance of getting him out. If I joined him— I don't know. Maybe I should have given myself up."

"You know better than that."

"I thought I did. But when I finally saw him, I couldn't help wishing I had. They beat him till he was nearly dead. This belligerent runt who wouldn't give in. The next day, they tossed him out in the gutter like so much rubbish. His eye was half out of its socket and nearly blind. Some of his teeth were missing. I could barely recognize his face, it was so—"

He stopped, his voice choked up. Then he went on. "I took him to the physician and had his eye sewn back, but he was never the same." He turned and looked at her. "You have to understand. He did that for me. To protect *me.* Can't you see how touched I was by that? He would have died rather than see me hurt. If you could have seen him at that moment—such devotion—he was so beaten, so heroic . . . I never got over the courage he'd shown. In spite of the fact that he was so pathetic and untalented as a flam man, he refused to give in. It was the bravest thing I'd ever seen in my life."

"Much like your feelings later for Pilar."

He hadn't thought of that—she could see it in the startled flicker of his eyes. "Perhaps. I didn't think anyone in my whole family had the courage to do anything so noble and unselfish. I'm not sure I ever would have. Right then and there, as I waited for the doctor to tell me if he'd live or die, I made a sacred vow. I vowed to protect Lance for the rest of his life."

"Is that why you broke him out of prison after he killed the American?"

"Of course. I meant to rescue my parents as well, but I wasn't in time. But at least I'd saved Lance. I couldn't bear to think of anything happening to him. I could never again look at him without recalling what he'd done for me —the look of worship in his one good eye even as he lay hurt and dying. I can't ever look at that eye without remembering his awful beating, and why he took it."

"I see," she said softly. "But, Mace, even the worst people are capable of great moments."

The look he gave her was racked with pain, his torn loyalties obvious. "I tell you, I can't even think of him without remembering. I'm not stupid. I know it's mostly illusion. I know he's done some terrible things, things I could never understand. But there's goodness in him, Saranda. I know it because I've seen it firsthand."

"It may be *in* him, but it's buried deep, in a hundred deceptions. He's far more cruel than he is kind. And I know that because *I've* seen it firsthand. He may have saved your life, but he ruined mine," she finished, her words devastating to him.

"You know if we're to have a future, we must put Lance behind us."

"I don't know how to do that. Not when you refuse to see the truth."

"What truth is that, Princess?" he asked wearily.

"That Lance is the demon of both of us. Until you realize that, there's no hope."

He took her arms in his hands and held her so

tightly, she trembled. "Don't say that, dammit. You're the first hope I've had in longer than I can remember."

"Don't you think I want to believe it? But you have to understand me, Mace. You can't look at his face without remembering what he did for you? Well, I can't look at *you* without recalling what he did to *me*. I know what it's like to live your life consumed by guilt because of what Lance Blackwood did. But how do you expect me to separate the two of you, when you can't even separate yourselves?"

CHAPTER 43

"So it's Lance that stands between us," he said quietly.

"You know it is."

"You can't forget what he's done."

"Would you expect that I could?"

"You can't make love to me without thinking of him."

She dropped her head, avoiding his eyes.

"You can't even look me in the face without seeing *his* face. Is that it?"

"Yes. I keep seeing him laughing at me as he hurt me. Seeing that awful glint in his eye. Like a rabid dog, tearing at my throat. Not caring what I was feeling, just taking his pleasure—if in his sick mind he even called it that—at my expense. You have that happen to you, then tell me you could look at the madman's brother and not remember."

"Yet you have little trouble looking at me at other times."

She didn't understand him.

"Times other than those when you're—aroused by my presence?"

She hadn't ever realized it, but it was true. "You're right."

He came closer. "So it's my touching you that causes this confusion."

"I'm hardly confused."

"What would you call it when a woman looks at a man who loves her and sees his brother instead?"

"Hopeless."

"Hopeless is not a word in my vocabulary. Not, that is, since meeting you."

"Do I inspire you then?" she asked, unable to resist a coy tilt of her head.

"You—inspire me in a number of ways." His voice, now hushed, sent chills up her spine. He moved closer still, used his hands to part the curtain of her silvery hair, slipped them beneath to grasp the sides of her neck. His touch was magic. Instantly, she felt the familiar wanting that had made her weak from the first. The effect on her no other man had ever had. She never ceased to marvel at the spontaneous leap of her flesh beneath his hands, at the responding vault of her heart within her breast. Her breath caught like a trapped butterfly in her throat. Yet when she raised her lashes and looked up at him, once again she saw Lance Blackwood's cursed face.

On the verge of tears, she turned her head away.

"I see," he said quietly, and dropped his hands.

She felt desperately alone when he stepped aside, adrift like a buoy in a restless sea. She wanted him with an inconsolable longing. Yet—

What was the use? Why go over it again? And again . . . and again . . .

"But you do want me?" he asked thoughtfully, sounding more like a scientist in the midst of an experiment than a man rejected.

"That's the worst of it. If I didn't want you, we wouldn't have a problem. Or—if I didn't love you," she whispered.

He raised a derisive brow. "It's your love for me that keeps you from my bed?"

"Maybe I always loved you. God knows, I didn't want to. There was a time when I didn't realize my feelings for you, so it was easy. You were a mark—nothing more, nothing less. I set my sights on you, and I was quite willing, thank you, to do whatever was necessary to bring you to your knees."

"Would that help? Were I to drop to my knees?"

"Don't be ridiculous. I don't want you cowering before me. Do you think I relish your fear of my refusal? The very thing that attracted me in the first place was the sort of man you are. A man who boldly took what he wanted. A man clever enough to outwit anyone in the room. Sly enough to fool them all. You see, I'm completely enamored of the confidence man in you. In spite of my father's wishes that I marry outside the profession, I can't help thrilling at your exploits. You're—everything my father didn't want for me."

"I'm everything you loved about your father. And more."

"Quite an assumption, that you're more than my father at anything."

"I'm assuming your feelings for me aren't daughterly in nature."

She blushed. "Not exactly."

"So, you despise the fact that I'm a confidence man, yet that's also what you love about me. Do I have it straight?"

"I despise the fact that you're a *Blackwood*! Nothing more."

"Ah, so we're back to that. But you were saying? Something about loving me and the problems that entails."

"When I didn't love you, I could close my eyes and sleep with you for the sense of control it gave me. It's always been that way. Once I'd been—manhandled—by your brother, I used the enticement of my body as a way of controlling men. Vowing never to get myself into a position of weakness again. So I gritted my teeth and made my *partners* weak with wanting *me*."

"Forgive me, love, but your responses to my attentions were hardly teeth-gritting."

Their eyes met, and a spark flared between them that they could feel from across the room. "I responded to you in spite of my best resolves. But things have changed, Mace. You're not asking me to share your bed. You're asking me to *make love* with you. I've never made love to a man. I don't even know how."

"You could certainly have fooled me," he murmured.

"I've slept with men when there wasn't any way to avoid it. Only as the very last of resorts. But I've never *made love* to anyone. Oh, this is an absurd conversation. I'm feeling embarrassed—not to mention awkward—about the whole thing."

She couldn't seem to figure out what to do with her hands.

He was still watching her thoughtfully, but there was a gentle amusement in his eyes. "Don't be embarrassed. It's charming. A flam woman caught with her drawers down—so to speak. I'm enough my father's son to enjoy the view."

"It's the fact that you're your father's son that's keeping my drawers on."

He continued watching her for a moment as she

moved restlessly around the cabin. "Then we shall have to do something about that."

"Whatever's to be done?"

"As I understand, it isn't so much that I'm a flam man that disturbs you. It isn't strictly that I'm a Blackwood, either. But rather that I'm *Lance* Blackwood's brother. And that being intimate with me brings back memories of the atrocities you suffered at my brother's hands."

"Yes, but—"

"And this only happens when you're in a state of arousal, which—fortunately or unfortunately—seems to occur with alarming regularity."

"Yes, so—"

"Then it's the association we must deal with."

"The—association?" She was confused—and intrigued.

"You know, we associate all sorts of things with other things. A brandy after a good meal. A cigarette after a rousing tumble in the sheets. A boy's hand is slapped for lying, and he believes falsehood to be wrong. But if he's *rewarded*—well, it's a different matter altogether. In the right hands, it becomes an art form."

"I can't say I like the look in your eyes."

"*Have* I a particular look in my eyes?"

"Would I comment on it if you didn't?"

He seemed suddenly in a boisterously good mood, as if he'd just figured out the answer to the question of the ages. He was looking about the room, running his hand ruminatively over the gold braiding along the curtains of the bed, picking up pillows from the settee and weighing them in his hand.

"What are you up to?" she asked suspiciously. Her instincts told her he had something brewing—something not necessarily to her liking.

Stepping into the bedroom, he glanced about, then went to the dresser and picked up the long white scarf she'd worn earlier that day. She watched as he drew the undulating silk with infinite slowness through the large fist of his hand.

"Are you attached to this?" he asked idly.

"You know in our business you never become attached to anythi—"

Spreading the foot-long width taut between his hands, he tested its strength, put it to his teeth, bit a tiny tear, then yanked down the length of it so he'd rent it in two.

"What in God's name are you doing?" she cried.

He sat on the edge of the bed. "Come here, Princess," he said, patting the mattress beside him.

She approached him cautiously, her hands thrust behind her back.

"Come, sit beside me."

She lowered herself with care next to him, sitting with her back ramrod straight. Before she'd had a chance to settle, he took her waist in his hands, and as easily as if she were a doll, lifted her up and back so she rested with her spine against the headboard of the bed. She felt suddenly enclosed, with the gold brocade canopy above and the curtains at the sides.

"What are you doing?" she asked as he reached beneath her and fluffed the pillows, inserting them behind her, shifting her legs so they lay easily along the length of the bed.

"Making you comfortable. Are you?"

"More curious than comfortable, frankly."

"Would you like more pillows?"

"I should like to know once and for all what you're about."

He took one of the lengths of silk and pulled it taut

between his fists. Pausing a moment, he looked into her eyes, and she was blasted back against the headboard. In spite of his bantering tone, the look in his eyes was intense, full of a resolute heat that spoke of powers that would be slowly, inexorably, unleashed. Suddenly, a panic gripped her heart.

"Teaching you the difference between my brother and myself," he told her in an unrelenting voice.

Then he fastened the scarf to her wrist and, with a bold tug, tied it to the bedpost.

CHAPTER 44

"Be a good girl," he said, "and give me your other wrist. I shouldn't like to hurt you."

She stared at him with disbelieving eyes. "Are you mad?"

"Not that I know of. But I suppose, as with everything else, that's a matter of opinion."

"I shan't give you my wrist. You must be as crazy as Lance to think I—"

He took her chin in his hands and held her tight, cutting off her words. "I told you. I intend showing you I'm not my brother. But I need your cooperation."

"I won't cooperate. You want to tie me to this bed like a—hog on a spit—and rape me, to show me how unlike your brother you are?"

"This is not about rape, and you know it. If you cooperate, as requested, no such vulgarity need enter into it. Now do as I say and give me your other wrist."

She thrust it behind her back. "No."

"Then," he said with a reluctant shrug, "I shall have to take it."

He stood and rounded the foot of the bed to the other side. As he did, she began to claw at the silk tie with her other hand, fighting to loosen the bond on her left wrist. Before she could budge it, however, he reached across, took her arm in a fist of iron, and patiently dragged it to the other side. There, in spite of her struggles, he tied it to the other bedpost, allowing the long sash to lie across her palm. Then he stood back to observe his handiwork, crossing his arms over his massive chest.

"Yes," he murmured, "that should do nicely."

Furious, she grabbed hold of the dangling white silk and balled her hands into trembling fists, pulling with a frantic strength against the ties that bound her. Panic engulfed her. The helplessness of her situation tasted like bile in her throat. She was at his mercy. More than that, she was all too aware of her vulnerability. For, love him as she did, she'd never been able to bring herself to trust him.

"I shan't cooperate," she spat at him, kicking her legs. "You'll have to prove yourself the louse your brother is by taking me by force."

He came and sat beside her. His finger traced the line of her brow, her temple, her cheek, the bridge of her nose. Jerking her head away, she couldn't shake him loose. He put a finger to her chin, turned her head toward him, and looked deeply into her eyes.

"You *are* going to make love to me, Princess," he said quietly. "To me—not Lance. Gently, lovingly, but without question."

She moved her head and bit his finger hard. "I'd rather die! You claim to love me. Yet knowing what you know, you tie me to this bed like some unwilling sacrifice—"

"It's knowing what I know that leaves me no choice."

"You're as mad as your brother."

"Perhaps. But after this night, I vow to you, you'll never look at me and see Lance again."

"I shall never *look* at you again, period."

"*That* will be your choice. The only choice, I might add, that you're to have this night. My brother warped you by what he did. He turned you into a terrified woman who craves control. Over situations, over men, over her life. You never had a chance to learn that control is an illusion. That the fear of losing control has a power over you that will never let you be free. That only by surrendering that need to be on top will you ever truly be in control of yourself and your fears. By allowing, by giving in, by surrendering—only then can you find freedom."

"So it's my freedom you're concerned with," she said furiously.

"It is."

"And what if, at the end of it, I choose freedom from *you?*"

"That's a risk I willingly take."

He put his hand to the flat of her stomach. Instantly, images of that night with Lance flooded her mind. She wrenched away from him, brought her legs around, and kicked him away.

He clutched his side, where her foot had attacked him. "I'm sorry you did that."

Reaching up, he began to rip the gold silk braid from the valance above her head.

"Oh, no," she groaned. "You wouldn't."

"What can I do? I can't have you using these feet like weapons every time I come near."

"I won't. I promise. Only don't—"

He gave her a look. "Are you asking me to trust you?"

"Damn you to hell! Damn you and all the other filthy Blackwoods who ever set foot on this miserable earth. Damn you to eternity and beyond."

As she cursed him with her words, he worked quickly, fastening her legs, spread-eagle, to the posts at the foot of the bed.

Even when he stepped aside, she began to squirm like mad, writhing frantically on the bed, pulling rebelliously against her silken shackles.

"That should do you for a spell," he observed, ignoring her histrionics. With a final nod, he picked up his valise and placed it on the dresser.

As he opened the drawer, she stilled.

"What are you doing?"

"Unpacking. Where would you like your things?"

"In hell. With you right along with them."

She continued to struggle and spit at him while he methodically unpacked first his bag, then hers.

Just as he was finishing, there was a knock on the door. They froze, their eyes finding each other's and locking. "Dare I trust you to silence?" he asked.

Her grin was malicious. "You may trust what you will."

With an air of exaggerated reluctance, he took a couple of crisp white handkerchiefs from the drawer where he'd just placed them. Shaking them out, he pried open her clenched teeth, stuffed one kerchief into her mouth, then tied the other over her lips and around the back of her neck, effectively silencing her. Then he moved with unhurried ease to open the cabin door.

"Evening paper, sir?" Saranda heard a male voice ask, soft and lyrical with the inflections of the South.

Mace affected his Yankee accent. "Thank you."

"Should I turn down the bed, sir?"

"Uh—no. The bed is quite satisfactory as it is."

Summoning all her might, Saranda yanked against the ropes and let out a muffled groan.

"What was that, sir?"

Mace glanced inside at the woman whose eyes spat fire at him from the bed. "I'm on my honeymoon. You understand."

"Why, of course, sir. And may I offer my most heart-felt congratulations."

"Thank you again."

"And many years of happiness ahead."

"Yes, well, if my wife remains as she is just now, I daresay it's probable."

"Would you care for a little honeymoon supper, sir?"

"Not a bad idea. We'll have some bread, some cheese, and some wine, if you please. Oh, and a good sharp knife."

"Very well. I'll only be a few moments, sir."

When the door was closed, he approached her with an amused smile. "Naughty girl. I may have to punish you for that." He ignored her venomous look and took a circuit around the room as he waited, hands shoved into his pockets, whistling all the while. Soon there was another knock.

"Your supper, sir."

Mace took the knife, held it up to the light, tested it with his thumb, then said, "Yes, this will do nicely. Thank you."

He paid the steward, took the tray of food, and closed the door.

Having discarded the tray, he returned to the bedroom. Carelessly, he tugged on the end of the gag, and it fell free. She spat the rest of it out, and tried vainly to wet her parched tongue.

"You reprehensible wretch! I only hope that knife is to slit your sorry throat."

Ignoring her, he went back to the sitting room, lit a cigarette, took the paper from under his arm, shook it out, and sat to peruse the contents.

"We've made the evening edition," he commented, as if she weren't tied, spread-eagle and waiting with murder in her heart, upon his bed. "Shall I read it to you?"

"Shall I tell you what I *really* want you to do?"

"Careful, love. I might have to gag you again."

The threat of it silenced her. She still couldn't moisten her tongue.

Time ticked away. The river rushed past. The sunset pinkened and receded, turning the sky lavender, then grey, then a deep midnight blue. She could see the moon from the cabin window, and a smattering of stars. And still he smoked and read, like a satisfied husband home of an evening. When it was necessary, he turned up the lamp and settled himself close to it, turning the paper to the light.

She continued to struggle, trying to loosen her bonds so she might slip from the bed, grab hold of the knife, and plunge it into his unsuspecting back. But he'd tied them so securely, they wouldn't budge. The blood was draining from her arms, leaving them prickly. The more she moved, the more chafed her wrists became.

Occasionally, he'd drop his paper to the table and come over to her, as if testing her mood. Once he asked, "Would you be more comfortable with your shoes off?"

"I should like to fling them at your head."

He removed them anyway. When he began to massage her foot, rubbing out the aches, a shot of longing rushed up her leg and settled in her loins. Angered anew, she kicked at him. But he'd seen the effects of his touch. With a smile, he moved away.

Another time, he came up and experimentally

touched her cheek. When she jerked away, he left as silently as he'd come.

She was, by now, consumed with curiosity. At first, her pride bound her to silence. She'd be damned if she'd give him the satisfaction of asking his intent. But as dusk deepened to night, she began to realize that her struggles, while making a statement, were accomplishing nothing more than wearing her out. Wearily, she dropped her head back on the pillows and swallowed her pride.

"For the love of God, Mace, when are we going to have done with this farce? Have you tied me to this altar just to persecute me with torturous imaginings?"

He came and stood over her. "I've told you. I intend making love to you. So thoroughly"—he ran his finger along the top of her still-clothed breast—"so satisfactorily, so goddamned lovingly, that never again will you feel my touch and think of another man."

"Then when," she asked through gritted teeth, "are you going to get on with it?"

His eyes ran the length of her bound and helplessly offered frame. "When you're ready."

"I shall never be ready."

"Then I'm content to wait. For understand this as you've understood nothing else. This is not a game. Neither is it something to be gotten on with, or gotten *over* with. This, Princess, is to be a night of nights. A night to remember. A night to make poets sing. The most enchanted of all nights when you, my lovely prisoner, will come to me, not with vengeance in your heart. Not with control as your aim. But out of love. When you will see *my* face and call *my* name. Because—and heed me well, my sweet—I shall accept nothing less."

His words had woven a spell, as he'd intended. In them she'd found the will to lose herself in his fantasy. To surrender herself to a confidence man's promise of brighter days. "If only it were possible," she whispered.

"Impossible—"

"Don't tell me. Is not in your vocabulary."

He ran his thumb along her lips and gave her a smile. "Why, Princess. Humor at such a tender moment? I do believe you're ready."

CHAPTER 45

The tray of food was placed, just out of her reach, on the bedside table. Taking the bottle of wine, he tipped it and drank, swallowing several times. Then he put it to her lips and helped her drink. "Better?" he asked.

She nodded. Her anticipation could be felt in every nerve, every fiber, every cell, of her body. Drawn out as the waiting had been, her imagination had taken over, conjuring up all sorts of desperate ruminations about her fate beneath his hands. Her senses felt strangely heightened. She could feel the wine slip cool and quenching down her throat. She could feel it burn along the hollows of her chest. Feel it settle in her stomach to warm and soothe.

Mace took a corner of her blouse in his hand. "Are you attached to *this*?" he asked.

Amusement at his words eased some of the frenzied pulsing in her throat.

"No?" he answered for her. Reaching for the knife,

he cut the blouse away. He tossed it aside and moved on to her skirt. "I trust you're not attached to this, either."

"I have a feeling I won't be for long."

He gave her a wink. "That's the spirit, sweetheart."

A shiver rushed through her as he cut away her skirt, then her drawers, until she was left in nothing but her corset, her chemise, and her stockings. The chemise he split up the middle with the knife, the corset he cut the strings from and yanked from her ribs, the stockings he surveyed with a narrowed eye, then decided to leave alone.

When he was done, she lay before him, bound and vulnerable, clad in nothing but silk stockings, a look of blue fire in her eyes.

He bent and kissed her foot through the delicate silk. Shivers ran up her legs as he kneaded his way up her calf, his lips following in the wake of his hands. Then he attended the other foot, nibbling her toes, running his tongue along the sensitive arch underneath her foot, moving slowly, deliciously, up the length of her calf to her knee. A sigh escaped her.

He rose and shed his shirt. In the meager light, his chest looked enormous, bulging with muscles, lightly covered with thick black hair. It was a body of beauty, of power. A body with no intention of taking no for an answer.

Bare-chested, he knelt between her legs. Leaning low, he took up where he'd left off, nibbling the inner flesh of her knees, raising them, and running his tongue underneath. She began to groan.

His mouth moved upward, playing with the soft, pliant skin of her inner thighs. Moaning audibly now, she shifted her hips, trying to move herself closer to his wickedly roving tongue. Each time she came close, he moved away. Bound as she was, it was impossible to guide him where she would have him.

"You're not in control, remember?"

"How can I forget?"

He bent his mouth to her thigh again, and she closed her eyes. "No, look at me," he said, raising his head. "Watch what I'm doing. Know that it's me who does it."

She tried. But as he bent his head over her pale skin, the memory of another such dark head assaulted her. She saw Lance, turned red as the devil by the light of the fire, loom before her with a deranged and cackling grin. Without so much as a rational thought, she flinched from him, backing with a jerk against the headboard.

Slowly, he lifted his head. She could see the hurt in his eyes. She was trembling, her flesh repelling him even as she longed for his touch.

"Mace," she whispered. "I'm frightened. I don't think I can do this."

He crawled up her body and rested himself upon her. The weight of him strained her wrists against her bonds. Sensing it, he leaned on his elbows and took her face in his hands. "You *can* do this."

"I can't. It's all tied up with the rape—with the fire, with my parents, with the baby. With the wrenching guilt I feel inside."

"That's why you must put it all aside. Just concentrate on me. On what I'm doing. Stop thinking. Just feel."

"I can't. It's those sensations that make me feel this way."

"I'm telling you that you can. Do you know why?"

Miserably, she shook her head.

"Because I love you, Princess. Because I'm not just another man who wants your body for his own selfish pleasure. Because I want your soul. I want to reach inside and heal you. To take away the pain so you can face life again unafraid. Without the need of a mask to hide behind. Because that's all we do. We hide behind one mask, then another. Our lives are a succession of stripping away the masks, only to find another underneath." He paused, his eyes serious. "For once, for one night, let's see what's underneath that final mask. Let's dig like seekers of treasure until we find something that's real."

"Even if what's real is ugly?"

"You listen to me. Nothing you can do—nothing you can say—nothing you can tell me would be ugly to me. I love you. Do you know what that means?"

"No," she whispered. "No one has ever loved me for myself. No one has ever really cared."

"That's in the past. Because you see before you a man who does care. A man who cares, in fact, so much, that he'll go to hell and back, if that's what it takes, to pull you out. I'm not asking you to pretend. If you can't feel passion for me, tell me. If you must curse me, then for God's sake, curse me to the skies and back. Whatever you feel, let me see it. Not what you think I want to see. Make me privy to what's buried deep inside. Somehow or other, together, we shall get through it. Wretched as it may be, painful though it is, you and I shall come out of it together. We shall face what we must together, holding nothing back."

"Is that what it means? To have someone love you? That you must strip yourself naked for their perusal?"

"No, Princess. It means you're safe. It means that nothing and no one can drive me away."

The words echoed through her, reverberating like a moving melody somewhere in her soul.

"Not even Lance?"

"Not even Lance. I'm powerless to change the past. But if nothing else, I can rescue you from what my brother's done."

"Are you asking me to trust you?" she asked lightly, parroting his own phrase.

He held her gaze seriously. "That's exactly what I'm doing."

She searched his eyes. She searched for all the identities she'd known. Archer. Tommy Ward. The greatest rake in all of Europe. She could find no trace of them in those dark, fathomless eyes. All she could see was a sincerity that threatened to break her heart.

He was the best of the best. A con man so good, he'd even conned her. And he was asking her to trust him with her wounded heart.

She took a deep, shaky breath. "You don't know what's inside me. You don't know the depth of my despair."

"Don't I?"

The woman he'd loved had been killed because of him. She and his unborn child. "Perhaps you do," she conceded. "I'm just afraid of scaring you away."

"Faith means nothing when things are easy and predictable, love. To trust is to suspend the tortures of your mind, to cease wondering at the consequences. I tell you with an open heart that you may trust me. Given the circumstances, if you choose otherwise, I shall understand."

He was opening himself to more pain than any man should have to suffer, that he might free her of demons that had driven her, sustained her, for more years than she could remember. He was willing to risk everything for the sake of her well-being. Her happiness. Her trust.

"Given the circumstances, how could I do anything *but* trust you?"

He could have misread her intentions. He could have assumed she meant that, bound as she was, she had no choice. But he didn't. He understood her words for what they were. A decision to risk as much as *he* was risking on a venture that held little save the promise of more pain.

She saw the relief in his eyes. He dropped his head

and lowered his lips to her brow. There he stayed for many moments, savoring the sweetness of her words.

"Then we've already won," he said.

Because her hands were tied, she nudged her head up, forcing him to look at her. "Then kiss me, Mace. You've helped me find the courage to face what we must."

HE DID MORE than kiss her. He showed her, with infinite patience, all that love could be. He caressed her with hands that gentled and soothed. He nuzzled her with lips that inflamed her body and pulled away when she grew afraid. Having been given permission, he took over the reins and drove her to the brink of passion and beyond.

It wasn't easy. They harbored no illusions that it would be. At times, the memories were so stark, she felt she was reliving them again. She cried out against him, fought to free her hands that she might beat against his chest and fight off the demon of his desire. But he put his fingers in her mouth to silence her and made her open her eyes. With her watching, he found her between her legs and caressed her with such consummate skill that she couldn't help but respond. Even when her eyes clouded over and she was on the verge of losing control, he forced her to watch, to lock her gaze on his face. Then, just as she began to feel the welcome tingling of release, he stopped what he was doing, put the flat of his large hand between her breasts, and said, "Bring the energy up here—right into your heart."

At first, she thought he must have lost his mind. But he explained that by allowing the sexual energy to rise, unspent, to the chest, she could open up her heart, and expand her capacity for forgiveness, for love. The greatest lover in Europe, she thought. He must know what he's doing.

After several tries, she was actually able to feel the energy rising. Frustrated because she wanted relief, she nonetheless forced the energy up past her loins and felt it settle in her heart. With his hand upon her chest, his words coaxing her efforts, she was continually snatched from the swirling of senses that she hoped might make her forget. But it wasn't forgetfulness he was after. It was a new awareness of what was transpiring between them.

Then, satisfied by her cooperation, he'd kiss her and begin anew. The midnight moon crept across the sky as still he taught her, with endless forbearance, the patterns of his touch.

She experienced a renewed sense of panic when he slipped inside her at last. By then, she'd almost spent herself countless times, beneath his hands, his lips, with him rubbing against her in preparation for penetration. But not yet had he satisfied his own longings and entered her.

He did so at last, lifting her hips high with his hands, teasing her with the throbbing head before plunging in. Facing him proved more than she could bear. She struggled against the damnable bonds that kept her pliable beneath him. She cried out as if in some agonizing pain. Raising himself up to an upright position, he put his hand to her face. She'd averted her head, and he turned her again, for perhaps the hundredth time, his way.

"Look at me, Princess."

She shook her head.

"*Look at me*," he ordered harshly.

When the fierce command of his strong hand registered his words, she finally dragged her eyes open and sought his face.

"That's it," he said, beginning to thrust into her

again. "Just watch. Just feel. Has anyone else ever felt like this?"

"No one," she gasped, shaking her head. "No one's ever felt so good."

"That's it, darling. Just feel what it's like to have me inside. Look at my eyes. What do you see?"

"I—"

He'd shifted position. He was moving against her so exquisitely, she couldn't find the words. She felt another climax building, felt her mouth began to slacken.

"Do you see malice?"

She shook her head.

"Do I look like I want to harm you?"

Again.

"What do I look like? Tell me."

"Like—you love me."

"That's it, love. Keep looking. Keep remembering this is how love looks."

He reached out and stroked her breasts as he increased his thrusts. Her breath caught in her throat, and her senses once again began to whirl. "Don't look away," he commanded. "Keep looking into my eyes."

She fought to keep her eyes open. He moved his hand and thrust his thumb into her mouth. She sucked on him all the while the sensations built. On the brink of release, he halted, and she felt the joyous flutters drift languorously, of their own volition, up her spine to the very depths of her heart. As they did, she saw in his eyes the approval, the light, the love. And she began to understand, at last, what this wearing night had been about.

"Mace," she whispered, when she'd come back to the bed, where her arms ached beyond endurance and her mind longed for sleep.

He leaned over her, taking her protectively in his arms. "What is it, sweetheart?"

"I can't go on. I'm so tired. I have to sleep."

He was still inside her, still as hard and rigid as a shaft of crystal in some deep, dark cave.

"We're almost there, love. Just a little more."

"*What is it?*" she cried, exasperated, and so exhausted she felt close to tears. "What is it you want from me?"

"You'll know," he promised her. And began anew.

The next time was easier. And the next. Her exhaustion began to release the hold of her mind. Too tired now to think, she abandoned herself, at last, to her feelings. To the sensation of his hot tongue against her breast. To the feel of his fingers tangled in the soft, dewy hair between her thighs. To the empty, aching longing when he withdrew and she was no longer filled with the matchless pressure of him pulsing inside.

And then it happened. The miracle he'd been waiting for. She no longer wanted her freedom so she could rake her nails angrily across his back, or beat him from her when her panic flared. Suddenly, all in a moment, she was consumed by a joy so immeasurable that it seemed to fill her heart and radiate out through every pore. Unbelievably, she felt her heart as a huge, glorious orb, pulsing love and compassion throughout her veins. It was as if she was being overtaken by an incredible surge of love so sweet, so overpowering, that it encompassed all the earth. She felt, for the first time, what it was to forgive.

He was nibbling at her neck when she could finally put voice to her transformation.

"Mace."

He stilled, waiting.

"Untie me."

"We've been over that."

"Untie me, Mace. I want to touch you. It isn't

enough to have you give this to me. I want to give something to you in return."

He looked at her suspiciously. Raising himself up on his knees, he knelt before her, thrusting against her mouth. "It isn't time," he said.

Her tongue was so hungry to taste him, it darted out and lapped at him with rare enthusiasm. She sucked him inside, the glorious throbbing length of him, too big to fit comfortably, yet her mouth seemed to stretch of its own volition, so greedy was it for the taste of him. She sucked hard, yanking at her cords as her fingers itched to touch.

For a moment, he caught his breath. His eyes closed, he moaned deep in his throat. As if the pleasure was so delirious, he couldn't find words to express it. Then, shaking his head like a fighter struggling for endurance, he forced himself away.

"No fair. I warned you. You're to have no control."

She couldn't blame his suspicions. Hours ago—or had it been days, now? She'd lost all sense of time—she'd tried to use her mouth to control *him* instead of the other way around. But she was beyond that now, transported as if by some divine intervention to a longing only to give pleasure in return for the gift he'd given her through the long hours of the night.

"Look in my eyes," she told him.

He did so, with a touch of amusement that she should turn his tactics on him.

"What do you see?"

He frowned.

"Something is different, is it not?"

He kept frowning, as if struggling to define it.

"More specifically, something's missing?"

"Yes . . . that's it. . . ."

"What do you see?"

Still, he couldn't define it.

"I'll tell you. You see a woman who loves you beyond all time and space. A woman who's so grateful to you that she wants to give, in part, as she's received. A woman whose eyes once held the pain of remembrance, but who now can see before her only the man she loves."

His eyes flicked over her face, and she saw a flash of hesitation, as if he wanted so badly to believe that he was afraid to hope.

"Untie me, Mace. Let me show you what you've done for me. Let me make love to *you* for a change."

Cautiously, expecting mutiny at every turn, he unleashed her limbs. As soon as she was free, she turned on him. She could see in his eyes that he expected retribution.

She lunged at him, wrapped her arms around his neck, and kissed him so violently, he fell backward into the shambles of a bed. Still kissing him deeply, she moved over him, rubbing her loins against the strong columns of his legs, running her hands over his chest, his shoulders, anything she could find.

She found him pinned beneath their bodies. He sprang to life at the touch of her fingers, filling her hands. Bending, she took him greedily into her mouth, running both hands along the sides of him, nudging apart his legs and cupping him underneath. She sucked with an avarice that made him growl as his hands buried themselves in her hair.

Her exhaustion was spent, replaced with a second wind that was born on her redemption. In that moment, she felt she could do anything. She could fly through the air with him and even look down. As long as she was safe in his arms.

"Oh, how I've wanted to touch you," she panted. "You can't know what it was like for me, to see you, so close, and not be able to run my hands along your body. Dear God, how I love your body."

He opened his eyes in surprise.

"That's it, darling. Keep your eyes open. I want to look into your eyes as you come for me." Shifting her weight, she lowered herself over him, impaling herself, inch by agonizing inch, until she was so full of him, she thought she'd split in two. Her eyes clinging to his, she began to move, up and down, up and down, slowly, teasingly, gripping him with muscles that should have been weary, but that somehow clung like a vise. Watching his eyes cloud over the way hers must have as he watched her.

She reached down and licked his nipples and heard his curse. Denied his own pleasure for so long, he was volatile and ready to erupt. She increased her pace as he grasped her buttocks and kneaded them as she moved.

She'd thought to give him pleasure. But as she moved, as she gazed lovingly into his eyes, she felt herself slipping and melding, like vapor, into him. Her climax was so unexpected, so intense, that it transcended bodily pleasure. It was a thing of the spirit, where two souls meet and, freed from their bodily prisons, realize their radiance at last.

"Oh, Mace," she said as if mesmerized, looking into his eyes. "Mace . . . Mace . . . thank you. Thank you for saving me."

They were so shaken by it all that they lay, locked in each other's arms, incapable of words. He clutched her tight as she clung to him, feeling her heart open and expand, feeling what it was to love. To give more than you had to give. To surrender it all.

To trust.

She settled her head into the crook of his arm and drifted peacefully to sleep. And knew, in her heart, in the newly discovered purity of her soul, that nothing could harm her again.

CHAPTER 46

They spent the next day in bed, dozing in each other's arms, nibbling on bread and cheese, being lulled by the ever-present rhythm of the paddlewheel on the river. The water churning against the sides of the boat, the tangy smells of the Mississippi, the gentle rocking of their enclosed quarters, all contributed to the feeling of peace and solace in the aftermath of absolution.

They pulled the curtains closed around the bed, shutting out the outside world as effectively as if they'd sailed to distant, enchanted shores. It was snug in their haven, cozy as a cave. They piled jewel-toned pillows about them and nestled deep, secreted in their own private world.

Away from judging eyes, they reverted to their natural inclinations. Shunning the civility of goblets, they drank wine from the bottle, passing it back and forth, and licked the wine, giggling, from each other's lips.

"I feel," she told him, "as if nothing in my life until this moment has been real. This time spent with you is like a reverie—a perfect escape from reality. Yet it seems more real than anything I've ever known."

"Often reality is the illusion, and the illusion more real," he murmured.

"You're the only one who'd think so," she said, giving him a kiss.

His grin was crooked. "Sometimes it's a curse, being a visionary. Seeing things no one else can."

"Do you feel you're forever holding your tongue? Incapable of saying things that seem so obvious to you, yet that snare others to the point that they can't see which way is up?"

"As if you're always having to slow down and wait for them to catch up."

"But when you're with me . . . ?"

He gave her nose a playful nip. "When I'm with you, love, I have to keep on my toes."

"I'm delighted to hear it. I should hate to think I was as plodding as all the rest of humanity. How was it, then, with Pilar?"

"Pilar represented something I wanted to be. She was as much a symbol as anything else."

"So, by loving her, you were really trying to find something to love in yourself."

He considered for a moment. "I hadn't thought of it. But I suppose you're right." He smiled, and she could see the relief in his eyes at the realization. As if he, too, had suddenly been set free. "Trust a flam artist to see through your justifications."

"Odd, isn't it? We've each been trained from birth to pierce the heart of every person we come in contact with. To see the hypocrisy, the weaknesses they never dare confront. And to use them to our own advantage. Yet when it comes to our own feelings—"

"It takes a kindred spirit to pull them out of us, is that it?"

They laughed companionably, rubbing their cheeks together. His was bristly with the stubble of a beard, scratching her soft skin.

"Mace."

"Yes, love?"

"Let's make a pact."

He drew away and pushed himself up higher against the headboard. "I confess to being leery of promises."

"Oh, you don't have to promise to marry me, or any such silliness as that. I just want us to vow that, come what may, we shall tell the truth from here on in. At least to each other."

He blinked and reached again for the bottle. "Well, Princess," he said quietly, "truth is a relative thing."

"Truth is truth. Something is either true or it isn't."

"I beg to differ. Truth lies in the way you perceive it. What's true for me isn't necessarily true for you."

She sat up, turned to face him, and crossed her legs beneath her. "You don't really believe that!"

"Of course I do. I've spent a lifetime proving it. So, I might add, have you."

"I've spent a lifetime running away from the truth. You've finally given me the courage to face it, and you have the audacity to tell me you don't believe in it?"

"I didn't say I don't believe in it. I merely said that truth is like a prism. You hold it this way and see one thing, you turn it and see something else. Truth is a concoction of possibilities. Made up of half-truths, ifs, and maybes. Nothing is absolute. Why do you think we scuttle artists can do what we do? We present a possibility as truth and make others believe it. Look at your friend Bat. I called him a killer of men. Was that the truth? Is it true if everyone believes it? And if they believe it long enough, does it become true? Perhaps your Bat will become a killer because the possibility was presented to him. So what's the truth?"

"That's nothing but double-talk. The truth is, Bat has killed only one man. He has a kind heart. He never sought to kill anyone. But that man was attacking a woman. Bat was shot—that's how he got his limp. So you see, circumstances forced him into something he otherwise wouldn't have chosen."

"So is he a killer, or isn't he?"

She opened her mouth to speak, then closed it again.

"You see. It isn't as simple as it seems."

"But what does this have to do with our being honest with one another?"

"How can I promise something that doesn't exist?"

"Are you telling me that, given the chance, you'd lie to me?"

"I'm telling you that what I accept as true may seem false to you. That each of us sees truth in his own way. That the pursuit of truth for its own sake is as fruitless an occupation as trying to find a lost shilling in the Hudson River."

"How can you claim to distrust truth and still honestly want to run a newspaper?"

"I'm not interested in dictating the truth to my readers. I crave nothing more than to make them think, to plant the one word in their minds that is the root of all wisdom: why? The true danger lies in those who profess to have the only truth and proceed to dictate that to the rest of us. I write editorials, remember. Not hard news."

"You write fiction, you mean."

"You've just proved my point. Your truth says that I create a fantasy. Mine says I create illusions that are often more true than the facts."

"I shall have to think about this."

"You do that."

"I have a sneaking suspicion I've been bamboozled somewhere along the line."

He grinned, showing wolfish white teeth, obviously pleased with himself. Thoughtfully, she traced a finger across the outlines of crisp dark hair along the sinew of his forearm.

"You're pleased at having bested me—temporarily, I might add—with your golden tongue. You swear that truth is an illusion, and therefore you have a right to manipulate it as you see fit. Yet you fought with revolutionaries who, surely, must have believed theirs was the only reality. You were amazed by my assumption that you were conning the Van Slykes—you obviously hadn't thought of it as such."

The grin had dropped from his face, to be replaced with a scowl. "What's your point?"

"No point, really. Just that your philosophy is so fully that of a con man, yet you've spent the last few years of your life opposing that fact. You seem rather like a noble gladiator, waging a battle for the rights of the downtrodden. So . . . I ask you, which is the real you?"

He was quiet for a few moments, taking another sip of wine. He offered it to her, but she shook her head. "Don't evade the issue."

"Shall I tell you a story?" he asked.

"Does it have anything to do with what we're talking about? Or is its purpose to distract me?"

"You be the judge."

"Very well." She settled back into the pillows.

"A man was traveling along the road one day when he came across a snake who'd been badly injured and was on the verge of dying. Being a kindhearted man, he took the snake home and cared for him until the snake had fully recovered. At which point, the viper turned around and bit the man who'd saved his life. As the man lay dying, he asked the snake, 'Why did you do that? After all the love and care I gave you?' And the reptile replied, 'What did you expect? You knew I was a snake when you picked me up.'" He paused, looking up at the canopy. "That's how I felt when I met Pilar. I no longer wanted to be that snake."

"Yet you're not averse to using your mastery of the art of deception to help others."

"We all work with what we're given."

"I wonder. Is it right to con someone for a good cause?"

"Sometimes it's all you *can* do."

"Odd, isn't it? I used to think you were evil incarnate. That you were coldbloodedly stealing the newspaper out from under the Van Slykes. I even thought you killed them. Yet, in your own way, you're every bit as compassionate as they were. All this time I've spent with you has shown me one thing: You, Mace Blackwood, whether you know it or not, are an honorable man."

"Honorable?" He sounded amused. "There are no half-measures with you, are there? Loathing or worship . . . is there nothing in between?"

"Look what you've done for me. You didn't have to face what you did. You sacrificed a great deal that I might feel whole and—happy."

His mouth curved in a smile, creasing a dimple deep in the side of his cheek. "It was a great hardship, spending the night making love to you."

"Do you know what I think? That you're more decent than you like to let on. For some reason, it scares you to admit that you're a good man inside. A man of deeply felt emotions. A man capable of a great deal of caring."

He laughed. "Oh, you do?"

"I also believe you want the *Globe-Journal* so you can make the Van Slykes' dream come true. Only somewhere along the way, it became your dream. And you became Archer."

"You think so, do you?"

"You know what else I think?"

"You think your father would approve of me?"

She bit her lip, considering. "If he got to know the real you. He'd be a fool not to see that you're the perfect man. And my father was no fool."

He turned on his side, propped himself up on an elbow, and grinned down at her. "Perfect, am I?"

"Oh, perfection. Considerate and caring with your clothes on—"

"And with them off?"

"Very . . . very . . . dominant in bed."

"Ah. This is a requirement of your father's, then? That the man who wins your hand be dominant in bed?"

"I don't know about my father . . . but it's certainly one of mine. Most men are so easily manipulated by a pretty smile that it's difficult to respect them. But you— you're different. Bat once said I'd met my match in you. While I'm not ready to go *that* far, I shall admit you're at least—worthy of me."

He gave her a slow grin as his eyes caressed her lips in a slumberous look that made her heart skip a beat. "You like dominant men, do you?"

"When I give them permission to be dominant. And so long as they're expending their efforts in satisfying me . . . and not just themselves."

"I shall have to bear it in mind."

"Darling—as far as you're concerned, I have no complaints."

"Ah, but you haven't seen the best of me."

She raised a delighted brow. "Haven't I, indeed?"

"We've spent so much time playing mental games

with one another that we've had precious little time to . . . play games in bed, so to speak."

"Keep talking. I rather like the way you speak."

He took her arm and pulled her on top of him. "Well, we've got me all figured out. Perfection personified, wasn't it?" he teased. "Now all we have to do is figure out what to do with you."

She straddled him, letting her hair fall and play against his chest. "I have a few suggestions."

"Such as?"

She wiggled her hips and felt him harden beneath her. "Why don't you show me what I've been missing? That is, of course, if you're not too depleted . . ."

CHAPTER 47

He extricated himself from her tangle of limbs and rose from the rumpled bed. "Come here," he said.

She got up, unconsciously tightening the wrapper around her waist. She felt an odd tingle of excitement curling in her toes, trying to anticipate what he had in store for her. Before, she'd always called the shots with men. It was a welcome relief to let someone else take over the reins. It was also a bit like playing blindman's bluff. She didn't know what surprise she might encounter when she turned around.

"You like me dominant, do you?"

"Yes." The word was like a caress.

In one swift move, he reached behind and heaved her to him. The air left her lungs.

"Dominant like this?"

Impatiently, he bent his head and took her breast into his mouth through the thin material of the wrapper. At the same time, his hands were shoving the covering from the other breast, baring the ripe, full globe to his view. At once, his mouth clamped onto her naked flesh, and the wrapper fell unheeded to the floor.

As he sucked on her breast, his hands found the downy hair between her thighs. He began to probe with exquisite skill so she dropped back her head in a helpless gesture. Her mouth gaped open in a gasp that filled the quiet room. His fingers moved in her with the dexterity and delicacy of a marksman. There was nothing hesitant or unsure about him. He moved as if he'd traveled the map of a woman's body so often, it was stamped forever in his mind. As if the journey was as pleasurable, as eagerly antic-ipated, as worthy of his wholehearted pursuit, as it had been the first time around.

"Let me see if I remember those conditions," he said, moving to the other breast. "As long as I give you pleasure . . . wasn't that how it went?"

And what pleasure he gave her! His masterfully rov-ing hands moved in ways she'd never imagined. She could feel those long, firm fingers sliding up her thighs, parting the lips, and slipping, one after the other, inside. When he bent on one knee and put his tongue to her, Saranda could feel the heated wet flick like a flame. He was an artisan, solicitously pursuing his craft, stroking, tasting, teasing, in-sisting. Her eyes, opening slightly, were as glazed and dreamy as if she were drunk. She knew how aroused he was —she could feel it in the fervor with which he devoured her. But still, as if he couldn't help himself, he took the time to thoroughly please.

And all the while, when it wasn't embedded in her flesh, Mace's prominent, wolfish mouth moved in a litany of uttered heat. He spoke to her continually, sometimes grinning, sometimes mouthing words around a slowly glid-ing tongue. Saranda licked her lips and expelled panting breaths. It made her hot just to hear his deep, lusty voice against her skin. Nothing aroused her like a man who talked in bed.

He began to whisper orders. "Turn for me just a bit." She did as he asked.

"Put your foot on the bed." She bent a leg and propped it up on the bed, affording him a better view.

His mouth moved again. She cupped her own breasts high for his perusal.

He stood after a while, took her waist in his hands, and lifted her high above his head. Shifting her, he brought the backs of her knees to rest on his shoulders, straddling him with her legs spread wide. Then he took hold of her buttocks, pulled her close, and buried his face in her moist heat. She had to grab his head to keep from falling backward as his tongue plunged into her, driving her wild.

She came, straddling the immense breadth of his shoulders, clutching his crisp black curls.

When she'd barely finished, he eased her back to the bed, propping her up so she was kneeling, legs spread wide in the disheveled sheets. Then Mace, in all his rough, hard-muscled glory, approached her. She put her hands together. She raised them, still clasped tight, high above her head so her breasts rose and swayed, and, making undulating motions with her torso, rubbed them all over his face. He snapped at them and sucked one into his mouth. As she threw back her head and let out a moan that could be heard from outside, he reached beneath her knees and gave a sudden jerk. The muscles in his arms bunched and strained as she flopped back onto the bed. The backs of her knees in his hands, he spread them wide, yanked her close, and entered her with a thrust Saranda felt in places she hadn't known existed.

Mesmerized, she watched her flesh open and greedily wrap itself around him. He slid in and out with forceful thrusts. By now she'd lost control completely and was wallowing in sensations too explosive to bear for long.

Saranda was so wet, so hair-trigger hot, she was afraid to move. Mace knew what he wanted, and he went after it with the same ruthless abandon with which he indicted robber barons—as if nothing and no one could stand in his way.

He took one leg in his large hand and pulled it high against his chest, raising her off the bed enough to rest the calf on his shoulder, letting the other leg fall free. Hanging on to her raised leg, he slammed into her with such passionate force that she flopped like a rag doll and, putting her hand over her mouth, let out a wild, impassioned scream.

He never held one pose for long. With the prowess of an athlete, he positioned her where he wanted, combining his acrobatic strength and agility with his vivid imagination to effect, not merely a quick romp to prove a point, but an artistic fusing full of power, majesty, and grace. His lovemaking was so imaginative, so creatively full of sound and fury, that it bordered on genius. She was swept away by such a maelstrom of emotions, such a tempest of erotic sensations, that she couldn't remember the last time she'd taken a breath.

"Is that what you like?" he asked as he thrust like a stallion, at the same time fingering the throbbing bud of her desire.

She felt her orgasm sweeping upon her like a tidal wave, washing away everything in its path. "Yes," she gasped, seeking something to hold on to and, finding nothing, grasping at the sheets. "Yes . . . yes . . . yes . . ."

CHAPTER 48

Several nights later, they were awakened by a heavy thud. They sat up, hearts pounding, listening in the darkness.

"What was that?" Saranda asked.

"Felt as if we ran ashore."

He rose and went naked to the window. "Oh, Christ."

She was holding the sheet to her breasts. "What is it?"

"We've been stopped by a small steamer. They're coming aboard."

They could hear voices now, abrupt, commanding voices that rang with the threat of authority. Saranda knew without being told why the men were here, boarding in the middle of the night. Rising, she began hurriedly to dress.

Mace pulled on his pants as he kept an ear to the window.

"What goes on here?" he heard the captain ask, indignant at the disturbance. Low voices confirmed Mace's suspicions, and he quickly pulled on his boots.

"Take a look at this," they heard a voice say.

There was a rustle of paper, and they heard the captain's startled response. "Why, yes, I believe he *is* on board."

Saranda had been opening drawers, gathering fists of clothes. She'd just shoved them in the bag when they heard footsteps stomping up the companionway.

"What are we going to do?" she asked. "We haven't got a gun. We'll never talk our way out of this."

He was busy looking about the room. Glancing upward, he spied the gaslight fixture that hung from the sitting-room ceiling. Hurriedly, he locked the door.

"When they knock, open the door fast."

Footsteps rounded the corner right outside their door. Mace flexed his arms, stretching them several times back and forth, testing the flexibility of his healed arm. She didn't know what he was up to, but there was no time for questions. She'd have to trust his ability to think on his feet.

Fists pounded on the door. "Open up in there!"

Mace nodded. Saranda turned the lock and flung the door wide. As she did, he leapt upward, grabbed the chandelier, swung himself back, then forward, and landed a fierce blow to the two startled men in the doorway, a boot in each face. After a stunned moment, they toppled to the floor, unconscious.

"What do you know?" he said, staring at them in surprise. "It worked."

"You weren't sure?"

"I never tried it before."

"Oh, great. Nothing like experimenting when our lives are on the line."

"We'll discuss it later, if you don't mind."

He grabbed her hand and pulled her after him, bounding over the bodies. Moving to the corner, he checked the hall. Several men had taken positions at the front of the boat. When they'd heard the commotion, they'd come running, but it was clear it would take a few minutes to reach the port deck.

"Can you swim?" he asked.

"Of course I can swim." More than once she'd escaped capture by diving to freedom.

"Then let's go." He pulled her behind him as he made his way stealthily yet quickly to the starboard side, away from where the steamer was tied up. They could hear footsteps approaching and voices arguing in the dark. The men must have come to, for they were calling to the others to halt their escape.

Mace took the bag and lowered it into the river without making so much as a splash. Then, putting his finger to his lips in warning, he helped her over the side and held her hands as she stretched her arms and lowered herself into the muddy Mississippi. It was an effort not to hiss as she hit the water. It was warm, but it felt thick around her. Bits of something slippery floated by, brushing against her legs. She bit her lip to keep from gasping. God only knew what was lurking in these waters.

"They're armed and dangerous," a voice called above them. "We've orders to shoot to kill."

Suddenly, the water, the mud, the possible river creatures, all seemed inconsequential. As Mace noiselessly lowered himself into the water behind her, she fished around blindly for the valise. If it was floating nearby, she couldn't find it. She was bobbing about when the current began pulling her under so the muddy water soaked her head and filled her nostrils. Mace pulled her up, took hold of her arm, and began to swim with powerful strokes away from the boat.

It was hard going, the current constantly threatening to drag them down. After a few minutes, Saranda was panting hard, water dripping in her eyes, her clothes sucking her down with every stroke. Her shoulders ached, and her lungs felt waterlogged. Large branches floated by, scratching at her skin, tearing at her dress. But when she looked back at the boat and saw the glow of the lanterns, heard the shouts of alarm when it was discovered they were gone, she renewed her efforts.

Still, she was slowing them down. Her skirts were so heavy, they weighted her down like an anchor, hampering their speed.

They swam toward shore and hid themselves among some reeds and brush. Saranda huddled against Mace, shivering in the night air, as the steamer passed at a snail's gait. Men hung over the sides, casting beams from their lanterns all around. Shots were fired into the water as the boat passed by. Saranda pressed her face into the swamp. There was no telling, in the darkness, whether one of the wild shots might find its mark.

Once, the light flashed across them, and she held her breath, certain they'd been spotted. But the boat steamed past.

"I can't see a thing," they heard one man call.

"Don't worry," called another. "No one can stay afloat in this river for long. If they don't drown in this current, they'll have to head for land. They can't get far on foot in these woods. We'll just patrol the area till morning. Then we'll have 'em."

Mace put his mouth to her ear. So overtaxed were her nerves that she jumped at the contact.

"Our only chance is to use the river to help us. If we can get past them, we'll swim downstream."

"But you heard what they said. No one can swim for long—"

"I'm an acrobat, remember? I'm accustomed to pushing my body to the limit." He turned her face to him. "Come on, love, don't give out on me now."

She nodded, encouraged by his confidence.

"Just hold on to me."

She did so, and they began to swim close to shore, gliding slowly, carefully, past the steamer, pausing only when a light was cast their way. It was a laborious process, throughout which Saranda could barely catch her breath. She knew these men weren't eager to take her back to trial. If she and Mace were caught, they'd be killed—probably under the claim that they'd been shot trying to escape. It was enough to render her limbs numb.

Yet glancing at Mace in the spill from the lanterns, she saw in his eyes the look of a man determined to rise to an impossible challenge. She remembered that he was a warrior at heart, accustomed to having men of corruption and power for breakfast. She drew comfort from it and took heart.

Once they'd successfully passed by the boat, Mace began to swim with determined strokes, putting as much distance between them and their pursuers as possible. It was a struggle for her to keep up with him. She was forced to grab hold of his shoulders and let him propel her along. Presently, when they were well out of sight of the boat, he stopped his metrical stroking and swam around to her. His breath heaving in his chest, he pulled her to him, grabbed hold of the waistband of her skirt, and yanked it open.

"What are you doing?"

"Getting rid of the dead weight."

He tugged the skirt from her and flung it aside so it began to float downriver. "Are you crazy?" she panted. "You've just thrown away the only thing I have to wear. After already having lost my valise."

"Better your clothes than your life. We'll figure something out when we come to shore."

"When, pray tell, will that be?"

"When I think it's safe. This is our fastest mode of travel for the present. Unless, of course, you'd like a wardrobe of prison stripes?"

So on they swam, sometimes floating on the river to rest themselves, sometimes swimming for all they were worth. Saranda had to admit it was easier without the burdensome weight of her skirts. But she was desperately tired, her arms crying out for relief from the continual strain of holding her afloat.

They must have swum for hours. Eventually, the sky began to lighten in the east. Just when she thought she couldn't go on, he pulled up, scissoring his legs to keep himself afloat. Not possessed of the muscles of an athlete, she began to sink, sputtering beneath the surface, until he caught her and heaved her above water.

"We'd best head for land," he told her, eyeing the sky. "At night the river's a safe haven. In daylight we shall be sitting ducks."

She didn't even have the strength to express her relief. In a lifetime of hard traveling, this night in the water had been the most uncomfortable she'd ever spent.

Sensing her exhaustion, he took hold of her and swam with her to the distant shore. Once there, they slogged out of the water with stiff legs and fell gasping onto the muddy banks.

Saranda lay there for some time, trying to catch her breath. The mud was cool against her face in the dawn chill. She felt herself losing consciousness, falling into desperately needed sleep. Only when Mace shook her did she recall their predicament and allow him to help her to her feet.

Once standing, her brain insensible from fatigue, she

took a look around. In the daylight, the Mississippi was as brown as she remembered it from the deck of the riverboat. From here, she couldn't even see the other shore. All she could hear was the whoosh of the water, the same sound that had lulled her for so many hours.

Her gaze fell upon her clothes, and a strangled cry escaped her lips as she realized what a bedraggled mess she was. She was covered in mud. Her blouse was torn to tatters, her satin drawers ripped and clinging wetly to the outline of her hips and thighs. Mercifully, the streaks of mud kept prying eyes from seeing through it. But her hair, now a murky brown, hung in wet tangles. Strings of bark and small twigs formed a nest in the snarls. She could feel the grit on her face; she could see it in the cracks of her palms and underneath her nails.

"Look at me!" she cried, forgetting her fatigue.

"I was doing just that."

She turned to him. Mace didn't look much better. His pants were as torn as her blouse, and just as dirty. His chest, shirtless in his hurry to escape, was so heavily smeared with mud that he looked like some pagan statue made of clay. Dirt streaked his hair and his face. When he ran a hand across his forehead, it smeared even more.

"I feel like I've been rolling around in a pig trough," she complained, trying to scrape the mud from her face.

"Actually, you look rather fetching," he said, taking her in his arms and pulling her close. "Maybe I should reconsider and call you Dusty. Or better yet, Muddy."

"Just the sweet nothings a woman wants to hear."

"Would it help if I told you you're as beautiful as the Nile in the moonlight?"

"No allusions to rivers, please. I've had enough of this blasted river to last me a lifetime."

They looked around. There was nothing in sight but the river on one side and woods on the other. The woods looked dense and hostile, but at least they weren't wet. "You may have to learn to love it yet again. I don't know where we are. Some way or other, we must get to the nearest town and from there to New York."

"I don't care how we get there, so long as we don't swim."

"Our first order of business is acquiring some clothes. Then we'll see about a ride into town. If there is such a thing in these parts. Which, given the lack of options, means we walk for now."

"Walk? When do we sleep?"

"When we no longer look like creatures from the netherworld."

She tried rinsing herself off with river water, but to little avail. "Oh, Mace. I've never felt more clammy or dirty or absolutely repugnant in all my life. How are we ever going to get clean?"

"You tell me," he suggested, a provocative twinkle in his eyes.

"By—finding some people and clipping them out of a bath, some clothes, and a ride into town?"

"Now you're thinking like the woman I fell in love with."

"This I'd like to see. What shall we say that might convincingly explain why we're in such a state?"

He kissed her and laughed when she squirmed away from his mud-caked lips. "Let's just see what the inspiration of the moment brings, shall we?"

"I must say you're in remarkably good spirits. Considering you're drenched to the skin, covered with mud, and without a possession to your name."

"Well, Princess, the way I look at it, we're alive and we've got each other. What's a little mud, compared to that?"

Her heart swelled with a sudden burst of love for

him. Suddenly, the muck didn't matter. She kissed him hard, thrusting her tongue into his mouth and clinging to his muddy skin. When she finally came up for air, she was as full of optimism as he. "Let's go con the pants off the next farmer we meet."

IT SEEMED HOURS before they detected the smell of smoke. Hours of trudging through the woods, of scraping their limbs on brambles, of feeling stiff as mummies as the mud dried and hardened on their skin. As the sun rose in the sky, the heat became oppressive. Soon, sweat mingled with the mud to form rivulets that ran down their faces and into their eyes.

They came to a clearing suddenly where the smell of cooking filled the air. All at once, Saranda's exhaustion fell away. Beyond the next wood was the promise of a bath, of clean clothes and warm food. With nothing but their wits to sustain them, they would have to think of something clever to make their situation seem plausible, even to simple farmers.

They stopped and gave each other one last preparatory look. Saranda could see the same thrill of the challenge in his eyes. She felt alive suddenly, felt her blood surging like the Mississippi through her veins.

"You lead, and I shall follow," she told him, and gave him a quick kiss for luck.

"I have the perfect story," he told her with a grin. "It's so absurd, they'll have to believe it."

Together, they stepped into the clearing. Walking confidently, they made their way across a small planted field. There was a structure in the distance; smoke wafted skyward from the chimney.

But as they approached, they slowed their steps. A

closer look showed it was little more than a sharecropper's farm. The structure was a meager shack, leaning and badly in need of repair. A single hog nudged around in the mud, surrounded by a wobbly fence. Out front, an old iron pot was boiling away over a fire. A woman, looking old and work-weary, scrubbed clothes on a washboard in a tub. She was surrounded by at least eight children, all looking to be under twelve years of age. They were scrawny, some with teeth missing, dressed in little more than rags. The hollowness of their faces clearly signaled their scandalous lack of food.

The woman looked up as they approached. At closer range, it was obvious she was little more than thirty years old. But her skin looked like leather and hung on her face. There was a look in her eyes that Saranda knew only too well. She'd seen it in the eyes of the desperately poor on the streets of London. It was the blank, hollow look of a person who'd long ago given up hope. Who didn't even remember that such a thing existed.

Mace touched her hand, and they stopped as one. No words were necessary. Looking into his eyes, she saw sorrow, pity, and empathy. She saw, too, that he couldn't go through with it. That, destitute as they might be, he'd starve before he'd bring himself to burn this family with nothing to give.

She felt a sudden surge of joy. The look on his face made her realize something she hadn't before. Because of him, she'd changed. Now she could open her heart and feel someone else's suffering. She knew she never wanted to hurt innocent people again.

It was the sweetest feeling she'd ever known. With a full and grateful heart, she put her arm about Mace's waist and held him close.

"You're not that snake anymore," she whispered. And knew that he understood.

CHAPTER 49

To make matters worse, the family dropped what they were doing and welcomed them like old friends. It was apparent that few visitors stopped by these remote parts. The excitement in the children's faces made Saranda feel even worse about their earlier plot to take advantage of them.

The one moment of tension came when the father, dressed in a tattered Confederate uniform, came limping over, frowning at their English accents. "You folks talk funny," he said. "You ain't Yankees, is you?"

"No," Mace explained. "We're British."

The farmer nodded philosophically. "I figgered you was from Britain or Asia, or one of them states."

The family even saved them the trouble of explaining their circumstances by refusing to ask. When Mace began his ingeniously designed story, the father said, "Oh, that don't matter none. Looks like you could use a scrub, though. Woman, toss that laundry water yonder. Let's get some proper use from the water what's boiled."

Clothes hung from a line stretched across the lawn, mostly children's pants and shirts, well-mended but scrupulously clean. These the farmer moved aside to accommodate the heavily patched quilt he threw across. Behind that, they set up the washtub, and there, first Saranda, then Mace, scrubbed themselves with harsh, homemade lye soap as the children stood before the concealing curtain and stared.

Once they were clean, they were given clothes to wear. Their protests went unheeded. "You cain't wear what you've got on," the farmer insisted. "Why, it wouldn't be neighborly if we didn't share what we got with folks that got less."

Meeting Mace's eyes, Saranda went behind the curtain once again and slipped into the farm woman's dress. Once it had been calico, but it was so faded from washings and wear that it now looked a dingy grey. It was too large for her on top—the woman must have been pregnant and nursing for most of her marriage—and the skirt was unfashionably wide in the style of a decade earlier. Saranda counted five separate tears that had been carefully mended, but the material was so thin, she knew a good tug would rip them open. Coming from behind the curtain, feeling dumpy and conspicuous, she caught the look of pride in the woman's eyes, and realized with a start that this must be her best dress.

Mace fared little better. The farmer was shorter than he, so the pant legs came halfway up his calves and the shirtsleeves barely past his forearms. The sleeves he rolled up, displaying a heady glimpse of thickly muscled arms. But the pants were so tight, he could barely move. The bulge in his groin was so noticeable, straining against the imprisonment of the breeches, that the woman's eyes came to rest upon it and widened in horror. As unobtrusively as possible, Mace pulled out the shirttail and let it hang.

Saranda was hard-pressed not to laugh.

They had a small pot of vegetable stew for their noon meal. It was hardly enough to feed the family of ten, yet they insisted on giving their guests the largest share. As they ate, choking guiltily on the food, Mace asked questions about the surrounding territory.

"I'd guess we're twenty miles from Memphis," said the farmer. "Hard goin' on foot, an' we only got a mule. We take a raft if needs be. Don't get much call to go to town, though. Ain't used it in a spell. You're sure welcome to it."

"We can't take your only raft," Saranda said, surprised to find herself preferring the thought of another moonlight swim.

The farmer waved his hand impatiently. "Heck, take it. You can see fer yourself, I got trees enough. If I need another, I'll jest build it. Woman, get these folks another helping of stew."

They declined, even though they'd eaten little for days and were still exhausted from swimming the river. "I'll take the raft, if you insist," Mace said. "We shall leave at dusk. As long as you tell me what we can do in return. Maybe fix some fences, or help you—"

"Now what would I need better fences fer? Ain't got nothin' to put in 'em. Naw, you're welcome to it. But if 'n it makes you feel better, you could talk to the young'uns. They don't get much sport, do you, kids?"

Solemnly, their eyes large in their faces, the children shook their heads.

"Pa, I'm ashamed of you. Cain't you see them folks is wore out? They need rest, is what they need. Ain't that so, folks?"

"Well," admitted Saranda, who was having trouble keeping her eyes open, "we could do with a bit of a nap."

"Well, use our bed!" cried the farmer. "You're both welcome."

They stared at each other, aghast. "We couldn't possibly—"

"Don't give it a thought. Me and Ma don't need it till nigh on seven o'clock. Go on in and settle yerselves."

They were ushered into the one bedroom with a small bed fashioned from rough-hewn logs. The quilt was retrieved from the clothesline, the faded curtain that served as a door was pulled closed, and the farmer and his wife returned to their chores.

Lying cramped together in the bed, Mace and Saranda shifted awkwardly. "We *could* do with some sleep," Mace conceded, "if we're going to travel all night."

"I feel so *guilty*!" she whispered. "Oh, for the days when I was heartless. At least if you have no heart, it can't break as it's doing now."

"Have no fear, love. As soon as the *Globe-Journal* is back in our hands, we shall send them some money. We'll say they've won some sort of contest. They'll never know the difference."

The prospect cheered her, but even more the fact that he'd used the word "we." She raised her head to comment, when a flutter of the curtain drew her gaze. There, on either side of the material, were six tiny faces, three on either side of the curtain, watching with unblinking eyes. She nudged Mace, and catching sight of them, he began to laugh. She joined in, and soon they were rolling in the strange bed, muffling their giggles in each other's shoulders.

When he could get a breath, Mace raised himself up and said, "Very well, my friends, come along. It's time for a story."

They flung themselves on the bed, surrounding the two strangers as if it were the most natural thing in the world. Mace grabbed a couple of them and held them to keep them from falling off the narrow bed. "Have you ever seen a circus?" They shook their heads. "Well, it's a sight like nothing else you'll ever see."

And he spent the time when he should have been sleeping weaving tales and painting word pictures for the children that were so full of color, magic, and inspiration that they felt they'd truly seen it all. From the elephants to the clowns to the flying men on the trapeze, they spent the afternoon in a world of fantasy and fun they might never witness.

Saranda watched him with a tender smile on her face. He held the children spellbound. If he described a near fall from the trapeze, they jumped and covered their ears. If he relayed the silly antics of a clown, they flashed toothy grins. They spent an afternoon forgetting the meagerness of their existence, all because this dear man cared more about their happiness than he did his own needs.

What a wonderful father he'd make.

Then, realizing what she'd just thought, she stared at him with terrified eyes. She could see his love for children in his face. After bearing most of the burden swimming the Mississippi, he had to be exhausted. Yet his eyes glowed with a gentle warmth as he spun delightful tales for the children's amusement. She thought she detected a wistful sigh in his voice, as if regretting the time he'd been denied with his own child. She understood in that moment what she'd only partially glimpsed in the tarot reading: that Mace's search for his own identity was tied up in his wanting a family. Wanting a child.

A child she could never give him.

Because as cozy as this afternoon had been, the reality was that she'd spent precious little such time with her own son. There'd never been the opportunity or the inclination to sit with him in her lap and tell stories about a world he didn't yet know. The reality of motherhood had been a nightmare for her. It had incinerated her heart and left behind nothing but ashes. And she knew in that freshly healed but still raw heart that she couldn't bear to go through it again.

So if Mace wanted a family as much as his eyes told her he did . . . what was her purpose in his life? She couldn't give him the one thing that would make him happy. And she couldn't rob him of a child a second time. After all the unhappiness and uncertainty in his life, he deserved the comfort of his own family.

He glanced over then and caught the torment in her eyes. Midsentence, he paused and pulled her head to rest on his chest. "Hush, darling," he murmured. "Whatever you're thinking, it doesn't matter."

She lay with her ear against him, trying to convince herself it was true. But she heard his voice rumble through his chest as he turned back to the children. She felt the accelerated beat of his heart. He was in his element. What better audience for a flimflam man with the gift of gab than an armful of innocent babes?

Presently, though, his heart began to slow. She could hear the weariness in his voice. Likely, his strength would be needed that night more than hers. She had to see to it that he slept.

She raised herself up and took the reins. "Do you know how to sing?" she asked the children.

They shook their heads.

"Let's see what you think of this."

Softly, she began to sing an old English lullaby. Her voice caught in her throat at first, for it hurt to think of all the times she should have sung to her own son and didn't. But soon she was singing clearly, with a voice as sweet as birdsong. Mace snuggled down under the quilt and closed his eyes. Still she sang. When one song was finished, she started another. It didn't matter what. Anything to rest his mind so he could sleep.

She could feel him relaxing beside her. With a sigh, he turned to his side and brought his head to rest upon her breast. At any other time, she might have suspected his motives. But he looked so peaceful, so trusting, that her heart spilled over with love for him.

"You sing like an angel," he muttered in a voice thick with fatigue.

She put her hand to his dark curls and stroked tenderly as he sighed more deeply.

Looking at him, so peacefully drifting off to sleep, she felt a moment of panic. This was too easy. What if the farmer had lied to them? What if he'd sent his children in as a distraction so he could run for the police? He could be lulling them to sleep, just as he was lulling them into trusting him. She'd never trusted a stranger in her life. Should she allow herself to sleep, only to wake and find they'd been set up?

She opened her mouth to voice her fears, but Mace was already fast asleep.

CHAPTER 50

Something was creaking. It had a swaying rhythm, like the swinging of a gallows rope. She could feel it tighten around her neck, feel the rope scratch and burn. Then, with a lurch, she was dangling high in the air, the noose choking off her last breath—

She awoke with a start to an empty bed. Springing up, she expected to find herself surrounded by guns, with Mace pinned to the wall. Instead, her lover watched her from a rocking chair, his eyes hooded. She fell back in the sheets with a strangled cry of relief. It was the rocking chair, and not the hangman's rope, that she'd heard in her sleep.

"I thought they'd called the constable."

"Did you?" he asked quietly.

"It occurred to me they might be waiting for us to fall asleep so they could run for help. For all we know, there could be a police station a mile away. I'd hate to be nicked at this late date."

The creaking stopped. He was silent for so long that she rolled over and looked at him questioningly. He was gazing at her steadily, seriously. But when he finally spoke, she detected an injured tone in his voice.

"If I'd thought there was any danger, do you think I'd have fallen asleep?"

Her breath felt trapped in her lungs. "Wouldn't you?"

He leaned forward, resting his elbows on his knees. "Know this, Saranda. Nothing and no one are going to harm you so long as I have one breath left. I would willingly die to keep you from being hurt."

A wayward curl had fallen over his brow. She reached up and brushed it back with shaking fingers. "What in God's name would make you presume your death wouldn't hurt me?"

He smiled. "I was hoping to reassure you that you're safe while I still live."

"Safety isn't something I've sought in my life, Mace. Given a choice between being safe and being with you, I most cheerfully choose the life of a fugitive. Yet—" She paused. "I confess your words leave me feeling empty-handed. I have nothing to give you in return that would match your willingness to sacrifice your life for my sake."

He took her hand from his hair and pressed it to his lips. "Don't you?"

She thought of the farmer's children and dropped her gaze. "How were you so certain the farmer wouldn't run for the authorities?"

"You forget, I'm an excellent judge of character."

"I don't know about that. You love me, don't you?"

"I've just told you. More than my life."

It was wondrous, that someone loved her so completely. So why did it fill her with such fear?

"I've run from trouble before," she told him. "But I

have to admit how much better it is, not having to run alone."

"When I'm through, you won't have to run ever again."

"Sweet words, but I doubt that's possible. My cover has been blown before the entire country. I've been exposed as a confidence artist. Even if we're successful in clearing my name, I still have no base of operation left."

"Do you require one?"

"I'm not certain what you mean."

"I mean is it your intention to continue with your career? If you could reclaim your anonymity, would you?"

She pulled her hand from his. "That's the question of the hour, isn't it? Having seen the light, will the lady libertine cease her despicable acts? I don't have an easy answer. What happened to Winston and Jackson horrified me, made me realize that, my code of honor not withstanding, my actions were hurting people."

She took a breath before going on. "I have a deep desire not to do so anymore. Being on this farm—if you can call it that—has shown me that more than anything. Yet what else can I do? I was trained from birth for only one thing. I can do a number of things well, but they all serve the larger purpose. I have only one real talent: to make people trust me so I can pilfer their goods. As much as I hate to link my name in the same breath as his, I'm much like Lance in that respect. Like you, I want to lead a more useful life. But I can't see a role for myself in the respectable world."

"You were willing to marry once."

"Yes, but I was doing it to con *you*. Had Winston lived, my life would have been one long pretense, playing the role of Mrs. Van Slyke to an unsuspecting world. This time, it's different. This time I have no role to play. I couldn't be married with nothing to do. I've spent my life working. So I seem to be caught in this vast nowhere land. Even if I don't hang for murder, there seems to be nothing I'm fit for." Saranda looked disconsolate.

"I don't know about that," he murmured.

"What do you mean?"

"I have a few ideas."

"What?" she asked. "Tell me."

He glanced out the solitary glassless window. "Some other time, I promise. It's growing dark now. We need to leave. We've but a week and a half left to make it back to New York. We can't afford to waste a moment."

The farmer had caught a rabbit, which was divided between the twelve of them in another stew. They ate quickly, eager to be off. Saranda wasn't looking forward to braving the river again so much as she was to questioning Mace further. She couldn't wait to find out what he could possibly have in mind.

THEY PUSHED OFF in the raft just at dark. It spun in the waters until Mace, using the oar the farmer had provided, was able to set it straight. Looking back at the family who stood waving on the banks of the river, lit by the pale glow of a single flickering candle, she wondered what lay ahead for them. Maybe she and Mace could help provide them with a better life—if they succeeded.

The raft began to pitch through the darkness, over the onrushing waters. Saranda and Mace settled at opposite ends, each using an oar, fighting to keep a steady course. The water sprayed their faces and dampened their clothes. Once or twice, they were tossed so perilously, they threatened to lose their balance on the slippery logs. But eventually they settled into a rhythm of alternate strokes to keep the raft straight and true.

Saranda brushed the sodden hair from her face and called over her shoulders, above the din of the torrent, "What did you mean when you said you had a few ideas?"

"Ideas about what you can do in the so-called respectable world," he yelled back.

"For instance?"

"For instance, something that will satisfy your new-found thirst for truth and utilize your talents all in one masterstroke."

"And what might that be?" Was he going to make her pry it out of him?

"A reporter."

"A *reporter*?"

"Why not? You want the truth, go out and find it for yourself. You'd be perfect."

"I know nothing about it. I don't even know if I can write."

"Ah, there's nothing to writing news. Who, what, where, when, why. I can teach you that. The *creativity* comes in having the ability to ferret out the real story. The story they don't want to tell you. That's something no one can teach you. That's where your particular genius comes in. I defy any man to look in your eyes and not be tempted to bare his soul."

The raft swayed to the left, and she paddled hard, bringing it around. Her arms were aching already from the effort. "I don't know, Mace. I'd have to think about it. I have this desire suddenly to help people better their lives. I keep thinking there must be a way of opening people's eyes to what harm they do to others with their narrow thinking and hypocrisy and greed."

"As a reporter, you'd have an obvious platform."

"I can't see how covering ladies' teas and factory fires

will help change the world. Besides which, it sounds awfully dull. Say what you will of my life, it's never been
boring."

"Suit yourself then. But I've found that most people
balk when they come face-to-face with their destiny. A
person destined to save lives with his skill as a surgeon
might just as likely prefer to be a carpenter. But reject it as
we may, I'm convinced that destiny is often staring us
in the face. Only we're looking so hard for it, we can't
see it."

As she considered his words, an idea struck her.

"I'm not interested in ladies' teas and such rubbish,
but there *is* one thing I could do."

"What's that, Princess?"

"Go undercover to get a story."

"Now wait a minute—"

"I could work in a factory and expose the awful conditions. Get myself admitted to an insane asylum and write
about how they treat the patients. It's perfect."

"Dangerous is what it is. You've risked your life more
than I'd like already."

"I see—it's fine for a man like *you* to risk your neck
for a story, but not a woman."

"Not the woman I love."

"But, Mace, think of it. You said I could be a reporter. But I've never been direct in my dealings. The
thought of interviewing someone *honestly* makes my hair
stand on end. But to do what I've always done—to play a
role, to make someone trust me, to extract something from
them as a result—information this time instead of money
—*that* I can do! It'd be a way to help change the world. A
way of conning people for *good*."

"You're wasting your breath."

Her throat by now was raw from shouting. It was

difficult to talk over the noise of the river, so she let it go. But she couldn't help thinking about it as they rushed through the dark night, pulled along by the current. *Could this be an answer? Could it be that what she'd been looking for was under her nose all this time?*

CHAPTER 51

In Memphis, Mace won enough money in a poker game to buy them a bath, some unobtrusive clothes, and train tickets to Ohio. Then he wired his people in New York requesting information and told them to reply under the name of Sanderson in Columbus.

The telegram was waiting for them when they arrived. Mace read it immediately. Saranda saw his face harden.

"What is it?"

He glanced up and noticed the telegraph officer peering at him with curiosity. "Let's get out of here," he said, and steered her down several side streets before he told her.

"McLeod is acting as publisher of the paper," he told her in a dull voice.

"Oh, Mace, no!"

He leaned back against a brick wall and closed his

eyes. His jaw was clenched tight, his hands convulsed into fists. His breathing was ragged.

"What are we going to do?" she asked.

"First we have to get back to town. Even though my contact warns against it. Says the authorities are checking every boat and train coming into the city. With the deadline close at hand, they're questioning every passenger. Even streetcars are being searched." He took the telegram from his pocket and read aloud: " 'Don't even try to come. You won't make it. They're out for blood.' " He balled it in his fist. "We could use disguises, but with that sort of scrutiny, we'd be risking too much. I'm not going to walk into a trap. And I refuse to put you in any more danger than I have to."

"We shall just have to find another way."

"How? With three days left, we haven't the time to ride in on horseback. We certainly can't walk."

For the first time, he seemed genuinely discouraged.

"There's always a way," she said. "If one idea doesn't work, it's simply a matter of finding something else. The word 'defeat,' " she added, mimicking him, "is not in my vocabulary."

She could see he wasn't listening. His handsome face was etched in angry lines. "If they're letting McLeod run the paper early, they must be terribly sure of the outcome. Which means they must have evidence that's irrefutable. Can you think what it might be?"

She thought for a minute, then groaned. *The letter of confession she'd shown Jackson the night before the wedding, outlining how she'd set out to con them and marry Winston.* She told him about it.

"I never thought of it again. There was no reason to. It had already served its purpose."

He shot her a bleak look. "Now it just might serve McLeod's."

.   .   .

HE WAS RESTLESS and gloomy all day. She tried to keep his spirits up, but all in vain. He couldn't sit still. So they wandered the streets of Columbus, talking little. Saranda spent the time racking her brain to think of ways of traveling undetected from Ohio to New York in time for the deadline. Nothing she came up with made any sense.

"Maybe we could get to the outskirts of the city," she mused. "Then your contacts at the paper could meet us and sneak us in."

"Impossible. They're being watched like bloody hawks."

"Well, there has to be *something* we can do!"

"I don't know. We may just have played into McLeod's hands."

"McLeod and your brother, Lance," she reminded him gently.

"Lance may have pulled the trigger. But it was McLeod who killed the Van Slykes. I swear to you before God, one way or another, I shall make him pay."

His defense of his brother sent her spirits plummeting.

THEY SLEPT THAT night in a hotel and ate their first real meal in weeks, but it did little to alleviate Mace's brooding. None of Saranda's efforts to cheer him were of any avail. Even her attempts to get him into bed went unheeded. He turned his chair back to the room and sat staring out the window for most of the night. Even when she fell asleep, he didn't abandon his vigil.

The next morning, he was in a foul mood. She bent

over him, wrapping her arms around him from behind, and kissed his cheek. "Haven't you moved?"

"Nothing," he said, his voice seething with disgust. "I've come up with nothing."

"You need some rest, darling. You can't expect to think clearly without any sleep."

"I don't have time to sleep. We're almost there. Two more days, and it might as well be two minutes. We're so close, I can taste it. But there's nothing I can do about it."

"Let's just ride the rails through Pennsylvania. Perhaps along the way we can come up with—"

"What? Shall we hide ourselves under a haystack and ride into town on a wagon?"

"If necessary."

"Don't be absurd."

"And don't *you* be rude!"

He looked up to see her glaring at him, her hands on her hips, and sighed. "I'm sorry. I just can't seem to—I'm not accustomed to being at a loss for ideas. If it were only me, it would be one thing. But I have you to consider now."

"Don't think about me, if it's causing you distress."

"You might as well ask me to stop breathing. But you're right. I shouldn't take it out on you. This is my problem."

She hugged him close. "It's *our* problem. Somehow, we shall think of something together."

He stood abruptly, shrugging her off. "Let's get out of here. I can't abide these walls for one minute more."

It was a gorgeous warm day with not a cloud in the sky. But his surroundings went unnoticed as Mace walked up one street and down another, his brow creased in thought.

They roamed the streets for what seemed like hours. Mace seemed to be on some sort of quest. Yet even he was hard-pressed to define what he was seeking. Some source of inspiration, something to spark an idea.

"Mace, I can't go on," she said when her feet were too sore to continue. "Let's just take the train east and—"

Suddenly, he stopped. His hand at her arm arrested her, and she lost her train of thought. She looked about to see what might have caught his interest. They were on the edge of town, surrounded by green fields. The only thing visible was a man standing beside some sort of huge wicker basket. On the ground beside him was an enormous bunch of brightly colored material in yellow and red stripes. A few onlookers were watching him as he spread it out on the ground. Propped beside him was a sign that stated: RIDES FIFTEEN DOLLARS.

"What on earth is that contraption?" she asked. "A buggy with a sail?"

He turned to her, alert and fairly vibrating with energy.

"Do you trust me, Princess?"

"To ride in a sail-driven buggy from here to New York?"

"Of course not."

"In that case—"

"Yes or no?"

She couldn't imagine what had him so fired up, but anything was better than the gloom that had besieged him. A current flowed from him to her, igniting her own sense of adventure. Whatever his idea was, it must be stupendous to have turned his mood around so completely.

"Do—you—trust—me?" he repeated, his voice intense.

"You know I do."

"Good girl. You won't be sorry."

Noticing the gleam in his eye, she hoped he meant it.

CHAPTER 52

After buying her a lunch so lavish it took on the trappings of a last meal, Mace steered her back to the edge of town, where they'd earlier seen the man offering rides.

Saranda halted when she realized where they were headed. "Mace, you told me we weren't going to do anything foolish."

He was grinning. "No, love. I said we weren't sailing to New York in a buggy."

She followed him out of the shadows of the outlying buildings. "Then what—"

Suddenly, she froze. Her heart seemed to leap into her throat, and her limbs turned to water. For the striped material she'd assumed was a sail had been inflated during their absence into a floating sphere, covered by a net that connected it to the wicker basket below. The curious contraption wasn't a sailing buggy, after all. It was a hot-air balloon!

"*Oh, no.*"

Her heartbeat was erratic. Her breath came in

spasms. She began to shake so that she could barely stay afoot. Surely, this was some kind of cruel joke, Mace's way of scaring her half to death. *Surely*, he didn't mean to take her in that contrivance up into the atmosphere. *Into the sky!* She, who couldn't climb a twelve-foot-wall without fear of her life!

"*Oh, no.*"

She felt dizzy. She barely noticed when he took her hand and pulled her with him toward the gathered crowd. Her heels dug into the ground, but still he strode forward purposefully, dragging her along behind.

The man in the red-and-white-striped jacket was hawking rides. He tipped his straw hat to them as they drew up before the brightly striped balloon, but Saranda didn't notice. She was staring up at the hovering beast, alarmed, trying to imagine the horror of rising in it to the clouds.

"Inflammable gas," the balloonist was saying. "That's what keeps it afloat. Helium, to be precise."

"Inflammable?" asked a woman in the crowd. "Does that mean it will catch fire?"

"Gracious, no, ma'am. But, sir, please refrain from smoking, or we'll all go up in flames."

Saranda couldn't stop staring at the monstrosity with panic-stricken eyes. "Please tell me this is just the curiosity of an acrobat," she said to Mace through tightly clenched teeth, "and no more."

He ignored her completely. "Tell me, my good man," he called to the pilot. "How do you make this thing rise?"

"Oh, no," murmured Saranda. "*Oh, no!*"

"I'm glad you asked that, sir. You may notice that the balloon is only half-full of gas. As such, it ascends more quickly. When I turn on the flame of my Bunsen burner, it converts water into helium and causes the balloon to rise without wasting precious ballast."

"Fascinating," Mace murmured, rounding the balloon and eyeing it appreciatively. "And how does one steer such a conveyance?"

"No such thing, friend. In a balloon, you ride whichever way the wind takes you. Of course, a knowledge of meteorology helps. At different heights, you run across different air currents. With any luck, you can find the current that's blowing in the direction you want to go. Of course, it takes a skilled pilot to determine such things."

"Naturally. But I'm curious. How do you land?"

"Now that's the tricky part, friend."

He droned on, proudly explaining the workings of his profession as only one who truly loves it can. But Saranda wasn't listening. She knew in her heart Mace wasn't simply passing the time of day. And she was frantically trying to think of a way to dissuade him from this madness.

Mace asked more questions, about the equipment, air speed, and methods of navigation. He was shown the compass, the barometer, the altimeter. His intelligent queries seemed to fuel the pilot's pride, made him eager to explain.

"Would you folks care to go up and see for yourselves?"

"Over my dead body," Saranda muttered.

A man in the back inquired after the safety of such a machine. As the pilot swerved to assure him, Mace took another turn around the balloon. It swayed slightly in the warm breeze.

Mace licked a finger and held it in the air. "This breeze is heading east, I believe."

"A good guess, sir. East and a little north, more precisely. You must have some experience with air currents."

"I used to sail," Mace replied absently.

"Of course, sailing is completely different from ballooning. In sailing, the boat is only half-submerged in water. A balloon is completely surrounded by air."

"But how does it stay up?" asked a woman.

Saranda went to Mace on wobbly legs. Her heart was stampeding in her breast.

"You can't do this to me. I shall die up there. Just turn me in and have done with it. Better to die hanging from a rope ten feet up than from a balloon fifty feet in the air."

"Fifty feet?" the hawker said, overhearing the last of her comment. "Why, little lady, we go *three thousand feet* and higher. Why, I've been six thousand feet in the air myself. 'Course, that's about as high as you can go before your nose starts to bleed."

She swayed on her feet.

"But don't worry, little lady. We won't be going that high today."

"Unless we run into some tall mountains," Mace said quietly, enjoying himself immensely.

"Although the higher up you go," added the pilot, "the better the atmospherical pressure, and the smoother the flight."

She grabbed Mace so hard, her fingers dug through his coat sleeve and bit into the muscles of his forearm. "You listen to me. I—*can't*—go up in that thing. I swear to you, I'll die!"

"Nonsense. After the first few minutes, you'll no doubt relax and enjoy the ride."

"*You* enjoy the ride. I'm going to turn myself in."

She turned to leave, but he swept her up in his arms, clamped a hand over her mouth, and turned her face into his chest, so it wouldn't be seen. "It's a good thing," he muttered, "that you like dominant men."

"In bed," she ground out against his coat, "not in a damn balloo—"

He tightened his grip. She tried to fight him, but when the balloonist and some of the crowd turned to stare, he held her pinned so tightly against his chest, she couldn't move. "It's just a bit much for her," he explained with a smile. "She should come to in a minute."

"Perfectly understandable," said the balloonist. "Happens all the time."

She kicked her legs frantically.

"Ah," said Mace. "She seems to be coming to already."

"Now who'll be the first to join me for a ride?"

The balloonist walked out into the crowd. While his back was turned, Mace backed up to the rope that held the balloon tethered and used his foot to stealthily kick it loose. Then he tossed Saranda over the side of the basket, jumped in, and turned up the flame. As the gas expanded, he took the massive bag of sand that helped pin the basket to the ground and heaved it over the side. The balloon lunged fifty feet in the air.

"Hey! Stop, thief! Come back!"

As Saranda clutched the sides of the wicker with trembling fingers, Mace gathered the last of his poker winnings, wrapped it quickly in some of the balloonist's twine, bit it off with his teeth, and tossed it down. "I've just purchased your balloon, *friend*. Thanks for the lesson."

"But—but—"

As the balloon ascended swiftly, the pilot ripped open the bundle and flipped through. Apparently, it satisfied him, for he looked up and called, "Don't forget, if your burner fails, you have to land. You've only four bags of ballast."

"We won't forget."

Hanging over the side, Mace gave a jaunty wave. The balloon swayed precariously. Transfixed by fear, Saranda dropped to the floor of the basket, too terrified even to pray.

CHAPTER 53

She sat, her back pressed against the wall of the wicker, clasping her knees to her chest, too frightened to open her eyes. The swaying of the balloon caused her body to tremble almost violently. She felt sick and faint. She had to fight to breathe. If she had any thought at all, it was to wish she'd never been born.

She was aware of Mace fussing with the burner, following the haphazard instructions he'd been given. Thinking of his lack of experience caused a new wave of panic. She was certain they were going to crash and burn. She just knew they were going to die.

"Stop moving around," she snapped. Her voice came out muffled, as her forehead was pressed into her knees.

"Do you want this thing to crash?" he answered.

She was so scared, she wanted to cry. Her fingers ached from clutching. His words conjured up visions of them soaring up out of control, or plummeting to the trees.

Endless minutes passed as she huddled and shook.

"Saranda," he said presently.

"Don't talk!" Any noise, any movement, made her aware of the vast distance between them and the earth. Aware that nothing lay between her and a fatal, who-knew-how-many-thousand-feet fall except a webbing of wicker, and a crisscrossing of wooden boards. "Don't even breathe!"

"Come up here. Look at this view."

When she refused, he put a finger to her chin and tipped her head up to look at him. "It's more glorious than you can imagine."

A white rage blinded her. That he could stand there like some bloody pirate of the air, barely holding on to the suspension rope, with a frisky grin as if this nightmare he was putting her through was all a splendid jest . . .

She lost her head. Like lava erupting from a volcano, she was on him in a single, vaulting lunge.

"You son of a bitch!" she screamed. "You said I could trust you!"

"You *can* trust me. Look around you. We're fine."

"Fine!" She choked his neck with fingers made strong from fear. "I've never been *less* fine in all my life. I've never wanted to kill someone as much as I want to kill you. *How could you do this to me?*"

He grabbed her about the waist and lifted her off her feet so she came crashing against his chest. As he did so, she caught a flash of scenery, a sensation of great height, and vast expanses of nothing but empty space. She gave a tumultous jerk and clutched his head so her arms were wrapped around it, his face pressed into the soft mounds of her breasts.

He was silent for a moment, feeling her tremble. Then, in a hushed voice, he asked, "*What* have I done to you?"

Panic was getting the best of her. Her breath was

coming too quickly. She knew she was panting, but she couldn't feel any air in her lungs.

He extricated his head from her hold and saw the dangerous green tinge of her skin. "I shall have to slap you if you don't calm down," he warned.

"Do it, and I shall throw you overboard."

"And land this contraption by yourself?"

Her knees buckled. He caught her beneath her arms and held her up. "I can see we're going to have to get your mind off this."

"Spoken like a man with no fears."

"Get you thinking of something besides the motion of the balloon."

"Don't even mention it," she groaned.

"Something so compelling, it will capture your full attention. Obliterate all other thoughts."

His words, along with his intimate tone, were beginning to penetrate the terror. She looked up and saw a raw arousal burning in his eyes. One strong hand dropped to her buttocks, and he pulled her close so she could feel him, huge and hard, pressing through her skirts and into her slender thigh.

"How," she gasped, "can you think of such a thing at such a time?"

"How," he asked, "can you not?"

"I'm so scared—"

"Don't think about your fear. Think of it as a grand adventure. Who knows where the wind will take us? What hazards we might meet along the way? Here we are, soaring through the heavens, seeing things few people will ever see. Look at those fields. Look how small the trees are. How vast the horizon. It's like being the only two people in the world. Just you and me. Transcending the mortal bonds, with our spirits flying free. Can't you feel it, love? It stirs the soul like nothing imaginable."

"Not to mention your animal instincts."

"Who says we can't mention it?"

He was grinning wickedly. Letting her go, he vaulted up onto the top edge of the basket, grabbing the rope with one hand, and leaned over the side. With his free arm motioning to the sky, he called, "Come on, Princess! Throw your cares to the winds. We're no longer mortals but gods. Nothing can harm us. We're young. We're in love. We're charmed. Let us take what pleasure we can. And tomorrow be damned."

As he called his words to the skies, gesturing extravagantly all the while, the balloon tipped perilously to the side. Grasping the edge behind her with desperate hands, she closed her eyes against the sight of onrushing land. She knew she had to do something before he killed them both with his cavorting. It was her worst nightmare come true: to be floating in a balloon thousands of feet in the air, with an acrobat who thought it *stimulating* to hang over the side.

Not only did she have to get her own mind off her panic. She had to distract him from playing pirate of the skies as well.

What you need is something so compelling that it obliterates all thought.

There was only one thing that compelling in all the world. He'd already made it clear that she'd meet with no resistance.

She forced her eyes open and looked up at him. He was leaning more precariously than before, with only one foot on the basket, one hand on the ropes. "Come down here."

"I like it up here."

"You can't kiss me from up there."

He arched a brow. "Can't I?"

Swinging himself expertly around, he leaned into the

ropes and gave her a quick kiss. Then he was back dangling from the side.

His motions had caused the basket to bounce wildly. This wasn't working as she'd planned.

Oh, God, please help me get this lunatic down off those ropes!

She'd used passion as a weapon before. What was one more time?

"Does this excite you?" she asked, trying to keep her voice from trembling.

"Madly."

"Have you ever"—she gulped down the knot in her throat—"made love in the skies?"

Now he looked at her. "Is that an invitation?"

"Come on down here and find out."

He leaped down to the floorboards, causing the balloon to sink. Clutching the ropes behind her, she willed herself with titanic effort not to scream at him for his folly.

He clasped her waist and pulled her to him so that her hands were forced to leave the ropes and clutch his jacket instead. In his eyes was a look of wonder.

"It's more than I ever dreamed of," he told her passionately. "I knew you were afraid. But I thought if I could just get you up here—if you could just see what I see, *as* I see it—that you, too, would feel the excitement—the very wonder of it all. That you could share the thrill of being high above the ground. The freedom. The exhilaration. The blood boiling in your veins. You really feel it?"

"Kiss me and find out."

He bent his head and took possession of her mouth. Never had his kiss been so wild, so trenchant, so . . . *appreciative*. And never had she felt more wretched in her life.

Because the truth was, she'd never felt less sensual. Try as she might, she couldn't forget her fear. She felt as dry as a month-old bone. She knew if he came inside her now, it would be like penetrating sandpaper. She was ashamed of herself for trying to con him. Their attraction was so great, it had never occurred to her she'd have to fake her ecstasy, as she'd done with other men.

If only he hadn't forced her into this fearsome contraption . . .

"You're wonderful," he murmured into her hair.

Feeling guilty, she was nonetheless determined that he wouldn't guess. She slipped her hands inside his jacket, easing it down over his arms. "You're not attached to this, are you?" she asked with a convincing grin.

Then she tossed it overboard.

"That's my only jacket."

She unbuttoned his shirt and ran her tongue along his chest. "Now you know how it feels."

She undressed him swiftly, avoiding looking out. The side of the basket rose above her waist, so by careful positioning, she could pretend she wasn't surrounded by nothing on all sides.

He stood with his hands above his head, holding on to the ropes. Naked and chiseled, dark and sinewy, he was a sight that by rights should make any woman weep. Saranda made a valiant effort. She made a great show of kissing him—his shoulders, the heavy coils of his muscular arms, the thick black hair that swirled about his chest. She sucked on his nipples and felt him go rigid beneath her hand. She followed the path of hair down his belly, gliding her tongue along the V that pointed, like an arrow, to the pulsing, tempered invitation of his sex.

Sinking to her knees, where her sight was blocked on all sides, she took him in her hands and brought him to her tongue. She teased him with it for a time before swooping down to take him inside.

He rewarded her with a satisfied growl.

"This is unbelievable," he told her, thrusting into her mouth. "You're more than a bloody princess—" She sucked harder, and he lost his train of thought. With an effort, he added harshly, "You're a dispenser of fantasies. A woman to make a man's every dream come true."

No, she thought miserably. I'm just a shuckster who's too bloody good at her job.

"You like it when I take you in my mouth?"

"Oh, Christ, yes."

She knew that dialogue, like nothing else, was the aphrodisiac of his heart. A master of language himself, he reveled in the use of imaginative descriptions and hot, raunchy words. Just a whisper could arouse him to a blood-pumping frenzy. She knew, too, that she couldn't excite him—or any man—the way he could excite himself, using his own fantasies as a means. All she had to do was ask him a question or suggest an image, and he'd take it from there.

"I love the way you feel on my tongue. I love the taste of you. The hot, manly smell. You're so hard, it makes me tremble. Like a sword of tempered steel. Tell me how much you like it, darling. Tell me what you want me to do."

He told her with words that were as poetic as they were explicit. Guiding her head as he spoke, he showed her what he wanted, his words lewd and lusty and spoken with a husky growl. They sizzled in the open air. She'd never known a man more appreciative of her wanton caresses, more willing to heap praise on the unholy impulses she inspired.

He propped a muscular leg up on the side of the basket, affording her easier access. Dropping lower, at his command, she reached under him and took him, one, then another, into her mouth—sucking, teasing, nibbling ever so softly as his breath rumbled through the deep chasm of his chest.

"Yes, darling, yes. Sweet Lord, you're unbelievable!"

She didn't doubt it. Channeling her fear—and her guilt at deceiving him—into her efforts, she focused all her energies on her task. She moved relentlessly, here and there, varying her touch, the flick of her tongue, the soft, moist succor of her lips—driving him wild with the lust licking through his veins and the heady anticipation of where her willing mouth might wander next.

When he moved to lift her, so she could share his pleasure, she declined. Looking up, running her tongue along the swollen tip, she asked coyly, "Didn't you say something once about wanting to come in my mouth?"

His eyes glazed over as he told her what he wanted in more specific terms.

Deftly, she rendered him incapable of speech. It didn't take long. Cupping his testicles with one hand, stroking his shaft with the other, she sucked hard, exciting the sensitive head with her tongue, then took him deep once again. She welded her mouth to him as he discharged with a roar. Yet he'd thrust so hard that, toward the end, he slipped from her mouth and spurted at her face. Lapping at him, she rubbed him along her cheeks, coaxing the last of his shudders as she put her mouth to him once again and sucked him dry.

That should calm him, she thought, sitting back on her heels.

He shook his head like a lion shaking himself free of a downpour of water. "Oh, God! Woman, what you do to me."

He caught her beneath her arms and lifted her, kissing her long and hard, looking at her tenderly all the while.

"You've made me so happy," he said. "Now it's my turn to do the same for you."

She shook her head. "For today let your happiness be mine. It's enough that I could—"

His eyes narrowed suspiciously. "Since when have you become Saint Saranda, dispensing unselfish offerings?"

"Can't I desire to make you happy without being interrogated like some—"

He shoved her back against the side of the basket. "Mace, don't—" she cried, flinging out her arms.

While she was busy straining to hold on, he flung her skirt up, yanked her drawers aside, and thrust his hand up between her legs. As before, she was as dry as dust.

"*You little bitch,*" he rasped, his eyes glittering in anger.

"Mace, for God's sake—"

She could feel the balloon swaying. Looking over her shoulder, she saw the countryside looming closer. If he didn't stop shoving her, she'd go over the side.

"So it excites you, does it? Flying like the eagles? Soaring above an unsuspecting world?"

"I never said it excited me. In fact, I said, if you'll recall, that if you brought me up here, I'd die!"

She bent her cheek to her shoulder and wiped the stickiness on her dress. The motion infuriated him, and he tightened his grip.

"Flam *me,* will you?"

"You deserve it! I told you I didn't want to come up here. I *told* you I was scared. But did you care? No! You go leaping from rope to rope like some ruddy pirate, regardless of my feelings."

The anger drained from him, replaced by a cold, resolute pause. He looked thoughtful, then a prankish gleam glowed in his eyes.

"You're altogether right," he said. "I *haven't* considered your feelings."

She didn't like his expression. It was the same look

he'd given her that night he'd tied her up and forced her to submit to his unusual form of therapy. He had the same unassailable glitter in his eyes that told her she'd gone too far.

"Take your clothes off," he ordered.

She stuck her chin out. "Why should I?"

"Because I won't be conned, darling. Especially not by you."

"It's happened before."

"It won't bloody well happen again. Now, are you going to take those clothes off, or must I rip them from you myself?"

He made a grab for the neckline, but her hands caught his and stalled them.

"I shall submit to your vile threats because I have nothing else to wear. But I warn you, it will do you no good. I couldn't get excited now if you were Casanova himself."

"We shall see about that."

CHAPTER 54

Naked and defiant, she stood before him. Her eyes were closed, against the awareness of height, and to hide her shame when she proved herself right. Mace might be the best lover in all of Europe—couldn't she attest to that?—but it would take more than any man possessed to excite her under the circumstances.

He rose to the challenge, but not in the way she'd thought he might. She'd expected rough demands. Instead, what she got was gentle hands at her shoulders. Lips at her eyelids, flitting as sweetly as butterfly wings. He lifted her face and ran his own lashes along her lids, her cheeks, her brow. It was a strangely soothing, playful, tender assault.

His mouth lingered at her temple, breathing in her scent, dallying to taste of her skin. In motions so slow they took on heightened expectations, he brushed his lips past her cheekbone, blazing a heated path to her ear. There, he idled, kissing the earlobe, frolicking with the tip of his tongue. She'd never realized how sensitive she was there. As he nibbled gently with his teeth, his fingertips grazed her neck, her throat, the slope of her shoulder, so lightly, so delicately, that her skin prickled in his wake. The combination of his mouth at her ear and his fingers on her skin caused in her body a rising craving of his touch. If he'd manhandled her now, she'd have gone numb and pulled away. But the delicious tenderness of his skillful technique caused the tingling to spread and fill her with onrushing currents of pleasure. Just as she might lean forward to hear someone whispering, her skin, barely fondled, sought the delectation of his touch.

No inch of offered flesh was neglected. Tilting her head, he tickled the area under her cheekbone, in front of her ear. He moved lower to nibble at the pulsating juncture of her jawbone, neck, and ear. As he did so, she gasped and threw her head back to allow him better access. Luscious sensations scrambled through her belly and raced down her thighs. He ran his tongue along the inner ear, his breath warm and seductive.

"You can't escape me," he said, very low, so that even the breathy quality of the words caused her toes to tingle. "Sooner or later, your surrender will be mine for the taking."

The way he spoke was casual, but the sexual confidence behind them was a decided provocation. She shivered and turned her mouth to his.

His lips were gentle, softly cushioning her own. His tongue just touched the inside of her lips, penetrating no farther, making her ask him to come in. He played with them patiently, and gradually she began to relax in his arms, softening her lips against his. His kiss deepened, sensitive, probing, exploring leisurely, giving her time to adjust, to enjoy, to *want*, what he offered. Only when she began to press herself against him did he proceed more boldly, slipping his tongue between her teeth and with-drawing it, until she began to follow his lead. Roguishly, he nipped at her lower lip, sucked it in her mouth, before finally crushing her lips in a kiss that vanquished her hesitation and made her dizzy once again.

Just as she was drowning in the sensation, he moved his mouth to her other ear. A mewing sound registered her protest, yet the rarefied torture evoked such exquisite longings that she was hard-pressed to complain.

She thought he'd kiss her for eternity. Never had a man used his mouth to excite her the way he was doing now. She could feel her blood bubbling in her veins. He hadn't so much as touched her breast or stroked her thigh, yet he was awakening longings of such intensity that would make a virgin in her parlor spread her legs and whimper to be taken. Unconfined by convention, he asserted his full manhood, shattering her defenses in the process.

Eventually, he moved to her breasts. Instead of crushing them in his palms, he fluttered his fingers over lightly, kissing them, licking them, sucking on them, nibbling the nipples. Holding both breasts in his hands, he brought the nipples together and ran his tongue along them, rapidly flicking back and forth. The sensation was so erotic, she thought she'd lose consciousness. She began to rotate her hips into his, seeking something hard to rub against.

He sensed that she was ready. Rising up, he took her slender waist in his hands and, with one powerful lunge, sat her atop the wide rim of the wicker basket. Suddenly, her heart began to pound, fear converging with arousal to create tremors in her such as she'd never known. It was useless to argue. Disoriented as she was by dread and desire, he had her at his mercy as effectively as the night he'd tied her to the bed. She clutched at the ropes above, obeying some destructive impulse to look over her shoulder at the patchwork of green and brown fields.

She jerked her head away. He was wasting no time, bringing one leg up and around the basket, weaving the ropes to hold her fast. He extended the other likewise, so she was helplessly pinned open. Perched so, she felt as if she could easily fall backward. She was forced to grip tight with her hands and wrap her feet as best she could around the nearest ropes.

"Mace—"

He towered over her. Taking her face in his hands, he forced her to look at him. "Just remember this the next time you're tempted to pretend."

She was gulping for breath. "I can't stay up here. I swear to you, I shall die."

His look was unrelenting. "Then, my deceitful little harpy, I shall make you one promise, and only one."

"You'll let me down?"

"Not on your life. But if you *do* die, I promise you'll at least go with a smile on your lying lips."

"I didn't lie, exactly. Anyway, aren't you the one who said my truth is different than yours?"

He came close and leaned over, his breath brushing her lips. "Not about this. Not about something as precious as this."

"Please let me down. I swear I shall love you with everything I have to give, only—"

"Not yet, love. But look on the bright side. The sooner you cooperate, the sooner you can come down. Now . . . shall we discuss it?"

"No! Damn you for the wretch you are."

He grinned and bent to put his mouth to her thigh. "That's it, love. Talk to me. Tell me what this does to you."

She blasted him with words of fire. But soon his mouth began to work its magic. Soon her concentration was centered at the juncture between her thighs. He touched her with questing fingers. She wasn't as dry but was still by no means begging to be touched.

He licked his fingers, then circled them along her inner lips, avoiding the bud of her desire, moving right, then left, until he slipped a finger inside and she felt the walls of her inner cavern, juicy and willing, convulse at his invasion. Her excitement was heightened by her awareness of danger. Even as she shifted herself, begging him now to touch her honeyed gem, even as she felt herself losing her will to fight, even as she welcomed the undulating sensations that heralded her climax, she knew too well the jeopardy. Losing control at such a height, in such a position, could be fatal.

At last he found her with his tongue. It was so heavenly, so wildly pleasurable after being denied so long, that she cried out her relief. She was throbbing, her hunger building, devouring her, burning away all thoughts of safety except one.

"Mace," she panted. "If I come like this, I shall fall. Please—"

He slid up her body and kissed her deeply. "I thought you couldn't come at all. I thought even Casanova—"

"Shut up. I want you so, only— Let me come with you inside me. Please. I swear to you, I shall never, ever, ever, try and fake it again."

"Are you asking me to trust you?" he teased.

Her body was throbbing, desperate for him. "I was a fool. To think a man like you couldn't excite me. Couldn't make me want you so badly, I'd suffer anything to have you. How could I know that even thousands of feet above the earth, you could turn me into an inferno aching only to be consumed by you? If we were to crash now, I'd first want you inside me."

"How do I know you're not flamming me?"

"You have only to feel me to see for yourself."

He did, and she cried out at his touch.

"Besides which, if you don't get me down, I shall foil you. I swear I'll grit my teeth and do everything—do you hear me?—*everything* in my power not to come. I'd rather fall to my death than give you the satisfaction."

"Is that a challenge?"

"Come inside me," she coaxed. And told him what she wanted.

He let her down. Her legs were so sore from being stretched that she could barely stand. It didn't matter. Lifting her legs to lock around his waist, he eased inside. As he moved, filling her with unbelievable might, her mouth dropped open. His fingers found her in front, and she lost control completely. Her senses swirled, and she bucked with him to a shattering climax. She slumped against him, kissing his chest, murmuring her gratitude.

"I shall never doubt you again," she promised.

"Then do something for me now."

He was still hard in her. Withdrawing, he turned her so she faced the open sky. Entering from behind, he bent her so she was forced to look over the side of the balloon and down to the farmlands below. His hands found her breasts, and he resumed his rhythm.

"Just once, look down and see what I see."

She did. It wasn't easy. It wasn't comfortable. But the sensation of fright, combined with the sweet agony of his thrusts, aroused her unexpectedly. She reached back and caressed him as he rammed himself into her.

"Isn't it incredible?" he asked against her ear.

"Incredible," she gasped as she began to lose herself once again.

CHAPTER 55

The rest of the day was like a dream. Once she began to look around, Saranda lost much of her agitation. She found, with her eyes open, that floating high above the earth as she was, there was no sensation of movement. It was as if they were suspended in space and time. As if the earth below moved, and not they. With the burner turned low, there was an eerie stillness, a silence such as they'd never heard before. As she relaxed, they put their arms about each other and savored the tranquility.

They spent the afternoon following their progress on the map, pinpointing cities and landmarks and checking them off. The wind favored them. Below, cities drifted by to be replaced by lush green farmland, and miniature forests thick with leafy spring trees. Winding roads looked like lengths of twine. When she was feeling confident, Mace moderated the flame, and they meandered down to take a closer look. Once, in a playful mood, he swooped down on a field of cows, herding them with the balloon before the farmer came running and fired his rifle at them. Turning up the flame to expand the gas, they soared once again, waving good-bye. The more proficient Mace became in the operation of the balloon, the more he enjoyed himself.

That night, Mace brought the balloon down, unwound the rope, and threw out the anchor to effectively lasso a tree. The anchor was little more than a huge, four-pronged hook, which gripped a thick limb and held the balloon hovering above. Then he scrambled down the rope, wrapped it around the limb several more times until the basket was flush with it, and helped Saranda out, lowering her by her hands to the ground.

"Just my luck," she muttered, "to fall for a man whose greatest thrill is cavorting in the air."

He took her waist in his hands and hoisted her high above so that she was forced to grasp his shoulders for balance. Then, spinning her joyously, he said, "But just think, love. We may be the first people in history to make love in the skies."

"Some consolation," she teased. But she was cheered by his buoyant mood—and by the feel of the ground beneath her feet when he finally put her down.

They ate a supper of the food they'd brought along— bread, fruit, and chocolates, washing it down with a bottle of wine. There was a blanket rolled up and fastened to the side of the basket, which Mace climbed the tree to retrieve. Then, as the sky darkened and the stars began to appear, they leaned back against the tree, huddled beneath the blanket for warmth, and gazed at the night sky.

"Hard to believe we were up there," Saranda sighed, appreciating her accomplishment more now that she was on the ground.

"Aren't you proud of yourself?"

"Actually, I am. Not that I have much reason to be. I only went because you forced me."

"Tomorrow it will be easier."

"I'm not so sure. I may panic again and refuse to get back inside. I find the feel of good earth beneath my feet is a comfort. I've never been much for digging in the dirt, but I may become a farmer yet, after my adventures with you."

"That I should like to see."

They were silent for a few minutes, holding each other close.

"I should imagine the thought of tomorrow should hasten you into the balloon with enthusiasm."

"Tomorrow," she repeated softly.

"Tomorrow we shall be in New York."

Her heart skipped a beat. Sensing it, he added, "Not afraid, are you?"

"A little. I've lived in terror of jail cells my entire life. I can't say I fancy even a short stay. There's no telling what a jury might do."

"Don't forget, I have some pull in that town as well as McLeod. I'm hoping the judge, on seeing my evidence, will dismiss the charges."

She bolted upright. "The evidence! It didn't get destroyed in the tornado—"

"Hush, love. I sent it with the paper you signed back to New York."

Relieved, she settled back into the haven of his arms.

"No matter what happens, I shall protect you," he promised. "No harm will come to you. Do you believe that?"

She nodded. She could feel the excitement surging through his veins.

"We shall make the *Globe-Journal* what it once was," he murmured softly, looking up at the stars. "A force for good, a champion of the downtrodden. This country's changing, Princess. More and more immigrants are pouring onto its shores. They're going to come seeking a better life, and what will they find? Men like Sander McLeod who will exploit them to line his own pockets. Men like me, flim-flam artists and grifters, who will take advantage of their ignorance. They look at the new world with a sense of hope and promise. A good con man—"

"—or woman—"

"—or woman—can use that, by making them believe what they want to believe. Cities pass laws to keep them from working. Well, it's not going to happen easily. Not while I'm alive. Not while it's in my power to prevent it."

"Nor I," she vowed, feeling truly a part of his dream for the first time.

"We'll do it together, you and I. You'll report the news; I'll write the editorials and steer the paper in the right direction. Make certain Jackson didn't die in vain."

"I'll go undercover and expose corruption on a more personal level."

He stilled. "We haven't decided that."

"No. But we shall."

"Saranda—"

"Mace Blackwood, if you honestly think I'd be content working under your thumb, you're out of your mind. Having you tell me whom and what I can report on. Handing out assignments to me like some novice reporter—I may not have much experience in writing, but I *own* that newspaper. At least I did before I signed it over to you."

"Then marry me."

She sat up and looked at him. His eyes were like moonlight on a dark river.

"Marry me, Saranda. Be my partner, in work and in life. Let's put an end to this bloody feud once and for all. For three hundred years, the Blackwoods and the Sherwins have been at one another's throats. Isn't it enough? Isn't it time our families came together for good? For a purpose worthy of our talents?"

"If only it were possible. . . ."

"It *is* possible," he insisted.

"There's still Lance."

"Lance won't be a problem. He'll do as I say."

"Are you so sure about that?"

He couldn't answer. Instead, he said, "I want our children to be the first Blackwoods who don't have to be ashamed. Ashamed of where they come from or who they are. Just think of the children we could bring into the world, you and I. With the Blackwood and Sherwin blood mixing together to make them strong. With the paper as their environment. If we pool our resources, our talents, the instincts that have been passed down through our families for generations—if we channel all that for good— nothing can stop us!"

"Stop it! How can you torture me like this?"

"*Torture* you?"

"You know how I feel about having children," she cried, tears tumbling down her cheeks. "You know the very thought of it terrifies me. Mace, I was a failure as a mother. I'm not capable of giving a child the love he needs. I'm not—"

"*Were* not. Of course you weren't. You were fourteen bloody years old. And raped, to boot. What did you expect? Anyone in your situation would—"

"But it didn't happen to just anyone. It happened to my child. And I'm afraid of what I might do to others."

"You were afraid to ride in a balloon, but I'd say you survived it rather well."

"You don't understand. I won't destroy any more children with my cold heart."

He leaned his head back against the trunk of the tree. "Princess . . . if you had a cold heart, I couldn't love you the way I do. The only way to transcend your past is to accept what you are."

"I *do* accept what I am."

"It's all an illusion. A belief that no longer exists. If you were truly heartless, you wouldn't care about what you'd done. Besides, who has loved and comforted me, and given me a sense of hope for the first time in so many years?" He gazed at her with such gratitude, she was stunned. "You must do the same, love. You must forgive yourself for being human, accept what's past. Allow your suffering to make you a more compassionate person. Use the paper to help other women who suffer the same despair. Work toward seeing that it doesn't happen to others. Use your pain for a purpose."

"I'd like that. But children . . ." Her words drifted off.

He pulled her back into the crook of his arm. In a kind and careful voice, he asked, "What are you doing to prevent becoming pregnant?"

"Mother taught me to chart fertile periods by the stars."

"You're joking."

"Not in the least. All you need to know is the correct month, day, and year of the woman's birth. There are only about two hours every month when a woman is truly fertile—when the sun and moon are exactly the same number of degrees apart as they were at the moment of the woman's first breath. So if you calculate by the day and time of birth and add a day or two on either side, you only have a few days every lunar month when you must abstain. Of course, if you want to ensure conception, it's more complicated. You have to know the hour and minute the woman drew her first breath."

"Fascinating. Where did your mother learn this?"

"From Madame Zorina. It was one of the reasons she

sought her out. She'd heard the Gypsy had the secret, and hoped she'd share it."

"And it works?"

"I'm not pregnant. Once, out of morbid curiosity, I went back and charted the time of the rape—to see if it happened during a fertile time."

After the briefest of pauses, he asked, "Did it?"

"Yes. Unlucky for me."

He used his hand to brush the hair back from her face in a gesture of supreme gentleness. "Didn't you tell me you believe there are no accidents in life?"

"Yes."

"Then what happened to you happened for a reason. Both of us lost children tragically when we were too young to fully appreciate or care for them. I'd like to think we shall be better parents because of it. That we shall love our children more. Give them all the love we have bottled up inside. No one knows better how precious our time with them is."

"I want to believe you, Mace. But I have little confidence—"

"Then take some from me. It matters not if you give me children. I shall love you all the same. But know this. I believe in you. I believe your heart was stepped on at a tender age, and that your fear because of it has kept you from realizing how much love you have to give. But I make you this vow. I shall happily spend the rest of my life showing you." He swallowed hard. "You may not believe this, Princess, but there's a goodly amount of love stored in this rusty heart, waiting to be given. All the love I hoped to give Pilar and my child but couldn't. It's all there, and it's multiplied over the years. I just didn't realize it till I met you."

"I *do* believe you," she said softly.

"Then do me one favor."

"What's that?" she asked warily, not certain she could comply.

"Believe in yourself. You, too, have a great deal of love waiting to be used. Let my devotion be your spark. Let it show you how much you have to give."

She looked at him lovingly. "You don't ask for much, do you?"

"Only that you see all the possibilities of life . . . dare what others only dream about. That's all I ask."

She smiled, because when he said it, her heart soared, and she believed it was all possible. "We've been a sorry lot up till now," she said.

"Ah, but that's the wonder of life. We can always learn from our mistakes."

"You make me believe it."

"Then marry me. Together, let's forge a different destiny for ourselves. A new life, a new love, a new purpose."

"Yes."

He sat up. "You will?"

"Yes." She laughed. "You sound surprised."

"You mean to tell me—knowing who and what I am —knowing everything I said could be a flam—you're still willing to throw your lot in with mine?"

"Mace, I know a flam when I hear one. What you just told me was no con. It was the real you, speaking from the heart. Given all that, what woman *wouldn't* want you? Besides," she added, lowering her head and kissing him joyously. "You have other talents that I find irresistible. I should be a fool to let you get away."

"We still can't live together openly," he warned. "But once I get the paper back and clear your name, I think I can come up with a way to make you out a heroine in this thing."

"I don't doubt it for a moment."

"But don't forget, they still think of me as Archer. They may know you were a con woman, but they still believe my story. Can you live with that for the rest of your life? Playing Mrs. Archer instead of living out your life as Saranda Blackwood?"

"You know me better than that. I would have done so had Winston lived, and had I not fallen in love with you."

"You'd have fallen in love with me in any case."

"Is that so? Well, don't forget, my smug friend, the name Blackwood isn't exactly one I've coveted in my life. I can live without it just fine, thank you."

She saw a flash of unbidden regret in his eyes.

"The question is," she added, "can you?"

"I shall have to," he said. "I have little choice."

"You could always come clean."

"And risk losing the paper? Our future?"

She went into his arms. "It doesn't matter to me what we're called, so long as we're together. You make me believe anything's possible. I should play a role forever rather than lose you."

He hugged her close, settling back to look at the stars. "Then tomorrow, Princess. Tomorrow, it begins."

They fell asleep in each other's arms, unaware how easily their dreams could be shattered.

CHAPTER 56

Their trouble began midmorning when the wind suddenly shifted north. Try as he might, raising and lowering the balloon to different elevations, Mace couldn't find a south-easterly current. Over northern Pennsylvania, the wind picked up, blowing them at a furious pace. Somewhere close to Albany, they ran into a patch of thick black clouds that threatened rain. In Vermont, the cloudburst was heavy and the winds gusting, forcing them to rise to nearly six thousand feet in order to steady the balloon. The air was thinner at that altitude, hearing and seeing more diffi-cult. Objects appeared distorted. Their ears ached. Still, they blew north, away from their destination. Once again, Saranda grew petrified.

Mace was more concerned with turning the balloon back toward New York. He refused to land and wait out the storm. There was no telling when the atmospheric condi-tions might suddenly change. He wanted to be in the air, so he could take advantage of every second of aid the wind could give them.

By afternoon, they knew it was hopeless. They'd been blown so far north, even a cyclone headed for New York would be hard-pressed to get them there in time for the five o'clock deadline. Still, Mace persisted, long into the night when flying conditions were all but impossible.

They finally landed in a downpour of rain. In the wet, it was impossible to keep the gas flame lit, so they had to bring the balloon to the ground. They spent the night under a grove of trees, soaked to the skin in spite of the protective overhang, shivering in the cold. Mace held Saranda close for warmth, but his mood was detached.

"I'm so sorry, Mace," she told him helplessly.

"Hush," he replied, not looking at her. "Try to sleep."

Of course she couldn't. It surprised her how disappointed she felt. She could feel his despondency as if it were a current flowing from him. She knew this was the end of his dream. By now, Sander McLeod had bought the *Globe-Journal*. But somewhere along the way, it had become her dream as well. A dream of a useful future, with the man she loved working by her side.

Now it would never be.

Still, some ember of optimism refused to die. "If we can prove my innocence," she murmured thoughtfully, "and implicate Sander McLeod, won't the paper revert back to me?"

"You're missing the point. McLeod owns the courts. He has the politicians in his back pocket. The only thing he didn't own was the power of the press. With the paper, we had a chance. We could print such a barrage of stories, the courts would have to take note. We'd print the evidence for all to see so no court or judge could possibly deny it. Without the paper, we haven't got a prayer. But with the paper in McLeod's hands, we're all but dead."

"Dead?"

"Even having secured the paper, we're still a threat to McLeod. He can't afford to be implicated in the Van Slyke murders. Besides Lance, you and I are the only ones who know the truth. I can't even take you in to the authorities for safekeeping. Once McLeod realizes we have proof, he'll be out to kill me. You he can leave to the mercy of the courts."

"What are we going to do?"

"I don't know. I'll be honest with you, Saranda, it doesn't look promising. In any case, we shall go into the city. I'll meet with my contacts at the paper while you hide out. Is there a place where you'll be safe?"

"I can try Stubbs' friend, Sophie. She's an old whore, but she'll do anything for money. I'll buy her silence by promising her a share of my inheritance."

"As long as you think you'll be safe."

"And then?"

He let out a slow breath. "Then we shall see."

Sometime during the long, wet night, she dozed against his chest. But even in her sleep she was aware of him, sitting rigidly with his back to the tree, scarcely blinking an eye.

THEY NAVIGATED THE balloon over the city after nightfall, hoping no one would detect their descent. They'd planned to land in Central Park, where there would be enough open space to set it down without being seen. But just as they began to drift down over the city, the burner began to fizzle. As Mace was struggling to moderate it, the flame went out completely. Denied fuel, the balloon sank at an astonishing speed, swooping down over the tops of buildings, barely missing them on its course to a crash landing. Frantically unwrapping the anchor rope, Mace hurled it into the air, and after several tries, finally succeeded in anchoring the hook to the corner of the Cooper Union Building. They had just enough time to scramble over the side and out before the basket bounced high and came crashing back down, dragging on its side halfway across the flat roof.

Shaken, they searched for a doorway that might lead them into the building. There was none. "Climb on my back," Mace instructed, "and close your eyes."

She didn't dare ask what he had in mind. Obeying him, she closed her eyes and clung to his back as he lowered himself over the side of the four-story building, sometimes sliding several feet before finding a foothold.

Finally, they reached the ground. The streets were deserted, although farther along they could hear the crowds around the Bouwerie Lane Theater. Suddenly, the time of parting was at hand.

Saranda was overwhelmed by feelings of despair. She hadn't been away from him in months. It troubled her that she'd be spending her first night away from him in the city that most wanted her dead.

"I can't bear to say good-bye," she told him, holding him close.

He kissed her, encircling her with strong, protective arms. For a moment, she felt safe, felt that in spite of the horrendous odds, all would come right in the end. But when he pulled away, the feeling left with him. She felt small and frightfully alone. She, who'd been on her own since the age of thirteen.

"You've spoiled me," she confessed. "I don't know that I can live without you ever again."

"Hang on to that thought. Hopefully, you won't have to."

"Mace—"

He took both of her hands in his. "Listen to me, Saranda. I can't make you any promises. But know that no matter what happens, I'm with you. I shall think of something. If I have to die protecting you, I won't let them harm you."

"That's small consolation. I wouldn't want to live if you weren't by my side."

He kissed her hands, which he still held in his. "Somehow, we shall get out of this. Just remember, there's always a way."

She knew he was saying it to comfort her. She could read his unspoken doubts in his eyes.

HURRYING DOWN AN intricate maze of side streets to make certain she wasn't followed, Saranda moved with all haste into the Bowery. There, she disappeared into the hordes of transient immigrants. The stench of the river mingled with the smells of food while somewhere she could hear screams coming from an open window.

Going back to Sophie's was like returning to a past she'd hoped she'd left behind. She'd stayed at Sophie's when she'd first come to New York. Nothing had changed. The girls were still turning tricks, and Sophie was still tucking the proceeds into her ample money belt.

"So you're back," she greeted, rarely surprised by anything life threw her way.

"Have you a room I might let?" Saranda asked. "Just for a few days?"

"My rooms don't come free, as you know—"

"I'll pay you more than they're worth. I just need a

little time to clear my name. When I've gotten my inheritance, I'll repay you with so much money, you can leave this rathole for good."

"Well . . ."

"Please, Sophie. I dearly need a place to hide."

"I don't want no trouble, you hear?"

Finally, they agreed, and Saranda shut the door and fell into the dirty sheets, too exhausted even to undress. Things looked so black, and the bed felt empty and huge without Mace at her side. Still, she was so tired that sleep began to steal her senses. She'd figure out what to do in the morning. Maybe things would look brighter then.

As she was losing consciousness, though, she was seized again by a feeling of doom. She was in a rat-infested brothel, while her lover risked his life to save her. Mace . . .

SHE WAS DEAD asleep when the door to her room was forced open, and she was dragged from her bed. Heavy with sleep, feeling drugged, she was surrounded by men in the blue uniforms of the New York police. It took her a moment to remember where she was, to understand why they were speaking to her in that surly tone as they shoved her out the door.

On her way down the stairs, she heard Sophie talking to the officer in charge. "That's her, Saranda Sherwin. Wanted to stay here for free. Gave me some garbage about paying me when she got her inheritance. Hah! Everyone knows she's going to hang."

In her stupor, Saranda heard Sophie's voice droning on, claiming the ten-thousand-dollar reward. On the ground floor, an inspector stepped forth and clamped handcuffs on Saranda's wrists. His mouth was moving, but she couldn't understand the words. She couldn't concentrate on anything but Sophie's voice echoing in her mind.

She's going to hang . . . she's going to hang . . . *everyone knows she's going to hang*. . . .

CHAPTER 57

She awoke to a foul smell of urine and decay. For a time, she couldn't remember where she was. Her surroundings were cold and dark, fashioned from stone, small and cramped. She lay on a hard cot with a ragged, dirty blanket her only covering. Across from her was a heavy steel door. There were no windows, no openings of any kind that would let in the light.

Suddenly, she remembered it all. Being dragged from her bed in the middle of the night, handcuffed, and shoved through the streets of the Lower East Side on foot. And her terror as she realized where they were taking her. *The Tombs*. Officially the New York House of Detention for Men, it was so nicknamed because of its resemblance to an Egyptian tomb. And, it was rumored, for the feeling of suffocation on being incarcerated in the horrid place. Her old friend Stubbs the safecracker had once done a three-month stint in the dreaded prison, and he'd never spoken of his experiences there to a soul.

Insensible as she was by sleep and shock, she'd had the presence of mind to ask why they were taking her to a man's prison. They muttered something about there being no maximum-security holding cell for women. One policeman grinned nastily at her, showing a gold tooth. "Ain't you heard?" he asked. "You're a desperate character." His partner only laughed.

She didn't know if it was day or night. As she sat on her cot, with her feet propped up, her arms wrapped around her knees for warmth, she began to shiver from more than the cold. The walls seemed to close in around her. In all her nightmares about prison, she'd never visualized such a closed-off cell. It was truly like being sealed off in a tomb. No light. No sound. No sense of her surroundings. Just alone in the dark with her own imagination.

It was her worst nightmare come to life.

She didn't know how long she sat, quivering in anticipation. There was no way of marking the time save the wild beating of her heart. The silence was unearthly. She began to listen for any sound, a footstep, a creak of iron, anything that would tell her she wasn't alone in this purgatory.

She became aware of her hunger. She couldn't remember the last time she'd eaten. Her stomach growled softly. She almost welcomed it. It was something real she could cling to, proof that she was alive, and wasn't, after all, losing her mind.

Finally, a key turned in the lock. The door squealed open and daylight spilled in, forcing her to shut her sensitive eyes. Then a figure stepped into the light. He was only a silhouette, the light outside reflecting behind him like rays of the sun. But she recognized the shape, the beloved form.

Struggling to her feet, she hastened toward him, awash with relief and joy. "Mace," she cried. But just as she was about to throw herself into his arms, he raised the lantern he held to his face and grinned.

"Guess again."

Horrified, she stumbled back. For it wasn't Mace who'd come to see her after all. It was Lance.

As her eyes grew accustomed to the light, she began to distinguish his features—the narrower jaw, the smaller forehead, the grotesque stare of his blind eye. It gave him the leering glint of a madman.

The door slammed closed behind him. He placed the lantern on a hook at eye level, then turned back to her, regarding her with a speculative gleam.

"So ye know who me brother is," he commented. "I wondered."

She was trembling horribly. The cell seemed suddenly too confining, too small to contain the both of them. To her eyes, he was the very essence of evil. She couldn't help remembering all that had passed between them. Yet her pride surged to the surface. She wouldn't give him the satisfaction of seeing how he'd beaten her.

"I always knew it," she said defiantly. "Why do you think I went after him? To make him pay for what you'd done."

"By gracing his bed, eh?"

She couldn't let him know the extent of her feelings for Mace. In a contemptuous tone, she said, "I'd die before I let another Blackwood in my bed."

He came forward and took a strand of her silver hair in his hand. It hung loose about her shoulders. She didn't know how beautiful she looked, or how vulnerable, with her blue eyes wide with fear. Watching her face as her hair slipped through his fingers, he asked, "Would you?"

Her hand lashed out to slap him. He caught it midway and wrenched it back, causing her to cry out. "Where's me brother?" he growled, his cockney accent pronounced, his pretense at civility abandoned.

"I don't know. For all I know, he's the one who turned me in."

He slapped her face hard, so her head snapped back and her cheek stung. "Don't tyke me for a fool, Sherwin."

"You just answered your own question. Since when did a bloody Blackwood ever do anything for a Sherwin but murder and rape them?"

"Me brother's only once risked his life for anyone. But he was willing to die to protect you. So don't try to bugger me. Where is he?"

"I don't know. Even if I did, I wouldn't tell the likes of you."

He slapped her again, this time jerking her forward and back in a half-circle. She lifted her head, shook back her hair, and stared at him defiantly. "Mace is right about you, you know. You *are* stupid. Too stupid to be able to figure things out for yourself. You'll never be the man Mace is, and you know it. It's what eats away at you, isn't it? Keeps you up nights. It's why you have to rape children. Because no woman in her right mind would want you of her own volition."

He lunged at her. His hands at her throat, he shook and strangled her until she couldn't breathe. Her eyes bulged, and she clawed at his hands, desperate to pull free. Finally, just as she was losing consciousness, he thrust her back so that she fell sprawling onto the cot. Gasping and coughing, she struggled to bring air through her burning throat and into her lungs.

"I should have bleeding killed you when I had the chance."

When she looked up at last, she saw him standing with his arms dangling at his sides, breathing like a furnace. There was a look of madness about him.

"I know wot yer thinkin'," he gasped wildly. "Ye think I'm daft, just like Mace does. I can see it in his eyes when he looks at me. Pities me, so he does. Thinks it's his fault I'm the way I am. It isn't, y'know. But I let him think it. Keeps him on me side. Thinks if he'd been better to me, I'd be different."

"You mean you were born crazy."

"*I'm not daft!*" He took a lunge for her but backed off a moment later, pacing the room with manic energy. "But I don't mind if Mace thinks so. Keeps him feeling sorry for me. Keeps him wantin' to help me. And all the while, I'm tykin' everything he ever wanted. Soon I'll have it all. Including you. I can't wait to see the look in me brother's eyes when he finds out you've been hanged."

"You'd do that to your own brother?"

"Me brother," he spat. "Me sainted, four-flusher brother. The man with the golden tongue. Butter couldn't melt in his mouth. Me brother Mace, who got everything and everyone he ever wanted. While I had to fend for meself. While he turned me away when I needed him most."

"When he found Pilar, you mean." She needed to hear him admit it.

"Aye. Bleedin' revolutionaries, wastin' me brother's talents on balmy ideals. I put an end to that nonsense, I did."

"Very clever, turning them in the way you did."

"Bloody right. Worked too. Soon as Pilar was tyken care of, Mace was free to go back on the con—with me."

"It must have been a shock, then, to find he'd taken up with the Van Slykes."

"Well, he ain't with 'em now, is he? He found the perfect world, created the perfect con. Well, I destroyed that world, and I put an end to his con. And like it or not, I'm tyking his place."

"What do you mean?" she asked leerily.

"Haven't you heard? McLeod's made me editor of the *Globe-Journal* in Mace's place. Wherever he is, I hope he's seething."

"What do you know about running a newspaper?"

"Not a ruddy thing, lovey. But I'm still enough of a clipper to cover me tracks. Once Mace is dead, it won't matter."

She felt chilled. "You'd kill your own brother?"

"I won't have to. McLeod will, once he finds him. You don't think he's goin' to let him get out alive?"

Before she could reply, the key turned again in the lock. "Time's up, Mr. Blackwood."

Lance came to her and rubbed his hand along her cheek. "Too bad. I'd have liked havin' another go. Maybe some other time—before yer hanging."

Chuckling to himself, he turned to leave. When his back was to her, Saranda raised herself up on her cot, full of loathing and a deep desire to cause him pain.

"I had your child," she told him.

He stopped. There wasn't a sound.

"He was a beautiful boy. Looked a great deal as you must have before your—accident. But he died because I couldn't care for him. If you'd been there, if you'd helped, he might be alive today."

Lance stood frozen, still with his back to her. She could feel his shock.

"But you know something, Lance? He's not the only child I shall ever have. One way or another, I'll get out of here. You can fool yourself as much as you like. But you know as well as I do what a master Mace is. He's going to beat you. And when he does, he and I will replace your child with his. And he'll have something you'll never have."

He didn't move. The guard finally prompted him, but

he waved him away. At last, he turned. He looked shattered. He gazed at her more closely, as if visualizing her pregnant with his child. As if imagining her holding the baby in her arms.

"I wouldn't be so sure," he said softly.

"Do you doubt Mace? Because I don't."

A cruel sneer turned his face ugly. "No, lovey, I don't doubt him. If what you say is true—if you do get out of this alive—Mace is bloody well going to have a choice to myke. You or me. When it comes to that, Mace will choose me."

"You don't know that," she insisted.

"I know it, Sherwin. He always has."

CHAPTER 58

The next time the door was opened—days later? She didn't
know.—It was Sander McLeod with another man, portly,
balding, with a stubborn set to his jaw and an air of self-
important authority. With McLeod's bulk, they effectively
filled the confines of the cell.

"Miss Sherwin," McLeod greeted her, scratching his
red fringed whiskers. "This is a long-awaited pleasure."

There was a note in his voice of smug satisfaction, of
savoring the notion of rubbing her nose in her defeat.

"May I introduce Warden Hull. You'll be his guest
until your trial."

The warden lifted a corner of his lip in a crude sneer.

"Why am I here?" she asked.

"Because, Miss Sherwin," explained the warden with
patronizing patience and heavy sarcasm, "you're wanted for
murder."

"Why the Tombs? Why a men's prison?"

Why, she wanted to add, the worst prison in the city?

Sander smiled. "My associate, Mr. Blackwood—I believe he paid you a visit, did he not?—is of the opinion that your partner in crime is more than capable of breaking you out of jail. Why he'd think so, I have no idea. He's a competent enough editor, I suppose, in his own way. But he never struck me as one to risk his neck in the sort of daring theatrics an escape would call for. Without the paper to hide behind, he's powerless."

"You may think so, naturally, if it amuses you."

"In any case, we've taken the necessary precautions. Your whereabouts are not being revealed to the press. Even my own paper, the *Globe-Journal*, is professing ignorance. But just to be safe, we'll keep you here for the time being. Even given the inclination, it would take a load of dynamite for Archer to break you out of this hellhole."

"Archer?" she asked, feeling more than a little dazed from her sojourn in the dark and her lack of food.

"You remember Archer, don't you? The man who aided you in eluding the authorities for so long. Who, by doing so, made himself an accessory to your crime."

It occurred to her that Lance was protecting his brother's identity. But for how long? What ammunition would he call forth to destroy him?

"Speaking of Archer," McLeod continued, "we're curious as to his whereabouts."

"Since you're aware Lance visited me, you know I've already said I don't know *where* Archer is."

"Please, Miss Sherwin, don't insult our intelligence. You don't actually think we're going to believe you?"

"It's the truth. Just as it's true I didn't kill the Van Slykes. But then, you already know that, don't you, Sander?"

She saw the flick of apprehension in his eyes before he turned to the warden. "See what you can do to loosen her tongue."

The warden nodded, and they turned to leave. Saranda stood in a single, impulsive gesture. "You're not going to leave me here in the dark, surely?"

The warden's uncompromising glower was made more menacing by the obvious pleasure he derived from her words. "That," he warned her, "is up to you."

"I'll just have a word with her alone, if you don't mind, Warden."

"Take all the time you need."

The door was closed behind them, and they were alone. The scene had told Saranda more than what was said on the surface. The easy manner by which McLeod secured the warden's cooperation spoke volumes about the power the man wielded. She had no doubt if Sander ordered her beaten, it would be done.

"I thought you'd like to see this morning's headline. It's exclusive, by the way. We were the only paper to get the news in time for the morning edition."

He withdrew a folded section of the paper from his back pocket and, unfurling it, held it to the lantern. She read the headline with a sinking heart.

PRINCESS OF THIEVES
BROUGHT TO HEEL AT LAST

"I'd let you read the rest, but it would only dishearten you. Suffice to say, by the time I get through with you, you won't have a supporter left in the whole country."

It was a particularly bitter blow. She and Mace had spoken often of how they'd use the paper to help vindicate her. To have the same powerful weapon turned against her seemed the final humiliation.

"It will prove difficult, nonetheless, to best us with trumped-up allegations," she bluffed.

"Trumped-up?" He withdrew a piece of paper from his coat pocket and unfolded it. "Tell me, Miss Sherwin, is this or is this not your own handwriting?"

As she'd suspected, it was the confession she'd written up in case Jackson learned the truth. Her heart sank.

"Now," he said, in a change of tone, "where is he?"

"You must be hard of hearing. I've told you I don't know."

"You might as well tell me. We're going to find him eventually."

"Then you don't need my help."

He studied her a moment as he replaced the paper. "The way I figure it—and tell me if I'm wrong—is, Archer wouldn't have brought you in if he didn't have proof you didn't kill the Van Slykes. Oh, don't look surprised. We both know you didn't. Behind closed doors there's no need for pretense between us, is there? Nothing I say here will stand up in court. They'll rule it as hearsay. Besides, who would believe an adventuress over a reputable member of society?"

"And if there were proof? To counter *your* proof?"

"That, of course, would make things more difficult. So I'm sure you can see why it's imperative I find your friend Archer before your case goes to court."

"I was under the impression that you had the courts —*sewed up*? Is that how you say it?"

"Well, it never hurts to be prepared for anything. No doubt you've found that to be true in your profession as well."

"Are you complimenting me?"

"I have to admit you had us all fooled. I'm not sure I'd even recognize you, without your Sarah Voors getup. It's why I sent Lance after you. He's the only one who knew what you really looked like."

"Has it occurred to you to ask how he knew?"

"That's unimportant."

"You're a fool if you trust Lance Blackwood."

"I trust no one, little lady. I merely reward people for services rendered. That way, they remain loyal."

"Some loyalties can't be bought."

"Have *you* ever found one that couldn't?"

She lowered her eyes.

"Just as I thought. You're a beautiful woman. I imagine men would walk through fire if you asked them."

She looked up with some of the old sexual confidence blazing in her eyes. "*You'd* walk through fire for me, if I wanted you to."

He smiled as if she'd proved his point. "And what would Archer do for you, I wonder?"

SHE'D BEEN IN prison for two weeks—or so she was told, while she grew weaker and more dispirited by the hour. For two torturous weeks, she was questioned day and night in a relentless effort to discover her lover's whereabouts. When she refused to speak, her inquisitors played cruel games with her mind—telling her one thing, then another, to throw her off-balance. They hit her with such a barrage of accusations and questions that she ached for peace and solitude. Yet when they left her alone it was worse. The darkness, the eerie, tomblike silence, the absolute isolation plagued her. She saw the guards in her cell, but a moment later couldn't tell if they were real or imagined. And always, she heard their snarling voices ringing in her ears.

They brought in trays weighted with tempting foods. Succulent meats, with vegetables so fresh, they looked as if they'd been picked that afternoon. Tender lobster in a cream sauce that smelled like heaven. Fluffy biscuits oozing with butter and dripping with sweet honey. Desserts to make her mouth water—chocolate concoctions and creamy fruit tarts. Each dish was carefully chosen not just for its physical presentation but for the aroma it exuded in the confines of her cell. As they questioned her, the rich odors distracted her, causing her stomach to cramp and growl. She was so hungry, she could barely concentrate on what they were saying. But when she refused to talk, they took away the sumptuous foods and left her only a bowl of broth and a cup of water.

The psychological games were more wearing and terrifying than any beating. She could have endured the lash of the whip. Eventually, she'd pass out and find merciful black peace. But they kept her on tenterhooks the entire time, telling her of the manhunt going on for her lover. How he'd been spotted and almost captured. How he'd been wounded getting away. How it wouldn't be long before he was dragged into an adjoining cell in chains. How he'd be hanged at her side as accessory to murder. And always—the endless interrogation: Where is he hiding? What are his plans? What evidence does he have?

All the while, she asked herself the same questions. *Where was Mace? What was he doing?* She'd half expected that, even safeguarded as she was, he'd miraculously appear and steal her away. *Mr. Blackwood seems to be of the opinion that your partner in crime is more than capable of breaking you out of jail,* Sander had said. Half-crazed by her stark conditions, she came to believe it was true. If Lance thought Mace would come, surely . . .

But in her saner moments, her rational mind told her it wouldn't happen. It wasn't Mace's style to swing in and rescue her with guns blazing. His weapon was his mind. If she was to be rescued, it would come subtly, brilliantly. In the most unexpected way.

Then one day Sander McLeod entered with a smile of satisfaction on his face. "We got him," he announced.

"Who?" she whispered.

"Archer—who else?"

Weak as she was, she forced herself to sit up in the gloom. "Where is he?"

Sander grinned cruelly. "Dead."

She wouldn't believe it. It had to be a trick, another twisted game to throw her off-guard, make her confess. But Sander told her of Mace's death in such gory detail that, even as she refused to believe, she put her hands to her ears to shut out the awful words. When she looked up, he was gone, leaving her alone to relive the ghastly images he'd planted in her mind. Had she found him after the tornado, only to lose him now?

So she waited. And despaired. Until one day the guard came in with her meager fare and a smile of anticipation on his face. "Your trial's set for Monday morning," he announced.

"Monday? What day is it?"

"Friday. Looks like the waiting's about over."

Two more days. She began to doubt for the first time. What, she wondered, was she waiting for? A miracle? Or a rendezvous with a noose?

Because surely if Mace were alive, he'd have found a way to send word. She hadn't been bothered by the warden in days. At first he'd made daily visits to taunt her, threatening retribution if she held to her silence. But lately the hours, the days, had drifted by, and no one had come but the guard.

She was weak and feverish. Sometimes, she caught herself talking aloud, just to hear the sound of a voice. Sometimes she realized the guard was standing there, and she hadn't even known it. Then, alarmed, she wondered what she'd been saying. Had she told them something that had led them to Mace? Was *that* why they'd stopped questioning her?

Once, a presence in the cell awoke her. Groggily, she was aware of three or four men standing in the gloom, watching her. When she stirred, one of them sat on the narrow cot and rubbed her arm. Another joined him, brushing her hair from her face.

"So this is the woman they say can drive men wild," one of them said in a faintly amused voice.

No longer caring what they did to her, she turned her back and went back to sleep. When she opened her eyes, they were gone.

It seemed only a blink of an eye before the guard came back, nudging her with his shoe. When she sat up, her hair falling about her face, she realized he was speaking. "What did you say?" she asked with difficulty.

"I said, say your prayers, lady. Your trial's in the morning."

FEEBLE AS SHE was, she couldn't sleep. Her defenses had been battered to the point that she could no longer hope. If Mace hadn't sent her word by now, it had to be one of two reasons: He didn't know where she was, or he was dead. He could be waiting to make his move when she arrived at the courthouse, but instinct told her it would be too late. Once McLeod had her in court, he wasn't going to let her get away. And if Mace showed up and presented his evidence, Sander would have him killed. Then Lance could discredit him by disclosing his real identity, and it would all have been for nothing.

If Mace didn't make his move before she was brought to trial, he'd never have the chance.

If he was alive.

.   .   .   .

SHE KNEW IT was morning when she heard the key turn in the lock. A matronly woman entered to ready her for court. She helped her change into a fresh dress, sponged the soot from her face and hands, and brushed and dressed her hair atop her head. Then the matron told her to wait, that they'd be along for her in a few minutes.

Saranda sat like a stone on her cot, staring straight ahead. The time had come. She'd be set up for derision and ridicule in a public courthouse. She'd be accused of murdering two people she cared deeply about. And she'd be found guilty and sentenced to hang. She doubted the proceedings would take more than a few hours.

She must steel herself to present a brave facade. She had to con them into thinking she wasn't as scared as she was. But she was so disoriented, so woozy from hunger and fever, that she couldn't seem to summon the effort.

The key turned once again. It was time. She rose on quivering legs and stepped forward like the walking dead— only to stop cold in her tracks.

She couldn't tell if she was dreaming or awake. Her head was spinning and her vision unclear. Had she completely lost her mind? For coming through the door were Bat Masterson and Wyatt Earp.

CHAPTER 59

They stood in the doorway in black suits and brocade vests, boots and spurs, with two guns strapped to their hips and Big 50 Sharps rifles cradled in the crooks of their arms. Rifles that could shoot a hole through a buffalo at fifty paces.

There was a scuffle as the guards protested the intrusion. Wyatt's voice cut in, harsh and curt, saying something about a warrant, a prior claim. Saranda's head was spinning so, she couldn't follow it. She took a step toward them, saying softly, unbelievingly, "Bat?"

Wyatt, with his uncanny hearing, heard her. He leveled his rifle at her and jerked his head toward Bat. "Get the cuffs on her," he ordered. "And keep her quiet. Move it, by God! I haven't got all day."

It was neatly accomplished. She was handcuffed and dragged, by virtue of the rifles leveled at the guards' stomachs, down the dank corridors and out into the blinding sun. They thrust her into an open carriage as the warden came running. "Guard her while I take care of this cactus burr," Wyatt told Bat under his breath. "If I'm not back in one minute, leave without me."

Bewildered by the sudden events, Saranda allowed Bat to settle her in the carriage, staring at him as if she still couldn't trust her eyes. He looked so dear to her, looked just the same with his thick black mustache and cold-as-ice eyes. "How did you . . . ?"

He held a hand up for quiet, listening through the carriage window as Wyatt explained the situation to the warden. Then Wyatt, with his best western swagger, returned to the coach and barked an order for the driver to take off. The warden and his guards were left staring after them in angry confusion. No one dared question the gunmen's authority. Not with a warrant from Washington to back them up.

As the coach lurched through the streets of the Lower East Side, Saranda tried to understand what was happening, and why. "You can thank your friend Blackwood," Bat told her.

"Mace is alive?"

Bat nodded, and Saranda leaned into him, collapsing with relief. "I was so worried," she said as Bat's arms wrapped around her protectively.

"You got no cause to worry about that one," Wyatt said, removing his hat and using his sleeve to wipe the sweat from his brow. "He wired us you were in trouble. Told us just what he needed. I pulled some strings with an old running mate in Washington. Had myself appointed U.S. marshal and made Bat here my deputy." He eased aside his jacket to display the marshal's badge pinned to his vest. His droopy gold mustache turned up as he snickered. "Mighty impressive for an old scoundrel."

"What was that about a warrant?" Saranda asked.

"Hell, we made that up. There was a holdup a few

years back of the federal mail. You were around Kansas at the time, so we drew up a federal warrant for your arrest—charging you with the crime. Since it happened before the murders, that gives Kansas a prior claim on you. They may throw it out, but it has to go before a federal judge in Washington. My *compadre* will see it's tied up for a spell. Meantime, we'll do what we can to keep you from hanging."

"Was all this Mace's idea?"

"Most of it," said Wyatt. "Although I supplied the holdup, having been acquainted with it."

"*Acquainted* with it?"

Bat laughed. "Acquainted with it from the standpoint that he *did* it."

"Well, it was before I got the marshal job in Wichita," Wyatt admitted.

Saranda smiled at them, shaking her head. "You two never change. But it's good of you to come. Particularly you, Wyatt, since we were never close."

"Hell, that don't matter none. Doc's come to lend a hand too."

"Doc Holliday?"

"Blackwood thought it might help if we had a doc to say you were indisposed," Bat explained. "Although, looks to me, sugar, like you really could use a pill roller. You're looking a mite off your feed."

"I'm all right. Not that Doc would do me any good, him being a dentist."

"They don't know that," Wyatt said. "By the time they find out—if they do—we'll be long out of this town."

"Where's Mace?"

"He'll be along as soon as it's safe. I reckon we'll be having visitors most of the afternoon. Don't worry, honey. We're going to put you in a hotel room and seal you up so tight, even the President of these United States can't get in."

"What if they force you?"

Bat and Wyatt exchanged level looks. "They won't," Bat assured her.

SARANDA HAD ALL but collapsed by the time they reached the hotel. She was forced to stand handcuffed in the lobby while Wyatt explained to the manager that she was in federal custody and not to be disturbed. Then they took her up in the elevator cage to the room where Doc Holliday was waiting. Bat didn't like him. He considered Doc to be the most vicious, hair-triggered man he'd ever known. But for some reason, Wyatt was devoted to the dentist-turned-gunfighter. Bat's loyalty to Wyatt had caused him to put aside personal feelings more than once and come to Doc's aid; now Doc was returning the favor.

Saranda was so weak by the time they arrived that they put her straight to bed. They ordered food sent up, but Saranda, who'd barely eaten for more than two weeks, couldn't keep her meal down. Doc responded by giving her a tonic made from whiskey with sarsaparilla roots and wild-cherry bark. By evening she wasn't feeling any more like eating, but she was comfortably drunk.

At one point, Bat sat on the bed next to her.

"Feeling any better?"

She gazed up at him with curious eyes. "Bat, the last time I saw you, you asked me to run away with you. You wanted to spend your life with me. Why, then, would you help Mace when he asked you?"

He lowered his eyes, as if embarrassed. "I reckon when you love someone, you'll do anything to help them. Even if you have to sacrifice your own feelings to do it."

"Yes," she said, understanding for the first time. "That really *is* what it's about, isn't it? Being willing to sacrifice yourself for the one you love."

"I reckon if you'd told them where Blackwood was, they'd have been easier on you. But you didn't, did you?"

As Wyatt had predicted, they had a steady stream of irate visitors throughout the afternoon. Bat and Wyatt, heavily armed, stationed themselves outside the door to the sitting room and refused entry to all. Police, reporters, court authorities, all came to make their claims or request an interview with the notorious criminal who'd successfully deferred her hour of judgment. But the gunfighters stood their ground, stating in no uncertain terms that the prisoner was too ill because of her treatment at the hands of New York authorities to see anyone. When a doctor was sent to validate this claim, Doc Holliday pushed his way out the door and asked in a sinister tone, "You doubting my word, you weaslly sonofabitch?" He was detained from drawing on the city doctor only by the combined efforts of Bat and Wyatt. No more doctors volunteered.

It was late that night before everyone had cleared out. Saranda had slept most of the afternoon. She was aware of the door opening and of someone entering the room. Forcing her eyes open, she wondered if the figure she saw was a mirage.

"Mace!" She struggled to sit up. Her hair had come loose and hung damply about her face. He went to her as Bat, Wyatt, and Doc entered behind him.

She rushed into his arms, savoring the feel of him, his warmth and strength. It seemed in that moment that he was everything she wasn't, everything she needed. She raised her face as he took it in his hands to kiss her. But he stopped midmotion and ran his hands over her moist face, shocked by the heat radiating off her skin. Coarsely, he swore beneath his breath.

"She's burning up."

"I take it they didn't treat her too hospitable," Wyatt said. "We tried to get her to eat, but she couldn't. Doc gave her a tonic."

Saranda was swaying dizzily. Mace laid her down gently on the bed, then sniffed the jug of tonic, tasted the rotgut whiskey, and almost choked. "Christ! Are you trying to kill her?" They began to protest, but he waved them to silence. "What did you feed her?"

"Steak, pota—"

"Jesus! Don't you gents know anything?"

He tossed off his coat and rolled up his shirtsleeves, pulling up the covers she'd kicked off and wrapping them tight around her. "Has a doctor been here?"

"We sent him away. Didn't figure we needed him catching on to the plan."

"Can't you see she's really ill? Doctor Holliday," he said in the same brisk, authoritative tone he'd used as Archer at the paper, "if you'd be so kind, call the physician back. Round up more blankets. I imagine he'll want to try and sweat out this fever. Sheriff, Marshal, return to your posts outside the door. Admit no one but the doctor. In the long run, it will help our plan to have an outside source attest that she's really ill. And call down for some broth. Any fool knows you don't give steak to someone who hasn't eaten in weeks."

"Out in the territories, we don't eat much excepting steak," Wyatt said, disgruntled.

"Does she look like a cowpuncher to you?"

She looked, in fact, frail and appallingly white, her changeable eyes feverishly blue-green and glittering in her pale face.

The gunmen left reluctantly, muttering to each other.

Mace sat on the bed and gathered Saranda into his

arms. "Not to worry, love. I'm here now. I shall care for you till you're well."

"You will?"

"You need to get well quickly. Then we're going to get the paper back," he told her, kissing her damp forehead. "Don't think about it now. Just concentrate on getting better."

"I want to help. I want to make McLeod pay for what he's done."

"Don't worry, love. You shall—"

"Oh, Mace, it was so awful. They told me you were dead. . . ."

CHAPTER 60

Under Mace's care, Saranda recovered quickly. She was driven partly by the knowledge that there wasn't much time—if they were going to make a move, it had to be immediately, and she was determined to be in shape to do her part. No one had ever taken care of her the way Mace did. No one had ever made sure she had the proper food or tucked her in at night and stroked her forehead until she drifted off to sleep. No one had ever told her funny stories to distract her from her worries, or rubbed the aches and pains from her body with sure and loving hands. She had never felt so safe, so cherished, so completely loved, in all her life.

Even knowing how crucial the timing was, he refused to rush her. Her health, he declared, was more important to him than the paper or any con. His understanding, his patience, his insistence that she take all the time she needed, spurred her to a speedy recovery. He was willing to put everything aside that she might heal as she needed. She wasn't about to let him down.

So she rose from her bed days before he thought it advisable, shaky on her feet but resolved to press forward.

Naturally, he protested. "If you don't care for yourself, how can you expect to take care of anyone else?"

"*You've* taken care of me," she assured him with a warm smile. "You've seen to the needs of not just my body, but my spirit. I don't require rest as much as I *need* to help *you* now. No, wait, I *do* need one thing first."

"What's that, love?"

"A bath."

She still felt gritty from her days in prison and clammy from her bout with fever. There was suddenly nothing she desired more than to submerge herself in a steaming bath.

The hotel room was equipped with a bathroom with running water, which seemed to her the height of extravagance. The only other place she'd seen such splendor was the Van Slyke mansion. After Mace had run her bath, she lowered herself into its welcoming depths, feeling voluptuously soothed and pampered as the scent of rich, exotic oils dazzled her senses. Normally, she wore no perfumes. A particular scent was dangerous to a confidence artist, could give her away even after she'd changed her appearance. So the aroma of lilies and jasmine seemed a forbidden luxury, making her feel sumptuously elegant, sophisticated, undeniably sexy. Entombed in prison, harassed, starved, and tortured, she hadn't felt like a woman for longer than she could remember. Now, she surrendered herself to her feminine element.

The warm water lapped at her shoulders, so hot her face began to glow. She washed herself leisurely, her hands lathered with scented soap, stroking her limbs with a languor that was heavenly. As she soaked, she washed away the grime and memories of prison, of helplessness, of her awareness of her own vulnerability. She found in her femininity a source of strength, a feeling of coming into her own and garnering her resources for the task ahead.

After she'd washed her hair and rinsed it well, she stood in the claw-foot tub and reached for a linen towel. But in her eagerness to get going on the plan, she forgot her unsteadiness and stood too fast. Blood rushed from her head. She tottered dizzily, groping for something to hold on to. But she could find nothing. In another moment, she knew she'd lose consciousness.

She called out to Mace. It seemed only a split second before he charged into the room and seized her in his arms just as she was about to tumble. Her senses anchored, she leaned her face into his chest, allowing him to carry her into the other room. She felt herself lowered to the softness of the bed.

"Now do you believe it's too soon?" he asked.

She opened her eyes and felt as if she were seeing him for the first time. His face seemed staggeringly handsome to her watchful eyes, with his black hair tumbling over his forehead in riotous curls, his eyes darkly blue, his brow puckered in concern. His lips had never seemed more sensual, pursed as they were in his disapproval of her impatience. His jaw had never seemed as strong. The white shirt was wet where she'd rested her head, revealing the faintest trace of black hair underneath. Like someone awakened from a dream, she became gradually aware that there was nothing between them but a thin linen towel. She could feel the wet material tickling her nipples as she was alerted to the swell of her bare breasts underneath.

She ran her hand along the wet spot on his shirt, suddenly wanting nothing more than to feel the thickly curling hair beneath her fingers, and lick his nipples with her tongue. Her eyes, darker with passion, sought his. The clash was electric. She felt heat rise from deep within her body that made her long for the touch of his skin on hers.

His dimples creased deep grooves in his cheeks as he slowly, incredulously, smiled. "That's hardly what I meant by taking care of you."

"You want me to recover properly, do you not?"

"Yesssss . . ."

"Well, it's neither food nor rest nor even whiskey that I need to effect a full restoration."

His smile was widening to a grin. "What is it, then, that will do the trick?"

"The taste of someone's flesh upon my tongue."

"Will just anyone's do?" he asked lightly.

"Yours would be preferable. But there are always other alternatives."

His expression turned sour. "Such as the three brutes standing guard outside your door?"

"No, darling. Such as this."

She inched the towel down off her breasts, tormenting him with the sight of her as she took one creamy globe in her hand, lifted it, bent her head, and put her tongue to the bright bloom of her own nipple. She heard the sharp intake of his breath as she continued to circle the rapidly puckering bud with the tip of her moist tongue.

The bed shifted. A moment later, his head came into her line of vision. His tongue joined hers, lapping at her aureole, twining with her tongue.

"Lock the door, darling."

He raised a brow. "Modesty at this late date?"

"I don't want Bat walking in."

"Oh?"

"I don't want him to see the evidence of how very much I love you."

His eyes softened. "Are you sure about this? I shouldn't want to overtax you."

"I need your loving to make me whole."

"Then how can I refuse?"

With a tender smile, he leaned down and kissed her lips. Then he crossed the room and turned the key in the lock. As he turned back, there was a distinctly carnal smoldering in the depths of his midnight eyes. He unbuttoned his shirt and pulled it from his trousers, displaying the wide expanse of delectably hairy chest. As he walked back toward her, he shrugged out of the shirt and tossed it negligently aside.

"Do you merely require the—taste of my flesh on your tongue? Or may I partake as well?"

Her eyes were full of promise, but her voice was provokingly remote. "Let's just see what happens, shall we?"

CHAPTER 61

After their loving exertions, Mace suggested Saranda sleep.
But instead she felt energized by their lovemaking, filled
with a new conviction that together they could accomplish
anything. So she put on the robe Bat had bought her—a
frilly peach ensemble, with ruffles at the low neckline and
along the lower half of the sleeves—sexy and flamboyant
in the way Bat liked women to dress. Hardly the style of a
woman who'd spent most of her life aiming for invisibility,
but she wore it to please him. Mace called Bat and Wyatt
into the sitting room, leaving the volatile Doc Holliday to
guard the door.

The men could scarcely help but notice the new
bond that existed between Mace and Saranda, so intense
was it that it seemed like another presence in the room.
Bat took a straight-backed chair, turned it backward, and
straddled it, settling himself grimly to concentrate on the
task at hand.

PRINCESS OF THIEVES 453

Saranda was eager to get down to business. "I want to hear everything," she said, looking at Mace.

"Our immediate problem is to get moving before the courts find a way to reclaim you. We can't hold you here for long. Already, we're surrounded day and night. They may cable Washington of their own volition and come back with another warrant. It isn't enough just to escape their clutches. We must do so legally, so Saranda is free from fear of further incrimination. To do that, we must regain the newspaper. It's the only way we can effectively prove her innocence."

"How can we help?" asked Bat.

"First, by making sure no one gets in here to discover Saranda's disappearance."

"Am I going somewhere?" she asked.

"That's the next step."

"But how are we going to get the paper back? You said yourself you're the last person McLeod would sell to—if he sells at all."

Mace sat back and gave her a mysterious smile. "You tell *me*, Princess. What's the one way we can get to McLeod?"

"I don't know."

"Think back, to before the murders. Who's the one person in the world he'd likely take counsel from?"

She was straining to think.

"His mother?" Bat supplied.

With a coaxing gleam in his eye, Mace leaned forward and urged in a low voice, "Think, Princess. The dinner party at Jackson's . . . the masked ball . . ."

Suddenly, it came to her. "Of course!" she cried. "Madame Zorina!"

He grinned and sank back in his chair. "Clever girl."

"Who in the Sam Hill," asked Wyatt, "is *Madame Zorina?*"

"I remember now," said Bat thoughtfully. "She's that Gypsy fortune-teller."

"*Madame Zorina*," Saranda corrected, "is not *merely* a Gypsy fortune-teller. She happens to be the greatest confidence woman the world has ever known. Better, even, than I am. She's such a smashing success, in fact, that no one can figure out exactly what her con *is*. As far as I know, every one of her predictions has come true. But where is she, Mace?"

"Doesn't matter."

"But I don't see—"

Mace was watching her with a complacent smile, as if waiting for it to dawn on her. Suddenly, it did. She fell back in her chair. "Perhaps I do."

"*You're* Madame Zorina."

Her hesitancy fluttered like moths in her stomach. "I don't know, Mace. Sander just saw me in prison. He might recognize me."

"Has anyone ever recognized you before—anyone you didn't want to?"

"No . . . but Madame Zorina's at least sixty."

"All the better. Less chance of him making the association."

"And her predictions—"

"I've already thought of that. All you have to do is play the role convincingly."

She took a breath. "Madame Zorina has been my heroine since I was a child. The thought of impersonating her—"

"Yes?"

"It's a bit daunting."

"Challenging, perhaps. Not impossible."

"I'm so weak . . . and thin. . . ." She ran a hand self-consciously over her collarbone.

"All the better to pass as an old woman." He leaned

forward again and took her hand in his. "You don't have to do this if you don't want to. I shall think of something else."

She saw in his eyes that he meant it. He was willing to sacrifice his plan for her feelings. She remembered what Bat had said to her the day he'd rescued her from prison. *When you love someone, you'll do anything to help them. Even if you have to sacrifice your own feelings to do it.*

"You needn't worry about me," she assured him. "I shall play my part superbly. More brilliantly than I've ever done before."

"That's the spirit, love. Remember, we're not just out to flam McLeod. We're going to gut him completely."

Their eyes met in a look of comprehension.

"I shall need backup, naturally, for a job of this magnitude," she reminded him.

"I have people at the *Globe-Journal* willing to help. We'll have to plant a few stories in the paper. I would warn you, though. It won't be easy. With Lance at the paper, we shall be working under serious handicaps. He'll be expecting something. He'll be checking everything. We must work carefully, and without mistakes."

Hearing Lance's name reminded her uncomfortably of his confession in prison. She'd have to tell Mace, but she wasn't certain how to broach the subject. She hesitated to say anything, now that they were feeling closer than they ever had.

Before she could respond, she was distracted by a scuffle outside. Doc's voice rose and was answered by another. A second later, a gunshot shattered the stillness of the hotel. As one, they surged out of their chairs and raced to the door.

Doc Holliday stood there with a smoking gun. A man with a similarly smoking backside was screaming that he'd been shot by a madman. Doc raised his Colt and shot him again in the seat of his pants, sending him running down the hall in a panic.

"Son of a bitch tried to force his way in," he muttered, holstering his gun. "Well, *compadres*, I reckon I'm headed West."

"Just a moment," Mace said. "We may need you at a later date. Is there somewhere the three of us might hide?"

"We can go to Stubbs," Saranda volunteered. "He's an old friend on the con. Maybe he can help too." She gave the address of the beer hall where she'd last seen him, before leaving town.

"Go, then," he told Doc. "Wait for us. We shall use the commotion you've caused to get Saranda out of here undetected."

CHAPTER 62

With Stubbs's help, they rented cheap hotel rooms on the Lower East Side and sneaked in past a sleeping night clerk.

Two days later, there was a knock on the door. Mace had just come out of the bath down the hall and was ruffling his wet hair with a towel. Saranda was eyeing him appreciatively as she opened the door and a newspaper was thrust in her face.

"Take a look," Bat said.

He'd already folded the paper to the item of interest —an article in the *Globe-Journal* announcing the arrival of Madame Zorina, the world's greatest psychic. The story made a great point of stating that, though the fortune-teller was much in demand, since reneging on her promise to appear earlier in the year, she was here on holiday and would be seeing no one professionally.

Saranda skimmed it as Bat read over her shoulder. As one, they began to smile. "Not bad if I say so myself," Bat said.

"I told you it was too dangerous for you to be seen here," Mace told Bat as he took the paper from them.

"Well," said Bat. "Just checking in."

When he'd gone, Mace tossed the paper aside. "What goes on here?" he asked Saranda.

"Nothing, darling. Bat's just happy to be involved in such a brilliant con. Have I told you how simply brilliant you are?" She wrapped her arms about his waist and brushed her lips along the hollow of his throat.

He moved her back so he could look at her, frowning. "Not trying to flam me, are you?"

"I should think I'd learned my lesson on *that* score. Now about this costume you brought me. I require a few more accessories to make it convincing. . . ."

THEY CHECKED INTO the Metropolitan Hotel, where, eighteen years earlier, the Prince of Wales had taken up residence on his trip to New York. Saranda had made herself up to look like an old woman, with an imposing charcoal-grey wig, fashioning crinkles, creases, and the illusion of crepey skin with carefully applied cosmetics. She'd even taken rouge and a thin brush and fabricated lines along her upper lip. When she pursed her mouth just so, it gave the impression of a woman whose mouth had once been sensually alluring but was now wrinkled and puckered with age.

She padded her figure and dressed in a heavy brocade suit lined along the neck and sleeves with dyed fur. The suit gave her a stately authority and a European air. It was dusty rose, yet she'd wrapped about it shawls and scarves in clashing colors of purple, orange, red. The orange was calculated. When worn close to her face, it turned her eyes a diverting shade of green.

All in all, with her bright ostrich-feathered hat and the thick heels that made her appear taller, she was the image of a Gypsy fortune-teller whose idea of dignified dressing was clearly less conventional than her more conservative sisters.

As Madame Zorina was known always to travel with her dog, Stubbs had gone to extensive trouble to procure a Hungarian vizsla—or at least a dog that looked enough like one to pass. This close-coated copper-red pointer tugged on the leash as they checked in, sniffing at the clothes of other guests and generally making a nuisance of himself.

"I said it," Stubbs grumbled. "Don't perform with animals. They'll upstage you every time." His father had been a carnival performer and had learned the hard way. But Saranda decided it wasn't a bad idea for a frolicsome hound to take the focus off her heavily made-up face.

Stubbs, in a conservative dark suit of European styling, was posing as her secretary. Mace, with a cap on his head to hide his eyes, carried the bags.

Once ensconced in the elaborate suite, they settled in to wait.

"I hope he comes soon," Saranda said, fanning herself with a newspaper. "This makeup is so heavy, my skin can scarcely breathe."

"How do you know he *will* come?" demanded Stubbs, who was skeptical of the plan. There were too many variables, he claimed, that could go wrong.

"We know nothing for certain," Mace answered, unconcerned. "But if he does, it's up to you to make him want to return. Now sit down and wait. Patience is the key to a success."

They waited three hours. Stubbs paced the room nervously. He was a safecracker by trade and was used to more action. Saranda concentrated on not rubbing at her face, which, beneath the heavy greasepaint, had begun to itch.

Only Mace was serene. He made use of the time by reading every story in the paper and making notes to himself. Whenever Stubbs asked again, "How do we know he'll come?" Mace simply replied, without looking up, "He'll come."

Within minutes there was a knock, and Mace and Saranda went into the bedroom, leaving the door slightly ajar. From their vantage point, they heard Sander McLeod's voice ask for Madame Zorina. Without looking, Saranda could feel Mace grin. Stubbs, holding the barking dog back by its leash, opened the door.

THEY WERE READY for him by eleven. Candles set all around the sitting room were the only illumination, casting eerie shadows that suited the mood and would keep him from too clearly seeing her face. Saranda was dressed in a costume inspired by Mace's Gypsy ancestors: deep purple silk shot through with gold, mixed with scarves of vibrant blues, pinks, and greens. In her ears were gold hoops, and dozens of bracelets jingled along her arms. She was careful to wear them over her long sleeves to hide the youthfulness of her skin. On her hands, she wore bright green gloves that, when she put them close to her face, reaffirmed the impression that her eyes were green instead of blue. As an added precaution, she wore a thin chiffon veil, also green, across the lower half of her face and around the steel-grey of her wig.

She was sitting at the table by the back windows when McLeod came in, necessitating a long walk across the room while she studied him with unflinching eyes. This was an added precaution, in case he should catch on to her act, and she was forced to make a speedy exit out the window. The dog Vizchy sat panting by her side.

"So you are the impertinent young man who demands my presence at this table," she greeted in a scolding tone.

"It was good of you to see me. I told your secretary you gave a reading to my father. Preston McLeod. Maybe you remember?"

"I see many people. Am I to be expected to remember every person who comes to my door seeking counsel?"

At the wave of Madame's hand, Sander sat down across the table. "A long time ago, when I was just a boy, you told my father what he must do in order to make his fortune. He followed your advice, and I'm now wealthy beyond my expectations."

"Naturally."

"But, Madame, I remember what it was like to be poor. I can still smell the stench of poverty in my nostrils. I don't ever want to be poor again. I *can't* be. Do you understand?"

"What do you want with me?"

"You warned my father about me. Something I was to look out for when I was grown. You told him never to tell anyone but me. I've kept the secret all this time. But I have to know. It's haunted me all these years. I *must* know what it means."

"What was it I told him then?"

He lowered his voice and leaned closer to her over the table. "That a newspaper could bring about my downfall."

Saranda had to fight to keep from glancing toward the door of the other room, where Mace and Stubbs had closeted themselves. It was too good to be true. In their wildest dreams, they would never have asked for such a gift.

As her shock receded, the implications began to register. Madame Zorina—the *real* Madame Zorina—had years ago warned Sander's father that Sander's downfall could come about through a newspaper. It made her feel that this was all part of some preordained destiny. Yet at the same time, it staggered her. *How had she known?*

"I never forgot your prediction. Even when it made no sense. I wasn't interested in newspapers. I made my money with railroads, factories, real estate. But then they started using this newspaper, the *Globe-Journal*, against me. Slandering all my associates. Ruining them. Implying ugly things about me. I knew I'd be next. And I knew your prediction was coming true. A newspaper *was* going to be the ruin of me. But I outfoxed them. I arranged to take over the paper."

"By illegal means?" she asked softly.

"I had to do anything I could to get it, don't you see? Or the rest of your prediction would come true."

Saranda understood for the first time why McLeod had gone to the lengths he had. He'd murdered, lied, had them pursued like dogs, and was willing that Saranda be hanged, all to prevent this prophecy from coming true. Thinking on her feet, she seized the opportunity.

"No, no, no," she told him. "You misunderstood. I said *owning* a newspaper would be your downfall."

Sander's face blanched beneath the red whiskers. "Owning?" She could see the panic in his eyes. "Holy God! I thought you meant—you mean—I was wrong all these years? Madame Zorina, you *must* help me! What can I do?"

"Let's see what the cards have to say, shall we? I believe I used the cards with your father, no?"

He nodded. Saranda marveled at the boyish trust with which he shuffled the cards and watched as she laid out the pattern. She'd never guess this was the same Sander McLeod who'd ordered her starved in prison and had arranged to tell her Mace was dead.

Stubbs had bought the tarot cards the day before. She'd spent part of the two days rubbing them in oil and crushing them beneath her shoes, trying to make them look as if they'd been used for years. In the candlelight, it was a believable facsimile.

She turned over the cards one by one, trying to ignore the images that flashed through her mind at the sight of them. The reading had been carefully discussed ahead of time. Yet Saranda was overcome with a sense of rushing water, of destruction. She shook her head to clear it and proceeded with the job at hand.

"The answer is simple. You must sell this newspaper."

"I can't do that. I had specific reasons for acquiring that paper."

"Yes, I can see that. Your enemy is here." She pointed to a card. "He is not of your country. He comes from across the seas. He is a sportsman, perhaps?"

"I wouldn't know."

"Perhaps he shoots arrows?"

"His name is Archer."

"Ah. But he is not what he seems. You must not sell to this man. He is for you a dangerous personage. But it is because of him that you must sell the newspaper. While you hold on to it, this man has the power to destroy you."

"But how can I sell? Who would I sell to?"

"I know only that he will seek you out. Then it is for you to decide."

"Madame Zorina, you don't understand—"

"No, my son, it is *you* who does not understand. If you do not sell this newspaper, your fortune and everything you've worked for will collapse. There is nothing that can be done about this. It is preordained."

"Preordained? How?"

She pointed to a card. "It will take the form of three

natural disasters. This is how you will know I speak the truth. You own a zinc mine in Bolivia, I believe?"

"Yes. It's my most productive mine. It nets me—"

"First an earthquake will bury your mine so that it cannot be mined again for fifty years. You own a hotel in Chicago, do you not? A fire will burn down this hotel. And your farmland in this country?"

"I own some of the richest farmland in Pennsylvania."

"Yes, but if you do not listen to Madame Zorina, a terrible flood will ravage this land."

"But how can this happen just because I don't sell the *Globe*? What you're asking is too much. If I give up the newspaper, I could lose everything else, my whole political base. With the newspaper—"

"You will be ruined. But without the newspaper, you stand a chance of continued success and happiness. Madame Zorina speaks only of what the guides reveal to her. The rest is up to you."

He would have asked her more, but she dismissed him, claiming fatigue. When he'd gone, the men came out of the bedroom. Stubbs turned up the gas lamps and went about blowing out candles. Mace came over and hugged Saranda, lifting her off her feet.

"You were splendid! I believed you myself."

When he put her down, she swayed a little on her feet.

"Are you all right?" he asked.

She nodded. "I'm afraid it tired me out more than I'd realized. I shall be fine, though. Don't worry about me."

"Then it's on to the next step. Stubbs, you're the buyer. Get your disguise ready and have everything set to go day after tomorrow. And don't forget to wear gloves to hide your hands."

Stubbs frowned at him skeptically. "You don't really think he's going to sell to the first buyer, do you?"

"That's what we're going to find out."

"Well, I'll be going," Stubbs said, moving toward the door.

"Oh, Stubbs," Mace called.

When he turned to face him, Mace held out his hand expectantly. "The thousand dollars?"

"What thousand dollars?"

"The thousand McLeod bribed you with to let him in." Mace wiggled his fingers, and Stubbs looked dejected.

"How'd you know?"

"Don't ask," said Saranda. "He knows everything."

Reluctantly, Stubbs turned over the money. Mace took half and handed the rest back. "Try that again, and you're out on your bloody ear."

"Well, you can't blame a fellow for trying," he said, and left with a salute of thanks.

"Looks as if we'll dine in style for a change," Mace said when he'd gone.

"Typical con men. Spending the take on the celebration."

He came close and turned her face to him, peering at her intently. "*Are* you all right? You seem a bit quiet. Not upset by seeing Sander, were you?"

"It isn't that," she told him. "It's just the feeling I got during the reading."

"What's that, love?"

"The most dreadful feeling of doom. As if something awful's going to happen. The only thing is, I couldn't tell if it was going to happen to McLeod"—she lifted her eyes to his face—"or to us."

CHAPTER 63

"Are you out of your ruddy mind?" Lance cried, pacing the corner office with the sweeping view of Park Row that once belonged to his brother.

McLeod sat at the corner of the desk. "Stop stomping, will you? And keep your voice down. Do you want everyone to know my business?"

Lance stopped pacing and stared at him. "You're going to throw everything away because a *fortune-teller* told you to?"

"I already told you. She's not just any fortune-teller. She's—"

"*It's a flam!*"

"What do you mean, a flam?"

"A con. Saranda Sherwin's *mother* was a fortune-teller!"

"Are you implying I'm capable of being conned? I tell you, my father saw her years ago. He described her to me. She *is* Madame Zorina."

"If she is, she's in on the flam."

"I have personal proof that Madame Zorina's the genuine article. I don't know where you'd get such a preposterous idea."

"Because your old nemesis Archer is the one who's flamming you."

"Impossible. For one thing, how could he get to Madame Zorina so quickly?"

"Any bloody number of ways. What do you know about this woman, eh? Don't you think it's just the slightest bit suspicious that she's shown up here, just at this time? And how is it the announcement of her arrival appeared only in the *Globe-Journal* and nowhere else? Did you approve the story? I sure as hell didn't. So where in the bleedin' blazes did it come from, I ask you?"

"How should I know? I don't check every story that goes in the paper. That's what I hired you for."

"You can bloody well be sure I'll check everything from now on."

"She told me specifics, made predictions no one in their right mind would make. It would be too easy to be discovered as a fraud if the predictions don't come to pass."

"Did she tell you *when* they'd happen?"

"No."

"You're being burned, is why."

"Why do you keep saying that?"

"Because Archer's involved, I'm sure."

"Archer's a—"

"*Archer*," Lance interrupted, "is one of the greatest flimflam artists who ever walked this ruddy earth."

Sander sat up straighter, interested now. "How do you know that?"

"Because Archer's me brother."

There was a moment of shocked silence. He peered

at Lance's face, as if wondering why he hadn't seen the resemblance before. "Your—"

"Mace Blackwood's the name. Me own big brother."

McLeod stood, his face suffused with red. "Why didn't you tell me this sooner?"

"There's such a thing as family loyalty. But not when he's makin' a ruddy fool o' you. He made a fool of everyone in this city, flammed them all for three bloody years."

"Archer . . . a con man?"

"That's the long and short of it, mate. But not just any con man. The best there is."

Sander circled the room, scratching his whiskers thoughtfully. "Madame Zorina *said* he wasn't what he appeared to be—"

"You're being hustled, you bloody fool!"

McLeod thought for a full minute. "Just in case, let's break the story. We'll expose Archer for who he really is. Get the public fighting mad."

Lance grinned. "It'll be me pleasure."

When he'd gone, Lance sat back in his brother's chair and put his feet on the desk. Leaning back, he placed his hands behind his head and smiled. "I know you're behind this, brother. But you're sure as bleedin' hell not going to get away with it. Not this time."

THE NEXT MORNING, the *Globe-Journal* was delivered with their breakfast. Saranda took it from the tray and was about to hand it over when the headline caught her eye.

"Oh, my God."

"What is it?"

She swallowed, wondering if there was any way to avoid showing it to him. He came closer, and she looked up at him, wishing she could hide the paper behind her back and ask him not to read it.

"Bad news?" he asked.

"The worst."

He took the paper from her and read the headlines.

FRAUD EXPOSED

NEWSPAPER DECEIVED

Confidence Man Posed as Editor for Three Years

Public Irate

He read the story as she watched him. She could see the flash of fury, then a hardening of his features as he steeled himself beneath the onslaught of facts and lies. By the time he'd finished, he'd wiped his face blank of any emotion.

"Lance's doing, no doubt."

"Mace, I'm sorry."

He shrugged. "It was bound to happen sooner or later."

"You expected this?"

"Didn't you?"

"Then what are you upset about?"

"Read the bloody article. He makes me sound like a cheap grifter. Doesn't even mention the Oxford scam. Or the job we pulled against the Lancashires. That was a mastery of planning."

She relaxed. "Ah! So it's professional pride that's got your back up."

"A more poorly written piece of rubbish I've never seen. Most of the facts are wrong. If I were still editor, these table scrapings wouldn't even have made the paper. And if I'd *written* it— What are you laughing about?"

She put her arms about his neck and kissed him on

the lips. "You. Worrying about your reputation. Here I thought you'd be devastated by having your cover blown, and the only thing you're concerned with is that you've been made to look like an *inept* confidence man."

He hugged her tight. "Just wait, Princess. When we get that paper back, I'm going to write an article that will not only make us look like the two greatest flam artists that ever lived, it will make bloody heroes of us in the same stroke. Just wait till the *irate* people of New York find out how it was *confidence artists* who used their skills—"

"—their *considerable* skills—"

"—to save their beloved *Globe-Journal* from the clutches of the evil Scotsman. They'll hoist us on their backs and carry us down bloody Fifth Avenue before I'm through!"

She'd been laughing, but she sobered at the thought of it. "If all goes well," she cautioned.

"Now to the next step . . ."

THE FOLLOWING DAY, a piece appeared in the *Globe-Journal* about an earthquake in Bolivia that took the lives of three people and effectively closed down production of several of the zinc mines in the vicinity.

"What about this?" Sander exploded, slamming the paper down on Lance's desk. "This earthquake just wiped out a third of my income. Madame Zorina's first prediction has come true."

"Give me that." Lance grabbed the paper and skimmed the story. "I didn't see this before it went to press."

"Now who's being hustled? You're so used to playing games, you don't know the real article when you see it. Thanks to you, I've just lost a fortune!"

"Don't jump to any conclusions, man. I know Mace is behind this. I just don't know how. We'll check it out, and you'll see I'm telling the truth."

Bat Masterson was waiting outside the *Globe-Journal* building when Lance came out. Armed with his sixguns, Bat trailed him from a safe distance. When Lance stopped at the telegraph office, Bat waited for him to begin writing out his telegram, then cracked the door and listened. Lance arranged for the telegram to be sent to Bolivia and asked that the reply be delivered immediately to his office at the *Globe-Journal*. By the time he left, Bat had hidden himself on the side of the building, where he wouldn't be seen.

A half hour later, Bat walked into the telegraph office and tipped his derby to the clerk. "Mr. Blackwood sent me over to see if that telegram he's expecting came in yet."

The clerk seemed flustered. "Why, no. I told him it might be some time. For all I know, it's night in Bolivia. Besides, if they've had an earthquake, the lines may be down. I explained all that—"

Bat leaned over the counter with a grimace. "Between you and me, patience isn't Blackwood's strong suit. I'll wait if you don't mind. It could mean my job if I go back empty-handed."

"Wait if you like," the clerk agreed. "So long as you know it might be a long one."

It was an hour before the telegram came in. The clerk read it over after he'd taken it down and muttered, "Well, that's strange. . . ."

Bat removed a few gold pieces from his vest pocket. "Just so this doesn't go any further," he explained.

The clerk seemed offended. "I *never* reveal the contents of telegrams. I don't care who asks!"

But he took the gold just the same.

Mace looked over the telegram stating that there had

been no earthquake in Bolivia and expressing surprise at
the inquiry. Then he handed it over to Stubbs. "Use your
contact to get that redone. 'Earthquake confirmed. Devastation
widespread. Mines closed permanently. Financial
help desperately needed.' That sort of thing."

"Sure thing, boss."

"Have it delivered to the paper at once. Then, in
disguise, seek out McLeod with an offer to buy the paper.
Let's just see what he has to say."

That evening, Stubbs returned, wearing a blond wig
and waxed mustache and dressed in an expensive suit. He
removed his grey gloves and tossed them aside, flexing his
stubby fingers. "He's being cautious. Says that even if he
does sell, he's not selling to just anyone off the street.
Wants to check me out first. I disguised my voice the best I
could, but he kept looking at me funny. Like maybe he
hears the Lower East Side when I talk."

"If he checks Stubbs out, we could be finished,"
Saranda warned.

But Mace just grinned. "You're never finished till
you've achieved your objective. It's time for the next step."
He picked up the copy of the paper with the story exposing
his identity. "Call me a cheap con man, will you?" he
muttered. "McLeod, you poor bloody bastard. You don't
know who you're dealing with."

CHAPTER 64

"What do you know?" Saranda said as she perused the next morning's paper. "A fire in Chicago burned down the Gresham Hotel. Poor Sander. Doesn't he *own* that hotel?"

Mace was shaving in the bathroom. "What does it say about us?"

She read him the article's high points. "City authorities are furious with the federals—a city policeman fired upon—courts waiting for a writ from the federal judge—looks like the crisis is coming to a head. We may not be able to stall much longer. Oh, it says we're sending a barrister to court to argue our case. Are we?"

"That's what I'm about this morning." He dried his face and came over and gave her a long kiss.

"My! You're certainly frisky lately. Don't tell me my Madame Zorina costume aroused you?"

"Planning the perfect flam arouses me. Too bad Stubbs is due any minute. I might be enticed to show you how much." He lowered himself over her so she was forced back into the bed where she'd been lounging, drinking her morning tea. She kissed him leisurely, then asked, "Is it the perfect swindle?"

"Do you doubt it?"

"There's the small matter of the hundred-thousand-dollar down payment we need to buy the paper back."

"What's the best way to buy something from a sucker?" he inquired.

"With his own money."

"Precisely."

"How do we do that? Convince him to bet it at the racetrack and have Stubbs and his men working there?"

"Too involved."

"Work on his superstition by telling him to bury a hundred thousand dollars to erase the curse?"

"Too unbelievable."

"What, then?"

"That's where Madame Zorina comes into play."

"You want me to go see him?"

"You won't have to. He'll come to you."

"How do you know he will?"

"Instinct." When she opened her mouth to speak, he kissed her into silence. Soon she lost her will to question him further. He looked up at her with a gleam in his eyes, but she sensed the seriousness of his words. "When a good flam is in motion, never question the planner."

"Oh? Pity. I had a question in mind that I fancied you might rather like."

"What's that?"

She found the rampant bulge in his trousers and unfastened the buttons. "Is this for me?"

"You don't have to ask," he said.

"Sure you're not a fortune-teller? You're so good at reading people's minds."

Just then there was a knock on the door. Saranda let

out a disappointed groan. "What beastly timing. Do tell Stubbs to come back later."

"Don't worry, love," he said, kissing her and buttoning his pants. "I shall be back."

She stretched her arms over her head and said sleepily, "Leave the bedroom door open. I rather fancy you conducting business in the sitting room, knowing I'm in bed waiting for you."

"The job comes first, remember?"

"How could I forget? It's your genius for the job at hand that gets me so excited."

LESS THAN TEN minutes later she heard him usher them out. "You certainly handled that with the utmost dispatch," she called.

He came to the door and leaned on the jamb, watching her appreciatively as she pulled her peach nightgown from under the covers and daintily dropped it to the floor. "I had a fair incentive. Now . . . what were you doing while I was away?"

"Come under the covers and find out. . . ."

LATER THAT EVENING, Stubbs arrived, agitated.

"I tell you, Mace, he's talking to another buyer. I swear he's going with him."

"Who has another buyer?" Saranda asked. "Sander?"

"McLeod's still not sure he wants to sell. But he found this other buyer on his own. Even *I* have to admit the guy sounds perfect. From an upstanding Georgia family. Someone in the medical profession. No ties to New York or the West, which McLeod'd have cause to suspect. I did all I could to convince him I'm his man, but he's waffling. I'm telling you, if he sells, he's going with this other guy."

Alarmed, Saranda said, "I never thought of him selling to someone *else*! What are we going to do?"

"Stubbs, go back tomorrow and push him. Make yourself as obnoxious as you can. Insist if you have to."

"I'm telling you, boss, he ain't going for it. I push him, and he's for sure going the other way."

"Just do it. We'll see what happens."

Shrugging as if he thought Mace was crazy, Stubbs said, "You're the boss" and left.

"Sander needs another push," Saranda told Mace when they were alone. "Why don't we go ahead with the flood story tomorrow? Show him we mean business."

Mace removed his jacket and draped it about the back of a chair. Taking her hand, he pulled her to her feet and into his arms. "Let's give it another day," he said casually, lowering his mouth to hers.

THE NEXT MORNING, it was Mace who was surprised by the headlines. He loomed over her as she sat at the vanity, brushing her hair. She looked up to find him glowering at her.

"You didn't have the flood story planted behind my back, did you?"

"Of course not. What—"

"Then it's real!"

He showed her the paper. Her hands trembled as she read it. "There was a flood in Pennsylvania . . . *just where we predicted!*"

Mace was staring at her with some of the same awe

she'd been feeling for him. "How did you do that?" he asked softly.

Saranda looked back at the paper, then at him. "I have no idea."

LANCE PACED HIS office that afternoon. He'd sent a man to Pennsylvania to verify the flood for himself. He was more certain than ever now that his brother was behind the strange occurrences. Once and for all, he would have his proof.

Just as he was beginning to feel complacent, his secretary handed him a telegram. As he read it, his face fell. He crumpled the telegram, tossed it in the wastebasket, and looked out his window over the busy street below. Somewhere out there his brother was smirking at him. He knew Mace was behind it, but he couldn't for the life of him figure out how. Disappointment tasted bitter on his tongue. Finally, he growled beneath his breath, "How the bleedin' hell did he *do* that?"

SARANDA WAS READY and waiting in her Gypsy garb when McLeod rapped frantically on the door. Stubbs opened it with unhurried dignity.

"I must see Madame Zorina," McLeod said without preamble. The quaking of his voice gave testimony to his panic. "It's a matter of utmost urgency."

Saranda came forth with the dog on the leash. "Come," she greeted him. "I've been expecting you."

CHAPTER 65

"My fortune's all but gone," Sander was wailing. "Everything you predicted has happened. I'm ruined, I tell you! You have to help me."

"What can I possibly do to help? I told you what you must do, but did you heed my counsel? No, you chose to ignore it. I am not accustomed to dealing with the faithless. Why do you ask my help, when you do what you want in spite of my words?"

"I swear to you, just tell me what to do, and I'll do it."

"What can I tell you that I haven't already? You must sell the newspaper. But why do I waste my time? It is already too late."

"No! It can't be! Madame Zorina, you must think of *something*. You told my father where to invest his money. You gave him a specific amount and told him he'd triple his investment in twenty days. It came to pass just as you said. You could do the same for me. I have a little money left. Not much, but if you'd help me—"

"How much will you receive for your newspaper?"

"A hundred thousand dollars."

"Very well, I will help you one last time. You must sell the newspaper as planned. But first you must invest just that amount in another venture. I will send an opportunity your way, something that will not only restore your fortune but will multiply it a hundred times and more. An incredible opportunity that only you will see the sense of. Do you understand me? Only you."

"Yes, yes. I understand. But what is it? What will it be?"

"I do not know yet. I know only that this opportunity will present itself to you tomorrow at your office. You must be vigilant and recognize it when it comes."

"I will, yes. Thank you, Madame Zorina, I'm sorry I ever doubted you."

When he'd gone, Mace handed some papers to Stubbs.

"Here are the stock options. Phony, naturally. Have O'Toole go to McLeod's office at the paper in the morning. Tell him to report directly to me with the results."

THE NEXT MORNING, Sander called his secretary into his office. He was a thin, efficient man with hair as red as McLeod's and horn-rimmed glasses. "Mr. Forbes, who's waiting to see me?"

"The customary assortment of men wanting you to invest in some project or other."

McLeod looked interested. "These men who want my investment, what are they selling?"

"Let me see. Office buildings, land in Florida—oh,

and two new ones. Man with a mine for sale. And another with some stock options."

"What kind of stock?"

"I don't know. I'll ask."

"What about this other fellow? What kind of mine is it?"

"Some rare element, so he says. I wrote it down." He flipped through his notebook. "Here it is. Aphroneium. I've never heard of it. He claims it's going to be valuable. No one really knows about it yet."

"She said only I would recognize it. . . . Forbes, run down to the morgue. See what you can find."

"Right away. And the gentlemen waiting?"

"Let 'em cool their heels until we get some more information. Then I'll decide."

IT WAS AN hour before Forbes returned. "I found two items in back issues," he said, referring to his notes. "The first, just a small announcement dated two years ago, describes a mine in New Mexico believed to be the only source of the element aphroneium. The second is more recent, about a year ago—an article about a man trying to sell options in this same mine. Unfortunately, he could find no takers, as no use had been found for this element. But here's the incredible part. You won't believe this. We're running a story *tomorrow* on this famous Italian scientist, Dr. Siffredi. He believes this element—aphroneium—can be used as a filament in electric-light globes. He claims by replacing tungsten with aphroneium, the bulbs would last ten times as long."

"My God!" whistled Sander. "With the city on the threshold of going electric . . . I could make a fortune. We're talking millions! What does he want for the mine?"

"I took the liberty of inquiring. Two hundred thousand, he said. Sir, I wouldn't mind putting a little of my savings in—"

McLeod gave him an annoyed look. "We'll talk about that later. I'll pay him a hundred thousand tops, which I'll get back on the payment for the paper— Shouldn't be too difficult. He's been trying to sell his mine for some time, so he'll be eager to sell. Ask him to wait. Check out his deed with our lawyers. I need some time to think. Plan my strategy. Tell the others to go home."

"HE WOULDN'T EVEN see me," O'Toole was telling Mace. "Kicked me right out. I never even got past the secretary. Who made it clear if I came back, the same thing would happen."

"Did you insist?"

"You better believe it! I made him tell me why McLeod wouldn't see me. He's already picked some other sap with a New Mexican mine to sell. I'm sorry, I gave it my best shot. Want me to try again?"

"No," said Mace. "It was essential that it be today."

"Some con men Stubbs came up with," Saranda complained when he'd gone.

"Now, now," Mace soothed. "Don't get discouraged."

"Discouraged? McLeod's going to hand over a hundred thousand dollars to buy some undoubtedly worthless mine in New Mexico, while we're left holding the bloody bag. I was afraid something like this was going to happen, something totally unforeseen. What about that flood— coming out of the blue the way it did? What else is going to pop up to surprise us? And where in bloody hell are we going to get our down payment now?"

He came behind her and rubbed her shoulders. "O ye of little faith. Save the panic, darling. It's under control."

She could hear the excitement in his voice, and the tinge of amusement.

"This setback doesn't bother you?"

"The secret to success is not to be bothered by setbacks. They're a part of the process. They can even *help* you, if you plan it right."

She turned to face him suspiciously. "What have you planned?"

He gave her a mysterious smile. "Something that will make this work *for* us instead of against us."

MR. FORBES OPENED the office door and poked his head into the outer office. "Mr. McLeod will see you now," he told the man who'd been waiting patiently.

The man stood. He was tall, with the self-possessed air of a man of the West. Just the sort of man for whom Mr. Forbes, a die-hard easterner, fostered great disdain. The man from New Mexico removed his hat and lowered his head as he stepped into the office, to make certain he didn't bump it on the door jamb.

"May I present Mr. McLeod, owner of the *Globe-Journal*," Forbes said with forced courtesy.

The westerner extended his hand. "How do, McLeod. 'Bout time you got around to invitin' me in."

McLeod shook hands, wincing at the viselike grip. "I apologize for keeping you waiting, Mr. Earp. Now if you'll have a seat, perhaps we can get down to business."

Mr. Earp sat in the proffered chair and crossed his boot over his knee with an affable smile. "Call me Wyatt," he said, and placed his hat on the floor.

CHAPTER 66

Saranda was offering suggestions, trying to figure out some way of raising the hundred thousand dollars.

"None of my father's methods apply," she mused. "He never endeavored to raise that much at one time. Since he was planning to marry me off to aristocracy, he didn't feel the need."

"You're wasting your time," Mace insisted. "Why don't you put your energies to better use?"

"I was under the impression we were partners. What are you not telling me?"

But he was frustratingly mysterious. This was his finest moment. He was in his element; he was in control. His eyes beneath the thick brows glinted and sparkled like bits of steel. He was so focused, his energy so electrically charged, that just being in the same room with him aroused her. She could feel her clothes brushing against her skin when she moved. She tingled with new awareness of him, wondering always what he was up to, what was around the next corner. Watching him in action was similar to watching her father in the early days. He, too, had sought to keep from her the details of his cons, not wishing to jinx them, but even more, determined that his daughter would have no need of such devices. Still, she'd pried from him every last professional secret.

She wasn't faring as well with Mace. He refused to divulge the components of his plan until he was certain of the outcome. Even then, she had the feeling he was teasing her, enjoying her attempts to outguess him. Though his amusement was apparent, however, all he would say in answer to her questions was, "You'll see."

She did see when Wyatt showed up a little later with a small black bag filled with cash. As he matter-of-factly began to stack it on the table, Saranda asked, "Where did you get that?"

"Sold my mine."

It was beginning to make some sense. "What mine?" she asked.

"My aphroneium mine." By now he was grinning.

"What's aphroneium?"

"A rare element used for electricity."

"For *filaments* in electric globes," Mace corrected.

"That's it."

Saranda was staring at the two smirking men with her hands on her hips. "I think you'd best start from the beginning."

"I went to McLeod to sell my mine. So happens it's the only known source for aphroneium, which, like we said, is fixing to—" Wyatt looked to Mace.

"Revolutionize the electrical industry on the eve of the great cities of the world switching to electricity."

"That's it right enough," said Wyatt with a satisfied nod.

"McLeod bought this?"

"Looked it up at the undertaker's—"

"The morgue," Mace corrected.

"—and found out for himself what a great deal it was. Shrewd businessman, though. Gave me half what I asked for." By now he was cackling. Wyatt Earp, who Bat always claimed was the most closemouthed man on the prairies.

"Do you really own an aphroneium mine?"

"Up till this morning, I owned a mine in New Mexico. Won it in a poker game. Worthless. Turns out it was salted. It was a right satisfying pleasure to see someone fork over a hundred thousand for the no-good hunk of rock."

"I'm confused. If there is no aphroneium mine, how was Sander able to look it up in back issues? Unless . . ."

"Unless my contacts at the paper planted those stories so McLeod would see them?" Mace finished.

He was standing with his arms crossed over his chest, waiting with a glint in his eye for her to figure out the rest.

"I see! So you sent O'Toole with phony stock options, knowing they wouldn't appeal to Sander, had him make an obnoxious fool of himself so Sander *wouldn't* pick him, and planted Wyatt there as the preferable choice—along with your manufactured stories in back issues of the paper."

"I couldn't be sure which one he'd go with. But I had a fair idea. Either way, he was going to choose one or the other."

"What about this element? This aphroneium? I've never heard of it."

"That's because it doesn't exist."

"But where did you get it? What is it?"

"It's from the classical Greek," Mace explained, enormously pleased with himself.

"And what does it mean?"

"Loosely translated?"

"However you bloody well choose to translate it."

The creases in his cheeks deepened as he showed his grin. "Loosely translated it means . . . sucker."

Saranda shivered with pleasure. "You're a ruddy genius!" she exclaimed. "You're the most incredible . . . brilliant . . . daring man on the face of this earth. What if he'd had the good sense to look it up?"

"When this is all over, I think we should mail him the translation. Or better yet, hand it to him when he's behind bars. I should give a great deal to see his face."

She flew at him, leaping into his arms and wrapping her legs about his torso while he laughingly swung her around. Grabbing hold of his head, she kissed him voraciously, on his lips, his brow, his nose, his rugged, handsome jaw. He fell back into the settee, and she straddled him, ripping at his tie, tearing the buttons from his shirt. Her realization of his intellectual superiority—of the depth of his brilliance—made her hotter than she could ever remember being. She suddenly cared about nothing and no one. She had to have him—now, this minute—to show him how wild he'd made her.

She was wrenching off his shirt when Wyatt cleared his throat. "Well—I reckon I'll be going along."

No one bid him farewell as he left the money and quietly closed the door behind.

Saranda was planting heated kisses all along the chiseled contours of Mace's chest. "You said not to doubt you, and you were right," she murmured. "My God, you're unbelievable! I always heard you were the best. But to see it happen—to be a part of it—you make me so ravenous, I can't bear it."

She tore open his pants and without preamble, without needing to ready herself in any way, impaled herself onto him.

"I never dreamed a man like you existed in all this

world," she panted as she rode him furiously. "Even my father would be hard-pressed to pull this off."

"Keep talking," he said, as he grasped the curving cheeks of her backside and squeezed hard, giving her playful little slaps as she reverted to her days out West and rode him like a bucking bronc.

"NOW ALL WE have to do," Saranda said, "is make sure McLeod sells to us and hands over the money. Just think, Mace! It could all be over with so soon."

"Let's not get overly confident, shall we? There may be an obstacle or two to overcome yet."

"I'm not worried. Not anymore. I know you'll handle anything that comes up."

"Well! This is a red-letter day."

Stubbs sat at the table reading through some copy Mace had written out for him to memorize. "I don't know, boss. Seems to me if I say this stuff to McLeod, he's likely to sell to that other—"

A knock at the door made them all jump. They weren't expecting anyone. Mace gestured to Stubbs, who, in his Hungarian accent, called out, "Who is it?"

"Lance Blackwood from the *Globe-Journal*."

Saranda's alarmed gaze flew to Mace's face. "It's all right," he whispered calmly, as if he'd been expecting this. He gestured for her to go into the bedroom, then whispered to Stubbs, "Find out what he wants and get rid of him. Don't let him in, even if you have to knock him out cold."

Stubbs donned his jacket, checked his appearance, and went to open the door.

They closed the bedroom door in case Lance forced his way in, but Mace and Saranda stood facing each other with their ears pressed against the door. They heard snippets of the conversation as the voices lowered and raised. Enough to know that Lance was demanding an audience with Madame Zorina and that Stubbs promised to inquire and send word to him at the paper.

By the time he'd left, Saranda had turned white. She flattened her back against the door and closed her eyes. "He knows," she said.

"He *suspects.* It's not the same."

"I can't see him. He'll know in a minute. I won't be able to keep my voice even. Mace, I can't do it!"

He took her arms in his hands. "I say you can. If you don't, he'll be even more suspicious. We'll arrange to meet him somewhere private—somewhere dark, so he won't get a good look at you. I shall be there with you, hiding in case you need me. Listen to me, Saranda. You have no reason to fear my brother. He's calling our bluff because he's scrambling to save his own position. *He's* the one we want to panic, not you. Do you hear me? If you don't show—"

"I told him about the baby."

He was quiet for a moment, his hands slipping to his side. "When?"

"In prison. When he came to see me. I tell you, I can't face him again."

"What did he say?"

She lifted her eyes to his. Her voice hardened at the memory. "He said you'd choose him over me. He said you always do."

"That's absurd. If we play our cards right, no choice will be necessary. That's why you must meet him. We can't afford to have Lance foul things up for us at this late date. Not when we're so close."

She paced around the room, clutching her hands together, trying to find a less painful way to say what must be said. There was none. "He told me something else. Something I'd rather die than tell you, but something I think you should know."

He didn't answer right away, as if instinctively dreading what was to come. "What's that, Princess?"

"He told me he was the one who informed on Pilar."

"Then he lied to you."

She stared at him. "Why would he do that?"

"I don't know. But I told you of his loyalty to me."

"Mace—"

"Listen to me." He took her hands and squeezed them urgently. "You just did for me in prison what Lance did all those years ago. No matter what they did to you, you refused to turn me in. So you tell me. After all that, could you turn around and betray me?"

"That's different. I love you."

"Are you saying my brother doesn't? Lance worships me. He always has. If anything, he worshiped me *too* much."

"That's precisely what I'm saying. Over the years, Lance's worship of you became twisted. You're everything he wants to be. He told me so himself. I don't think he merely wants to be *like* you—he wants to *replace* you. Tell me the truth. Didn't he find ways to take advantage of your vow to protect him? Didn't he push it to the limit time after time?"

He closed his eyes and wearily ran a hand through his hair.

"He as much as boasts about it! Mace, if he doesn't want you dead, he at least wants to destroy everything that belongs to you. He's mad. He'll stop at nothing—"

"Stop it!" he rasped. "Do you know what I have to do to believe you? I have to face the fact that he went insane because of me."

She couldn't believe she was hearing this. "That's not true!"

"Isn't it? If Lance is deranged, it's because of the beating he took for my sake. If I recognize that he's evil—that he's twisted in some way—I have to take the responsibility. He wouldn't do the things he does *if not for me*."

"Don't even say that!"

"Do you know what a terrifying prospect that is? *He's my brother!*"

She threw her arms around him, determined to keep him from mouthing such atrocities. "It isn't true, darling. You're such a consummate con man, you've conned yourself."

With an effort, he extricated himself from her grasp and pulled himself together. "It's Lance we have to flam now. But I need your help. We don't have time for anything else."

Clearly, he wasn't going to face this now. There was work to be done. Gutting McLeod must come above all else.

"He'll know it's me. I shall give myself away."

"I don't believe that. What I believe in is *you*."

She looked at him for a few moments, shaking visibly. "Is it true?" she asked softly.

"Is what true?"

"I've wondered ever since he said that. *Would* you choose Lance over me?"

CHAPTER 67

Dressed as Madame Zorina, Saranda met with Lance at midnight on the Chelsea wharf. The night was dark, with only a gas lamp at the entrance to the wharf lighting the way. She stood along the dock by the river, concentrating on the current in an effort not to think. Somewhere in the darkness, Mace hid. It seemed little comfort at such a time. Unlike Mace, Saranda knew disaster lurked in the shadows. How she knew, she couldn't explain. It was the same feeling that had come over her when reading Mace's cards, and again Sander McLeod's.

The current was unusually swift. Boats anchored at the dock bumped against one another, causing her already-jangled nerves to jump. She'd chosen the most secluded spot she could find, far enough away from the gaslight that she could see without revealing any details of her face. Still, she trembled. Perspiration beaded her brow beneath the heavy makeup. Her mouth was dry, her tongue like sandpaper. She was openly walking into a trap set by her worst enemy—the man who'd stolen her youth, her dreams, and everything she'd ever loved until that time. A man who cared nothing for her—who was threatened by her closeness to the brother he both loved and hated. A man who would gladly see her dead.

She heard his step behind her. He stopped so she was forced to turn toward the light. She did so gradually, with a squaring of her shoulders and a grand show of dignity. Frightened she might be, but she wasn't about to let Mace down.

"So this is the world's greatest fortune-teller," Lance greeted her sarcastically. "I knew a soothsayer once. Her name was Sirena Sherwin. Turned out she was a sham, however. Palming herself off—don't mind the pun—to the aristocracy. Burned to death in a fire. Pity, that. I heard she screamed and screamed and no one helped. Not even her lovin' daughter." He paused to savor an ugly cackle while Saranda fought her heaving stomach. "A rather tasty daughter, as I recall. Though the memory's a bit dim. Wouldn't mind refreshing me memory, at that. Tell me, Madame Zorina, since yer so good at predicting. Any chance of havin' another whack?"

Her fury was so intense, she had to dig her nails into her palms to keep from lashing out at him. In the darkness, his face looked eerily like Mace's. She steeled herself and raised her chin a notch. Ignoring his words, she asked imperiously, "Is this for what you demanded Madame Zorina's presence?"

He stepped closer. In the dim light, she saw two pistols stuck in his belt. She averted her eyes. "I just thought you could tell me fortune, seein' as yer so good at it. Better yet, tell me why I'm here."

"Ah, but you ask so little of me! You are here because your petty mind grapples for control. You live your life in the shadow of one of greatness. This shadow haunts you always. Your life is lived not for yourself, not for the good of others, but for the senseless pursuit of besting one who cannot be bested. Your desires are evil; therefore, your very existence is tainted. But you don't need an old woman to tell you this. You know it already."

"If yer so bloomin' clever, then, wot do you see in me future?"

"Death." She didn't know why she'd said it. Suddenly, she was overwhelmed with the feeling of death on the horizon. And somehow she knew it would be his. "You are about to be killed."

He was grinning grotesquely, his bad eye visible even in the dimness. "And who's goin' to kill me?" he taunted. "You?"

"Why would an old woman stoop to killing someone like you?"

Suddenly, he grabbed her, pulling a pistol from his belt and turning her away from the river. "Come out, Mace," he called.

There was no movement. The rushing of the river and the bumping of the boats were the only sounds. He jerked her around, searching the darkness for a sign of his brother. As he did so, she recalled the other gun in his belt. She was a master pickpocket. She could easily retrieve it without his knowledge. But could she use it? Mace had refused to bring a weapon. Dear God, if she had to pull the trigger, could she?

Lance cocked the pistol and put it to her head. "I'll kill her, Mace. You know I will."

After a long moment, Mace walked out. He moved slowly, cautiously, carefully. "Put the gun away, Lance," he said in a patient tone.

"I finally got you, brother. Now you *have* to choose. Yer brother or yer lady. Which'll it be, eh?"

"Why give him the chance?" she taunted in her own

voice, loudly enough that Mace could hear. "You never
gave him a choice when you informed on Pilar and had her
killed. Or when you put bullets through the heads of the
Van Slykes."

"Wot's she babblin' about, Mace?"

If only she could get him to confess, Mace could see
for himself what sort of man his brother was, see the face
Lance showed everyone but him. He had to see that he had
nothing to do with it. That Lance's madness went far beyond the aftereffects of a childhood beating.

"There's no need for pretense among us. Not at this
late date. Not after all we've been through. Mace knows all
about it, and he's already forgiven you—haven't you,
Mace?"

Mace was coming closer. "Lance, there's no need for
this."

"Tell him the truth, Lance. How your jealousy has
eaten you up all these years. How being the runt of the
illustrious Blackwood family made you dependent on
Mace's talents—even as you hated him for being so good.
How you couldn't stand the thought of anyone taking him
away from you—because then where would you be?"

He laughed so close to her ear that it hurt her ear-
drum. By now she had the gun safely in hand. As he
laughed, she cocked it silently, so he wouldn't hear.

"You goin' to believe this fairy tale, Mace? From
some bloody princess-come-lately who wasn't even there?
Who doesn't know the love we have fer one another, eh?"

Mace was walking ever so deliberately toward them.
"Put the gun away so we can talk," he said soothingly. "I'd
say it was about time we talked, wouldn't you?"

"Talk! All right, brother, let's have that chat. We'll
just dispose of the excess baggage first, eh?" He was growing wilder by the minute, choking Saranda in his fervor. "I
should have killed her long ago!"

"Talk all you want," Saranda goaded. "Kill me if you like. It won't change the fact that you're the most pathetically poor con man who ever lived. It wouldn't have been so bad, would it, if your own brother hadn't been the best there was. Admit it, Lance, you sniveling coward—didn't you despise him for it?"

She could feel him shaking with anger.

If Mace heard what she was saying, he gave no indication. He continued on his steady path forward, talking in a monotone. "Lance, you're the only family I have left. I love you. Let me help you."

"*Help* me? Help yerself!"

Letting Saranda loose, Lance lifted the gun and aimed at Mace. Without thinking, she raised her own gun, pointing it at Lance's face. "Pull the trigger, and I shall kill you," she declared.

He turned back to her, his face showing his contempt. "Yer goin' to shoot me, are you? Who are you flamming? You had yer chance. You couldn't do it then, and you bleedin' well can't do it now."

Incensed, she pulled the trigger. The retort blasted in her ear, sending her backward. In the dim light, she saw, as in a dream, Lance's hand slap his forehead. His hand dropped back down, and she turned away in horror. She'd shot him in the head. Blood oozed down his face. Staggering backward, he lost his balance and fell, arms flailing, into the river. The current was so strong, he was immediately carried away.

The gun dropped from her hand. She saw Mace racing toward the dock. In her shock, she realized he meant to dive in after Lance. She ran for him, her heart pounding in her ears. Grabbing hold of his arm, she tugged with all her might and spun him around. "You're not going after him," she screamed.

He glanced helplessly toward the water and back again.

"He's dead," she told him. "It's done. I won't allow you to kill yourself for nothing."

She was shaking now, from shock and relief. Lance was dead. He could never threaten her again. Yet when she saw Mace's face, her heart turned to stone. As if she weren't even there, he pulled his arm away and walked in a daze to the dock. There he dropped to his knees and watched the river as it flowed swiftly by. There was no sign of Lance. By now, his body was on its way out to sea. Yet Mace stayed as he was, staring out at the watery grave of his only brother, alone with his grief.

Saranda watched, and something inside her died.

CHAPTER 68

Their epic con proceeded as planned, but nothing was the same after that; it was no longer the fun it once had been. Even when the deal was made for Sander to sell the paper to the "upstanding Georgian," she couldn't summon enough energy to care. She went through the motions, spoke as before, and listened to their plans. She wasn't a conwoman for nothing. But her heart was never in it. Her mind was far away, unable to forget the Chelsea wharf where she'd tried and failed to convince Mace of his brother's treachery, and where Mace had betrayed his true feelings.

Before Lance's death, she'd worried because of his assertion that Mace would always choose his side. That night on the wharf, when Saranda had shot Lance, Mace had made it clear where his loyalties lay. If she hadn't stopped him, he'd have tried to fish his brother's body out of the river and save him somehow.

Perhaps if Mace had been forced to make a clear

choice, if he'd saved her life at Lance's expense, she'd be sure of the depth of his feelings for her. Now she would never know.

It shouldn't matter. Lance was dead, and they need fear nothing from him ever again. Yet it nagged at her endlessly. Once more she saw Lance's face every time she looked at Mace. She couldn't gaze at him without wondering. What would he have done? Had Lance been right about him?

She began to ask herself questions she thought she'd long ago put to rest. She was a Sherwin; he was a Blackwood. The feud between the families had persisted for so many hundreds of years; was it by now in the blood? She'd thought for a time that they could transcend it with the power of their love, that they could band together and use their combined forces to destroy the evil Blackwood influence. She'd thought Mace wanted it as much as she. But she was haunted by the knowledge that it was she, a Sherwin, who'd put an end to the Blackwood tyranny, while Mace had stood by and mourned his brother's death.

Who would he have chosen, if she hadn't pulled the trigger? Was the Blackwood tie so strong in him that he'd have sacrificed her in the end for family loyalty?

SANDER MCLEOD SIGNED over the deed to the *Globe-Journal* in high spirits. "When do you want the next payment?" the buyer asked.

"Next payment? Hell, take it. I got it cheap. Truth to tell, it's a relief just to get it off my hands."

He could afford to be magnanimous. He was set to rake in a fortune that would make the newspaper look like small potatoes. He passed the paper along so the buyer could sign.

"It was fortuitous, you showing up when you did. I know I'm leaving the paper in good hands. Just don't forget our deal now. One slanderous story appears in this paper about me and—"

"Don't worry yourself, Mr. McLeod," drawled the buyer. "So long as I own this here paper, you can put your misgivings to rest."

He took up the pen, gave a little cough, and signed his name on the line provided. Dr. John Henry Holliday, of Griffin, Georgia.

SUDDENLY, IT WAS over. Bat showed up with the deed to the *Globe-Journal* in his hands and a triumphant smile turning up the corners of his mustache. "You're a lucky man," he told Mace. "It was only Wyatt's influence that convinced Doc to sign the paper over to you. He was fixing to hang on to it."

Mace took the deed and shook his hand. "You've been a tremendous help," he said. "If there's anything I can do to help you in the future, don't hesitate to ask."

"Why don't you stay and celebrate your victory?" Saranda suggested.

"No, thanks just the same. I reckon you two would like to be alone at a time like this."

Alone was just what she didn't want to be. Bat gave her a wink and turned to Mace, extending his hand. "You'll do to ride the river with," he said gravely. It was the highest compliment a westerner ever bestowed.

When Bat had gone, the room seemed suddenly too small, too confining. Saranda glanced up, and their eyes met for one intense moment before they looked away.

"Congratulations," she said quietly. "You got what you wanted."

"At one time, I thought it was what *we* wanted."

She heard the hurt in his voice. "It was," she said. Then she corrected herself: "It is."

Mace turned and went to the window to look out over the street below. Tapping the deed against the knuckle of his other hand, he stood there, looking out for a long time without saying a word. When he did speak, it seemed he did so more to himself than to her.

"Odd," he murmured, "how empty some victories can be."

She stared at him for a long time. Again, she knew without knowing how. Knew he was thinking of what he'd sacrificed for this victory. Knew he was thinking of Lance.

She turned quietly and left the room.

CHAPTER 69

A month later, Saranda stood on the rail of a riverboat heading south, looking out over the muddy Mississippi, remembering happier times. It was here on a boat like this that she and Mace had once confessed their deepest feelings for one another. She'd left feeling healed, feeling that nothing could harm them again. But like everything else in her life, it had been an illusion. . . .

They'd been successful in taking over the *Globe-Journal* as planned. Once he was back at the helm, Mace wrote a series of articles disclosing the truth. His words were so audacious, they seemed to have been fashioned from lightning and hurled from stormy skies. Once again, he proved the power of the press. With Jackson's letter printed in the *Globe-Journal,* the other papers quickly picked up the story. Sander was arrested, and Saranda cleared of all charges. But that wasn't all. Bluffster that he was, Mace painted such a heroic picture of his and Saranda's participation in the deed that overnight they became glamorous figures.

Two confidence artists who, having discovered the murder of two of New York's most beloved citizens, had conducted an elaborate deception to bring the murderer to justice. They were welcomed back, not just to the *Globe-Journal*, but to society, with open arms.

Since Saranda had been cleared of all charges, the *Globe-Journal* reverted back to her. The courts ordered McLeod to refund the payment he'd received—leaving Mace and Saranda with an extra hundred thousand dollars of McLeod's money in the bank.

They should have been happy. They tried their best. They'd never spoken about it openly, but each knew that something vital had died. In an effort to rekindle the love they'd had, they decided to go through with their marriage. Tired of public spectacles after the ballyhoo of Sander's arrest, they chose instead to be married, quietly and simply, by a justice of the peace. It should have been the happiest day of their lives. But at the final moment, they looked into each other's eyes and saw the doubt.

Since Lance's death, Mace had been behaving strangely. He'd taken to carrying a gun, something Saranda hadn't been able to convince him to do in the wilds of the West. Often, when he thought she wasn't looking, he'd stop with his head cocked, as if listening for something. He never told her what it was he feared, which served to distance them all the more.

But she knew he was mourning Lance's death. And she suspected he blamed her. Could he be thinking that if Lance were still alive, they could help him? Even now, she decided, Mace refused to understand the extent of his brother's madness.

After the wedding, they'd returned to the hotel where they'd been living. It had been too painful to go back to the Van Slyke mansion after all that had happened, but buying a house seemed somehow too permanent in their present state. So they'd been content to remain in the hotel. On their wedding night, however, it had seemed a sterile, empty place. They'd lived too long like vagabonds, yet now that they were married it seemed that nothing in their lives had changed.

They'd been undressing for bed—awkwardly, almost dreading what was to come—when suddenly, Mace had grabbed her by the shoulders with some of his old spirit. "Let's get out of here," he'd pleaded. "Now. We'll take the first train out to Saint Louis. Take the riverboat back the way we came. Call it a honeymoon. What do you say?"

She knew he was trying desperately to recapture what they'd discovered on that fateful voyage, yet standing on the deck now, looking out over the mighty Mississippi, she could feel herself trembling with trepidation. That trip north had been a surrender of sorts. A time when she'd learned to trust him, when she'd freely given him her heart and soul. She wasn't sure she could do it again. She wasn't sure she believed it would do any good.

Yet Mace swore to her that it would be worth the pain. He was so insistent that she'd finally agreed to reenact the entire night, to allow him to tie her to the bed and try to rediscover the love and trust that had perished that night along with Lance.

The smell of the river was recalling memories of her first journey on the boat when he came up from behind. They'd been traveling for hours, and night was falling. The sky was a deep purple, streaked with midnight blue—the color of Mace's eyes. She knew the moment was upon them. Yet she'd been delaying it for as long as she possibly could.

"Ready?" he asked, as if a stranger was inquiring after her health.

She turned and looked at him. At the dear face that made her heart ache to gaze on it. *If only* . . .

She couldn't think of that now. She'd made a commitment. She must honor it as best she could. Perhaps Mace was right. Perhaps it *would* help.

Then why did she feel as though she were being given a last cigarette before the firing squad took aim?

She squared her shoulders and moved from the safety of the rail. "I'm ready."

THEIR CABIN WAS larger than before, more luxurious since they now had all the money in the world to spend. Mace, however, had gone to a great deal of trouble to reconstruct the scene as it had been. He'd brought along a white scarf to bind her hands to the headboard. And as before, he used braid from the canopy to tie her legs.

Naked and spread-eagle, waiting for him to finish his handiwork, she'd never felt more exposed in all her life. It was as if she were bared before a stranger. She was beginning to wish she'd never agreed. But the look in his eyes kept her from speaking. She saw there a love for her she couldn't deny. Squirming uncomfortably in her bonds as he rounded to the other side of the bed, she had to wonder, Was it enough?

Because the truth was, she still felt betrayed. Mace had had his opportunity to prove his loyalty to her, and he hadn't taken it. He could have carried a gun with him the night they'd gone to face Lance. He could have done the killing himself, as one would mercifully end the life of a rabid dog. He could have kept her from having to do it for him. He hadn't. He'd stood by and watched as Lance threatened her. As he'd almost killed Mace. Did Mace even realize how close he'd come to being murdered by his scoundrel brother? Alone at night, did he ever face the truth? Or did he still think he could have talked him out of it?

Now, when it was too late, he kept a gun tucked inside his coat. Did he think that would make up for it? That he would protect her from now on?

It pained her just to think about it. Because in spite of everything, she loved him more than she ever had. She'd given him all she had to give. She'd changed because of him. In spite of her fear, she'd been willing even to give him children, because he'd made her believe she could. But how had they come to this point where they had to play games just to make love to one another? Just to feel close.

Maybe it was the nature of the beasts, she thought as he tightened the cord at her ankle. Maybe con artists needed a role, and without it, they felt naked. The sad thing was, it hadn't always been that way.

Mace was just taking her last hand to fasten it to the bedpost when there was a knock at the door. "Mr. Black-wood, come quick," came a steward's trembling voice. Mace's fingers stilled, and they exchanged startled looks. He'd asked not to be disturbed. Something must be wrong. The steward was banging on the door as if the ship were on fire.

"It's an emergency," came the urgent voice.

"I'll be right back," he told her.

"Don't leave me here like this!" she cried. But he was already striding off.

She heard the door open and close again, then some sort of thud. She listened for the turn of his key in the lock. It didn't come. Had he left her here, tied naked to the bed, with the door unlocked? What if someone came in?

She reached over with her free hand and tore at the knot binding her other wrist. Something was amiss. What sort of emergency would require Mace's immediate presence? Why only him? Because if all the men had been similarly summoned, wouldn't she hear their footsteps on the floorboards outside?

As she was struggling to untie the stubborn knot, the door opened. "Mace?" she asked.

She heard a soft gasp. Very softly, almost unintelligibly, he spoke. "Holy Christ."

"What is it? What happened?"

"Nothing," he whispered.

"But why did they call you?"

"It was a mistake."

He was coming toward her from behind. She could hear his soft footfalls on the carpet. Pausing on the threshold of the bedroom, he turned down the gas lamp, casting the room into dark shadows. The porthole curtains were pulled. For a moment, there was an eerie expectant stillness in the gloom. Her heart was beating an odd rhythm. Usually, Mace left the lights on when they made love. He liked to see her face, to watch every nuance of her body as it moved beneath his. But tonight the shadowy dimness was a relief. A damp sheen of perspiration dotted her naked skin. Even now, she didn't know if she could go through with this. Some instinct was screaming at her that it wasn't right.

As he came closer, she reached out to him with her free hand. She just wanted to hold his hand a moment, to calm herself, to feel some intimate contact without pressure. Just some time to ready herself for what was to come. Physically. Emotionally. In every way.

But he misread her intentions. Instead of taking her hand in a tender caress, he grabbed the wrist and, retrieving the silk tie, bound it with quick efficiency to the bedpost. The scarf was tied tighter than the other, cutting into her flesh. "That hurts," she protested.

He walked to the dresser and picked up something, dangling it in his hand.

"Mace, it hurts. Just loosen it a bit."

He came toward her, and she felt something soft graze her cheek. She could see him silhouetted before her for just a moment before he brought the length of silk to her mouth and tied it behind her head. With a start, she realized he'd gagged her. It was utterly unexpected. A blindfold, perhaps, to play into his love of masks. But what was the point of silencing her?

She struggled madly for a minute, pushing with her tongue in an attempt to expel the gag from her mouth. He'd tied it too tightly—so tightly, in fact, that it was cutting off her breath.

What was going on?

The bed shifted as he sat down beside her. His hand touched her belly and wandered up to touch her breast. She arched up, moving away from his hand, but bound and gagged as she was, she couldn't escape his grip.

She tried to think of other times with him. Of the night he'd bound her wrists with ropes at the masked ball and kissed her breathless, then left her suddenly, stunned and aroused by his maleness. And the sweet and tender time they'd spent at the dirt farmer's in Tennessee. When they'd lain in that dilapidated bed with the children all around them, and Mace had spent the afternoon, when he was so tired, entertaining them with stories of the circus. Odd she should remember that as the happiest of times— how warm and cozy they'd been . . . and how very much in love.

He leaned over and kissed the round of her shoulder, but it was more as if he was inhaling her skin rather than showing his love. Then his mouth moved to her breast. He seemed different—more possessive, more aggressively inquisitive. His teeth nipped at her flesh.

He groaned against her skin. He began to touch her more insistently, as if he suddenly couldn't help himself. His hands gripped at her breasts so hard they hurt. She cried out beneath her gag, but he didn't seem to hear. He shifted and moved on top of her with his clothes on, the roughness of them scratching at her sensitive skin.

She groaned vigorously, trying to convey to him through her gag that she wanted him to slow down.

He ignored her completely, reaching between them and hurriedly unbuckling his belt. Was he just going to take her, with no preparation, no—

All at once, her heart froze. This wasn't like Mace. Even at his most dominant in bed, he'd always geared himself toward her pleasure first. It had, in fact, been a challenge to him to prove to her that here was a man who could satisfy her as no one else ever had. But this frantic grappling with clothes . . . as if hurrying before he was interrupted . . . was more like rape than—

She understood in that moment a horrifying truth. She struggled wildly, fighting to break the bonds that bound her helplessly beneath him. Using every ounce of strength she possessed, she fought like a wildcat to push him from her.

To no avail.

Suddenly, she heard the doorknob turn. It must be locked, for someone was pounding frantically on the door. She heard a series of hard thuds as the man on top of her began to laugh. The laugh of a ghost. She could feel him against her like a spear, ready to enter her. Even as he moved toward her, the door crashed open.

The gas lamp flared and fizzled as someone turned the knob to its highest setting with a sudden jerk. She hardly had time to let out a muffled scream when the intruder staggered into the room. Blood flowing from a gash in his head, it was Mace!

The man on top of her raised his head, and she found herself staring into the lifeless, deformed eye of a dead man.

Lance Blackwood was doing his best to reenact that long-ago rape.

CHAPTER 70

Lance was alive. Cackling as he had that awful night when she'd been nothing more than a girl. It brought it all back to her in stark detail. The flames leaping around them. Her mother's screams. Her beloved father, banging on the door, trying frantically to find a way out before the smoke choked them to death. And all the while that crazy laughter sounding in her ears . . . just as it was now.

She didn't realize she was screaming. All she knew was that, one moment she was staring into that hated face, and the next he was ripped from her by a force so violent, it seemed to sweep through the room like a hurricane. Lance was thrown up against the wall so hard the wind was knocked from him. And Mace stood before him, his breath heaving in his chest.

"You son of a bitch," Mace growled.

"Don't lose yer temper, mate. I thought you left her there fer me. A present, like. Fer comin' back from the dead, eh? Ain't it lucky yer *wife* is such a poor aim. Grazed me head, that bullet did. Left me with another scar, but wot's another one, eh?"

For once, Mace seemed completely caught off-guard, as startled as Saranda by this turn of events. He looked so shaken, as if for once in his life, he couldn't think what to do. "You had me called away," he said between ragged breaths, "and clubbed on the head, so you could—"

"Have me revenge? Ye wouldn't expect less of a Blackwood, would ye now? She may have fancy-talked ye into thinkin' she was good enough to marry, but she almost killed yer baby brother. Would have, too, if I hadn't washed up against a nearby boat and been fished out of the drink. I've been watchin' you, the happy couple. Waitin' to make me move. Never realizing the—entertainment that was in store." The last was said with a contemptuous glance at Saranda, who was struggling to get free.

Mace glanced at her and saw the panic in her eyes. Stepping over to her, he slipped the gag from her mouth, tossed a cover over her, and asked, "Are you all right?"

She couldn't believe what she was hearing. "For God's sake, Mace, kill him!"

Lance assumed a cocky sneer. "Yer goin' to kill *me*, Mace? Tyke a look at me eye, brother. A good look. I got that because of you. Or mayhap ye don't recall the vow ye made? To protect yer baby brother till the day I die?"

For a moment, the room was silent as Mace glanced at Lance and back again at Saranda. Saranda wasn't sure he'd ever make a move, but she did know one thing: Lance had no intention of letting them out of here alive. She could see it in his eyes.

Caught unawares, and with a wicked blow to his head, Mace had been robbed of his customary control. Blood from his wound dripped into his eye. He swiped it away as if he were in a daze. Not since the tornado had she seen him look so helpless, so at risk of losing against an unbeatable foe. Except that his foe this time was his love for his brother. On the heels of wishing him alive, how could he now bring himself to end his brother's life?

He saw the sudden despair in her eyes and turned back to Lance.

"The day you die?" he repeated dully. "That day has come, Lance. You've caused enough misery for one lifetime."

"You and yer blasted tongue, Mace. You talked yer way into everything I wanted and couldn't have. When I think of all the times I begged fer yer help—"

"When did I refuse you my help?"

"When I went to you and asked ye to leave Pilar. I was sufferin' right enough. All I asked was wot one brother should expect from another. But no, ye had to stay with that bitch while yer only brother starved. That's why I turned her in. She was turnin' yer head, she was. I knew once you got shy of her, you'd come to yer senses and go back on the flam with me. But what did ye do? Joined up with the Van Slykes. Never offered to cut me in on the action. All ye had to do was make me a part of their con. Share and share alike, eh, brother? Ain't that wot ye promised me all those years ago?"

By now, Mace was shaking with visible fury.

"We've shared one thing, we have," Lance went on. "This little Sherwin piece. Wot do ye say we bury the hatchet and have a go together?"

Mace closed his eyes. Then he reached into his coat pocket and slowly withdrew his pistol.

"You goin' to shoot me, brother? Look in me eye and tell me ye can go through with it. No girl on earth's worth a brother's love. And ye *do* love me. Y'said ye did."

Mace looked into the bad eye of his brother—the eye that had caused him so much guilt over the years. He made himself look, forced himself to face the truth. That Lance would have been this way even without the beating. That he'd been protecting a madman. That it had to end. He faced it squarely. "Love?" he spat. "You took my love and turned it into something vile. You never knew the meaning of the word."

He took a breath and, like a man putting an end to the suffering of a dying beast, pulled the trigger.

The shot exploded in the confines of the room. Lance's cocky countenance changed to one of utter shock. Blood spurted from his chest, where Mace had shot him through the heart. Stunned, he stumbled across the room and out the shattered front door as if running from a retribution he'd never thought would come. He clutched at the rail, only to lose consciousness and fall with a splash into the river.

"My aim isn't faulty," Mace muttered, staring after him. "This time there'll be no returning from the dead."

Footsteps sounded outside. Shaking himself to his senses, Mace dropped the gun and moved to swiftly untie Saranda and hand her a robe. Gasps and screams were heard from the deck. He hurriedly went to join the people on the rail.

With the robe tight about her, Saranda joined them just in time to see Lance's body drift into the paddle wheel to be crushed against the side of the boat. Sickened, she leaned against Mace, turning her head away.

Pandemonium had broken out all around them. But through it all, she was aware of a great stillness in Mace. He didn't move. He didn't seem to breathe. She looked up to find him looking down at her with a deep sadness in his eyes.

CHAPTER 71

Most of the night was spent answering the captain's inevitable questions as to why and how Lance Blackwood had been shot. After an inquiry, Mace was exonerated of any wrongdoing. They were given another cabin, and Mace's head was cleaned where Lance had hit him from behind, but he refused a bandage. He still hadn't come to bed when she finally fell asleep.

Saranda slept most of the morning, too emotionally exhausted to do anything else. When she awoke in the afternoon, she found Mace sprawled in a chair, sleeping.

She dressed silently and crept out the door to stand by the rail. Even while they were answering the barrage of questions, an unearthly stillness had settled about them. They'd avoided each other's eyes, as if it was too soon to give voice to what must be said. Saranda knew now that she'd been wrong about Mace. But she didn't know what that meant or how it would affect their future. Had Mace been feeling as betrayed by her as she'd been lately feeling about him?

She wished, looking out at the banks of the river, that they could just put it all behind them. That they didn't even have to say the words. That they could just look at one another and know what the other was thinking. That it could be free and easy.

But when had it been free and easy between them? Only in those days when they'd been running for their lives.

She felt his presence beside her. Looking at him, she saw a heartbreakingly handsome man dressed in the expensively tailored clothing of a publishing magnate. He looked sleek and elegant, as he had when she'd first seen him in New York. The only things that belied his aura of respectability were the wild black curls, the wolfish mouth, and his Gypsy eyes. Otherwise, he was a shining example of New York sophistication. She knew she looked equally conventional in Paris silk. She couldn't help recalling what he'd looked like in the Tennessee farmer's clothes, two sizes too small, with the bulge of his groin so noticeable, he'd had to pull out the shirttail to hide it from view.

She smiled tenderly at the memory.

"Why are you smiling?" he asked—the first words he'd spoken to her since after Lance's shooting.

"Oh, I was just remembering how you looked in that farmer's clothes. Just wishing—"

"What?"

"That we were back there, wearing those clothes again."

It wasn't all she wished, but it was all she could bring herself to say.

He put his elbows on the rail and leaned over the side to study the landscape. "Funny you should think of that now. We must be close to Memphis."

His words settled on the breeze. Again the stillness descended.

"Mace . . ." she said presently.

"Let's not talk about it now, shall we?"

She sighed and looked back at the riverbank. He didn't want to talk any more than she did. But what were they to do now? Where were they to go from here? She knew what she wished would happen. She wanted nothing more than to be off this boat and away from the remaining memories of Lance.

Minutes later, the terrain began to look familiar. She was seized by an eerie sense of *déjà vu*. As if she'd done this before. Thought these same desperate thoughts while looking out on the same terrain. They rounded a bend in the river, and she stood up straight. There, before them, was the huge jutting rock where the farmer had kept his raft.

Her gaze flew to Mace. He was looking at her with the same sudden awareness in his eyes. His teeth flashed in his prominent mouth. What a glorious smile he has, she thought, answering it in kind—what a hell-bent-for-leather grin.

It was as if a single thought flashed from his mind to hers and back again. They didn't bother to ask each other, Can we really do this? There was no time for questions, or even rational thought. As one, they began to tear off their clothes and drop them to the deck. His city hat he tossed into the river. His expensive dark suit lay in a heap at his feet. The traditional dark blue frock she'd spent hours having fitted was kicked aside in a pile of petticoats.

By now, they were laughing, feeling as carefree as children, as full of anticipation as if this were their first day on earth. They stood, as one, on top of the rail, tottered for a moment, then dived, together, into the rushing current of the muddy Mississippi.

Before they'd swum far, people called to them from

the rails, believing they were in need of help. But when they looked back and waved, laughing all the while, the would-be rescuers shook their heads. Perhaps, they whispered, after the shock of the night before, the newlyweds had completely lost their heads.

"Where are we going?" she called to him as they swam.

"Does it matter? So long as it's away from here?"

She shook her head, shaking the water from her eyes. The current was strong, but she didn't care. She felt wonderful suddenly, bathed clean of memories and that awful punishing silence. It was good to move, to stretch her muscles, to feel alive.

"The farmer's family did, after all, win that contest," she called. "Ten thousand dollars of McLeod's money, wasn't it? We could always drop by and give them the happy news."

He was grinning. "And we never really saw New Orleans. Certainly not in its best light."

"Who cares where we go?" she called to the winds. "As long as we're—"

She paused. In one last moment of uncertainty, she cast a shy glance his way.

"Together," he finished.

He swam to her, took hold of her waist, and kissed her hard. The water dripping from her eyes mingled with her tears. "Can you ever forgive me?" she asked.

He put a hand to her mouth to quiet her. "There's nothing to forgive."

"You killed your brother because of me."

His eyes clouded momentarily. "The man I killed wasn't my brother."

"Mace—"

"Hush, love. One thing about being reformed confidence artists . . . we know how to start with a clean slate."

"Are we? Reformed, I mean?"

"Well . . . maybe after one last hurrah to sow some wild oats."

"Before settling down. We do, after all, have a newspaper to run."

"We shall go back and run it," he promised. "But first, I say we do what we set out to do. Have a real honeymoon. Strike out—have some fun—leave the past behind."

"There's so much for us to adjust to. There hasn't been much time."

"Do you doubt that we can do it?"

"Not anymore," she said, and found to her intense joy that it was true. "Then I say let's honeymoon for all we're worth. Before you return to running the paper, and I go undercover to expose the evils lurking in the heart of the great city."

"Now wait just a minute. We never agreed—"

She broke from him and swam like a demon toward shore. Once they'd reached the banks, they were panting and giggling at the same time. Saranda stumbled from the water and set out to run from him, but he fell on her, propelling her with his weight to the ground. They rolled in the mud, laughing and squealing, until he captured her mouth with a kiss. She clung to him then, grateful beyond words that they'd been given this second chance.

"I love you so," she told him. "I want to put everything behind us. Make love to me, Mace. Let it be like the very first time."

"Here?" he cried mockingly. "In the mud?"

"It's just about the only place we *haven't* made love."

He smiled at her with all the love and gratitude he

felt shining in his eyes. "I think I'm going to have my hands full with you."

She took his hands and ran them along the hollows and swells of her body—just to show him how very right he was.

ACKNOWLEDGMENTS

I received so many wonderful letters from people after the publication of my first book, *The Last Highwayman*, that I wanted to take this opportunity to thank you. I can't tell you what it meant to me, not just to hear your kind words about the book, but to read expressions from readers such as "I'm glad you didn't give up" and "You've really inspired me." That, I think, was the most gratifying of all.

Thanks to Meg Ruley, who proved herself not only the delightful person I knew her to be but a brilliant agent as well. And Andrea Cirillo, for her behind-the-scenes wisdom and encouragement. Nita Taublib, for her superb insights that helped make this a better book and for her incomparably fun company. Susan and Craig Johnson, for their unselfish generosity and for, along with Nita, sharing in the memory of the illustrious handshake. Jayne Ann Krentz, whose quotes helped me so much and whose willingness to give of herself and her time, not just to me but to the genre as a whole, is an inspiration. Similarly, Iris Johansen's generosity has touched me deeply. Jennifer McCord and Kathe Robin, for such enthusiastic support. Katie Kocis, for reading the proofs, for the COJK autographing, for the insight into characters, and for showing me how openheartedly one writer can support another. Joyce Sparks, Chiara Guerrieri, and Kate Mulgrew, for their excitement about the book and their continued unconditional friendship. And of course, Mary Cunniffe McKinney, who has always been there for me and who teaches me continually about the concept of selfless love.

I'm not sure I'm supposed to acknowledge them in the dedication, but I just have to add a final note. This book came about because of two people. First, my husband, Bill, who dedicated himself to seeing that it was accomplished in the time allotted and who taught me what it is to be loved, just as Mace taught Saranda. How can you thank someone for being everything to you? And Barbara Alpert. She's been such a friend, such an inspiration, such an influence in my work, my creativity, my life. She's been so much more than an editor. Her mark is on this book every bit as much as mine is. Thank you, Barbara. Without you, none of this would have happened.

ABOUT THE AUTHOR

KATHERINE O'NEAL is the daughter of a U.S. Air Force pilot and a fiercely British artist who met in India in the fifties. The family traveled extensively and lived for many years in Asia. Katherine is married to William Arnold, a noted film critic and author of the best selling books *Shadowland* and *China Gate*—a man she feels makes her heroes pale in comparison. It was he who said, "You're a romantic person; why *not* write romantic fiction?" Together, they continue the tradition of travel whenever possible. They also enjoy their dogs, cats, horses, and each other—not necessarily in that order. They have a daughter, Janie, who isn't sure if she wants to write, but who's definite in her love of horses. They currently live in Seattle, Washington, where Katherine is working on her third novel, a swashbuckler set in the exotic far East.

Katherine loves to hear from readers.
Please write to her at:
P.O. Box 2452
Seattle, WA 98111-2452
and enclose a self-addressed stamped envelope for a response and news of forthcoming books.